John Colter

The Legend of the First Mountain Man

D1599433

Don Amiet

PublishAmerica
Baltimore

ISBN: 978-1-60749-071-5 (softcover)
ISBN: 978-1-4489-0895-0 (hardcover)
PUBLISHED BY PUBLISHAMERICA, LLLP
www.publishamerica.com
Baltimore

Printed in the United States of America

This book is dedicated to my wife, Deborah Lynn Amiet, for more than words can ever say. I love you.

25% of the author's royalties from the sale of this book will go to Best Friends Animal Society in Kanab, Utah, to assist them in their goal of No More Homeless Pets. Please visit their website at bestfriends.org for more information.

John Colter

The Legend of the First Mountain Man

PROLOGUE

My name is John Colter.

Back in 1803, I was one of those crazy fools who signed up to join Meriwether Lewis and William Clark on their journey across the continent. Back then, it seemed like every person who knew or learned about our journey told us we were out of our minds. If the hostile natives didn't kill us, the Spanish would, they said. There was no chance of our being successful. No chance at all.

Well, we proved them wrong, didn't we? We sure did! We went up that massive Missouri, crossed the mountains, reached the ocean, and then did it all again in reverse. None of us were killed by the natives and none of us were killed or enslaved by the Spanish. But when President Jefferson's famed Corps of Discovery floated back down the Missouri and landed in St. Louis in September of 1806, I wasn't with them. Nope, I stayed up there in that beautiful and wild country to make my fortune. What I ended up making was a legend.

Anyone with a lick of sense will tell you that every legend is a lot of fantasy mixed with a little truth. Such is the case with me. Sometimes when I hear a tale about something I supposedly did, I wonder who in tarnation they're talking about! But that's all right. There's nothing wrong with mixing fantasy and truth. Fantasy can add to a story and make it more interesting and romantic than it really is, which is fine as long as the truth isn't lost entirely in the telling.

It's a beautiful night, isn't it? The stars are bright overhead and the moon is shining a path across the sluggish waters of the Missouri, or, as we used to call it back when we were forcing our way west against its current, the Misery. I can hear coyotes and wolves in the distance, and the darn skeeters seem to be leaving us alone. So pull up a log by the fire and sit a spell, and I'll tell you a story. And I'll do my best to hold fantasy at bay.

CHAPTER ONE

When I was about five years old, my family moved me away from our home in Virginia and across the Alleghenies to the new land of Kentucky, forever changing my destiny. Now, I'm not saying I would have settled down, married and become a farmer if I had stayed in Virginia; my adventurous nature would have drawn me across the mountains into the wild west at some point, I'm sure. But growing up in the raucous and untamed Kentucky country certainly molded me into the man I would later become, the kind of man I needed to be to survive. And the Ohio River that flowed through the bottomlands always made me dream of faraway places.

In my younger days, I did a few things that almost elevated me to legend status, including fighting alongside the great Simon Kenton with General Wayne at the Battle of Fallen Timbers, but it is in 1803 where I want to start my tale. 1803 was the transitional year for me, the year that changed everything. That is when it all really began and I set off down the road to becoming the first "mountain man."

You see, prior to the summer of 1803 I had no definite plans for my future. I didn't know what I wanted to do and I wasn't looking any further ahead than to plan for the next day's meal. Then a man named William Clark approached me with a proposition. He said he was looking for a few tough and fit young men to join him on an expedition. He wanted men who knew the outdoors, men who could live rough off the land and who weren't afraid to get into a skirmish, should one become necessary. I was intrigued.

"Simon Kenton gave me your name," Clark told me on that hot afternoon. He stood with one booted foot resting on a large rock, and his shrewd eyes watched me closely from beneath shaggy brows.

"He did, huh?" I said, tossing the last of the beaver pelts onto the shore from my canoe. I had just returned from trapping up the Scioto River and my rewards were pretty slim. The beaver were getting scarce around those parts by then.

"Yep." Clark was a tall man, and confident. He stood smiling down at me from atop the bank, the afternoon sunlight glinting off the stock of his rifle and the red in his hair. "Thinks fairly high of you, does Mr. Kenton."

I straightened up and rubbed the small of my back. A day spent working beaver traps followed by rowing down the Scioto and the Ohio to reach Maysville had left me with a sore spine and not a lot of patience for small talk. "What can I do for you, mister?" I asked.

He walked down to where I stood, one hand extended. "My name's William Clark."

I shook his hand. His grip was strong and sure. I liked him already, don't ask me why. "Any relation to George Rogers Clark?" I asked.

"My brother," Clark said easily.

"He's a legend around these parts."

"I know."

I hauled my canoe up onto the rocky bank and tied it to a stunted tree. I looked into Clark's eyes and made a decision. "How about a drink, Mr. Clark?"

"Don't mind if I do," he said. "I'll even buy."

"You're my kind of man."

* * *

Clark helped me carry my few beaver pelts up to the store in town and waited on the cluttered porch while I collected my pay, then we walked along the muddy main street of Maysville to the town's only tavern. Clark headed for the bar while I settled down at a table near the door. My back was sore and I was tired and sweaty and that whiskey Clark was carrying toward me sure looked like it would go down good.

"Here's my proposal, John," he said as he sat across from me. "I need good men, strong men, to join me on a great expedition. The going will be rough, you'll work harder than you've ever worked in your life, but you'll also see places few, if any, white men have ever seen."

I took a swallow of the whiskey while my mind raced. Danged if he didn't have my interest up! "Where you headed, the moon?"

"Almost as far," Clark replied with his easy smile, throwing back his own whiskey. "But not quite. You see, John, where we're going is the Pacific Ocean."

I looked at him carefully, not sure if he might be pulling my leg. "White men have seen the Pacific," I said. "What's the big adventure in that?"

Clark laughed. "You're right. White men have been to the Pacific, by ship. We're going by land."

"By land." I was now wondering if maybe Mr. Clark had already downed a few too many whiskeys before finding me, because he sure wasn't making a lot of sense.

"Technically speaking," he said. "We plan on following the Missouri River to its source, then crossing over the mountains to the Columbia and taking that down to the Pacific. We'll travel with a small, select group of men, winter on the Pacific coast, then return, either by ship if we can secure passage or by land. Your pay will be $5.00 per month, plus there will be grants of land upon your return. Interested?"

I took another swallow of whiskey, biding my time while I thought about what he had said. Beaver pelts were fetching a dollar to two dollars each, so five dollars for a months work didn't seem like a fortune, but the beaver were running out along the Ohio. A steady pay would be a nice thing to have. And the idea of land sounded pretty good to me.

"Can I think on it?"

Clark nodded. "Yep. I prefer that you do. My partner, Meriwether Lewis, will be passing down the Ohio with our keelboat in the fall. If you decide to join up, he can pick you up on the way through."

I looked out through the grimy window, across the narrow dirt street toward the green hills of Ohio rising beyond the wide river. All I really knew in the entire world was here, along these swampy bottomlands and in the forested hills that rose up on either side of the river. Virginia was only a vague childhood memory; Kentucky was my world. I had roamed these woods most of my life and I knew every creek, every hollow, damn near every tree. But in my mind I was seeing much farther, to those lands beyond the Mississippi, lands of which only rumor and conjecture had ever reached the hills of Kentucky. Rumor spoke of savage Indians and giant beasts, like the ones whose bones sometimes appeared in the sides of the hills after heavy rains washed the covering dirt away. Rumor also spoke of endless plains swept by the wind and buffalo and deer so thick you had to elbow them out of the way to walk. What would it be like to visit those lands and see those amazing wonders? A chill passed through me at the thought.

From the corner of my eye I could see Clark watching me, studying me, a small smile on his face. I had the feeling he knew what I was thinking.

"All right, Mr. Clark," I said, facing him. "I'd like to go along on this adventure of yours."

He looked surprised. "I thought you wanted some time to think on it."

I nodded. "I just did. Where do I sign up?"

"Well, when Captain Lewis brings his keelboat down in the fall, introduce yourself to him and tell him you spoke to me. He'll get you taken care of."

I was thrilled. This sounded like it might be fun.

CHAPTER TWO

"Welcome, Mr. Colter. I'm proud to have you along." Meriwether Lewis shook my hand and that quickly I was sworn in, a private in the army of the United States. It was October 1803, and I had just gone from Citizen John Colter to Private John Colter.

I studied the captain's face. Meriwether Lewis was an enigma to me then, and so would he remain during all the time I knew him. He was an intense man and I didn't warm to him the way I had toward Clark during the summer. Lewis was a far different type of man than Clark, a man driven by something beyond my ability to understand. Understand him or not, though, I was in this thing now and there was no turning back. Not that I had any intention of changing my mind. I was thrilled to be included.

"Thank you, sir." I said. "I think I'm making the right choice."

Lewis nodded and smiled, though his smile didn't seem to touch his eyes. He had strange eyes, eyes that seemed to be seeing things nobody else could see. I wondered what those things were.

"It will be a decision you won't regret," he said, then moved on to speak with another of the new recruits.

I hoped fervently that he was right.

"What do you think of all this, John?" A strong hand clapped me on the shoulder and I turned to look at my old friend, Charles Floyd. Charles and I had hunted together many times over the years and I knew him to be a man you could trust, a man who always had your back in a sticky situation. I had been a little surprised to see him joining up with this outfit, until I heard rumors that he was a distant relative of William Clark. Then it all made sense.

"I think I might be crazy for going along with this scheme," I said, "but I'm in it now. I hear they're making you a sergeant?"

Floyd nodded proudly. "Captain Lewis likes me," he said. "I just hope I can live up to it."

"You'll be fine," I told him, and I knew he would be. Floyd was the kind of man that other men just naturally followed. He had the charisma and the instincts of a born leader. I had followed him into a few apparently hopeless situations in the past and had come out alive on the other end, including one skirmish we'd had with some Shawnee up Ohio way. But that's another tale for another day.

Captain Lewis wasted no time in moving us along down the river. By dawn the following morning all the gear was stowed on board his impressive keelboat and on his two pirogues and we were under way, heading down the Ohio toward the mighty Mississippi. The going was fairly easy on that first section of the Ohio, though the water level was low and we occasionally had to force that big boat over sandbars and rocky shallows. We did that by unloading the cargo and using push poles, mainly, and by God that is hard work! Standing at the prow of the boat, placing the long pole against the bed of the river with the other end against your shoulder, then walking toward the stern, moving the boat forward with the force of your legs. Or another method was to send a group of men ashore or into the water with a rope tied to the bow and pull that heavy boat forward. Then, of course, we had to reload all that cargo once we were past the obstruction!

Obstacles notwithstanding, we were on our way, and the excitement was thick within our ranks. We all felt like we had been chosen, singled out as something special. And the winnowing out wasn't complete yet. Only a handful of men, carefully picked during the planned winter camp on the Mississippi, would set out on the journey up the Missouri River in the spring, and I was determined that I would be one of them.

I'm not the kind of man to accept failure, especially in myself.

The trees along the Ohio were filled with their autumn colors, and their orange and red and yellow leaves floated on the smooth surface of the river. Clouds moved across the blue sky, propelled by a cool breeze, warning us of winter on the way. I didn't mind winter. I had lived outside during almost thirty winters, hunting deer and turkey, fighting Indians. Winter I could handle.

The journey wasn't all idyllic, though. All of us on the boats kept one eye peeled toward the Ohio side of the river. Shawnee still liked to shoot at passing boats along the river in spite of their defeat in the wars and their signing of peace treaties, and all travelers on the Ohio knew to be careful.

That first day moved past like the banks of the river as we rowed. Our captains spent a lot of time in their small cabin in the stern, discussing their plans for our arrival at the Mississippi, or in the bow, taking measurements of every bend in the river. I would spend a lot of time over the next few years watching those two measure and count their way across the continent and it never failed to impress me. I was never much of a book person, though unlike most men of that time I could read, and all the math they were doing so assiduously eluded me, but watching Captain Clark work on his map or watching Captain Lewis measure the sun and the river touched something inside me and made me realize that there was a lot more to this expedition than it seemed on the surface.

"President Jefferson wants a lot of information, gentlemen," Captain Lewis said to us during our swearing-in back in Clarksville. "He wants to know if there is a navigable water route across the northern portion of the continent. He wants to know all we can learn about the Indian nations of the interior. He wants to know about the plants and animals that we might find along the way. He wants a detailed map of all the waterways and mountains that we encounter. Our nation is growing, boys, and we will be at the very forefront of that growth."

It was a heady time for me.

* * *

That first night, we stopped on the banks of the Ohio and made camp. Two of the men were sent out to hunt, and they returned shortly with two fat does. The fire blazed high and the talk was loud and boisterous. I knew a couple of the men, other than Floyd, and had heard of two others through reputation; a man's reputation has a tendency to spread far ahead of him in those parts. Several of the men had made their reputations fighting Indians up in the Ohio and were tough as nails. Nate Pryor was a neighbor of mine and was married; I was surprised to see him on this expedition. I would have thought that a married man would want to stay near his bride instead of traipsing off across an unknown continent, but then again I knew nothing about the thoughts of married men, never having been one myself. William Bratton was a local hunter with a great sense of humor who had once been apprenticed as a blacksmith, and was strong as a horse. It would be a pleasure to have him along. And George Gibson, who I was acquainted with through reputation only, was known in Kentucky as an exemplary hunter and woodsman.

The two brothers, Joseph and Reubin Field, had been recruited in Kentucky by Clark, and seemed familiar with him. They were solid characters and I was glad to have them along.

The other men in camp that night, the ones who had been with Lewis when he reached Kentucky, were strangers to me, but already I was forming my own opinions of them. Several stood out in my thoughts as strong men who seemed like they could be counted on, while others seemed a little weak, character-wise. I just couldn't envision them making it all the way across the continent on a journey as arduous and dangerous as this one promised to become.

Mostly, though, I watched the interaction between the captains. Obviously familiar and comfortable with each other, they seemed to get on quite well, and their demeanor encouraged me. It was easy to see they were friends of long standing, and both gave the impression of being strong and competent. Following weak or petty men on a dangerous mission is one sure way to get killed. These did not seem like weak or petty men.

"Hey, Colter," Charles Floyd said from his seat on the other side of the fire.

"Yeah?"

"Tell us about Simon Kenton."

The men around the fire grew quiet, listening intently. Simon Kenton was a legend on the western side of the Appalachians.

"What do you wanna know?"

"Is the man as big as the legend?"

"Bigger," I said quietly. I could clearly remember fighting alongside Kenton during the Indian wars of the late 1700's, long after his reputation had been made, and it was truly like fighting alongside a legend. The man was larger than life.

"By the time I knew Kenton he was already a legend in the Ohio country," I said. The flames of the fire crackled and snapped, sending sparks up to mingle with the stars overhead, and I heard an owl's low call in the woods. "This was after he had fought at Chillicothe Town and had been captured and sent to Detroit. Most of the Shawnee had been pacified but there were still enough to cause problems for settlers. And there was the campaign under General Wayne."

Captain Clark wandered over and sat down near me. "My brother has a lot of respect for Simon Kenton."

"As Simon did for him," I said.

"You fought with Kenton under General Wayne?"

I nodded. "Summer of 1794, it was," I said. "I was nineteen, just a kid. We chased Blue Jacket's Shawnee up the Maumee to a place where some long-ago tornado had knocked down a whole bunch of trees. It was a mess of broken trunks and branches and brambles, just a nightmare. The Indians were hiding in there, taunting us to come in after them. A lot of those same Indians had been back in Chillicothe when Kenton was captured and tortured in 1778, and I think Simon wanted to gain a little bit of revenge. So we went in after them." I shook my head, remembering. "That was a damn bloody battle. It was all close quarters, and we fought more with bayonets and knives than we did with bullets. We drove the Indians out from their cover and chased them up past Fort Miamis. When the Brits wouldn't let the Indians into the fort for protection, we knew we had won."

Crickets chirred in the woods as we sat in silence, thinking about the war being waged against the natives by the government, a war that had been going on for years and which seemed never-ending. Then Lewis spoke.

"Part of our reason for going up the Missouri is to work out peace treaties with the natives up that way," he said, and in the firelight his eyes seemed to dance. "If we can meet them on peaceful terms and convince them that they are now under the protection and rule of the American government, then maybe we can impose peace upon them and turn them toward more settled lives."

I listened respectfully but inside I wasn't so sure. In my experience with the Indians of the Kentucky region, it seemed to me the natives were pretty happy living the lives they'd been living for generations. If our mission was to pacify Indians, it was going to be a bloody toil.

"If nothing else," Lewis continued, "we can move them away from trading with the British and Spanish and establish our own trading forts in their territory. That would be a huge boon not just for them but for the United States as well."

"Better turn in, gents," Clark said, stretching and yawning. "We'll be on the river at first light."

That night, laying there under the stars, I thought about all I had heard that day and I was a little surprised to feel the excitement still growing inside me. For the first time in a long time, I was aiming for a goal instead of just wandering through life. This enterprise dreamed up by Jefferson seemed like it might be doomed to failure, but I was curious to see it through.

* * *

First light saw us back on the Ohio, with a strong tail-wind that allowed us to hoist the sails on the keelboat and on the two pirogues. Clouds had moved in during the night and were threatening rain, though the temperature was staying fairly warm for October, which suited us all just fine. I had seen winters along the Ohio where there'd been a foot of snow on the ground by October. We saw a lot of deer along the banks of the river, and thousands of pigeons on their annual migration. Geese and ducks also flew high overhead, aiming south in their long vee patterns, honking away for all they were worth, and we all knew what that meant. Winter was tapping on our shoulders.

Midday saw us stopped for a while for dinner, and after eating Floyd and I were assigned to shore duty, hunting down some food for that evening's camp. So as the keelboat and pirogues swung out into the current and headed downstream, we hiked inland instead, into the thick, cool forests.

Signs of deer were everywhere on that gray afternoon, and the woods were filled with the sounds of life. The rustlings of small animals were all around us, along with the incessant calls of birds. Those were comforting sounds to any hunter in territory known to also be the hunting grounds of Indians. I'm always more wary in a quiet forest than in one noisy with animal life, and that wariness has saved my life in the past.

The first part of the day Charles and I spent talking more than hunting, conversing in hushed tones about Lewis's plans for the journey and what might become of us all. Needless to say, the future was of a concern to us. Finally, though, we settled down to our task of finding meat for our new friends on the river. By mid-afternoon we had killed and butchered four deer and a turkey and had caught up to the keelboat, which had been unloaded once again and was negotiating another of the cursed sandbars.

And that was how we spent the next several weeks, working our way down the Ohio as the weather turned steadily colder. I took my turn in the keelboat or in the pirogues, rowing, poling or pulling, or on shore hunting to help keep the men fed. Evenings were spent in camp, talking around the campfires, getting to know one another and getting to know our captains. Camaraderie was slowly building between us, as we learned about each other and learned how to work and get along together. Personalities were revealing themselves, as the familiarity of our situation forced us to speak out loud of ourselves and reveal our talents, and weaknesses. Some of the men could row from sunup to sundown but were terrible hunters, couldn't hit the ground from two feet away. Others could find game without seeming to try but weren't a lot of help in the boat. And then there was the small core group who seemed able to perform any task placed in front of them, no matter what that task might be. Sergeant Floyd was one of those, as was Nate Pryor and the Field brothers, and, I like to believe, myself as well.

And I could see the captains quietly evaluating us all, making their minds up about us and deciding who would be retained as members of the permanent party, the ones who would be heading up the Missouri come spring. They often consulted with Sergeant Floyd, as I had to become used to calling him, being a private myself now, so I felt confident that I would be retained for the full journey. Floyd knew me well enough to trust me, and that meant a lot to me, since I trusted him implicitly.

For one month we floated down the Ohio, through waters in which I had never dipped an oar. The Ohio and its tributaries around Maysville I knew the way I knew my own hand, but this lower section of the Ohio was new to me, and exciting because of it. Floyd said that he had never traveled this far down the Ohio, either. In fact, our captains may have been the only men on board who had ever been this far down the Ohio, but they never said one way or the other. They seemed to be comfortable with where we were going, as if they had traveled this route before, but at the same time they spent most evenings in their tent, writing about the activities and sights of the day. Strange men. It would be interesting crossing the continent with them.

"What do you think about all this, John?" William Clark asked me one day.

It was late in the afternoon. We were on a high bluff on the south side of the Ohio, looking down at the sparkling ribbon of water that wound its eternal way toward the west. From this height the keelboat was no larger than a toy, the voices of the men thin and distant. Clark and I had set out early that morning to hunt, and I could see him evaluating my skills throughout the course of the day. I had the feeling his question was another part of my test and I thought about my response carefully before answering.

"I'm divided, Mister Clark," I said.

His eyes surveyed the magnificent scene below us. "In what way?"

"I'm plumb excited to be invited along, but I wonder if this whole enterprise isn't crazy as a loon."

Clark laughed, that booming infectious laugh that always made people want to laugh right along with him. "You may be right at that, John," he said. "But I think we can pull it off. If we can get a crew of good men, like Floyd and yourself, why, I don't see how we can be beat."

That made me feel good.

"We picked up some fine men at Fort Massac," he continued, "including that half-breed hunter, Drouillard. And now that Captain Lewis has downed his doses of his favorite Rush's pills and is starting to get over whatever illness has been plaguing him recently, I think we're in as good of a position as we could hope to be in right now."

I nodded.

Clark looked down at the keelboat's slow but steady progress. "What say we get this venison down to those men? I think they're going to need it."

I hoisted my doe over my shoulders and we started down.

CHAPTER THREE

"There she is, boys!" Lewis's voice rang out from the bow, and I looked to see him pointing ahead. He was an almost indistinct shape, difficult to see through the pouring rain.

"The Mississippi River!" Lewis said happily. "Let's take her to starboard, lads. Aim for that point."

I could feel a sense of awe washing through me as we angled the keelboat toward the spit of land which formed the junction of the Ohio with the Mississippi. As I pulled on the oars, I reflected back on the previous month. It had been an interesting month, stopping at the Falls of the Ohio and meeting the legendary George Rogers Clark, then stopping again at Fort Massac, where we took on some new men, including an interpreter by the name of George Drouillard. Drouillard was part-Shawnee, and I'm not sure what he thought about being hired by a brother of the man the Shawnee had hated and feared, and had called Town-Burner Clark. If Drouillard had feelings one way or another, he didn't say. I, for one, welcomed having George along, especially after hearing the soldiers from the fort exclaiming their disappointment at losing their very best hunter to our crew.

We wrestled the keelboat to the shore and tied her tight, then set about making camp for the night. The captains had told us just that morning that it was their intention to take readings of our latitude and longitude and the width of the two rivers where they met using their chronometer and something called a circumferentor, so I expected to spend at least two days at the confluence. Which was fine with me. A month on that damn boat made me realize how much I disliked rowing.

Pryor and I prepared to set out to hunt as soon as the camp was complete. Clark's slave, York, was employed at the river's edge catching fish for our dinner, a role he seemed to relish. Myself, I'll take venison over fish any day.

"Let's head east along the Ohio," I suggested. "I saw deer back that way as we came down."

Nate nodded in agreement and then shook some of the rain water off his hat. "Fine by me, though how you could see anything in that damn monsoon, I have no idea."

I grinned. The weather had been steadily declining as we moved down the Ohio, culminating in heavy rains the past couple of days, but that was to be expected and it didn't bother me at all. Next would come the snow, which I was actually anticipating with some pleasure. I prefer hunting in the snow as tracks are much easier to follow.

We watched as Drouillard set off toward the north to do some hunting of his own, then Nate nudged me. "What do you think of him?" he asked.

I shrugged. "Don't know him well enough to say," I said. I knew Nate didn't like Indians, and I didn't care for most of them myself, but I wasn't going to pass judgment on Drouillard until I knew him better. "The soldiers at Massac speak highly of him."

Nate sniffed, and then spit. "We'll see how great of a hunter he is. He can't be all that good. Besides, I ain't too big on traveling with an Injun."

"According to Clark, we can expect to meet a lot of Indians up the Missouri," I reminded him, needling him a little. Sometimes it was fun to needle Nate. It was so easy to get his back up.

"I know that. But meeting up with Injuns ain't the same as spending all day with 'em."

We spent that afternoon in the woods east of the camp and came back with two fat deer, feeling pretty proud of ourselves. As we set to work butchering them, Drouillard came into camp and dropped several large bundles of dressed meat on the ground.

"What didja get, George?" Clark asked, stepping out of his tent.

"Three deer and a bear," he replied. "Dressed 'em out in the woods.

If I can borrow a couple men, we can go get the rest of the meat and fat."

I glanced at Nate as Drouillard set out with two of the men from Kentucky, John Shields and George Shannon, to bring in the meat. Nate was scowling. I tried not to laugh.

* * *

The next morning, the captains started out with a small group of men to cross the Mississippi in one of the pirogues and explore the western side. "Scouting out a spot for a fort," Floyd told me. "This here is a prime spot to put an American fort, to guard the two rivers and control the traffic up and down 'em."

That made sense. But I was confused about one thing. "Isn't that Spanish land over there?" I asked.

Floyd grinned. "For now," he said mysteriously, but he wouldn't say more. I wondered about that, and about the vague rumors I had heard recently that the United States was taking over the lands west of the Mississippi. I wondered if that was what Floyd was hinting at.

I spent the morning helping Floyd and some of the other men empty out the keelboat and spread the contents on the bank to dry. The heavy rains had dampened everything, and the small bit of sunlight peeking through the clouds was something of which we had to take advantage. Clark had said we would be making a winter camp opposite the mouth of the Missouri prior to setting out in the spring, and had prophesied that it would be a wet winter, so I had the feeling that the drying of supplies would be something we would do a lot of.

"I'm told it rains a lot in those parts in the winter," he had said, smiling cheerfully all the time. "Gonna get us a bit damp. Hope you all brought along your webbed feet."

I'm no duck but it'll take a lot of rain to stop John Colter.

In the afternoon we ran to the shore at a shout from Shannon, who had walked down with York after lunch to do some fishing. Shannon's pole was bent almost double, and the fish that was thrashing in the shallows looked like some kind of sea monster. Nate and I jumped in to the water and wrestled the fish to shore, amazed at its size and weight.

"What the hell is it?" Shields asked as we landed the monster on the rocky shore.

"Looks like a catfish," York said, wonder in his voice. He stood high on the shore, hands on his hips, shaking his head slowly back and forth as he stared down at the fish from a safe distance away.

"Biggest damn catfish I ever saw," Nate said breathlessly. We were both soaked to the skin, our arms marked bright red where the fish's tail had repeatedly smacked us.

"Maybe it's a puma fish," someone quipped, and we all laughed. That was one big damn catfish!

That evening, the captains measured and weighed the fish, after declaring that it was indeed a catfish. The fish was over four feet long and weighed just less than 130 pounds! We feasted on catfish that evening and toasted young Shannon's fishing skill, each toast becoming more creative and colorful as the whiskey flowed.

Shannon, who looks to be about ten years old but is said to be nineteen, just smiled and blushed.

* * *

I was awakened in the night just a couple days later by frenzied shouts, accompanied by the howling of a banshee-like wind and the splintered cracking and crashing of trees falling to the ground. Rain was coming down in buckets, driving horizontally across the campsite, obscuring everything, and as I ran toward the shouting I had to dodge flying branches and tents and small pieces of equipment. The shouting was coming from the vicinity of the river, where I found the men hastily attempting to rescue our pirogues, which had been driven against the shore and were in danger of being swamped. Waves were crashing against the rocky bank with surprising force, flooding over the gunwales of the pirogues and filling them with river water. It was a desperate situation.

"Turn that pirogue over!" Clark shouted, his voice barely audible over the howling of the wind. "Pour that water out. Move it, man!"

I ran down to the water's edge, vaulting over Lewis's black dog, Seaman, who was running in circles and barking maniacally. One of the pirogues was being pulled to higher ground and several men were struggling with the second, which was filled almost to the top with river water. The spray being thrown off the river by the wind was blinding, and the waves that were slamming against us made it almost impossible to turn the pirogue over to be drained.

"Grab 'er amidships, boys, and turn her with the wind," Clark said, jumping into the water beside me. What he said made sense. We had been fighting against the wind to drain the pirogue, but with Clark's help we rolled it toward the shore instead and it went fairly easily. A lot of river water flowed out of the pirogue, making it possible to finally lift the boat to safety.

"Good work, men!" Lewis shouted above the wind, as we carried the second pirogue away from the water's edge. He had to raise his voice to be heard above the shrieking wind and the crashing of the waves against the shore. "Now let's get this camp in order!"

* * *

In the morning we surveyed the damage, which was surprisingly light. Neither pirogue had been seriously damaged after being battered against the rocky shore, which was a miracle in itself. None of the gear had been damaged or lost when the pirogues had filled, all due to Captain Lewis's insistence the night before that all the gear be unloaded and stowed on shore. Several tents had been torn, and we never did find Silas Goodrich's blanket, but none of the men had received anything more serious than scratches and bruises. We were pretty lucky.

"What a night," Nate said in the morning, standing with his hands on his hips and looking around at the damage. Several trees were down and broken branches were strewn across the camp. It looked like a war zone.

"Well, guess we oughta get started," I said. The captains had expressed their intent to remain at this camp for another couple days before heading up the Mississippi, and they wanted the debris cleaned up.

"Guess we better. Wanna grab the other end of that tree?"

"Colter! Pryor!" It was Clark's voice.

"Yes, Captain," Nate shouted back.

"Get your rifles and come with us."

Nate glanced at me and I shrugged. Grabbing our rifles, we hurried down to the shore. Lewis and Clark and several other men, including Sergeant Floyd, were lowering one of the two pirogues into the water and clambering aboard. Lewis's dog sat proudly in the bow of his master's boat.

"We're gonna head downriver a ways and take a look at old Fort Jefferson," Clark explained. "Climb aboard."

Pryor and I jumped into the pirogue and took up oars. Clark pushed us off from the shore and climbed into the stern and we headed out into the water.

The Ohio was running fast on this morning following the storm, and was littered with floating branches and other debris. We struck out due south across the width of the Ohio, aiming toward the far shore. To our right, the waters of the Mississippi met the waters of the Ohio in swirling patterns, the muddy waters of the Mississippi mixing with the cleaner, clearer waters of the Ohio. Somewhere far below us, those mixed waters would eventually empty into the Gulf of Mexico.

"My brother, George, built Fort Jefferson back in '80," Clark said as we plied our oars. "I'm curious if it's still there."

The wind coming down the Ohio from the east was gusting and cold, and tried its best to blow us out into the flow of the Mississippi. We dug our oars deeper into the water and propelled the pirogue to the southern shore of the Ohio, then turned toward the west. The combined rivers at this point angled toward the southwest and we headed down that way, hugging the eastern shore. The Mississippi was running low for the time of year, according to Lewis, and the surface was choppy, frothed with whitecaps. It seemed smoother near the shore, and that's where we stayed.

"Look there," Lewis said, pointing across the Mississippi toward the west. Several canoes were struggling north against the strong current, manned by Indians who were leaning hard into their own oars, and they stared at us with as much curiosity as we were showing them.

"What tribe, do you think?" Lewis asked.

"Probably Shawnee," Clark surmised.

"Way down here?" I asked, surprised.

"A lot of Shawnee came this way after they were defeated by General Wayne," Clark said. "They joined some more of their people who had migrated here before the war, the ones who voted against any more fighting with the Americans. The Spanish gave them refuge west of the Mississippi. Now pull on those oars, John, and let's get to that fort!"

We pulled on the oars and the pirogue shot down the broad Mississippi, racing for a while with a large tree that, fortunately for us, stayed to the center of the river. Lewis kept up a running dialogue from the bow of the boat, pointing out different trees and animals, surmising possible places for forts and trading posts. I could sense in his mind a wide picture of the continent and the role of the new American government in it, and it was a thrilling picture to me. I have never been a learned man, have never been educated beyond basic schooling, but I am not a stupid man by any means. As an American who had been born in Virginia, I had a strong sense of my young country's place in the world. Lewis's translation of Jefferson's goal of making America into a great international power enthralled me. And I was a small part of making those grand dreams come true.

We secured the pirogue to the shore below a tall bluff on the eastern side of the Mississippi a few miles down from the Ohio and climbed to the top. The splintered and burned remains of an old fort littered a field that was itself returning to wild, and the view of the descending Mississippi showed George Rogers Clark's genius in placing the fort in that location. The wide river flowed past this bluff, visible for miles in both directions, and there was no way a force of any size could move past this point on the river without being spotted.

Captain Lewis was walking back and forth across the fort site, followed by his faithful dog. He was taking measurements, as he always seemed to do, and jotting entries in his ever-present notebook. Captain Clark was taking his own measurements, using some fancy instrument the workings of which I couldn't figure out, and so I took my ease on a log that looked as if it might have been part of the old fort's wall.

"Gonna snow soon," Nate said, plopping down beside me.

"Yep," I said. The air was sharp and crisp, and did seem to speak of snow to come.

Nate chuckled and shook his head slowly. "Someone woulda told me back in the spring that I'd be spending my winter on the Mississippi, I woulda laughed out loud."

I grinned and nodded. I knew what he meant.

He watched Lewis and Clark for several minutes. "You think them captains are gonna measure every hill and curve all the way to the Pacific?"

"Kind of appears that way, doesn't it?" I said, watching Lewis as he practically trotted through his self-appointed chores. The captain moved rapidly in everything he seemed to do. Made a body tired just watching him.

Nate shook his head again. "All those numbers must weigh awful heavy in their heads."

* * *

We got back to the camp that evening and found that some of the men had met up with a whiskey seller and were quite drunk and acting like fools. The captains were extremely disappointed and angry, and I vowed right then to maintain my own sobriety and not incur their wrath.

It's a vow I unfortunately broke before spring arrived.

CHAPTER FOUR

We left the camp at the mouth of the Ohio on a morning that was spitting snow and started north up the Mississippi. Captain Lewis had plans to part company with us soon to make his own way north to St. Louis with the intention, according to Captain Clark, of speaking with the governor of the Spanish territories concerning our little expedition up the Missouri.

"Them Spaniards won't be happy about our plans, but the choice isn't theirs to make," Clark said, some of his typical ebullience gone this morning. I had heard him complain to Lewis about not feeling well, and it showed. He seemed haggard and run down, and his normally sharp eyes were clouded.

The Mississippi was awash with floating trees and debris, as well as the more dangerous submerged underbrush that had anchored itself in the muddy bottom and floated just below the surface, there to rip or puncture the hull of a boat. I was assigned to one of the pirogues, the one with Lewis on board, and we made frequent calls to the shore so the captain could investigate some rock or hill that interested him. I thought about President Jefferson way back east in Washington and his demands to know everything about this land, and I wondered what he was going to do with all this new information once Lewis and Clark were finished scribbling it down. It all seemed a little foolish to me. But I was just a private in this army. My opinions weren't asked for and didn't matter.

We stopped that evening and made camp about thirteen miles up from the place where the Ohio and the Mississippi met. The weather had moderated a little, though the wind still blew strong from the north, carrying with it more snow, but right then I was more concerned about Nate Pryor than I was about future inclement weather.

"He is not the kind to desert, Captain Clark," I said. "I'd swear on the graves of my ancestors. Something must have happened. Let me go look for him."

"No, John," Clark said, and I could see the worry in his eyes. "Then we might have two of you missing instead of just one. Nate knows we're going north, and the Mississippi is too damn big to miss. He'll catch up."

"But if he's injured…"

"John, he set out to hunt eight hours ago. He could be anywhere. We'll fire a few rounds to signal him and that's about all we can do." Clark went into a spasm of coughing and I watched him worriedly. He really was feeling sickly.

"You all right, Captain?"

"I will be, John. I will be. Now how about throwing a couple more logs on that fire? I just can't seem to get warm tonight."

* * *

The next morning Nate had still not appeared and we set out without him. This day was a repeat of the one before, with many stops to gather plants or measure islands and sandbars, and by that evening we had traveled only a short distance north, stopping opposite a small settlement called Cape Girardeau. After sending Captain Clark with the keelboat and the other pirogue on north to anchor for the night above the town, Lewis directed us to put him ashore by the village.

"Got a man here I need to see," he said, tucking his leather pouch beneath one arm and taking up his rifle. "Sergeant Floyd, Private Colter, you come with me. The rest of you take your leisure and watch the pirogue, and no drinking!"

We left the other men grimacing on the shore and made our way up to the town, to a small and crowded general store and trading post. Floyd and I waited on the cluttered porch while Lewis went inside, only to emerge soon after with a frown on his face.

"He's at a horse race," the captain said, his voice tinged with disgust, and I hid a grin. For a man like Lewis, whose work occupied him all hours of the day and night, the idea of a store proprietor attending a horse race in the middle of the afternoon must have rankled greatly within him.

"Louis Lorimier used to be in the Ohio country," Captain Lewis said as we walked across the town toward a field where he had been told the races were held. "He did a lot of trading with the Shawnee and Delaware in that region. George Rogers Clark destroyed him in a raid and drove him from the area." A skinny dog ran at us from a side street, barking and snarling, but retreated when I waved my rifle at it. "I probably won't tell him that I'm traveling with Clark's younger brother," Lewis finished with a grin. "He might not be willing to trade with me."

We found Lorimier at the race grounds and he was a remarkable figure. Not a tall man, he was broadly built and had a head of dark hair that fell almost to his knees, tied back in a thick queue. Given his name, I had expected a Frenchman, but Lorimier appeared to be of full native blood. His horse had just won its race and he was busily collecting his winnings, but as soon as he had settled with his fellow bettors, he turned his full attention to Captain Lewis.

I wasn't able to hear all of their conversation, but they seemed to be speaking in a friendly enough manner, for an American Army officer and a man who had had his fortune taken away by the American Army. As we left the race grounds, Lewis pulled Sergeant Floyd aside. "Take the men and catch up to the keelboat. I'll be taking dinner with this man and his family and will join you this evening."

"Yes, Captain."

* * *

We caught up to the others after they had set up camp, and we spent a restful though rather chilly night. By seven o'clock the next morning we were back on the river, fighting the current north. I was looking forward to reaching the winter camp just to get off these boats for a while! The life of a riverman would never be the life for me!

Shortly after we set out, a shot rang out from the eastern shore, and we all turned to see Nate Pryor, waving his rifle from the shore and beckoning to us. A feeling of relief shot through me at the sight of him. The red pirogue turned and made its way to where Nate stood on a large rock and gathered him aboard before launching back onto the river. As the pirogue came up beside the keelboat, I could get a closer view of Nate, and he looked tired and worn.

"Where you been, man?" Clark called out.

Nate tried to grin. "Where haven't I been?" he replied.

Later, when we had stopped for lunch, he told us how he had gotten lost while trailing a wounded doe, and had ended up on the north bank of the Ohio rather than the eastern bank of the Mississippi. Rather than try to cut back to the Mississippi cross-country and possibly lose his way again, he had followed the Ohio down to the juncture before turning north.

"I been walking day and night," he said tiredly. "Didn't think I'd catch up to you boys before spring."

* * *

The following days passed in much the same manner as they had since leaving the camp at the Ohio and Mississippi junction, which meant rowing. The Mississippi ran moderately fast and the hazards remained the same as we were used to, with trees and floating branches being the largest of those hazards. We saw very few other boats, just some keelboats heading down toward New Orleans and a few canoes belonging to hunters and Indians. Lewis, who had rejoined us, was diligent with his measuring and exploring and the pirogues were often at the banks of the river while he wandered inland. The day after finding Nate alive and well we passed a tall and impressive column of rock just offshore from the western bank, a marker used by the river men to determine where they were in relation to the scattered cities, what Clark called a "landmark." Trees and shrubs grew on the top of the rock column, and it could be spotted for several miles along the course of the river.

"Fascinating," Lewis said, shaking his head as he studied the column from all sides. I half-expected to see him climb to the top in order to view it from that angle. "Imagine the years it took for the river to wash the dirt and softer rock away from this harder rock column. It is amazing to think that this column was once in the middle of a field or hills, and the river was hundreds of yards away, slowly eating away at the banks until it got where it is now. Truly fascinating."

I looked at the rock column again in a new light. It was pretty fascinating, when one looked at it the way Lewis did.

Numerous smaller rivers emptied into the Mississippi from both sides, along which could sometimes be seen small villages, mostly of Indians. On several days I went ashore to hunt and had the opportunity to see some of the land beyond the high banks of the river, and I have to say it seemed a lovely country, especially if you were of a mind to farm the land. The low lands along the wide river appeared capable of producing fine crops, and those same lands were thick with deer and other game. On my first foray onto the eastern shore I returned with two deer and a turkey within an hour of stepping off the pirogue.

My second hunting expedition was just as successful, and I was impressed with my companion on that particular trip, a man by the name of John Shields. This was my first chance to hunt with John and he was a man obviously at home in the woods. He was tireless and seemed able to smell the presence of deer. He would be another good man to have along in the spring.

Captain Lewis parted company with the main party along this section of the river to head up to St. Louis, and we continued north under the command of Captain Clark, who proved to be just as industrious at taking observations as Captain Lewis. Our progress was slow but steady as a result, not that any of us on the oars minded. It was always nice to take a break and rest our sore and tired muscles while the captain explored on shore.

The weather along the Mississippi turned regularly colder and wetter the more to the north we proceeded. The wind increased with the rain, strong enough at one point to break the mast on the keelboat. I heard several of the men lament the coming of winter, but I didn't know what they thought we could do about it. Winter always comes, followed by summer, then winter again. It's one of those things that is pretty much out of human hands. It's best to just learn to live with it.

Our journey up the river ended on December 12, at the mouth of a small river called Wood River. Captain Lewis had rejoined us several days earlier following his meeting with the commander of the Spanish garrison, a meeting at which Lewis had received just about the sort of welcome he had expected.

"He was civil," Lewis said to Clark over that evening's meal at our camp near Cahokia. All the soldiers were gathered around the two roaring fires, bracing against the chill wind off the river and the icy rain that fell steadily from leaden skies.

"That's about all he was," Lewis continued. "I offered Mr. Jefferson's greetings and explained the purpose of our expedition, and he hemmed and hawed for a while before saying that he could not give us permission to proceed up the Missouri until he conferred with his superiors." The captain smiled.

Clark grinned also. "Did he say he would attempt to stop us?"

"Of course not. He isn't foolish enough to go that far out on a limb. He knows that his control is limited and of short duration." Lewis looked around at us, his eyes bright. "It's time you men know what is taking place, those of you who don't already know, and I think it will help to shed a different light on this business we're about. The United States government has recently purchased the area west of the Mississippi, as far as the base of the Rocky Mountains, from the government of France. In a very short time, that land will belong to the United States."

"France?" Shields asked. "I thought that there land belonged to Spain."

Lewis shook his head. "Spain has ceded the land to France, who has in turn sold it to us to help finance their war in Europe. In a few weeks there'll be a ceremony, turning all the land from this river to the mountains over to American control."

Stunned silence greeted his words, followed by whoops and cheers from the assembled soldiers. I nodded in understanding. The whole reason behind this expedition was suddenly clearer than it had been. We weren't going up the Missouri to simply satisfy the curiosity of Thomas

Jefferson or to find some kind of water route to the Pacific. We were going up the Missouri to explore and report on our new land.

"So you men see the importance of what we are doing," Lewis continued when the celebration had quieted down. "We'll be the first Americans in that land once it becomes part of America. It's vital that we learn all we can about it, and implement our plans to create a trading empire with the natives."

The natives. Now there was a thought. I was kind of curious what their perspective on all this might be.

* * *

Our arrival at the camp on Wood River coincided with the arrival of a strong storm that came barreling down the Mississippi, complete with large hail and snow, and it made for a miserable first evening. We set up our tents and unloaded the keelboat and pirogues in that driving wind and snow, and were thoroughly soaked and shivering with the cold by the time the storm finally abated. Captain Clark, feeling much better after his recent illness, worked shoulder by shoulder with us, his cheerful voice booming out regularly above the howling of the wind, and my respect for him continued to grow by leaps and bounds.

Shields and I were sent out shortly after our arrival to scout the land around the camp and bring back some food. The land that surrounded the camp was hilly, but nothing like what I was used to along the Ohio back in Kentucky. The snow was filtering down through the trees, leaving a dusting of white on top of the autumn's fallen leaves. Remnants of Indian camps were scattered through the woods, abandoned now, and we saw several small farms and homesteads through breaks in the trees. We returned to the camp later that evening with several large turkeys and a couple of fat opossums, meager fare but the best we could get in a short time. We ate that night hunched over the fires, our backs turned toward the wind, which carried only small amounts of snow at this point but was just as chilly as it had been earlier.

"We'll set to work on building a camp hereabouts. This is where we'll winter," Lewis said, gesturing off across the Mississippi. "And there is why." Far across the wide river, through the squalls of snow, could just be seen the mouth of the Missouri, the river that we would begin to ascend in the spring. Finally seeing that river, distant as it was and shrouded in fog and snow, was a proud moment for me. This is where it would really begin.

And it was where it almost ended for me, through my own stupidity.

CHAPTER FIVE

"I'd like your opinion, Mr. Colter," Clark said the next day.

We were taking a breather from chopping trees and hauling wood and I was glad to sit down for a few minutes. Earlier that morning the two captains had drawn out their plans for the camp that would act as our winter quarters and now work had begun in earnest. All of the men were busy, clearing the trees away at the camp site and felling other trees to be used in the building of the huts. A light snow was falling from a leaden sky but we were in high spirits, shouting cheerfully to each other while we worked.

"What can I answer for you, Captain?" I asked. Our breath frosted in the chilly air as we talked, though several large fires helped keep the worst of the cold away. There was nothing, however, that was going to stop that wind.

"Captain Lewis and I have been working on the roster of men to go up the Missouri," Clark said, looking around at the busy camp. "We've concluded our opinions on some of the men, but I'd like your opinion on a couple others."

"I'll answer you best I can, Captain."

Clark nodded in satisfaction. "We're both impressed with your skills and attitude, John, and you're definitely going upriver with us, if you're still inclined."

"I'd be heartbroken if you excluded me, sir," I admitted.

He laughed and clapped me on the shoulder. "That's about what I reckoned. Obviously Sergeant Floyd is going along, and we've also decided on John Shields and the Field brothers."

"They're good men," I said.

"We think so. Give me your thoughts on Shannon."

I looked across the camp to where George Shannon was working with Joseph Reubin, the two hacking their way through a thick log with a long crosscut saw. They were perfectly in time with each other and were getting through the tree with swift ease. "He's young," I said thoughtfully, "which can be a hindrance if he allows it to be. But I like him. He's strong, works hard, and never complains."

"So you'd be all right traveling upriver with him?"

"Yes, sir."

"How about Nate Pryor?"

"I'll admit to being a bit prejudiced there, Captain Clark."

He studied me. "In what way?"

"Old Nate and I have been friends for a long time. I know him well, and I know his wife, and I know how excited he is to be on this journey. My opinion might not be the best one."

"I trust you, John. Just tell me what you think. After all, you're going to have to travel with him through some dangerous lands. I don't think you'd put him forth if you didn't honestly trust him."

"Thank you, sir. Given my choice, I would have Nate along any day."

"And Shields?"

"Another good man, sir."

Clark named several others, some of whom had come downriver from Pittsburgh with Lewis, and I answered him as honestly as I could. I could see him filing away all my words in his head as we spoke.

Clark finally nodded in satisfaction. "There's another group of men being brought up by Drouillard who should be here just about any time, and I guess we'll have to judge them over the winter. But for now, if you'd be so kind as to keep your eyes open, I'd appreciate your further thoughts on any or all of the men here." He grinned, possibly sensing my discomfort. "I'm not asking you to spy on them, John. Just tell me if you're comfortable with them on a long and arduous journey."

"I can do that, Captain," I said.

* * *

The camp came together slowly but steadily, and I had the growing impression that slow and steady would mark most of what we were to do in the following months. Captain Lewis was back down the river securing supplies, leaving Captain Clark in charge of the construction and running of the camp, which was fine with me. Lewis might be a smart and driven man but he was distant and aloof. I liked Captain Clark much better.

Every day the camp buildings moved forward toward completion, though the work was back-breaking. Some days there was no discernible progress then the work would race forward. We spent most days felling trees and hauling the logs to the clearing to be used for the huts and walls, then cutting them down to length and placing them in their proper positions. When we were assigned to hunting it came as a reprieve from the labor, though we all took our turns at all aspects of the construction. Captain Clark planned everything with a meticulousness that matched Lewis's, and all the men knew what was expected of them.

The snow continued to fall, mixed occasionally with rain or sleet, making the conditions in camp miserable. We all let out a loud cheer when the first hut was completed, and the rest quickly followed, allowing us to move indoors. The final hut went up just five days before Christmas, and those huts were a gift all by themselves.

"You boys comfortable?" Clark asked, sticking his head in the door of the hut I was sharing with several other of the men. A log fire was burning, and despite the narrow gaps between the log walls that let in the stiff breeze, the air was warm and cozy.

"Getting there, sir," Nate replied.

"Good. Then maybe we can finish my hut now."

That's one thing I have to say about Clark. He insisted on our huts being completed before the work began on his, and I admire that in an officer.

The following day Drouillard appeared in the clearing, leading a line of men recruited from army posts in Tennessee, and bringing with him several packhorses laden with supplies and fresh venison. The men were a welcome sight to see, though most of the work was done, but it was the fresh venison that had most of our attention! And it was good to see George again.

The new men were immediately taken aside by Captain Clark and interviewed. I could tell that he wasn't very happy with them.

"They're giving me the dregs," he said to me that afternoon. Ice was flowing fast and heavy down the river and several men had been pulled from the fort detail to construct wedges for under the keelboat. The boat had been emptied to reduce the weight, its cargo stored in several of the huts.

"What do you mean, sir?" I asked.

"Ah, the captains at those Tennessee posts probably don't want to give up their best men," he said. "Can't really blame them, I suppose. But, damn it, I need men of strength and character!" He took off his hat and scratched his forehead. "I need your help, John."

I waited.

"I've already asked Floyd to talk to the new men and work with them, give me an idea of their characters. I'd like you to do the same."

"Yes, sir."

"I'm going to send you out on a hunt tomorrow with one of them, a man named John Potts. I already know and like Corporal Warfington, but the rest I'm unsure of. Talk to Potts, feel him out a little, then let me know what you think, will you?"

"Yes, sir."

He smiled. "Thanks, John. I want the best group I can gather on that boat in the spring, you understand?"

"I do. I want the same."

* * *

Potts and I left the camp before dawn the next morning and angled off toward the east, following the meandering Wood River up and away from the Mississippi. It was a very cold morning, the frost heavy on the ground, and I wasn't surprised to see that the ice was almost full across the water.

"I wanna get as much meat as we can today," I told Potts before we left. "Christmas is in a couple days, and the captains want a fine celebration."

Potts grinned and nodded. I could already tell he was a man of few words, which suited me fine. But Clark had tasked me with learning more about the man so I had to try.

"Where you from, John?" I asked. We were following the north bank of the Wood River, stepping carefully across the frozen ground, and I kept my voice pitched low so as not to scare off any game. I expected we would have to walk a fair distance to find anything; the area around the camp had become hunted pretty low.

"Germany," he said, and grinned again as I glanced at him in surprise. "Didn't count on that, did you?"

I grinned back. "Not really."

"My family came to America when I was fairly young," he said, his eyes sweeping the woods ahead and around us. "I worked as a miller before joining the army."

"So how'd you end up out here on the edge of the wilderness?"

"Captain Purdy assigned me to it," he said simply. "I don't think he likes me very much."

"Wanted you out of his hair, did he?"

Potts nodded, though his eyes never stopped their search of the woods. I liked his concentration and attention to the job at hand. He was doing better than me at watching for something to shoot!

"What do you think about being assigned to this mad venture?"

He grunted something that might have been a laugh. "Better this than the pointless make-work details I always seemed to get stuck on back in Tennessee. Besides, this sounds like it could be a load of fun."

We walked for a while in silence. Then Potts said, "What about you, Colter? I hear you volunteered for this duty."

"I did."

"Could be a dangerous mission. Are you having second thoughts?"

"Not at all," I replied. "I was at Fallen Timbers."

He glanced at me for a moment, clearly evaluating me just as I was doing with him, then returned his attention to the woods. Without seeming to move, he brought his rifle up and squeezed off a shot, and I turned my head to see a doe take one faltering step and then drop to the ground about a hundred yards away.

"I guess we'll find out sooner or later if your decision was a right one," he said, and I laughed. I liked old John Potts already.

* * *

Christmas morning was greeted with much celebration at the camp. Floyd, Pryor, the Fields brothers and I awakened the camp with a round of rifle fire and loud war whoops, laughing as the other men ran from their huts to find the source of the commotion.

Shields and one of the Tennessee recruits had engaged in a drunken fight during the night, apparently after the Tennessean had made disparaging comments concerning Shields's ancestry, and I could see the anger and disappointment on Clark's face. The captain tried hard to keep whiskey from the camp but there were too many locals and pacified Indians in the area with whiskey to sell and too many soldiers with money, and time, to spare. Bored men and whiskey would never be a combination to inspire peace and harmony.

Later in the day, we feasted on deer, turkey and grouse, much of the meat having been brought in by George Drouillard. Drouillard was as good of a hunter as the troops at Fort Massac had claimed. The quiet half-breed was proving his worth in the camp, not only with his hunting skills but with his diplomacy. He kept mostly to himself, staying clear of the petty squabbles that broke out on a daily basis. He seemed solid and dependable, a worthy man to have along.

The year of 1803 concluded with the work still going on at the camp, along with the commencement of training for the soldiers, both newly recruited like me and old hands like the boys from Tennessee. Many of the men in camp who had been in the army prior to this assignment knew all about drill and rifle practice, but it was new to me. I understood the need to ingrain obedience in soldiery, to learn to obey the commands of an officer without hesitation, but I was an independent man, used to going my own way. It required a lot of self-discipline on my part to adapt to my new role of soldier. Captain Clark had us all on guard rotation, and

I usually pulled the shift during the darkest part of the night, due to my ability to see quite well in the dark.

"Sergeant Floyd tells me you're part cat," Clark had said. "Wanna take the night shift?"

"Okay by me." I studied his face. "You expecting trouble here?"

"What's the best way to avoid trouble?" he asked in return, then answered his own question. "By always expecting trouble. That way you're never surprised."

I nodded. It was the kind of advice Simon Kenton would have given.

My first night on guard duty I worked with Joseph Field. Joseph shared a similar background with me, born in Virginia and moved to Kentucky as a child. I had known him and his brother since I was a teenager and I was glad they would be with us as we set out up the Missouri.

"I heard Captain Clark sent some of them Tennessee boys back home," Joseph said quietly. The woods around the camp were silent and still and a light rain was falling, a change from the snow and sleet of previous days.

"Can't blame him," I said. "They weren't much good."

I could sense him nodding to himself. "And they're making Nate a sergeant."

"They know what they're doing."

"Shoulda been you, John."

I laughed. "Me, a sergeant? I don't lead men. Floyd and Pryor can lead men."

"And Ordway?"

I grimaced. Sergeant John Ordway was a thorn in my side. Something about the man just rubbed me the wrong way and Joseph knew it. That was why he was ribbing me about him. "Ordway's a big bag of gas," I said. "He gets in my craw." I nudged Joseph's shoulder and pointed into the woods, and we watched a doe lead two medium-sized fawns down to the river's edge. Pretty late in the year for fawns, I thought.

"Well, I can tell you this about sergeants," Joseph said. "Most of them want to be junior officers, and are often more of a pain than a real officer. But you still gotta obey them."

He was right, of course, and they were words that I should have kept in my mind.

* * *

After the turning of the year the weather deteriorated even more, and the temperatures steadily dropped, dipping into the single digits at night. Snow lay heavy on the ground and both the Missouri and the Mississippi froze clear across. A comment made by Clark earlier in the winter, about being able to walk up the Missouri on the ice, seemed to be coming true. The wind that came down the two massive rivers cut through all layers of clothing, leaving a man shivering constantly, and the act of thawing mud to fill the chinks between the logs of the cabins became an all-consuming task. We also spent a lot of our time fixing and repairing the braces we had built for keeping the keelboat safe against the bank. The shifting river ice was a constant danger to the big boat.

We passed our time hunting or drilling, or sneaking out to find the whiskey sellers, going against the captain's express orders to stay away from those men. It wasn't that we didn't have an allotted amount of whiskey per man, we just wanted more. It was boring and tedious in that camp, with the icy weather and nothing really to do, and the whiskey was an escape that we all craved the way we craved oxygen.

The closeness of the huts led to frayed nerves, and fights were common. Some the captains learned about and others were kept secret. I tried my best to steer clear of men with whom I didn't get along, in order to avoid trouble, because I'm not the kind to walk away from a fight if it's forced on me. Potts and a soldier named Werner got into a real knuckle-buster one night and both were reprimanded by Clark for their actions, and threatened with dismissal. That could too easily be me if I wasn't careful.

The icy weather also helped to keep nerves on edge. Frostbite was a danger among hunters, and I almost broke my leg one day when I fell off an icy rock while hunting. On another day, Clark broke through the ice on a pond while attempting to reach an old Indian ruin and Floyd and I had to pull him out, getting good and wet in the process. All of us had frozen fingers or toes at one time or another, and many of the men were sick.

Drouillard, Shields and I were the primary hunters during that long winter and spent a large amount of our time in the woods and on the prairies surrounding the camp, hunting anything we could find that would bring nourishment to the men. The weather stayed near or below freezing and the ice remained on the rivers all through the month of January, and the deer seemed to have gone into hiding. Couldn't blame 'em. I wanted to go into hiding myself at times.

Captain Lewis returned to the camp from Cahokia at the end of January, and then just as quickly was gone again, heading across the Mississippi to St. Louis. He stated his goal of spreading diplomacy and making important contacts with the influential people there, but most of us at the cold, dirty camp could picture the fancy balls and wine and ladies and we didn't buy the captain's explanations. Dissatisfaction was setting in.

In February, both captains set out for St. Louis, leaving Sergeant Ordway in charge in the camp. Most of the men were ambivalent but it bothered me to no end. I hadn't signed on to this expedition to take orders from a man I didn't respect. My temper sizzled, until one night when he pushed me too far. That was when I almost threw everything away.

CHAPTER SIX

"Reubin, you're on guard duty."

I watched as Reubin Field opened one eye and looked up at John Ordway. "The hell I am."

"Come on, get up. I said you're on guard duty."

"I was on duty last night," he said, closing his eyes. "I'm off tonight."

"Reubin…"

"Listen, Ordway, I'm not on guard duty!"

"You tell him, Reubin," I said.

Ordway took a deep breath. "The captains left me in charge of this camp, and I say you're on guard duty right now!"

Shields sat up on his bunk, weaving from side to side as he stared blearily at the sergeant. We had been out of camp earlier, paying a visit to a nearby farm for the purpose of securing some whiskey, and now the tension was building in the small hut. I could see that this conversation was heading down a dangerous path but the whiskey had my brain fuddled and, besides, I had had just about all I could stand of Sergeant John Ordway.

"We all heard what Lewis said," Shields said, his words slurred. "How could we not have? Little pipsqueak talks all the time. Now go away!"

Reubin laughed.

"Damn it, Reubin," Ordway exploded. "Get up out of that bunk and get on that guard post or I'll put you on report!"

"So put me on report or don't, you big bag of wind. Either way, get out of my hut."

I couldn't help but laugh at the expression on Ordway's face. I knew I shouldn't but the whiskey had more control over me than I did.

"You think that's funny, Colter?" Ordway asked.

"Yeah, I do."

"Fine. You're on report, also."

I sat up on my bunk, suddenly furious. "It'll be kinda hard to write your damn report if I shoot you, you pompous ass."

Shields fell over laughing.

Ordway stared at me coldly. "You've just bought yourself a ticket off this expedition," he said quietly. "I'll make sure you're court-martialed and sentenced for that."

I would have shot him then, with God as my witness, and I had even got as far as grabbing up my long rifle, but Pete Weiser grabbed me and held me back, and I'm eternally grateful to him for that. Because with the mood I was in right then and with the whiskey flooding away my common sense I probably would have killed Ordway and spent the rest of my days looking out at the world through the bars of a stockade.

As it was, I did face court-martial upon the return of the captains. Clark sat me down in his hut and told me what would happen.

"I can't believe this of you, John," he said.

I sat with my head down. I couldn't believe it of myself.

"I wish I knew what you were thinking. I know you don't like Sergeant Ordway, whatever your reasons, but as a private in this army your likes and dislikes mean nothing. We put him in charge of this camp in our absence and that is all the authority he needs. Let me ask you a question."

I listened.

"If I had come in to that hut and told Field to get on guard duty, do you think he would have done it?"

"Yes, sir."

"And would you have threatened to shoot me?"

"Of course not, Captain Clark."

"If Captain Lewis or myself have to spend all our time in this camp issuing the simplest of orders, we'd never have time to gather the supplies and the knowledge we need to be successful on this expedition." His voice was low and calm, but I could sense fury behind his words. "That's why we have sergeants. You don't have to like them but you damned well better obey them!"

I nodded slowly. He was right. I had nothing to say in my defense. I was sober now, and sober I never would have threatened Ordway, but that didn't matter in the slightest. Once words are spoken out loud they can never be taken back.

"Am I off the expedition?" I asked.

"That's not for me to say, John. There'll be a trial. That much I know. You, Shields and Reubin will be given a chance to tell your side. If I were you, I'd stay in this camp and stay away from the damn whiskey sellers until that trial has come and gone. As it is, you're confined to this camp for the next ten days, minimum. Is that clear?"

"Yes, Captain."

"And if Sergeant Ordway tells you to do something, you're going to keep your mouth shut and do it. And in that way you just might save your own skin."

* * *

John Potts stopped me as I walked across the camp later that day.

"I put in a good word with the captains for you, John," he said.

"I appreciate that. Hope it does some good."

"It can't hurt," he said. He nodded toward his left, where Sergeant Ordway was talking to Corporal Warfington near the sergeant's hut. "An apology to him would go a long ways, also."

He was right. And as much as my pride didn't want to take that step, it was something I had to do. Thanking Potts, I took a deep breath and walked toward the sergeant.

Ordway looked at me as I approached, his gaze level and without emotion.

"Sergeant, can I speak with you for a moment?"

He nodded noncommittally. Warfington didn't make any move to leave us alone, which was fine with me. What I felt I needed to say wasn't private.

"I want to apologize to you, Sergeant Ordway," I said, and I was

49

surprised and pleased that the words weren't as difficult to speak as I had thought they might be. "What I did and said in that hut was completely out of line and inappropriate. I know it's no excuse, but sober I never would have said or done those things."

He watched me, saying nothing. I couldn't tell if what I was saying meant anything to him or not.

"Anyway, I just wanted to say I'm sorry, and I hope we can start over again and work together," I finished. As I turned to walk away, he caught my shoulder in his hand, stopping me.

"I'd be lying if I didn't say that a part of me wants to hate you, John," he said evenly. "I've never been keen on any man who threatens to shoot me," he added with a small smile. "But I also know you're a man of integrity, and this apology just proves that. I'd be happy to have you along on this voyage." And he shook my hand.

"Thank you, Sergeant," I said.

"Just do me one favor."

"Name it."

"Don't threaten to shoot me again."

I smiled. "I think I can guarantee that."

A short time later, the official list was posted in the camp of who was going up the river with the Corps and my name was on it. And I was on Sergeant Ordway's squad.

* * *

The month of April passed in a whirlwind of activity, as final preparations were made for the imminent journey up the Missouri. On several occasions the captains were absent from the camp, traveling to Cahokia or St. Louis, and in all of those instances Sergeant Ordway was left in charge. There were no more incidents between us and we even went on a short hunting trip together around mid-month. I'm not going to sit here and tell you we became fast friends, because that wasn't the case, but we did resolve our differences, learned to respect each other, and found out we could work together.

Several local men from neighboring villages and farms came by the camp toward the end of the month, imagining themselves smarter than us, and challenged us to several games of chance, thinking they would win our money. We took them up on their offers because we were nothing if not confident. It was quite humorous to see them walk away with empty pockets instead of carrying our hard-earned pay as they had supposed they would.

Whiskey still appeared in the camp on a regular basis and several of the men found themselves in trouble with the captains for being drunk, but after my earlier experience I did my very best to stay out of the whiskey's grip. I'm not saying I didn't drink it when it was offered to me, but never again did I get drunk enough to act like a fool. I wanted to go up the Missouri with the Corps of Discovery.

Other visitors made regular appearances at the camp, from territorial leaders to traders, all of them eager to learn of some way in which they could benefit from the expedition. In early May I was introduced to one of those men, a man who would be instrumental in my life in later years, though I did not know it at the time. His name was Manuel Lisa, a fur trader from the St. Louis area. He visited the camp along with some other men, accompanied by Sergeant Floyd, and I could tell by Captain Clark's expression that he didn't care for the man. At that time, Lisa was just another stranger passing through, and nothing indicated that one day I would be in his employ, or that I would almost die as a result of that employment.

But that was later. For now I was busy redeeming myself, and I was quite proud when Captain Clark gave me the task of delivering several letters to Captain Lewis in St. Louis, returning with his replies. It showed me that the captains were beginning to trust me again, and that meant a lot to me. I had stumbled, granted, but I'm not the type to stay down long.

Preparations to depart continued into May, as the weather warmed and the level of the rivers rose. We took the keelboat out one afternoon for an experimental run north up the Mississippi and it rode fine in the water, showing no apparent damage after the brutal winter. Now it really felt like we were close to leaving the Wood River camp and getting on our way.

And, finally, on May 14, after what seemed like an eternity, we set out for the Missouri.

CHAPTER SEVEN

May 14th started out cloudy and cold, and rain was falling heavily by afternoon, but in our hearts the sun was blazing down from a clear sky, shining directly on us. We were under way! All the planning, all the preparation, all the rainy gloomy months stuck in that muddy camp, were culminating in this moment that we had all been dreaming about. The keelboat was loaded, the two pirogues were alongside, and we were pulling on the oars, leaving Wood River behind. In later months I would roundly curse those damn oars and that damn keelboat but on the afternoon of the 14th I was exuberant and excited, and the keelboat felt like it was floating on air.

Captain Lewis was still in St. Louis working on whatever he was working on, and we were only going up the Missouri as far as a small island near the village of St. Charles to await his arrival, but distances didn't matter yet. What mattered was forward motion! This was the symbolic moment for me, the dividing line between my old life and my new. While it was true that I had started this journey way back in the summer of 1803 when Captain Clark met me on the bank of the Ohio, everything since then had felt like, well, an interlude.

Not any more. Now the true expedition had begun.

All around me the men were in very high spirits and they pulled on the long oars with enthusiasm. Behind the keelboat, our two pirogues trailed along with us, one filled with soldiers and the other with French boatmen, hired by Lewis and Clark as guides and possibly interpreters between our party and the natives up the river. Optimism and excitement were the ruling emotions of the day.

"Pull them oars, boys," Sergeant Floyd called out cheerily. "Let's make this big hunk of wood fly like a bird!"

Groans and good-natured catcalls greeted his words and he laughed, a large friendly man embarking on the final journey of his life, though of course we didn't know that then. I can still picture him in my mind as he was on that day, sitting there on that keelboat in a driving rain, calling out cadence and smiling like a little boy on Christmas morning. God, how I miss him.

We entered the flow of the Missouri and fought our way upstream against the strong current. One mile passed, and then another, the first of thousands to come. Due to our late start we weren't able to reach St. Charles that day, so we put ashore on the northern end of a large island just below the town. At Captain Clark's direction we set up a temporary camp, something that we would become very good at over the next couple of years. We were a little rusty that first time, I'll say that, but we did improve with time.

It rained all through that first night and into the next morning. The Missouri was running high and swift, and, much like the Mississippi, was a roiling danger of floating debris and sawyers, trees that had fallen into the stream yet retained their roots in the banks. The floating logs and debris seemed to pose the worst hazards and we were having major problems with them. Eventually we determined that part of our problem stemmed from the fact that we had too much weight toward the bow of the boat and not enough in the stern. I would have thought that our experienced French river men could have warned us of that danger when the keelboat was being loaded, but the subject apparently never came up and they never thought to volunteer the little bit of information that could have saved us a lot of trouble.

Another day on the river took us to the small village of St. Charles, described to us by Clark as the last civilized city on the Missouri. Many of the inhabitants of the village came down to the riverbank to see us and to see the boat, and they were cheerful and friendly and much curious about us and our intentions. Captain Clark went up to the village in the afternoon, saying he would most likely be spending the night, and left us under strict instructions not to leave the camp. We would be remaining at the camp until we were rejoined by Captain Lewis in a couple of days.

We enjoyed a large fire that evening to go along with our daily dram of whiskey, and we danced to the fiddle music provided by one of our French boatmen, a happy little man named Cruzatte. The mosquitoes were fierce that night, droning in our faces and ears, but none of us were willing to let that small distraction dampen our enthusiasm.

"Hey, John, you wanna get away from this damn boat for a while?" The whispered question came from John Collins, one of the men who had been assigned to the expedition while we were at Wood River. I didn't really trust Collins, who had been in trouble already for stealing a hog from a farm near the Wood River camp and then lying about the incident to the captains.

"What do you have in mind?" I asked.

Collins looked around to make sure we weren't overheard. "Me, Hall and Werner are gonna go up to that village and have a look around, maybe find us some good whiskey and one of them French lasses as seem so easy with their favors. Wanna go with us?"

I shook my head. "You know you're going to get caught, don't you?"

"Nah, we ain't," he replied indignantly. "Come on, what do you say? Wanna go along?"

The idea of slipping away to the small village was appealing, for just the reasons Collins had mentioned, but there was no way I was going to take that risk, especially this soon after my earlier infractions and the leniency shown to me by the captains and Sergeant Ordway. And there was another factor. St. Charles was just too small of a village for word of us being there to not get back to the captains. I could sense disaster looming.

"Thanks for the invite, John," I told him. "But I think I'll take a pass."

"Hell, you used to be fun," Collins said with disgust, shaking his head. "You're turning into an old woman."

"That may be," I said easily. Collins' opinion really didn't carry much weight with me. "You go have your fun."

"You gonna tell the sergeant on us?" he asked, eyeing me suspiciously.

"That's not my way, John. I'll keep your confidence."

* * *

I had been right. Our three wayward boys did get in trouble, mainly for being drunk and making idiots of themselves. Collins even went so far as to harass several of the womenfolk in the town and was subsequently reported to Captain Clark for it. Needless to say, Captain Clark was infuriated.

The court-martial took place the next day, with the three miscreants still hung-over from their adventure and not seeming to really understand the seriousness of what they had done. At one time, I most likely would have been standing there beside them, listening to Captain Clark harangue us for bringing disrepute down on the entire Corps, and my head would have been hung in shame like theirs were. I silently thanked whatever force had made me decline the invitation to accompany them. Maybe I was just becoming more responsible.

Hall and Werner were convicted of being away from the camp but were not punished. Collins is the one who took the brunt of Clark's anger. Fifty lashes on the bare skin of his back, applied heavily. I winced as the lashes fell, feeling badly for him, but I understood the reasoning behind the harsh punishment. Besides the damage to the reputation of the United States Army among the citizens of St. Charles, a city newly annexed into America, there was the question of establishing discipline prior to leaving civilization behind. Disobeying orders in the middle of hostile Indian country could get us all killed.

It was a lesson Collins was a long time in learning.

* * *

The next day was dedicated to shifting the load on the keelboat, and Collins worked right along with us, flayed back and all. It was hard, sweaty, back-breaking work. We had several tons of equipment, supplies and Indian gifts on that boat, all of which had to be taken off, sorted, repacked, and then returned to its new location on board with the idea of transferring some of the weight to the stern. We worked all through that long day, glad that the rain had subsided for the time being, and by dusk the keelboat had been loaded again.

"You men did a fantastic job," Captain Clark said to us that evening, as we sat tired and sore on the sandy bank next to the boats. "That work wasn't easy."

"Was our work worth an extra dram of whiskey tonight, Captain?" someone shouted out. I think it was Potts.

Clark grinned. "I think so."

We cheered.

Clark continued. "And I might have some news you'll all appreciate. We've been invited to a ball in the village tomorrow evening. I can't go but I'm planning on sending quite a number of you men up to represent us. We'll have to leave a guard, and Collins, Hall and Werner will not be going, but the rest of you are encouraged to clean yourselves up and make yourselves presentable." Clark fixed us all with a stern glare. "Represent us well, gentlemen. If I hear any reports like two nights ago…" He held up a thick stick and snapped it abruptly in half, tossing both ends into the fire.

We got the message.

For our final fling in civilization, it was a fine affair. St. Charles was a small village, and the people were poor, but they threw us a great party, with music and food and beautiful women, not to mention all the wine and spirits that thirsty men could consume. I drank but didn't get drunk, though if I had known this was my final visit to a true city for more than four years, I might have imbibed a little more than I did! But I didn't know, and I was still worried about my standing in the eyes of the captains, so I behaved.

CHAPTER EIGHT

Shortly after that final fling, Captain Lewis came up from St. Louis to rejoin us, and our last preparations were made to depart upriver. Lewis was accompanied by several prominent men from St. Louis, and his arrival coincided with the arrival of several strong thunderstorms. I secretly think the captain enjoyed the image he presented that day, of the intrepid young explorer appearing out of the wind and rain and swirling darkness, intent on his mission to the exclusion of all else. It is the kind of thing that would walk hand-in-hand with Lewis's image of himself.

"He's like a struttin' rooster," I heard a soldier named Moses Reed say one time, as we watched Lewis give one of his speeches to some Sioux upriver, and I knew what he meant. Lewis was a man who was full of himself and his role as Jefferson's hand in the west.

Not that I want to be down on Captain Lewis. He was a strong man, and his leadership was good. He treated us well, and with Captain Clark he held us all together on our unprecedented trek across the continent and back. We only lost one man on the entire journey, poor Charles Floyd, even though we faced innumerable life-threatening dangers along the way. Hostile Indians, deadly cold, deep mountain snows, illness, injury. Yet we all came through it and the leadership of those two captains played a vital part in that.

* * *

Boom!

The roar of the swivel gun mounted in the bow of the keelboat echoed off across the flat prairie land, followed by cheers from the men. Quite a few of the townfolk from St. Charles had gathered on the bank to watch us depart and they cheered in response, waving their hands above their heads. Low clouds raced by overhead, promising more rain that day, as the big lumbering boat started up the Missouri. Like our departure from the camp on the Wood River, or River Dubois, as Captain Clark had called it, this felt like a true beginning.

The Missouri was flowing fast, probably as a result of all the rain we'd been having, and pulling against that current was a chore, but I was used to hard work and it didn't bother me. Somewhere in my mind I'm sure I realized that rowing that boat would become more of a bother as the months went by, but on that warm afternoon, as St. Charles disappeared to our stern, my attention was on the river and the mission ahead and I had all the energy I could ever want.

"This is it, Colter," John Potts said from his seat across from me. The creak and splash of the oars punctuated his words. "Last chance to jump over the side and swim back to civilization."

I grinned.

"No jumping now, lads," Captain Clark called out. "We are on a grand adventure!"

Another cheer split the air, and then we all settled in to our work. The breeze coming down the river was cool and clouds kept the worst of the sun off of us. Intermittent rain helped keep things cool as we pulled on the oars and passed seemingly endless prairies. This would become a familiar setting for us, the wide river lapping at the bow and gurgling past, the voices of the men as we sweated on the oars, the vast sky above our heads. At that moment I was very glad to be alive and to be right where I was.

The going wouldn't always be easy, as anyone who has ever paddled a large boat against a river's current can attest. We had the same problems that were faced on the Ohio and Mississippi, that of submerged logs, sawyers, sandbars and other obstacles. We spent as much time poling or dragging the boat using ropes from the shore as we did paddling, but we made progress. There were days when we would collapse by our fire at night in a state of complete exhaustion after only making two or three miles, and then there were the days when a favorable wind would allow us to hoist our sail and we would make fifteen or twenty miles with relative ease. We would have incidents like the one just a few days out of St. Charles, where a strong current wrenched the keelboat around, breaking the tow rope and landing her hard on a sandbar, sideways, almost flipping her over. Or the time in early June when Sergeant Ordway steered the keelboat too close to the shore and broke the mast by snagging it in some overhanging tree branches. We battled mosquitoes, biting flies and gnats, and received our share of drenching from heavy rain. All of us had blisters and sores from days spent laboring as we forced the keelboat up the Missouri, but we always seemed to have enough energy to dance and laugh around the fire in camp at night.

The hunting was easy at the beginning, with wide prairies and shady bottomlands that supported a myriad of game, including buffalo, deer and fowl. On the Missouri we never went hungry, and you could hear guns blazing at just about any time of the day. As a hunter, some of the indiscriminate killing bothered me, such as the day two wolves appeared on the shore, curious about us, and one of the pirogues stopped so a man could go on shore just to shoot one. We didn't need the food at the time, and we didn't eat the wolf, anyway. Or the time Lewis went out of his way to kill a large rattlesnake that was sunning itself on a sandbar. The snake was no danger or hindrance to us and there was no reason to kill it. Killing for food is one thing. Killing just because you can is foolishness.

One afternoon Captain Lewis shot at a wolf that was just minding its own business, then ordered me to shoot it after his bullet simply wounded the animal. I shot the poor wolf more to end its pain than through any desire to kill it. Lewis was impressed with my shooting and seemed ecstatic about the kill. I was just disgusted.

Our captains were often as busy as we were, but in a different way, measuring every bend and twist of that river and jotting down their observations. Lewis continually reminded us of his responsibility to Jefferson and the other learned men of the east to report back to them on this vast land, every detail he could learn, until most of us were tired of hearing his voice, yet those times when we would stop to allow him to explore something on the shore that had caught his interest were welcome reprieves from rowing. And I often had the opportunity to get off the boat to hunt and the pleasure of walking or riding one of the horses on that vast and fertile land is hard to describe.

We occasionally met up with boats coming down the river, loaded with beaver and otter pelts and other animal skins, and heard the stories told by their occupants of the richness of the land into which we were entering. The sight of the canoes and pirogues piled high with beaver pelts caught my attention. Here were men coming down from the upper Missouri with enough pelts to sell to make a body live comfortably for a long time, and the ease with which they described the gathering of those pelts drew my imagination.

"Them beavers just about line up to be trapped," one heavily-whiskered man said as he joined us in camp. "Can't hardly walk up there without stepping on one."

It was barely spring and those men were already finished with their seasons trapping and were heading down to St. Louis to sell the skins. I would learn later in my life that winter in the high country was the best time to catch the beaver, and I would learn firsthand of the hardships those men endured, but at the time it seemed like a life of leisure, to be finished with your labors just in time for the warm and pleasant weather.

It was a thought that stayed with me for a long time.

* * *

Ahead of me, George Drouillard motioned downward with one hand and I stopped. The cottonwoods lining the south bank of the Missouri were thick at this place, their leaves rustling in the ever-present wind that flowed down the river from the north and west. We had parted with the keelboat at dawn and set out to hunt. The amount of meat being consumed by the men struggling and straining against the swift current was awesome to behold, thus the need for several hunting parties to be sent out daily.

I squatted motionless, watching George as the mosquitoes buzzed around my face. The pesky mosquitoes were so prevalent that I barely noticed them anymore.

George slowly raised his rifle to his shoulder, sighted, and then squeezed the trigger. The roar of the rifle sent birds flapping away from the branches of the cottonwoods, and then George was motioning me forward. As I followed him down into a shallow ravine, I could see the fresh blood splashed across the thick green underbrush. He had gotten another one.

As we followed the trail of blood up out of the bottomlands and onto the wide prairie, I had to marvel again at this half-breed's hunting skills. Drouillard seemed able to find meat where nobody else could. I don't consider myself unskilled in the act of hunting for my food, but where I could spend a day stalking a single deer, George would come back to the boat with three. I had no love for Indians but I had to admire George.

"There she is," George said, pointing. The doe had fallen to the ground about a hundred yards out onto the prairie.

As we knelt beside her, I heard George say something in his native tongue.

"What was that?" I asked.

"Just a little prayer," he said.

I nodded.

"My people pray to Creator when we make a kill, thanking the animal for giving its life to sustain ours," he said.

I nodded again, though it all sounded like superstitious nonsense to me. Later in my life I would interact with Indians on a more personal level and their customs and beliefs wouldn't seem so strange and alien to me, but that was in the future.

We dressed out the deer and carried the meat down to the river, tying it up in a tree for the men to find as they brought the boat up. Even now we could hear them coming, the groaning of oars, the muffled voices of the men, the occasional curse or shout. Far away on the northern side of the river we heard a gunshot and knew that more meat had been obtained to feed our friends, and George smiled.

"Whaddya say we find us one more deer then call it a day?"

"I like that idea," I concurred.

We headed back into the trees.

* * *

"Hey, Drouillard, tell us an Injun huntin' story," Joseph Field called out.

We were camped for the night on a small island near the southern bank of the river. Heavy rain had fallen as we were making camp but had since moved on, and stars were shining brightly overhead. The fire was blazing high, the only light for leagues in every direction, and it seemed mighty small against all that dark prairie. We could hear the howling of wolves in the distance, and the high-pitched yipping of what Cruzatte called coyotes.

Drouillard grinned but said nothing.

"Yeah, come on, Chief," Potts chimed in. "You gotta have a good hunting story."

"In fact, I do," Drouillard said. "Back when I was a child, I had a friend named Limping Deer."

"Hell kind of name is that?" someone muttered and was quickly shushed.

"I'll tell you what kind of name that is," George said. "Limping Deer got his name when he was out hunting one summer afternoon. He had prepared carefully, bathing in a stream near his tipi to remove his human scent and checking his bow and arrows to make sure they were ready. Then he set out. He followed a stream down from his village toward a place where he knew the deer were plentiful.

"He had just hidden himself up in an oak tree when a deer came down the trail. It was a large buck, and it was walking with a limp. One leg had been injured, and the buck could only hobble along as it headed down to the stream to drink.

"My friend felt bad for the buck, as our people believe we are not above animals but are their equal. But his family was hungry, so he brought his bow up and took aim. As he did, one of the buck's antlers caught the tree in which my friend was hiding and shook it severely, and the branch under my friend broke. He fell out of the tree, right onto the back of that buck.

"Well, that old buck went about plumb crazy, leaping around trying to shake the man off, but his hurt leg buckled and he fell over, pinning my friend under him and injuring my friend's leg.

"Several other men who were out hunting heard the commotion and came running to see what was going on. When they got to the clearing they saw a sight they would talk about for years, a limping man being chased around that clearing by a limping deer. They shot the deer and saved my friend's life, but from that moment forward my friend was known by the name 'Limping Deer.'"

The men laughed at the image of a limping deer chasing a limping man and George grinned. To this day I still don't know if that was a true story or if Drouillard was just pulling our legs.

CHAPTER NINE

Sergeant Ordway took me aside one morning shortly after. "We need your assistance, John," he said.

We had been at our camp at the junction of the Missouri and Kansas Rivers for several days, drying our equipment and making repairs to one of the pirogues, and we were planning on leaving in the morning. I had slept well most of the nights we were there, as I did on almost every night when I wasn't on sentry duty, but the previous night I had been awakened by a loud argument. I felt sure that was what Ordway wanted to talk to me about.

"We're convening a court-martial," he continued. "You heard what happened last night?"

I nodded. "I heard a little."

"Will you be a member of the court-martial?"

I nodded again, and marveled at my transformation in the eyes of the captains and sergeants. At the Wood River camp I had been the person in trouble. Now I was being chosen to be one of the men presiding over another man's fate.

We convened at eleven o'clock, on the wide rocky bank that held our camp. The other members of the panel were Patrick Gass, John Newman and John Thompson, with Nate Pryor presiding and John Potts acting as the Judge Advocate. The men charged were John Collins and Hugh Hall, and their crime affected every man on that journey.

The night before, Collins had been on sentry duty, a vital role the deeper we moved into Indian territory. We didn't know if the local natives were aware of our presence on the river, or if their reaction would be hostile once they did learn of us. If they did react to our presence in a hostile manner, it was most likely they would attack us during the night, when we were in camp. Because of that potential threat, sentry duty was an extremely important role.

During his tour, Collins was accused of accessing the whiskey rations and getting himself good and drunk. There was only so much whiskey to go around, and some of that was set aside for treating with the Indians upriver. Each man knew just how much whiskey there was, and we all relished our evening dram.

But it wasn't just the theft of the whiskey that had everyone riled. A drunken sentry wasn't going to be aware of an attack until it was too late and men were being slaughtered in their blankets and tents. Which is why drinking on sentry duty was punishable by death. Collins had put all of our lives at risk by his stupidity and greed and he deserved to be punished harshly.

Hugh Hall had come along and caught Collins in the act, but instead of turning him in to the sergeant, Hugh had joined him in pilfering the whiskey. Sergeant Floyd had conducted an inspection and found both of them drunk, hence the hurraw of the night before.

"John Collins, you are accused by Sergeant Floyd of being negligent in your duties as a sentry by being drunk on your post, and of theft for stealing the whiskey with which you became drunk." Nate Pryor's voice was appropriately serious as he read the charges. "Negligence of duty of this magnitude is punishable by death, should the panel deem it so. How do you plead?"

"Not guilty," Collins said immediately.

"Sergeant Floyd."

Floyd stood up and related what he had found the night before while inspecting the guard. His voice was level, without emotion.

Nate turned to face the men on the panel. "You have heard the testimony given by Sergeant Floyd and have heard the defendant's plea. It is up to you to determine the defendant's fate."

Well, it didn't take us long to come to a decision. We all knew Sergeant

Floyd's reputation for fairness and honesty, and we also knew John Collins. Collins's word wasn't worth much to us.

"If Floyd says he caught them drunk on our whiskey, then he caught them drunk," Patrick Gass said, spitting in disgust. We had moved off to one side of the camp to talk. "That whiskey wasn't given to them by the captains, that's for sure."

"I agree," I said. "But I don't think we should apply the punishment of death."

"Why not?" Newman asked. "If some Injuns had attacked us while he was thieving our whiskey, we could all be dead right now."

"And I agree with you," I said. "But I get the feeling we're going to need every man we currently have if we hope to be successful on this expedition. If we put Collins to death and then run into some hostile Sioux upriver, we'll wish we had him there to fight by our sides."

Gass nodded thoughtfully. An educated man, he was one of the few tasked by the captains with maintaining a journal while on the expedition. "Colter's right," he said.

Newman grunted. "All right then," he said. "So we don't kill him. But we gotta punish him severe enough that he don't get any more stupid ideas like this in the future."

When we reconvened the court-martial, it was recommended that John Collins receive one hundred lashes on his bare back, the punishment to be delivered by the men of the expedition, since they were the ones who had suffered most at the loss of the whiskey and who were in danger of being killed by his negligence as a sentry. Hugh Hall, when his testimony came up, pled guilty, and was sentenced to fifty lashes.

The men chosen to punish Collins and Hall were exuberant in the swinging of the lashes, as they were justified in being. Those two miscreants would be feeling the pain that resulted from their actions for a while to come, especially as the days grew hotter and the sweat of their exertions on the oars ran down their flayed backs, sometimes in rivers.

It was no less than they deserved.

CHAPTER TEN

"Damned if old George didn't bring us back some Injuns," Potts said, and I could hear a combination of disgust and awe in his voice. John Potts hated Indians more than most of the men on that journey, and he couldn't seem to decide if Drouillard was an Indian or a white man.

I looked where Potts was pointing and saw Drouillard standing on the bluff above the camp, waving down at us. By his side stood a figure clad in buckskins, long black hair tied back with a piece of rawhide. A true-to-life Indian.

"Well, that's what the captains sent him to do," I said, taking another bite of venison. Smoke from the fire swirled around my head. "Can't hate the man for doing his job."

Potts just grunted and went back to his own dinner, a deer shot earlier that day by Reubin Field.

I smiled to myself. I probably should have kept my mouth shut but I really got a lot of enjoyment out of ribbing old John. "Yep, I gotta say, that there half-breed might be the most important man on this mad venture. Where would we be without him and his hunting skills? Now he's gonna be our interpreter with the natives upriver." I shook my head in exaggerated admiration. "Good man, that Drouillard."

"Oh, shut the hell up, Colter," Potts said. "You yap worse than an old woman."

Across from us, Silas Goodrich laughed and tipped me a wink. "After being out on this river, rowing and pulling that damn boat up this here

Misery River, I kinda admire them Injuns. They ride across the prairie on horses, free and wild and tied to nothing. Hell of a lot smarter than us white boys, eh, Potts?"

John slapped his leg in frustration and stood up. "The company around here is starting to get annoying," he said. "Think I'll go sit by the river a spell."

"More skeeters down there," I said.

"Fine by me. At least the skeeters keep their fool mouths shut!"

We smiled as we watched Potts stalk away. Then Silas's grin slid from his face. "Old Dorion's talking makes me a bit concerned about meeting up with them Sioux," he said. Pierre Dorion was a Frenchman who had gone up the river to live and trade with the Sioux quite a few years back, and he had hinted to the captains that he had a lot of influence with them. His lurid descriptions of that nation's ferocity and overwhelming hatred of Americans had all of us nervous about meeting them. There were less than forty of us in this party, and hundreds of Sioux warriors.

I nodded. "I know what you mean. But did you see Captain Lewis's face when Dorion told him that the Sioux might not let us pass? He got that stubborn look that says he's planning on walking right over them Sioux if'n he has to."

Silas grunted. "That might be easier said than done."

"The Sioux are for another day, boys," Clark's voice rang out from behind us, and I almost dropped my venison. That man could sneak up on himself if he really tried and he wouldn't even know he was coming!

"We got us a real live Indian here now," Clark continued, waving us to our feet. "Come on, up, up! What say we meet this fellow with a show of finery and strength, eh?"

The Indian turned out to be a member of the Missouria nation, according to Captain Clark, a tribe closely related to the Oto people. Drouillard had met up with three of their hunters out on the prairie and had convinced one of them to return to the boat, while the other two were sent to their village to ask their headmen to meet with our captains for a parley. I knew Lewis would be ecstatic. I had heard him practicing his speech from President Jefferson on numerous occasions as we came up the river, and I suspected he was more than ready to try it on some real Indians.

Drouillard brought the Indian into the camp and he seemed much impressed with our display of weaponry and goods. He sign-talked with Drouillard, who translated as best he could for the captains, and the gist seemed to be that his leaders would be interested in meeting with the captains at a point up the river. The majority of his tribe was out on the prairie hunting buffalo and their leaders were with them, so it might take some time to bring them to the boat for a meeting. The captains assigned one of the French hired men who could converse in the Oto tongue to accompany the Indian back to his people with the invitation for a parley.

After our very first wild Indian departed, the rest of the Corps continued on our way up the river, continually watching out for the arrival of the tribe's headmen on the banks and hoping that they wouldn't bring all of their warriors with them to attack us. We finally stopped at a high bluff, determined to set up camp there and wait for the Indians to arrive.

It took almost a week before they did, and they were a sight to behold, with their buckskin attire and painted faces. There were six men who were indicated to us to be leaders of the nation, and with them they had brought eight warriors, enough, according to Drouillard, to maintain their honor without appearing threatening. The captains met them under an awning made from the keelboat sail stretched to provide shade from the sun, and Captain Lewis finally had the chance to give his carefully-rehearsed speech. The gist of his speech was simple, though I am not sure how well it translated for the natives. The country of America was the new owner of the land upon which those natives were living, meaning they were now subjects of the United States. President Jefferson, therefore, was their new "great father." They were to trade only with the Americans, and were to live under American rules and laws.

The Indians listened patiently as Lewis droned on and the translations continued, faces expressionless. I tried to imagine what I would be thinking if strangers came into my ancestral land and told me what these captains were telling them, but my imagination wouldn't stretch that far. The Indians, bearing such colorful names as Little Thief, Big Horse, White Horse and Hospitality, ingested what they were being told without giving any indication of their feelings or thoughts, and I could see Lewis becoming frustrated. But there was nothing he could do except press on.

* * *

Moses Reed deserted from the party while we were in camp waiting for the Missouria delegation to arrive, and George Drouillard was sent after him. Captain Clark had originally asked me to go in search of Reed, and then decided it was better to keep me in camp in case there was trouble with the Indians. Maybe he didn't believe that Drouillard, being half-Indian, would take up a weapon against fellow Indians, should the need arise.

Or maybe Clark just felt that Drouillard was a better tracker than me, and in that he was probably right.

In either case, it took Drouillard a few days to catch up to Reed, who was foolishly trying to walk back down the Missouri to St. Louis. Reed was looking pretty poorly when he was brought in, like a man who had realized the stupidity of his actions only after it was too late. He was filthy and hungry and I almost felt sorry for him.

The Indians who were in the camp when Reed received his punishment didn't look very happy with what they were seeing, and I asked Drouillard about it later.

"They don't like seeing a man whipped, especially a man who is a part of our own 'tribe.'"

"Even after what he did?"

"You don't understand, John," he explained. "In their culture, a man is free to make his own decisions and follow his own mind and heart. There is no such thing as 'desertion' in their minds because no man is forced to follow a path that he doesn't want to follow."

I wasn't sure I understood even after his explanation. "Then how do they keep control of their people?"

George smiled. "They don't."

"Huh?"

"They don't have to keep control of their people," he said patiently. "Control is an invention of the white man. Out here, the people are one, and they work together for the good of the people as a whole. They don't live just for themselves. That's the difference between them and white folks."

* * *

We concluded our parley with the Missouria Indians and continued our slow progress up the river. And it wasn't long before we were forcibly reminded of our mortality in the worst way possible, with the death of Charles Floyd.

Ever since leaving the camp at Wood River we had battled strong storms in which our keelboat and pirogues were in constant danger of being swamped. We had dealt with the harassment of the vicious mosquitoes that made the low wetlands their home, and viewed us as fair game for their bloodthirsty attentions. We had learned to adapt to blisters and boils that made our days a misery at times, and there wasn't a man among us who wasn't ill or injured at one time or another. So when Sergeant Floyd became sick with sharp pains in his stomach, we all figured he would pull through.

He didn't. Charles Floyd, a man I had known and admired for several years, died on the banks of the Missouri on a warm and sunny afternoon from an unknown cause, and in the end, despite his intense pain, he was as composed as a man facing death might hope to be. I can only pray that when my time has come I can face it with the fortitude and strength shown by Charles Floyd.

We buried him high on a bluff overlooking the slow-moving Missouri, and erected a cross above his grave. It was a beautiful site, with a broad view of the endless prairies and the majestic Missouri, and it's the kind of place I think Floyd would have enjoyed standing atop and looking out from. I remembered that day the previous fall on the Mississippi, at the site of the burned-down Fort Jefferson, and the way Floyd had stood at the edge of the bluff, the wind blowing back his hair as he gazed at the wide river passing below him. That was the image of him that would always be in my head.

We continued upriver the next day, and mine weren't the only eyes that looked back toward the high bluff that held Floyd's grave until the meanderings of the Missouri hid it from view.

CHAPTER ELEVEN

On a very hot and muggy morning shortly after Floyd's death, I joined a large party that included the captains, Sergeant Ordway, Corporal Warfington, Shields, and several others, and went ashore. Dorion had told us about an immense hill located several miles inland that was rumored among the natives of the area to be haunted by devils, and both captains were determined to see it for themselves.

We walked across the wide prairie for close to three hours, the hill visible and slowly looming larger on the horizon. The heat was coming up off the prairie in shimmering waves, and the sun beat down mercilessly on our heads. Sweat poured off of us in streams, and our breath came in gasping draughts. It seemed to take forever to get close enough to really see details of the mound, and sure enough, it looked like there was some kind of little devils buzzing around its top. As we drew closer, we could see that the "little devils" were actually small birds.

"Probably chasing insects," Lewis said, shading his eyes as he looked up at the hill. "Let's go up to the top and see."

"You're really planning on climbing up there, Captain?" Ordway asked, and I could sympathize. He was breathing heavily and mopping sweat from his brow, as were all of us. The day just seemed to get hotter by the minute.

"Yes, I am," Lewis said, and we could see that he meant it. I wondered if he ever grew tired of killing himself to satisfy Jefferson's curiosity.

"You men can stay down here," Clark said, though I had the

impression he wasn't any more excited about climbing that hill in the oppressive heat than we were. "Take a breather. We'll be down shortly."

He didn't need to tell me twice. I'd seen hills and birds before. A hill is a hill and a bird is a bird. No sense dying from heat stroke just to see more of the same. I sank down onto the ground in the shade cast by the hill and was quickly joined by most of the other men.

After close to an hour, the captains came down from the hill, both drenched in sweat and breathing heavily. They looked about as hot and tired as any two men I'd ever seen. "Sure could use some water," Lewis said. "I drained the last of my water up there."

I let him drink from my water flask. "There's a creek just over there," I said, pointing toward a line of trees a short distance away.

"Then let's go there," he said, handing back the flask with a nod of thanks.

We gathered our gear together and walked to the narrow river, where the cool water was just as refreshing as we had imagined it would be. After quenching our thirst and refilling our water flasks we retraced our path to where we had left the pirogue.

"So no devils up on that hill, Captain Lewis?" Shields asked as we walked.

Lewis scoffed. "Superstitious savages," he said dismissively. "They'll place any credence on a myth rather than take the time to determine the truth. Look around," he finished, waving at the flat prairie with one arm. "The wind blows across the prairie and hits that mound. The insects are carried on that wind and the birds are waiting for them on the leeward side of the hill. It's that simple." He shook his head and snorted in derision. "Little devils. Ridiculous savages."

I glanced sideways at Drouillard but he walked facing forward, not saying a word.

* * *

"I can't find him, Captain," Drouillard said two days later.

He and Shannon had been sent out to try and find some of the horses that had strayed from the party. That had been on the day we returned from the hill that had been supposedly inhabited by devils. Shannon had headed off in a different direction from Drouillard and had since become lost.

"Can you tell what direction he's moving in?" Clark asked.

"It's hard to say. He's meandering all over the place, from what little sign I can find. But it looks like he's heading mostly upriver."

Clark shielded his eyes against the glare off the water and peered toward the north. "You think he believes we're ahead of him?"

"It's all I can figure, Captain," Drouillard said.

"That Shannon," the captain said. "I'm not so sure of him at times."

"Yes, sir," Drouillard said. "I'll set out again later to look for him but I needed to get some food and rest first."

"Of course, George. Shields!"

"Sir!"

"Get Joe Field and see if you can chase Shannon down. Damn fool's gone and got hisself lost!"

After the two men set out in pursuit of Shannon, the rest of us guided the keelboat and the pirogues out into the current and continued our seemingly endless journey. The river had turned toward the north in recent days, though the way it twisted and wandered all over the prairie it was hard to judge its ultimate direction. At one point, several days prior, we had worked our way around what seemed to be most of a circle, and when the captains had sent a man across land to check, it was discovered that the river had bent back within a thousand yards of itself. Our distance by water had been over eighteen miles to get back to just about where we had started!

We rowed and poled until about two that afternoon, when a lookout shouted, "Indians, Captain!"

We stopped rowing and looked toward the eastern shore, where an Indian boy was swimming out toward the keelboat. We had set the prairie on fire a few miles back as a signal to the Sioux to come to the river, as we were in their country now. I assumed that this boy was Sioux.

Drouillard helped him aboard and called for the pirogue that carried Pierre Dorion, our Sioux interpreter. Through him we learned that the Sioux were camped a few miles up a side river. Two more Indians were standing on the shore and we halted the keelboat by them. After a brief consultation, Captain Lewis assigned Sergeant Pryor and Dorion to travel to the Sioux camp and ask them to meet us at a bluff further up the river.

"I'm extremely anxious to talk with these Sioux," Lewis said, as he watched the men disappear over a bluff.

We continued up the river. The Indian boy who had stayed with us was wide-eyed as he watched us work that ungainly boat upriver against the current, and I wondered what he was thinking. Back on the Ohio and Mississippi, the keelboat had been a source of curiosity among the white settlers, but they had seen keelboats before. Now we were out here on this great vast plain where modern inventions would appear alien and strange. What would a boy who lived his life free and wild on the prairies think of the sweating cursing men who were chained to moving this big boat up the wide river?

He must have believed we were all mad.

He might have been correct!

Once he had determined where we planned to stop, the Sioux boy left the boat to meet with his people and guide them to us. We made camp near the high bluff that Lewis had learned about from our French hired men and set about preparing for a council with the Sioux. Around that same time, Shields and Joe Field caught up to us and said they had been unable to find Shannon and believed he was still somewhere ahead of us.

I was getting worried about Shannon. He was just a kid, and not very skilled in surviving on his own. I could tell the captains shared my concern, and I heard Patrick Gass, newly promoted to sergeant in Floyd's place, mutter that Shannon was most likely a goner.

"Losing two men in a week," he said, shaking his head. "Not a good sign."

"Shannon's not lost yet," Weiser said. "The kid's smart."

"Not smart enough to realize we're behind him."

"Colter!" Captain Clark was motioning me.

"Yes, Captain?"

"Get some provisions and head upriver. See if you can locate Shannon and the horses and bring them back here."

"Yes, sir."

"Don't you get lost, too," Drouillard said, grinning. "I don't want to have to find two lost white boys."

I laughed. "I'll keep that in mind."

CHAPTER TWELVE

I was walking through the most beautiful land I had ever seen.

The prairie stretched as far as the eye could see in every direction, marked occasionally with a low hill or dark smudge of treetops, indicating some small creek or draw. The sky was immense, almost overpowering. I was walking through a land of incredible bounty, with massive herds of buffalo darkening the grass, with deer and elk in every direction, and I marveled that there could be a land like this. I had lived my entire life in a hilly forested land, where the sky was something you saw up through the branches of trees and deer had to be stalked, sometimes for hours. In this land, the deer were so unused to humans that they would practically walk up to you and say howdy.

I picked up Shannon's trail pretty quickly, and I had to agree with the other men who had tried unsuccessfully to find him. It was fairly obvious that he was heading north, keeping the river to his right as he struggled to catch up to the keelboat, obviously not realizing that the keelboat was down the river from him, not up. And I could almost understand his confusion. Down on the river, working the oars or the poles, it was easy to make that boat the center of your universe, and believe that it was much larger than it was. Out here, under this massive awning of sky, you came to realize that the keelboat was just a tiny dot on the landscape, and was therefore easy to miss.

Eventually, though, he would have to realize that the slow-moving boat couldn't have gotten that far ahead of him and he would turn back.

I hoped. If not, George Shannon would likely die out here on this prairie.

I followed Shannon's trail as the day wore on and the sun rose higher and higher into the sky, then began its descent into the west. In the afternoon I shot a rabbit and cooked it over a low fire and watched as dark clouds reared up in the western sky, quickly blocking the sun. The clouds were as mighty and vast as the prairie sky itself. Lightning flashed inside the towering clouds and the distant rumble of thunder rolled across the waving prairie grass. Another storm was coming.

Finishing my meal, I quickly set out after Shannon's trail once again, knowing that if a heavy rain did fall, any sign of his passing would be obliterated. But I could tell that I was fighting a losing battle. The wind had picked up ahead of the storm and the clouds were racing toward me, moving in that fast manner so peculiar to prairie storms, and I knew the rains would reach me long before I caught Shannon. As the first fat raindrops fell, I sought out a sheltered place to spend the night.

The rain fell heavily throughout the night, accompanied by periods of high wind. I had found a dry spot beneath a bluff on a side stream that emptied into the Missouri, and I spent the night as comfortably as could be expected. In the morning the rain stopped, though the sky stayed cloudy and the wind continued to blow, bending and whipping the tall prairie grass. And all signs of Shannon's passing were gone.

I stood for a while in indecision, trying to decide if I should continue trying to follow him or return to the keelboat, but eventually I just shrugged. What else could I do? I continued north.

I figured by now the Sioux would have met up with the captains at the bluff, and I was missing out on all the fun, but that was out of my hands. What would happen in the council would happen with or without John Colter being there, not that I was needed in the first place. And I had to grin when I thought about what my mother would have told me when I started thinking too highly of myself, of how the world had gone around for a long time without my help and would continue to do so in the future long after I was dead and gone.

Chuckling quietly, I pushed on toward the northwest.

* * *

For over a week I followed George Shannon across that endless prairie. Sometimes I found signs of his passing that seemed just hours old, but I never seemed to catch up to him. His trail sometimes led far from the river as he looped and meandered around, apparently in search of game, but it always came back toward the Missouri. Several times the signs were right at the river's edge, as if he had stopped to gaze up and down the muddy river, and I could almost see him standing there, desperately hoping for a sight of our boats.

As I walked I hunted, leaving the elk and deer meat on scaffolds at the river's edge for the men on the boats to find as they came up. Finally, out of ammunition and seemingly no closer to Shannon, I made for the river and the keelboat.

"He's still moving," I told the captains that afternoon. I was resting on the keelboat, having heard all about the meeting with the Sioux from Sergeant Gass, and now I was giving my report.

"He obviously still believes we're ahead of him, though how he can think we're moving that fast is beyond me. I don't know what's he's eating, and I'm sure he must be out of ammunition by now. But he's still going."

"You think he's killed one of the horses for food?" Lewis asked.

I shook my head. "No, sir. The tracks would let me know if he had one less horse, and they haven't changed."

Lewis shook his head also. "I can't expend any more time or men on looking for him. He'll have to find his way to us. Eventually he'll figure out that we are downriver from him and reverse his course."

I disagreed with that decision, not wanting to leave one of our men lost and alone on that prairie, but I was just a private. Captain Lewis's word was law and his mind was made up.

* * *

So we continued up that wide Missouri, the story of our lives. Game continued to be plentiful on the prairie and in the low valleys, and you could practically reach your hand down into the water and come up with a fish. This truly was, as Captain Clark often stated, a land of plenty. Deer, elk and buffalo darkened the plains, huge herds trailed by wolves. Birds of all kinds filled the skies and the trees along the river banks. I sometimes envied the native people who had lived in this wonderful land for generations.

One afternoon we stopped while the entire party labored to capture a small rodent-like animal that lived in burrows beneath the ground. They looked almost like the squirrels of Kentucky, save for the lack of a thick bushy tail. Captain Lewis was determined to kill one and send it back to Jefferson.

The small animals, called Prairie Dogs by the French traders who were with us, would stand up on their hind legs watching us approach, and then emit sharp whistling chirps before diving into their underground burrows. For several hours we dug into the soft dirt, yet the tunnels seemed to go down endlessly. Finally Captain Lewis ordered water to be brought up from the river and poured into the holes to flush them out.

It was a long tedious chore. The day was hot. We hauled water up from the river in buckets and poured it into the holes until I thought we might drain the Missouri and still not capture any of the little rodents. Meanwhile, at other holes, more of the elusive creatures would stand and watch us, chirping away, and I almost believed I could hear them laughing at us.

Finally, after hours of fatigue, Lewis had his prize, a live Prairie Dog he could send back to his President. The animal was placed in a cage made out of small branches in which it sat huddled, staring out at us, and we could finally start back up the river.

* * *

"Up ahead, Captain! Man on the shore!"

The call came from Corporal Warfington from his seat in his pirogue, and we all gazed toward an upcoming bend in the river.

"God above, it's Shannon!" Captain Clark laughed out loud. "Pull her hard, lads! Let's pick up our lost man!"

When we reached the place where Shannon stood, there were tears in his eyes. "Sure happy to see you fellas," he said hoarsely. The man looked like death walking. He was thin and gaunt, with dark circles by his eyes, and his hands trembled as he climbed onto the keelboat.

"Get him some of that elk jerky," Lewis commanded, and Whitehouse came forward with the food, handing it to a grateful Shannon.

"What happened to you?" Clark asked.

It took a few moments for Shannon to start talking. He was gnawing at the jerky as if he hadn't eaten in days, and from the look of him I felt sure he hadn't.

"I got lost after locating the horses, and ended up on a smaller river rather than the Missouri," he said, stopping his narrative occasionally to take a bite of the meat, given to him sparingly by Clark. "Once I realized my mistake, I headed north, hoping to come across a bend in the Missouri. When I finally did, I followed it northwest, thinking you fellas had already passed. I saw some tracks, thought it was our hunters, and just kept going." He shook his head slowly. "'Bout gave up on ever seeing you all again. I finally decided to start back down the river and hope for a trading vessel to come up or some trappers to head down."

"What've you been eating?" Potts asked.

Shannon gave a shaky laugh. "A whole lot of nothin'," he said. "Some grapes, berries, a rabbit I shot with a stick."

"A stick?" Lewis asked, as if he hadn't heard correctly. The rest of us glanced at each other, wondering if maybe Shannon hadn't lost his mind.

"I was out of bullets. I put a stick in the barrel. Shot a rabbit."

I thought about all the life out there on those plains, all the buffalo and elk that covered the land. Yet this man had almost died because he had run out of bullets. This land of plenty was obviously also a land of great danger.

CHAPTER THIRTEEN

As we continued moving slowly up the river, the air turned steadily colder. The wind had shifted during the first days of September, coming straight down at us from the north on most days now. Large flights of ducks and geese were passing above us, heading toward the south, and the trees that lined the river were beginning to shed their colored leaves. The cooler days brought relief for those rowing the boat or on shore pulling on the tow ropes, but in the back of all of our minds was the thought of the upcoming winter.

The French trappers who had been hired to travel with us told tales of winter that sometimes belied belief, with stories of snow drifts dozens of feet deep and temperatures so low they would freeze the sap in trees and cause them to split open with a sound like a gunshot. Just the idea that a river as wide and ever-flowing as the Missouri could freeze solid enough from bank to bank that a horse could be ridden across it was enough for most of the men to shake their heads and mutter about impossibilities. That attitude sort of surprised me, since those same men had seen the Mississippi frozen clear across when we were at Wood River.

Impossible as those stories might seem, though, the rain that fell on most days now was cold, sometimes laced with ice, and when I thought about the ferocity of some of the summer storms we had seen on those prairies, I could believe those tales of winter blizzards and deep freezes. The water, when we had to wade in it to pull the boat over sandbars, seemed to run colder with each day, also.

Winter was coming, there was no doubt about it. I just hoped we would be in a position to weather it out when it arrived.

* * *

Barely breathing, I moved at a snail's pace through the cottonwoods, one slow step at a time. A light breeze rustled the remaining leaves above my head and I paused, not taking my eyes off the large bull elk there on the edge of the sandbar. So far, he gave no indication that he was aware of my presence. I took another step closer and raised my rifle to my shoulder.

This would be the fourth elk that I would kill on this day, and I knew the captains would be pleased. After meeting-up with three more Indian boys on the river bank the day before, we fully expected to have a council very soon with the group that Captain Lewis called the Teton Sioux, and this was the group he most wanted to impress.

The trappers we had met earlier in the summer had been full of stories about the Teton Sioux and how they were the force to be reckoned with on the upper Missouri. They were said to be a people filled with their own importance, and fierce as the storms that scoured this high wide land.

"They control the Missouri," Dorion had told us. "If they don't want you to pass by, they won't let you pass by."

That put Lewis's back up! "We are soldiers, Mr. Dorion," he had said firmly, "not a band of old women. This is our country now, and those Sioux need to understand that. They do not tell us where we can go."

Dorion had tried to explain. "You can tell them it's your land now, Captain Lewis, but they have been living on it for generations. They may not choose to believe you."

"President Jefferson bought this land from Napoleon," Lewis trumpeted. "It belongs to us!"

Dorion just shrugged.

Now it appeared that our meeting with those fierce Teton Sioux was about to take place, and everyone wanted to make a strong first impression on them.

* * *

The rifle jumped in my grip, its blast echoing across the river, and the elk dropped. Moving forward, I quickly dressed the meat, a job that had been reduced to routine for me, as many times as I had done it. But when I went back to get my horse to bring in the meat, the horse was gone.

A sound on the prairie above sent me running up onto the bluff, and I could see several Indians racing away across the prairie, one of them on my horse. Cursing loudly, I raced down to the river's edge, where I could just see the keelboat and pirogues rounding a bend below. I flagged them down and one of the pirogues came over to collect me.

After they picked me up and I told them what had taken place, we continued up the river. Everyone was fully alert now, expecting trouble.

"Indians, Captain," Ordway called out, pointing toward the shore.

Five Indians stood on the shore, waving to us. We drew abreast of them and held our station in the river.

"Keep your eyes open," Lewis said. "Where's my interpreter? Cruzatte, get up here!"

The five Indians were Teton Sioux, sent to tell us that their chiefs would be at the river the next day to meet with us. Lewis demanded the return of our horse, but the Indian men professed to know nothing about its fate.

"I don't believe them," Lewis declared. "Cruzatte, tell them that we are soldiers and are not afraid of them. Tell them that we will not speak with them until our property is returned to us."

The message was passed along, though I could see that Cruzatte was reluctant to do so. The Indians, however, didn't seem offended by Lewis's words and simply stated that if their people had the horse, it would be brought up with the chiefs and returned to us.

This seemed to mollify Lewis and the five Indians were brought on board the keelboat. We continued up the river until we found a likely spot for a council and anchored near the center of the Missouri.

"All right, men," Clark said. "We're in hostile territory now, and we need to be prepared. I'll send a small group on shore, the cooks and a guard detail, and the rest of you will stay on the boat. As you see, we've anchored out here in the river rather than on shore. I don't plan on giving them a chance to overrun us."

You could feel the tension rise among the men at his words. Everyone was aware that our grand journey could end right here with the deaths of all of us.

The following day dawned hot and hazy. An awning was rigged up on shore in preparation for the council, and a group of men, including the two captains, went ashore to await the Indians arrival. On the keelboat, the rest of us waited also, weapons ready, for whatever might happen. Nobody spoke, and none of us took our gaze away from the banks of the river. At any moment we expected to see hundreds of Sioux warriors appear, intent on killing us all.

Late in the morning the chiefs appeared with a strong party of their warriors. The captains greeted them civilly and led them to the shade of the awning. Though we were too far away on the keelboat to hear what was being said, we could tell by the gestures and activities that the captains, after smoking a pipe of peace with the chiefs, were reciting their usual speech from Jefferson. We had all been through this before and we knew that the speeches could drag on for a long time.

As the morning wore on into early afternoon, the talks continued, and from what we could tell they were peaceful enough, though the Indians were beginning to look restless and maybe even a little bored. I'd sat through the Jefferson speech. I knew how they felt.

"I don't like looking at all them Injuns up on that bluff," Potts said beside me.

"Just relax, John," I told him. Sweat ran down my face and I wiped it off with my sleeve. "They're not doing anything against us right now. We'll just watch them and be ready."

"Still don't like it."

After what seemed a very long time, the captains led four of the Indians down to the red pirogue and they all climbed on board. As the boat began to cross the river toward us, Sergeant Ordway called out, "Visitors coming, lads. Look lively."

We would later learn that three of the Indians were chiefs of their nation, and the fourth was a bodyguard. The three chiefs were called

Black Buffalo, Buffalo Medicine and Partisan. The first two seemed like honest men, while Partisan carried the air of a trouble maker. His insolent smiles and hooded eyes put my nerves on edge and I vowed to keep my eye on him.

All of the chiefs seemed properly impressed by the boat and its contents, and smiled openly when the captains presented them with gifts, including some of our whiskey. Clark, through Cruzatte, told them of our plan to continue up the river, and that was when they began to get belligerent.

"They want us to stay here and trade with them, Captain," Cruzatte said.

"That's neither here nor there," Lewis said. "Tell them we are not traders but soldiers. Other traders will follow with many goods, but only after we continue up the river."

Cruzatte translated his words, and then listened as the Indians spoke. "They say you have a lot of nice things on this boat and that you must be traders. They think you're going up the river to trade with their enemies, and they're not right happy about it."

I could see Lewis getting angry. "Then you set them straight, Mr. Cruzatte. We are soldiers on a mission to the mountains and beyond. We are not traders. Tell them."

Partisan snorted derisively as Lewis's words were translated. Holding the empty whiskey bottle by the neck, he began staggering around the deck of the keelboat, acting like a drunken fool, much to the hilarity of the Indians on shore and the rising anger of the captains. Finally tossing the empty bottle to the deck, he shouted something in his native tongue, gesturing angrily all the while.

"He says we give them scraps while taking better gifts upstream to their enemies," Cruzatte interpreted, sweating profusely. "He says we are insulting them."

"This is preposterous," Lewis stated. "Tell them that we have a long way to go and can not be detained any longer. We have treated with them and have explained our mission. We have communicated as friends and have given them gifts. Tell them that we leave now."

With much gesticulating and shouting, the Indians were put on board the pirogue and rowed toward shore, Captain Clark accompanying them. We could see the Indians on the riverbank milling about, and the voices that carried across the water held an angry buzz.

"This doesn't look good," Lewis said. "I want men on the swivels and every one ready to act." As several men moved to man the swivel guns and the rest of us held our arms in readiness, the pirogue reached shore.

We were too far away to hear conversations, but the actions we could see spoke volumes to us. As the boat ran aground, the warrior who had accompanied the chiefs grasped the mast with both arms, refusing to let go. At the same time, several other warriors grabbed the rope attached to the prow of the pirogue and held on to it, preventing the boat from leaving. We could see numerous warriors nocking arrows in their bows and I felt sure we were all going to die right there on that damn river that we had struggled so mightily to ascend.

Partisan was stalking up and down the shore, shouting and shaking a fist. Then he walked down to where Clark stood and shouted directly into the captain's face. With that insult, Clark drew his sword, pointing it straight at Partisan, and just that quickly the entire scene froze like a statue or painting.

"Be ready, men," Lewis said softly, and I can guarantee that we were ready. I had my rifle aimed straight at Partisan, and I'm sure I wasn't the only one. If it all came down to shooting, that belligerent chief was going to be the first to die.

More words were passed on the shore, Cruzatte translating like a mad man and, I'm sure, pouring even more sweat. Clark must have had a hundred arrows pointed at him but he never flinched and he kept the tip of his sword just bare inches from Partisan's nose. I could hear Clark's voice, though I couldn't understand the words, and his tone never changed. Later, the men who were with him in the pirogue would tell me the main points of the conversation, how Clark never wavered in his determination that we were soldiers and would continue up the river whether the Sioux liked it or not, and how the chiefs told him they would follow us and kill us off one by one if we did. All I know is how he stood there like some military hero of legend, never taking the point of his sword away from Partisan's face.

I don't know how long we stayed frozen in that manner, but it seemed like hours had passed before one of the chiefs, I think it was Black Buffalo, ordered the warrior off the mast and retrieved the rope from his other warriors, thus freeing the pirogue to return to the keelboat. The men quickly rowed back to the keelboat, leaving Clark, Cruzatte and Drouillard on the shore. Lewis swiftly loaded twelve more soldiers on the pirogue and launched it back toward the shore in defense of Captain Clark.

The Indians who were gathered on the riverbank backed away as the pirogue landed and the soldiers clambered out. Captain Clark continued talking with the chiefs, and even offered his hand, but was rebuked, and finally he climbed back into the pirogue and cast off from the shore. Those of us on the keelboat had no sooner breathed a sigh of relief than Black Buffalo and Buffalo Medicine were wading into the water after the pirogue, talking earnestly.

"What is he doing?" Potts breathed, as Clark stopped the pirogue and took the two chiefs on board. My rifle never wavered from Partisan, who stood about thirty yards up the shore, arms crossed and a disgusted look on his face.

"Haven't a clue," I said tersely.

"Keep alert!" Lewis barked out. "We're not out of this yet."

Trust me. We were all alert.

The pirogue finally made it back to the keelboat and was unloaded. I caught a brief glimpse of Clark's face and he looked about as mad as a wet hen.

"All right, men, let's move this boat upriver a ways. Colter, Potts, Shields, Drouillard, stay in your positions and yell out if those Indians on shore make a hostile move." Lewis looked just about as angry as Clark, and his voice was tight with rage. "If you have to shoot, take down Partisan first. Is that clear?"

"Yes, Captain," we said.

We got the boat moving and headed slowly upstream. The Indians on shore followed along the banks, keeping pace with us, and we could hear the babble of their voices over the splashing of the oars. The warriors, however, seemed reluctant to make any move toward us, possibly fearing for the safety of the two chiefs on board. Looking back at that day, I wonder if those two chiefs had known that Partisan would order the warriors to attack and the only way to keep that from happening would be to join us on the keelboat. It's an interesting thought.

We anchored about a mile upriver from the council site, just off an island and far enough from shore to have plenty of warning should the Sioux decide to attack. I had the feeling that none of us would be getting much sleep that night.

"Captain Clark?" Shields said.

"Yes, John?"

"You been naming every island all the way up this bedamned river." Shields jerked his head toward the island. "So what are you gonna name this one?"

Clark uttered a short bark of a laugh. "How does 'Bad Humored Island' sound?"

We all thought it sounded just fine. We were all in a bad humor.

* * *

The night passed slowly. None of us slept as we listened to the endless murmuring of Indian voices from the riverbank and watched for any hint of an attack. My eyes grew tired from staring into the darkness. The captains had taken the two Indian chiefs into the cabin at the stern of the keelboat and spent most of the night talking with them, but we didn't hear much of what was being said. I figured Captain Clark would tell us what we needed to know when the time came for us to know it.

Early the next morning, a pale ball of sun rose in the east, hazy in the mist that hung above the river. The Indians were still gathered on the shore, the warriors having been joined by hundreds of women and children, all of them staring at us and talking among themselves. We pulled the anchor and set out upriver, the act of rowing even more of a chore this morning due to our lack of sleep during the night, and again those Indians followed along on the shore.

"Don't they all have anything else to do?" Potts asked grumpily.

"Quiet, Mr. Potts," Sergeant Ordway said, not unkindly. "Just do your job."

The chiefs stood on the deck, speaking with the captains in low tones, motioning toward the shore where their people were following along. The chiefs' demeanor appeared urgent, and it wasn't long before Lewis ordered the keelboat stopped.

"These chiefs want us to come to their village," Lewis said.

"Is that a good idea, Captain?" Nate asked.

"I guess I won't know until I go. Jefferson wants a peace treaty signed with these Sioux, so I have to take the chance."

"Let us send a strong guard with you," Sergeant Ordway said.

Lewis pondered the idea for a moment. "We don't want to insult their hospitality," he said finally. "I'll take five men with me. That way I can be somewhat guarded while still honoring their courtesy."

Ordway shook his head but didn't say anything more.

I was one of the five soldiers assigned to accompany Captain Lewis to the native village. I had to agree with Ordway; it seemed like a small number of soldiers to guard Lewis's life against the hundreds of natives lining the shore, but we had to follow the captain's lead. The two chiefs who had spent the night on board with us seemed friendly enough this morning, and I didn't see Partisan among the Indians on shore, but my nerves were still on edge. This whole scenario had the potential to explode into a massacre, and we would be the ones massacred if that happened.

On the shore, we were led into the Sioux village, a grouping of stout and well-constructed tipis placed in a rough circle around a larger council house. The people were very curious about us and we walked in the middle of a crowd of men, women and children, all of them staring and whispering. The men had a fierce appearance and were attired in buckskin and robes made from animal hides, all armed with bows and arrows and many sporting hawk feathers in their hair. The women wore long robes decorated with porcupine quills and some were quite pretty, disturbing for a man who had gone long months without seeing a woman. But I forced my mind to pay attention to the dangers at hand instead of the females.

The chiefs led us to the council house where they motioned for us to be seated in a circle on the floor. A pipe was passed. On the walk up from the boat, Lewis had told us of the chiefs' desire that we spend at least one more night with them, so they could show us their hospitality and dance for us.

"I think our obvious intention to not back down before them has impressed them," Lewis said. "They seem to understand strength and they know now that we are soldiers who are not afraid of them."

"I gotta confess, Captain," Pete Weiser said. "I am just a bit afraid of them."

Lewis grinned. "Nothing wrong with that. Just don't let them know."

It sounded like good advice to me and I did my best to appear calm and confident.

The morning passed slowly as Lewis spoke with the chiefs through Drouillard and Cruzatte. I did my best to follow their conversation but it was a tedious process and I often allowed my attention to drift away, to study the myriad faces that were gathered around us. There was open hostility on a few faces but most of the people simply seemed curious about us and they studied us as intently as I was studying them. I knew from the captains that white people were not unknown in Sioux lands, that traders from the English, French and Spanish made regular visits up the river, but we were not traders, and thus were a source of curiosity. I wondered what they thought about us.

Around midday Sergeant Pryor came up from the boat and joined us. "Captain Clark was getting a mite concerned about your welfare," he explained. "You've been gone a while."

"Tell him we are fine, and the chiefs are preparing a feast in our honor," Lewis told him. "Tell him we are spending the night here."

Pryor departed and the talking continued. At one point Lewis excused himself and returned to the boat, and Captain Clark was brought up to the council house, carried on a robe by eight Sioux warriors. This, we learned later, was a great honor. Lewis was brought back later in the same manner. Speeches were given by some of the older men, whom I assumed to be the elders of the nation, and those went on for a long time. The gist seemed to be that the Sioux were eager to be the friends of their new great father, Jefferson, and would abide by his rules and laws.

They were grand words, just the words we wanted to hear, but I wasn't convinced, and I don't believe the captains were, either.

After the speeches and meal were done, the people put on a demonstration for us, with music and dancing. A lot of the dancing seemed to be their way of telling stories, as the warriors pantomimed acts of courage in battle, jumping up, slashing with imaginary tomahawks or knives, pulling back the strings of invisible bows and launching invisible arrows. The women danced also, celebrating the heroics of their men and waving scalps and other trophies of war. The natives danced with a lot of energy and spirit, and the steady pounding of the drums combined with the occasional loud whoop or yell gave the entire scene a primitive air that made my heart beat faster. It was frightening and fascinating all at the same time.

The dancing and singing went on well into the night, until the captains finally thanked our hosts and told them that we were very tired and needed to return to our boat. Most of the village accompanied us down to the shore and Black Buffalo and Buffalo Medicine spent another night on board the keelboat.

"Keep alert again tonight, boys," Sergeant Pryor told us, nodding his head toward the shore, where many Indians appeared set to continue their vigil. "I'll spell you in shifts so you can try to get some sleep, but we'll need to be ready for anything."

It was another sleepless night.

CHAPTER FOURTEEN

In the morning, which dawned clear and cold, the captains accompanied the two chiefs to the shore, fully prepared to bid them farewell and continue on our journey up the river. I remained on the keelboat this time, allowing other soldiers to spend some time ashore, though I'm not sure that was much of an honor for them. After all, it would be the ones on shore who would be the first to die if hostilities broke out.

Sergeant Ordway said later that the chiefs almost begged the captains to stay one more night, claiming that many people of their nation were on their way to the river just to meet the white men and it would be impolite for us to leave. The captains were not enthusiastic about staying there any longer but felt obligated to do so. That night the dancing and singing went on again until late, the sound carrying down to the river, almost drowned out by the voices of those Indians who were perpetually sitting and standing on the banks. I would have thought it would have been boring for them, sitting and staring at a bunch of white men on a boat, but I guess anything new and unusual was cause for excitement among them.

Around midnight we could see the captains coming down to the bank and climbing into the pirogue. They had Partisan with them.

"What are they doing?" Collins asked quietly.

I shrugged. Partisan was the last one I thought would be invited back onto the boat.

"They're not bringing him on board, are they?"

"Appears that way," I muttered.

"This could get ugly," Sergeant Ordway said. "Clear your heads, men. Be ready for anything."

The pirogue cut a vee shape across the surface of the water, aiming for the keelboat. None of us realized until it was too late that the boat was headed straight for the anchor rope.

With a surprisingly loud snap the rope broke and immediately the keelboat began a slow lazy swing into the current of the Missouri. Captain Clark was the first to recognize the danger and his shouts for the men on board to get on the oars roused Partisan to shouts of his own. I'm sure he had no idea what was happening or why Clark was suddenly shouting, but I'm sure he suspected some kind of treachery. Within minutes dozens of armed Sioux appeared on the shore.

Meanwhile, the men on the oars were struggling to get control of the keelboat before she could get sideways to the current and be overturned, while the rest of us hunkered down and prepared for the barrage of arrows and gunfire that we felt sure would be coming our way any moment. The pirogue had headed back toward the shore, with Partisan still riled and shouting for all he was worth, and the yells of the other Indians on the shore drowned out the curses of the men on the keelboat.

Within a couple of minutes the keelboat was under control and stopped against the far bank, beneath an overhang of roots and dirt. The pirogue had reached the shore, where Clark was struggling to explain what had happened to an anxious and suspicious crowd of Indians. Eventually the voices of the Indians calmed as the explanation was conveyed, and we could see the warriors lowering their arms, many of them returning toward their town.

"Everything okay over there, Captain Clark?" Ordway called out.

"We're fine, Sergeant," Clark replied. "We'll be across momentarily."

"Yes, sir."

The captains came across to the boat shortly after that, and they had the three principal chiefs with them. "Everything's all right, men," Clark said.

"What in tarnation happened?" Gass asked.

"When I started yelling, the Indians thought we were all under attack from one of their enemy nations. That's what Partisan was yelling about."

"Those warriors appeared awful quickly, Captain," Sergeant Pryor said.

"I know," the captain said. "Hardly seems like a coincidence, does it?"

It was another sleepless night.

* * *

"I can't see a thing, Captain," Silas Goodrich said, water streaming off his hair and clothes as he clambered aboard the keelboat. "It's nothing but mud and sand down there, and cold as a trollop's heart."

"That's it, then," Lewis said, shaking his head in anger and disgust. "The anchor is lost. Probably buried under the bed of the river by now."

"We'll just have to go on without it," Clark said reasonably. He clapped Silas on the shoulder. "Good try, Silas. I thank you. Now go put on some dry clothes before you get sick."

I stifled a huge yawn and blinked my eyes blearily. Two nights without sleep was taking its toll on me. My head was pounding like the inside of a drum.

"Let's get these chiefs off the boat and get on our way," Lewis said. "I'm tired of spending any more time here."

Getting the chiefs to shore proved to be more difficult than expected. And, again, it was Partisan who was the troublemaker as he demanded more gifts. Eventually, though, the chiefs were put on shore and we were able to get under way.

Several more times over the next days we stopped to talk with various chiefs of the Teton before finally moving up out of their territory, and we all breathed a sigh of relief. The captains had been forced to bribe, cajole and threaten the chiefs in order for us to continue on our journey, and I heard Lewis express his disgust and hatred toward the Sioux on several occasions. It looked to me like Jefferson's grand plan to pacify and integrate the Sioux had ended in failure.

* * *

And so now we were back to our standard routine, making our slow but steady progress up that wide river. We faced the usual culprits that we had been facing all those long weeks, including so many sandbars the captains stopped keeping track of them when writing in their journals at night. With each passing day the wind seemed to grow colder, and rain was a constant reminder to us of the winter to come. On several occasions we saw Indians along the shore, but the captains ignored those Indian's pleas for us to stop and take them on board. Many of those Indians seemed to think we were traders and wished to inspect what goods we had on board, and they seemed dismayed when we continued up the river without stopping.

Our hunting opportunities were limited due to the captain's desire to keep everyone close to the keelboat, but fortunately many of the animals seemed to be in their season of migration and we were often able to kill elk, antelope or deer right from our boats as they swam across the river.

The land along our course was a combination of timber and wide prairies, and we came across numerous other rivers and streams that emptied into the Missouri. In most cases, we would stop so the captains could explore up those rivers and write about what they saw for Jefferson to read. Geese and ducks were numerous along the shallow bottomlands, and the sky was filled more every day with fowl heading south.

On the eighth of October we arrived at a large village of Indians. The village seemed to consist of dozens of earthen lodges, like those we had seen in abandoned villages ever since leaving the Teton Sioux, and the captains said that these people were called Arikaras.

To our surprise, a Frenchman named Joseph Gravelines was living with the Arikaras and he came on board with us as an interpreter. A trader, Gravelines had lived among the Arikaras for almost two decades and was quite well known and apparently well liked by them. We stopped and made camp a short distance above the village and Captain Lewis went with Gravelines to meet with the Indian leaders.

This was a pattern that would be continued as we moved up the river. The captains were following Jefferson's directions to spread the news about America's purchase of the territory and to try and create a new trading empire. All of the Indian nations we came in contact with were familiar with white men as traders and seemed to welcome us and our promises of building trading posts along the river that would bring new and exciting items to their people. I never learned what they thought of the concept of some distant nation buying their land, or if that idea even translated properly to them. If they did understand the full import of Jefferson's message, they seemed to take it with an astonishing level of equanimity.

After parting company with the Arikaras, we continued on our journey. Our final destination for that year was to be the Mandan villages that were located somewhere above us, and that were known to be friendly to the white traders and explorers who had met with them in the past. The captains wanted to winter near the Mandans in the hope of not only making a lasting friendship with them but to learn as much as possible about the land and rivers beyond their village. Details about the country above the Mandan lands were sketchy, coming mostly from trappers traveling down to St. Louis with their beaver and otter pelts. Since we would be venturing into that country in the spring, the captains wisely wanted to learn all they could about it.

* * *

"I tell you, I'm sick and tired of it," John Newman said. Known as a perpetual complainer and whiner, he normally kept his voice pitched low so as not to be overheard by the captains or sergeants. On this day, for whatever reason, he wasn't bothering with propriety.

"We're nothing but slaves," he said from his seat where he was manning the oars of the keelboat. "Working our fingers to the bone, and for what?"

"Keep your voice down, John," Moses Reed warned. Reed was Newman's only friend. He glanced to his left, where Sergeant Ordway was seated. I couldn't tell if Ordway was listening, but knowing the sergeant's hearing prowess I would have been very surprised if he wasn't absorbing every word.

"Why the hell should I?" Newman was red-faced with anger. "I'm a free man, not some damn slave!"

"Is there a problem, Mr. Newman?" Ordway had heard, just as I thought he would.

Newman grumbled something under his breath, and for a moment I thought he was going to be smart and keep his fool mouth shut. Then his head came up. "Damn right there's a problem! I ain't no slave. I'm sick and tired of hauling this heavy boat up this river day in and day out, risking my life on this fool venture!"

"Mr. Newman, I suggest you..."

"And I suggest you go to hell!" Newman said. "I am not a slave! None of these men are slaves, and we shouldn't be treated like slaves!"

At the stern, I could see Captain Lewis get up from his seat and walk to the door of the small cabin he shared with Clark.

"Take up your oar, Mr. Newman," Ordway commanded.

"The hell I will!"

"Sergeant!" Lewis's voice split the air like the crack of a whip.

"Sir!"

"Remand that man to custody immediately!"

I shook my head as I bent back to my work. With the kind of mood Captain Lewis had been in since our encounter with the Teton Sioux, Newman couldn't have picked a worse time to rile him.

* * *

Newman's court-martial took place the next day and he was found guilty of treason. He was sentenced to seventy-five lashes on his bare back. Worst of all for him, his name was removed from the permanent party and he was assigned to whatever drudgery work that needed to be done until he could be sent back down to St. Louis with the keelboat in the spring.

"In an enterprise such as we are on," Lewis pronounced, "I can not allow this kind of dissension in the ranks. You, John Newman, have been found guilty of uttering words of a highly criminal and mutinous nature, with the intent of creating disharmony and destroying morale and military discipline. Your words carried your obvious intent to drive a wedge between these honorable men and their sergeants and officers.

"From this point forward, your name has been removed from our permanent party, as I will not sully the fine names of these upstanding soldiers by allowing your name to be associated with theirs. You will immediately surrender your arms to Sergeant Gass. You are no longer a soldier in the Army of the United States of America.

"Your role from now until you can be sent down to St. Louis in the spring is to relieve these honorable soldiers of that distasteful work of which they should not be exposed as long as you are with this party. You will be assigned to the red pirogue as a simple laborer and will only do those tasks assigned to you to relieve the remainder of the party."

Newman sat with his head hung as his sentence was read. Reed, who had unwisely spoken up in defense of Newman the day before, kept his mouth closed, though I could see that he was angered by what was happening to his friend. I expected more trouble from them both before all was said and done.

CHAPTER FIFTEEN

Now this was more like it.

I drew in a deep breath and slowly let it out, savoring the moment. The Arikara squaw who had just given me much sensual pleasure was already sitting up, drawing her robe around her shoulders. I didn't know her name, and probably wouldn't have been able to pronounce it if I did, but that didn't matter to me. After almost a year without feeling the flesh of a woman, this moment had been like experiencing a slice of pure heaven.

The Arikaras were a nation of people who, quite simply, seemed to love us, and their women shared that sentiment. I had heard Drouillard talk about ceremonies where men offered their wives to other men, choosing men with great prowess as a hunter, assuming in that intimacy that the other's hunting skills would be transferred to the husband. Apparently the Arikaras saw us as great hunters.

We had been among the Arikaras for several days, and the men had all sampled the pleasures of these women, all the men except Newman and Reed, that is. Those two were confined to camp. Even the captains had taken their pleasure among the willing squaws, if the rumors among the men were true. And who could blame them? They were men of flesh and blood, just like we were, and the Arikara squaws were beautiful and lusty.

Besides that, it was considered an insult to the Arikaras to not accept the favors of a squaw when they were offered. And who were we to insult our hosts?

"I hear tell that if you sample the pleasures of these squaws, your luck will change for the better," Shannon said one afternoon.

"And then you'll find a pot of gold at the end of the rainbow," Goodrich teased, and Shannon turned red.

I don't know about my luck changing, but I was more than willing to share the pleasures of the squaws.

* * *

We continued to meet up with trappers heading down to the Mississippi, their canoes laden with furs, and with each of those encounters my interest and excitement rose. The pictures their words drew of rivers teeming with beaver and otter and mink made my head spin. There was a fortune to be made up here in this land and I wanted to be a part of it.

"Think about it!" Lewis said to Clark one afternoon. He had also been dwelling on the tales told by the trappers but as usual his thoughts turned toward his country. "Think of how the nation can be enriched if we can just establish a trade network in this land!"

I agreed with the part about enrichment. But my interest was more in the enrichment of John Colter.

Much of my time was now dedicated to hunting, and I spent fewer and fewer hours working aboard the keelboat. The captains often compared my hunting skills to those of Drouillard, who was, without a doubt, our best hunter. I enjoyed those solitary times, on the wide and open prairies, with the wind as my only companion. And I enjoyed bringing the meat back to those men who were struggling so hard to keep that boat moving up the river.

But my goal as we moved deeper into Mandan country was to get a shot at one of the legendary white bears that the Indians spoke of with tones of the deepest reverence. I had found the tracks put down by those bears and they were huge, bigger than any track I had ever seen. I pointed out one of those tracks to Captain Clark one day and all he did was whistle in a low, awed manner. The Indians went in fear of those bears, and to own the claws of one was considered by them to be great medicine. All told tales of deadly encounters with the massive animals and I itched to see one of those bears.

However, it was Cruzatte who became the first of our party to encounter one of the bears, and it was almost the death of him. Having shot at and wounded the bear, Cruzatte dropped his rifle and took to his heels when the bear towered up on its hind legs and emitted an earth-shaking roar. The rest of the crew ribbed him mercilessly in camp that night, but all of us secretly wondered how we would react when we first encountered one of those fearsome monsters.

We arrived at the principal Mandan villages just about the same time that winter really began to show its face. Snow fell almost every day now, and the icy wind cut through our clothing no matter how many layers we put on. We stopped at the Mandan villages to hold a council and to learn as much as we could about the neighboring tribes and the course of the river to the mountains. I also knew that the captains wanted to establish a winter camp near these villages.

"The ice will be on the river soon," Gravelines told them. "Once the ice closes in, that boat of yours won't be going anywhere."

Lewis and Clark understood this, so the establishment of a winter camp was at the top of their list of things to accomplish. And the bluff just a little ways south and across the river from the upper Mandan village seemed like the perfect place, especially after Captain Clark scouted a ways upriver and couldn't find a location anywhere else with wood and game. There were several acres of forest near the bluff from which we could get trees for building and we were close enough to the village to associate with the people there. The trees in the wooded area were mostly cottonwoods, not the best for building, but they were the only trees for hundreds of miles in any direction.

"We'll build a fort right here," Lewis said, standing on the top of the bluff as the wind blew around us. Small snowflakes flew with that wind, not enough to cover the ground but enough for us to know that more was on the way. The sky was filled with gray clouds as far as the eye could see in all directions, and small chunks of ice floated in the river. Winter had found us.

"You want a fort this time, then?" Clark asked.

Lewis nodded. "Yes. I don't fear an attack from the Mandan, but there are still Sioux out there, and I sure don't trust them. I want a fortified camp, inside a wall, that we can defend if we have to."

Clark nodded in agreement and he and Lewis set out for the keelboat to draw up their plans for a fort. In the meantime, Drouillard and I set out in another direction. If we were going to be building a fort, we would need a lot of meat to feed the men. And finding meat in this cold and windswept land was going to be a challenge.

Once the captains had completed their drawings for the fort, the work began. Sergeant Gass oversaw the construction, and all of the men pitched in, including Newman and Reed. The almost-daily snow showers and the perpetual cold wind were enough to keep the men working hard, as we all wanted to be indoors before the full force of winter was upon us. I took my turn felling trees and hauling them to the fort, though my main job was securing meat for the party, and I'll be the first to admit that construction and carpentry are not my top skills.

One thing I have to say about Captain Lewis at this juncture is that he was a natural leader of men. His personality may not have allowed me to feel comfortable with him, and there were times when he seemed morose and withdrawn, but as the leader of an expedition such as this one Jefferson couldn't have picked a better. In his style, he was like a strict father, always making sure the men were fed and clothed properly, that discipline was meted out when necessary, that the best interests of the men came first and foremost but with the ultimate goal always in mind. He seemed able to tell when we had reached our limits and he would call for a rest and ration out a dram of whiskey. Yet, no matter what we thought our limits to be, Lewis always seemed able to move us just enough beyond those limits to show us we could do it. And he knew to assign men to the tasks that best suited their skills. Gass had been a carpenter so he was put in charge of building the fort. Drouillard, Shields and I were the best hunters so the responsibility of providing the Corps with meat was ours. Like him or not, Captain Lewis knew his business.

It took about two weeks to complete the fort, and we were just in time. The first heavy snow of the winter fell shortly after we moved into the huts, and the walls were still being completed as the heavy wet snow piled deep on the ground. The Missouri seemed to ice over in a remarkably short amount of time, and the temperature plummeted.

"She's looking mighty fine, Mr. Gass," Clark said, his breath frosting in the air as he stood with his hands on his hips, surveying the work. Two rows of connected huts angled out from each other, forming two sides of a triangle; the third side was just being completed as a high palisade wall. The roofs of the huts sloped inward, rising up to almost eighteen feet in height at the outside. At the apex of the triangle, where the two rows of huts came together, a storeroom had been added for holding our gear and perishables from the keelboat.

"A good job of work, Sergeant," Lewis said, smiling widely. "This will be a fine place to spend the winter."

"Thank you, Captain."

I stood to one side, and I certainly agreed. All of the men had worked long hours to complete what Clark was calling Fort Mandan and we were happy to be living indoors. Smoke curled up now from the several chimneys, and, having just returned from a two-week hunting trip about thirty miles south, I was eager to sleep inside four walls with a roof over my head!

Our hunting trip had been a success, and we had returned with a good supply of meat, but the hunting had not been easy. The animals seemed to have headed south, or were hunkering down in hidden draws and valleys that had to be searched for on the wide plains. Winter was affecting them in many of the same ways it was affecting us.

The captains were spending a lot of their time at the Mandan villages, and had even managed to broker a peace between the Mandans and the Arikaras further south. So far they were considering our short stay with the Mandans as a success.

"I just wish we had gotten that boat up to higher ground sooner," Clark said, looking down the hill to the river.

The keelboat was frozen against the shore, locked in by the ice that seemed to have covered the river overnight. Our hunting party had taken the red pirogue downriver and we had had to drag it across the ice coming back up, that's how quickly that river had frozen over. The bow of the pirogue had been damaged by the ice and had to be repaired before we could use it again. No stranger to cold winters, I had the distinct feeling that this would be the coldest winter I had ever experienced.

"We may still have a thaw," Lewis said. "If we do, we'll drag her up onto the bank."

Many of the men were making regular visits to the Mandan village across the river, where they were greeted warmly by the people there, especially the women. The rumor making the rounds was that those women valued men of pale skin as good medicine, and we did nothing to dispel that notion. Spending a cold day outside working on the fort or hunting was not as bad when there was the promise of a good meal and a warm woman later in the evening.

* * *

As the full force of winter closed in, we were all amazed at the Mandan's seeming nonchalance in the face of howling winds and temperatures that dipped to an incredible seventy degrees below freezing. They went about their business as if each day was warm and sunny, and the regular stream of visitors to the fort never diminished. They regularly brought us bushels of corn in exchange for some of the meat we brought in, and we were happy to trade. Our hunting trips became exercises in agony, as we struggled through snow drifts that were hip deep while guarding against frostbite and keeping an eye out all the time for raiding parties of Sioux.

With the cold weather came illnesses, from colds and rheumatism to the ever-present venereal complaints, though I never heard any man vow to stop visiting the women across the river. Frostbite was common. Injuries were also common as men struggled to use axes and knives with hands numbed and frozen with the cold, including Drouillard who cut one hand almost to the bone and was pulled off the hunting rotation. Nate Pryor dislocated his shoulder when taking down the mast on the keelboat during our winter preparations, and it pained him all through the winter. And on top of that the snow continued to fall and the temperature continued to drop.

All in all, I knew it was going to be a winter I would long remember.

CHAPTER SIXTEEN

"Sergeant Ordway, Sergeant Gass, rally your men!" Captain Clark's voice rang out across the fort. "Bring your arms!"

We scrambled out of our bunks and rushed into our warm clothing, knowing that if we were under attack the alarm would have been different. The intensity in Clark's voice, however, told us that something serious was happening. Grabbing my rifle and shot pouch, I ran out into the open area in front of the fort's gate, where the two captains stood with an Indian man and our interpreter.

Both squads gathered within minutes and Clark told us what was happening, his face grim. "The Sioux from down below attacked this man's hunting party and killed a warrior. They also stole their horses, and some other hunters are missing. This is our chance to prove to the Mandans that we are their friends and allies."

I glanced at William Bratton. Just the night before we had spoken about the rumors we had heard, that some of the Mandan chiefs believed we were allies with the Sioux and would eventually turn against them. Both captains were desperate to dispel those rumors.

We crossed over to the Mandan village and were met outside the town by one of the main chiefs. While we stood shivering in the snow, the chief took Clark into his lodge and spoke with him for what seemed an extremely long time. When Clark came back to where we all waited, there was a satisfied smile on his face.

"Sorry to keep you standing out here, lads," he said, "but it was for a good cause."

"We goin' after them Sioux, Captain?" Sergeant Gass asked, his teeth chattering with the cold.

"Not today, Pat," Clark said. "The chief feels that it's too cold and the snow is too deep to possibly catch up to them. But they now know that we're willing to fight on their side if the need arises. Can't ask for much more than that, can we, boys?" He shook his head and his smile faded away. "The chief tells me that some of the men who attacked their hunters were Arikaras, working with the Sioux," he said. "Looks like peace agreements don't mean much out here." He blew out a slow breath, which froze in the air even as it left his mouth.

"Well, can't do anything about it standing out here in the cold. Let's head back for that fort," he said finally. "And I think we all deserve an extra dram of whiskey tonight!"

* * *

Several days later, Big White, one of the Mandan chiefs, mentioned that a massive herd of buffalo was passing near the village on their annual migration. Being short of meat by this point, Lewis immediately gathered together a large group of men, including a healed Drouillard, and we set out in pursuit. The weather had warmed slightly over the previous days, though it was still quite cold, and we were able to make good time over the hard frozen ground. The wind was coming at us from the southwest, but we could feel it turning, angling down more from the north, and we knew that colder weather would soon return.

The buffalo were passing from north to south several miles to the northeast of the fort and it didn't take us long to catch up to them. A large number of Mandans were already busily engaged in their own hunt and we joined them, bringing down ten of the large animals within a few short minutes. By the time the rest of the herd had thundered away across the icy prairie, sixty of their number lay dead and the Indians were rejoicing.

The butchering and transport of the meat took most of what was left of the day, and we feasted that night on buffalo and whiskey. Several of the chiefs and their warriors joined us and the dancing and celebrating went on well into the night.

In the days following the hunt, the temperature continued to drop, becoming so cold that all the hunting parties were called in and we hunkered in the fort, our only goal being to stay as warm as possible. The visits from the Mandan villages continued in spite of the deep cold, a fact which never ceased to amaze all of us. Our newest hired French interpreter, a man named Charbonneau, was a regular visitor, along with his two wives, and the chiefs of the villages came often to consult with the captains.

Snow fell on most days, and the wind never seemed to cease. On many nights we could hear the sound of the cottonwoods cracking open with a report like a gunshot as the waters inside their trunks froze solid and expanded. It seemed the wild stories told to us in the fall were coming true.

On Christmas Eve we finally completed placing the last of the pickets around the fort, making our outer wall complete. Our little Fort Mandan was now finished, and we all felt as warm and cozy as could be expected. To many of us, the small fort was rustic and barren when compared to the homes we had left behind in the east, but from the evidence we had, namely the fact that the Mandan chiefs seemed to want to spend every night in it, our fort was luxurious by western standards.

At daybreak on Christmas morning, we greeted the holiest of days by firing off several rounds from the swivel gun that had been transferred from the boat to the fort, and then raised our flag for the first time over Fort Mandan. The sight of our little flag, with its fifteen stars and fifteen stripes fluttering in the stiff prairie wind, raised a cheer from the men gathered to watch. Whiskey flowed freely throughout the morning, and we cleared one of the rooms for music and dancing. The Mandans stayed away all through the day by request of the captains, who were becoming a little tired of the constant presence of the Indians in the fort.

"Tomorrow is our big medicine day," Lewis had told Big White through an interpreter the day before. "Please ask your people not to disturb our celebrations and reveries."

I wondered what the Mandans thought about a big medicine day that involved the firing of weapons and the consumption of large amounts of whiskey.

* * *

As the year turned from 1804 to 1805, the pace of our lives settled into routine. Hunting parties went out to bring back buffalo, deer, elk, or any other meat we could find, and sometimes stayed out through the night, though it was normally too cold to allow that. The Indians brought corn and other food to us in exchange for small trifles and articles, and also for the services of Shields and Willard, our blacksmiths. The Indians had pots and tools made of metal which they had obtained through trade, and many of those items needed mending due to being damaged or broken. During some of the coldest spells, it was Shields and Willard more than the hunters who kept us fed.

Most of the men, including me, continued our relationships with the happy and willing women of the villages, and some even found women who became more than just partners of convenience. Shannon was the first to indicate that he had a special friend in the town, but other men also seemed to direct all of their attentions toward one favorite woman. When we weren't sharing the warmth of a woman's blankets, we were dancing with the people of the village in spirited outbursts of music and laughter that would often continue deep into the night.

The captains spent many hours with the chiefs, and with the traders from the Hudson Bay Company and the Northwest Company, mapping the course of the river and the lay of the land above the Mandan villages to the base of the mountains that lay to the west. Even in the deepest cold of the winter their minds were already on spring and the next leg of the expedition.

* * *

"This is an exercise in futility," George Shannon gasped. His face was red, and sweat ran from him.

I had to agree. For two days every man not out hunting had been at the river, struggling to break the ice around the boats in order to free them from its grip. We had used axes, pry bars and saws in a failed attempt to cut through or break the ice, which was almost two feet thick, and had even resorted to boiling water and pouring it over the ice in an effort to melt it, all to no avail. I would have wagered all the money due to me from this expedition that the boats would remain where they were until spring thaws melted the ice and freed them. We could only hope that the thick ice didn't crush their hulls before those spring thaws came.

"I agree," I said. "But we have to keep trying."

Shannon nodded and attacked the ice again with his axe. This was the third spot around the hull of the keelboat where we had tried to break through and we weren't having any more success than we had had on our two other attempts.

Corporal Warfington and John Potts slipped and staggered their way across the lumpy ice toward us, each clutching the handle of a large bucket. Steam rose from the sloshing water inside the bucket, water that had come off a fire built on the shore for just this purpose. The two men slowly poured the hot water onto the ice and Shannon and I began hacking at it again with our axes.

All around us, men worked at the stubborn ice, many moving sluggishly in the bitter cold. We were all bundled up in furs and heavy gloves, making an impossible task even more difficult. And the sweat generated by our exertions was freezing to our faces and bodies as soon as it appeared.

"Don't forget to check your hands and feet for feeling," Clark said loudly. "If you're getting numb, get to the fort and get warmed up. We've had enough frostbite to last us for three winters!" Captain Clark was armed with his own axe and was flailing away at the ice right alongside us, a fact that impressed the men no end.

I feared frostbite ahead of just about anything else, and I knew what Clark was thinking about as he spoke. Just the day before, Lewis had been forced to amputate the toes of an Indian boy who had been frostbitten during a hunting trip. Though the operation had gone well and the boy would recover, I had no intention of reaching the point where I would need Lewis to start removing my body parts!

At last, we gave up on breaking the ice around the boat and decided we would have to wait until spring came and then pray there was no damage to the hull. Tired and dejected, we trailed back to the warmth and comfort of the fort.

CHAPTER SEVENTEEN

The winter continued, so long and so brutal it seemed we had been hunkered in that fort for a lifetime. The wind howled across the open prairies like something possessed and the temperatures dropped to levels that were almost amazing to behold. Meat was scarce, as the game animals had all migrated south for the winter, those animals being apparently smarter than we humans! Hunters went out every day scouring the countryside for anything to shoot, and the variety of animals we brought back ranged from small deer to mangy elk to porcupines and badgers. Even the meat of a skinny wolf was a welcome change from old dried-up corn that we received from the Mandans in trade.

I was part of a large party that went out in February under the command of Captain Clark with the intention of staying out until we had secured enough meat to last us well into the following month. We loaded up three horses and two flat sleighs with provisions and set out, bearing south across the frozen river. The air was so cold it hurt to inhale, and only by moving could we keep from freezing. The land before us rolled and dipped, a mixture of open prairie and scattered woods, crossed with narrow creeks and rivers frozen as solid as the Missouri. From what we could see, we were the only living creatures in that icy and barren land.

"What do you think, John?" Joe Field asked, the fur trim around his hood dotted with ice from his breathing.

"About what?" I asked.

"All this," he said, waving out across the prairie.

"I think all the animals have gone down to New Orleans for the winter," I said.

Joe laughed. "You might be right, my friend."

"Oh, they're out there," Clark said. "They're just better at hiding than we are at finding. Let's keep moving, men, before we freeze to the ground."

We continued south throughout the days that followed, and camped at nights along the river in whatever cover of trees we could find. As the days went past, we were able to kill several deer and elk, their numbers increasing the further south we went. Clark directed us to build pens to hold the meat as we traveled, to protect it against the scavenging of the wolves, which seemed to be everywhere. They seemed to be having as hard of a time finding meat as we were!

"Them wolves ain't too dumb, are they?" I said one day, watching a small pack that was sitting on a low rise to our west. They were staring in our direction intently.

"What do you mean?" Captain Clark asked.

"Look at them there, waiting for us to do their hunting for them. They're smarter than we are, that's for sure."

Captain Clark just grinned and nodded.

We spent almost two weeks away from the fort and managed to gather a large amount of meat in the wooden pens. Some of the elk and deer were so scrawny that we left them for the wolves, since their meat would be stringy and inedible.

Clark shielded his eyes against the glare of weak sunlight off the snow as we finished securing several elk in the last pen. The horses and sleighs had been sent back with our newest interpreter, the one called Charbonneau, several days prior. "Good work, men," he said. "What say we head back up and send some of those men who've been warm and cozy this past week to gather up this meat?"

Nobody argued with that plan and we started back up the river toward the fort. Going north proved more difficult than walking south had been, due to the fact that the wind was coming down into our faces from the north, and we walked most of the time with our heads down against its icy blast. Finally, though, we saw the squat, friendly shape of the fort loom up ahead.

"Home never looked so good," Clark said.

Inside the fort, we unloaded the dressed meat from the horses and sleighs while Clark drew a quick sketch showing the locations of the meat caches.

"Anything exciting happen while we were gone?" Clark asked.

"That little wife of Charbonneau's had a baby boy," Lewis said. "Called him Jean-Baptiste. It was touch and go for a while but mother and child are doing fine."

Clark grinned. "That's good." I knew that the captains had hired Charbonneau to travel up the Missouri with us to act as an interpreter, and their intention was for him to take one of his wives along. Clark was hoping it would be the one called "Bird Woman," or Sacagawea. But with a brand new baby, I wondered if they would now decide to leave her behind. She was of the Shoshone nation, and the captains hoped to meet with those people and possibly secure horses for the journey across the mountains, and it would sure help our negotiations if we had someone along who could converse with them.

We would just have to wait and see.

* * *

"Smoke, Captain Lewis," Ordway said, pointing ahead.

Two days earlier, Drouillard, Goodrich, Frazier and Newman had been attacked and robbed by a group of Indians assumed to be Sioux, who stole two of their horses. The men had been traveling down to retrieve the meat left behind by our hunting party when they were surrounded by dozens of Indians on horseback. Only by sheer bravery and bluff did they manage to keep one of the horses and their weapons and escape with their lives. Now Lewis was leading a party after the Indian marauders in an attempt to retrieve what was ours.

Lewis called a halt and we looked at the smoke rising above a hill to the south. The smoke seemed to be coming from the vicinity of several old Mandan camps, where we had stored some of the meat.

"Could be those Sioux," Sergeant Gass said.

"Probably at that old Mandan camp."

Lewis nodded, and then turned toward the east. "Follow me," he said.

We crossed the river and headed up a small rise, into a thick copse of trees a little ways above the Mandan camp. Securing the horse and sleigh we had brought along for the purpose of taking the meat back to the fort, Lewis gathered us around him.

"Here is what we will do," he said. "Sergeant Ordway, you will lead a group of men with me and we will circle that camp to the northwest. Sergeant Gass, you will take the remaining men and get on the southeast side of the camp and prepare to attack." He held up the horn from the boat that he had brought along for the purpose of signaling if our group were to get separated from each other. "We will advance on the camp, and if you hear gunfire and we sound the horn you will know to attack from your side. Understood?"

We all nodded our understanding and set out. Sergeant Gass was in charge of the squad to which I was assigned, and I followed him along the bank of the river until we determined that we were southeast of the camp. The smoke could still be seen, gusting toward the south ahead of a strong and bitter wind.

"Okay, men, get ready," Gass said. Motioning to his sides, he spread us out in a line facing the camp and we took cover as best we could. Silence descended, broken only by the thin cry of a hawk, circling high overhead.

I checked my rifle, making sure it was fully primed and ready to go. It had been several years since I had been in a skirmish with Indians, not counting the little stand-off with the Sioux back down the Missouri, and I wasn't surprised to feel my heart beating faster. The prelude to a battle is often more stressful than the battle itself, when instinct can take over and you just do whatever you have to do to survive. In the prelude, you think about what might happen and what your role needs to be, and you think about the fact that you could be looking at the final moments of your life. I didn't want to die in this icy and barren land, not over some stolen horses that didn't even belong to me.

After what seemed a very long time but which in reality was only a few minutes, the horn sounded, echoing across the frozen land. There had been no gunfire, so we knew the Sioux must have moved on, but Gass still had us advance forward cautiously. When we reached the camp Lewis and the other men were waiting.

"They burned some huts," he said, motioning at the smoldering ruin. "And they took the meat. Ordway says the tracks show them heading toward the south and they're at least a day old. There's no way we'll catch them now."

He seemed disappointed. I sensed that Captain Lewis would have welcomed the opportunity to engage the Sioux in battle, whether to avenge the problems and headaches they had given us during the summer or just due to the ruination of Jefferson's grand plans for upriver commerce.

"There's another cache of meat about a mile west of here," I said.

"Let's go over there and see if they found that one, also," Lewis said. "If not, we'll gather the meat and head back to the fort." He looked one last time at the burned hut, and then gazed longingly toward the south. Finally he shook his head. "All right, men, let's move out."

* * *

Slowly, over the course of several weeks, the temperature started to rise and the snows began to melt. The river remained frozen for a long time, stubbornly holding onto its winter covering, but eventually that too resigned itself to the coming of spring. The winds gradually changed their course and brought with them warmer temperatures from the south, and the flights of geese and other fowl passed overhead on their own tracks toward the north, more of them going by with each day. Snow changed to sleet and finally to rain, a pleasant change from the snow and sleet with which we had been bombarded all winter. The first buds started to appear on the cottonwoods, and we all knew that the long, incredibly vicious winter was coming to an end.

Hunters went out more often, and were able to find plenty of food as the large herds of bison, elk and antelope returned from their wintering grounds. Spirits rose within the men as winter's grip eased, and even Sergeant Ordway was able to laugh one evening when his hat fell into one of the fires and was burnt to a cinder.

As the weather warmed, a crew of men was assigned the task of felling trees to make canoes for our continued journey up the river. The keelboat, under the command of Corporal Warfington, would be returning down the river to St. Louis, taking with her all the myriad specimens and notes gathered by the captains on our way up the river. Sergeant Gass wasn't excited about the prospect of making canoes out of the stringy cottonwood trees but they were all we had to work with.

"Damn things gum up a saw like nothing I ever knew," he grumbled. "This'll be a job to make a priest cuss."

"Then I'd say you're just the man for it," Captain Clark said and walked away, leaving Gass looking after him with confusion on his face.

* * *

February passed and March rolled around and our preparations proceeded at a feverish pace. Every man was busy with some important chore, be it making rope, drying meat, sewing skins into moccasins and clothing, working at the canoe camp, or just doing whatever was needed to prepare us for our journey up the river in the spring. Hunters continued their regular forays into the woods and we all kept a wary watch for the Sioux, especially after learning that they had confided in the Arikaras their intention to kill all of us.

We had finally succeeded in freeing the keelboat and pirogues from the frozen river and inspections were carried out to make sure there was no damage. Our supplies were also pulled out of storage and inspected, and Lewis spent many hours planning the distribution of every item we would be carrying upriver with us to make sure the loads were evenly distributed amongst the boats.

In late March the new canoes were floated down from the canoe camp and carried to the fort, where we set to work tarring and patching them, making sure any flaws or splits were filled prior to setting out.

With work racing forward, we still found time to continue our visits to the villages, though crossing the river had become a hazard with the ice breaking up and floating away. Most of us who had female friends in the village were willing to take the chance, though, as we didn't know how long it would be before we saw another female.

One benefit we reaped from the melting and dispersing of the ice on the Missouri was the number of buffalo that came floating down to us. Apparently, when trying to cross the thinned ice further up the Missouri on their migration, they would fall through and drown. The Indians were especially dexterous at pulling the huge bodies from the river as they passed and it was a time of great feasting for them.

Then came the month of April. We were completing our final loading of the keelboat with the tons of material Lewis was sending to his President and also loading the two pirogues and the new canoes for the journey toward the mountains in the west. It seemed as if every waking moment was devoted to our final preparations and we all moved with the knowledge that time was everything. We were fully aware and continually reminded that we had to cross the mountains, reach the coast, and recross the mountains before winter closed in again, which would mean leaving the Mandan villages the moment the river became navigable. We had to be ready.

We were also fully aware of the line we were about to cross. Our entire journey up the Missouri River so far had been through land well-traveled and well-documented by white traders and explorers who had come before us. The land above the Mandan villages was a different story. Though known to a few trappers and the Indian tribes that lived up that way, it was almost wholly unknown to everyone else. It would all be new. And with that unknown land would come unknown dangers.

And on April seventh we departed Fort Mandan for the final time.

CHAPTER EIGHTEEN

We stood on the bank in front of our little fort, waving and shouting farewells as the keelboat pushed off from shore and floated away on the current of the river. Most of us were happy to see the last of that big unwieldy monstrosity, though the large keelboat would have provided more protection than the pirogues and canoes in the event we were attacked by Indians. But the captains had spoken at length with the Mandan chiefs, who had stated the Missouri above the Mandan villages was too shallow to allow the keelboat's passage, so off it went, bound for St. Louis, and good riddance.

Newman and Reed were among the passengers departing with the keelboat, and none of us were sad to see them go. Throughout the long cold winter they had been sullen and taciturn and generally unpleasant to be around, though Newman had reportedly acquitted himself well during the showdown with the Sioux raiders who had stolen the horses and meat. Drouillard had praised his bravery in that incident when, armed only with a non-working musket, he had stood alongside the other men and held the gun pointed at a nearby warrior, bluffing desperately. In spite of that, we were all glad those two were not continuing with us. Our shouted farewells were not for them.

The other men traveling down the river had known from the Wood River camp that they would be returning to St. Louis, though some had expressed their desire to continue on with us to the Pacific. I knew how they felt. Once adventuring gets under your skin, then adventuring is all you want to do, and this was an adventure like none other. None of us had any idea what lay ahead between the Mandan villages and the Pacific Ocean, what kinds of dangers and hardships we might face, but we were all eager to get under way.

"All right, fellas, let's get on that river!" Clark shouted, and we quickly clambered aboard the pirogues and canoes and took up the oars. Our little fleet of two pirogues and six dugout canoes, as Captain Clark had said that morning, might not have been as impressive in appearance as those fleets belonging to Christopher Columbus or Captain Cook, but to us they were a thing of beauty. And with them we would conquer the continent.

Oh, yes, we were confident, but we felt we had every right to be. We'd made it that far, hadn't we?

Hundreds of Indians lined the banks on both sides of the Missouri, shouting and waving in farewell, and several dozen others surrounded our pirogues and canoes in their little round bison-skin bull boats. It was an emotional farewell on both sides, as we had come to enjoy and like these Mandan people over the long winter. They were friendly and affectionate and had gone out of their way to be hospitable and helpful to the strange white people who had appeared in their midst and demanded so much from them while delivering only promises in return.

Behind us, the little fort stood empty on its rise now, the gate standing open. The flag no longer flew above the palisade wall and the normally ever-present smoke no longer hung above the chimneys. I felt a little sad to see it like that, as if it was being abandoned after serving us so well, but Fort Mandan now belonged to the Mandan people.

Captain Lewis chose to walk along the north bank rather than begin the journey in the boats, claiming that he had not had enough exercise of late, but I heard Captain Clark tell Sergeant Ordway that Lewis wanted some time to be alone to contemplate the meaning of this day. It made perfect sense to me. A thinking man like Lewis would find a lot of significance in a day as important as this one.

Five minutes up the river, Richard Windsor grinned at me. "Just like old times, eh, John? Rowing against this damn Missouri current?"

I nodded and laughed. It was like old times. And it felt good to be moving on.

"It could be worse," Hugh McNeal chimed in. "It could be that dang keelboat."

We all agreed with that statement.

Sergeant Gass slapped his arm and looked at the bloody spot left behind. "Damn skeeters are back, too," he said, wiping the smashed mosquito on his leggings.

Windsor laughed. "Just like old times."

* * *

Our journey up the Missouri over the following weeks was fairly uneventful, though we did have our small incidents, like always. One of the dugouts sprung a leak a short distance out from the fort and we had to spend a day repairing it and drying the goods that were dampened. Lewis chafed at the delay but there was no way to speed the process of fixing a canoe or drying wet papers and equipment. All he could do was bite his lip and accept the inevitable.

George Drouillard spent a lot of his time hunting on shore, as did several others including Shields and me, but the results were not very good, as the Indians had hunted this portion of the country pretty thoroughly. The river itself was fairly easy to navigate, though we did have to contend with the standard floating debris and sawyers, not to mention the caving in of the high banks as the current washed out the dirt underneath. The weather wasn't very remarkable, mostly sunny, with some days of rain and wind. The temperature rose on an almost daily basis, and flowers could be seen covering the vast open plains on both sides of the river.

The wind blew mainly from the south and southwest, allowing us on some days to use the sails on the pirogues, though it did shift at times and blow down on us from the north or northwest. There were days when the wind caused such high waves on the river that we could not travel for fear of the canoes filling with water, or it would blow sand and dirt into our faces until we were blind.

I had my chance to walk on the shore and do some hunting, and sometimes I was joined by Captain Clark. It was on one of these walks that we had an interesting conversation.

""Stop for a minute, will you, John?" We were about two miles ahead of the pirogues and canoes, climbing up a long bluff totally devoid of trees or shrubs. The prairie around us stretched to the horizon, with only small clumps of foliage to be seen. We had killed several deer and one big elk already that day and had left the carcasses at the river for the boats to collect on their way up and we both felt pretty good about our efforts.

I stopped walking and we stood for a while, looking back at the twisting course of the river.

"I'm feeling powerful content today, John," Clark said, resting his hands on the barrel of his rifle and leaning on it.

"In what way?" I asked.

"Well, for the first time since leaving Wood River a year ago, I feel like we have the perfect crew to make the journey a success."

I nodded, knowing what he meant.

"Our malcontents are gone, our temporary crew is gone, and we're left with the best of the best. Up ahead, we have no idea what we'll face. Hostile natives, storms, even death for some of us, maybe. Anything is possible. But this group of men we have now...well, I just feel good."

I nodded again. I couldn't think of anything I could say to add to his words.

"Charbonneau is of little use to us, but that squaw of his could be worth ten times her weight once we reach them Snake Indians in the mountains. And I'll tell you something Big White said to me just before we left the fort which I think is mighty important. A crew of men traveling through the upriver country may be viewed as a war party. A crew of men traveling with a woman and a baby, especially a native woman and baby, are far less likely to be attacked out of fear."

It made sense to me, knowing what I did of the workings of the native mind, a subject I knew far more about then than I had a year earlier.

Clark had more to say. "Our sergeants are like an extension of Captain Lewis and me, and they have been doing a fine job. I wasn't real sure about Gass replacing poor Charles Floyd but he has exceeded my expectations. And I wasn't sure if you and Ordway could get through without one of you killing the other, but you have."

I grinned.

"And the men have come together with a cohesiveness and spirit that I couldn't have imagined back in the Wood River camp, when you all spent half your time trying to beat each other to death!"

He was right, for the most part. There were still small incidents, like the morning when a beaver became ensnared in two separate traps and the owners of the traps got into a shouting confrontation over who could lay claim to the animal. But generally we were working together in the manner a good team should.

"We have a long way ahead of us, John," he said. "Are you ready for the challenge?"

"More than ever, Captain," I said.

He clapped my shoulder. "Good man. Then let's get us some more meat and get back to those fine boats and fine men."

* * *

"By my calculations, we have traveled one thousand, eight hundred and eighty eight miles from the mouth of the Missouri River to reach this point," Captain Clark said, and I could hear a combination of pride and wonder in his voice.

We were camped on a rocky shore at the point where the Yellowstone River flowed into the Missouri. The juncture of the two rivers lay in a beautiful land thick with cottonwoods and animals of every variety and was surrounded by low bluffs, some still showing traces of that morning's frost. The tops of the bluffs offered excellent views of both rivers and their meandering courses for miles to the west and south.

That was an important moment for all of us, as that joining of rivers was one of the landmarks we had so long anticipated. We stood that evening as a group on the point of land between the two wide rivers, watching the waters of the Yellowstone mix with those of the Missouri, and felt our own sense of pride and accomplishment growing. Captain Lewis ordered an extra dram of whiskey to be given to the men to celebrate, and the dancing and fiddling went on long into the night. All the pains and toils of the day were forgotten in this moment of happiness and pleasure.

"Next goal is the Great Falls of the Missouri," Lewis proclaimed. The Mandans had spoken at length about the great falls we would encounter on our journey, and the captains expected we would have to spend at least a day or two portaging the canoes and gear around them. "From there, we'll dance across the Rocky Mountains and sprint down the Columbia to the ocean!"

We all cheered his words, as though the remainder of the long journey might really be that simple, or that close to an easy conclusion. I think we all knew better, in our minds, but we were caught up in the euphoria of the instant.

"We'll stay here for a day or two," Lewis said. "I want to take some celestial readings and we can procure some meat. And then we will be on our way."

As we bedded down that night beneath the millions of stars that glittered above, I think we all felt like we were really something special and elite. I thought for a while about all those people back in the east laboring away at their jobs and sleeping in stuffy airless rooms and I felt sorry for them. I took a slow deep breath of the cold clear air and let it out, savoring it. Yep, I was right where I wanted to be.

* * *

Captain Lewis held a finger to his lips and motioned me forward, pointing excitedly toward a stand of willow near the bank of the river. We had left the boats far behind on this day and had walked up the north bank to hunt, and now it appeared our hunt was to be successful.

The forks of the Yellowstone and Missouri were behind us now and the boats were continuing up the Missouri. We had entered a land of high stony bluffs and hills that lined both sides of the river, an area that was beautiful in a stark sort of way. Like all the wild land we had passed, this part of the journey offered its own challenges and rewards, and the amazing scenery was one of the rewards.

"White bear," Lewis whispered now, and I could feel my heart pump faster. We had had several encounters with the white bear, an animal much feared and respected by the natives all along the Missouri, though we had yet to shoot one. Lewis's driving desire by this point was to kill one of the bears so he could examine it and report his findings to Jefferson. Plus, I think Lewis just wanted to disprove the native myths and legends about the animal by showing once and for all that it was merely a mortal being and was no match for a white man.

We crept forward, all senses alert. A light breeze rustled the leaves around us, and I was glad to see that it was blowing away from the bear and toward us, reducing the chance that the bear might detect our scents. I moved to the captain's left to give myself room to shoot. I could hear rustlings and cracklings in the dense shrubbery ahead, and my nose caught the unmistakable scent of the bear. As long as the wind continued to blow toward us, we should be able to get close enough to shoot.

Lewis knelt down and slowly raised his rifle. Ahead of him I could see a brief glimpse of tan fur through the new green leaves, and then the captain was pulling the trigger.

His shot was answered by an enraged roar and the crashing of branches. We ran forward, just in time to see not one but two white bears break from cover and run. One headed straight out across the prairie, running away from us, and I fired at that one, catching it a glancing blow that didn't even slow it down. It just kept running away. Meanwhile the other, catching sight of us, let loose with another earth-rattling roar and charged straight toward us. This bear was the one Captain Lewis had shot and it ran in a strange lopsided lope, obviously injured. Just as obviously it fully intended to injure us if it could. I was able to reload quickly and fired at the bear while Captain Lewis beat a hasty retreat, reloading his own rifle on the run, and my shot hit it in the hindquarters. The bear roared again, whirling toward me, and by this time Captain Lewis had reloaded and was able to fire once more. The bear he had hit twice and I had hit once finally stumbled and fell. I glanced around to make sure this one's buddy hadn't decided to circle around seeking revenge but he was still running away from us, and as I watched he vanished over a rise with an amazing turn of speed for so large an animal.

"Hallelujah!" Lewis shouted. "I finally got one!" He was practically dancing with excitement and I couldn't help but smile at his enthusiasm.

"Good shot, Captain!" I said.

"Thank you, John. And thank you for your good shot. If you hadn't hit him when you did, he might be dining on me right now! Now, if you'd be so kind, head down to the river and bring up some men to assist us. I want to get this big fella down to the river and get some measurements."

"Yes, sir."

The boats were just coming around a bend as I reached the shore, and I fired a shot to flag them. The red pirogue was rowed over to me and I told them what had happened.

"Yahoo!" John Potts shouted across the water to the other boats. "Captain Lewis done shot him a white bear!"

* * *

The boats put ashore and Captain Clark ordered off ten men to accompany me up to where Lewis waited. Captain Lewis was walking around the dead bear, examining it from all sides, and was rubbing his hands together in excitement and pleasure.

"He's a beauty," Clark said, shaking Lewis's hand. "Congratulations, my friend."

The bear, on close examination, was a young male, probably not fully grown, yet still a formidable animal, one that could easily have killed both of us. The captains estimated the bear to weigh about 300 pounds, but I thought it looked a lot larger than that. Of course, I had seen it coming at me with fangs bared, and at that moment it had looked about twenty feet tall and two thousand pounds! My opinion was a little bit biased by that.

"I can better understand the savage's reluctance to confront this animal," Lewis said, looking down at the dead bear with an expression on his face that was almost fond. "With their crude weapons, it would be a terrifying animal to go against."

"I guess that's why there is so much glory for them when they kill one," Clark said.

Lewis nodded in agreement.

Clark finished measuring all the parts of the bear that he could reach and jotted down his final notes, then sat back on his heels. "What an amazing animal," he said in undisguised admiration. "I can not wait to see a full-grown adult in close proximity like this."

"I agree," Lewis said. "And I hope I am the one to get him."

"Not if I beat you to it," Clark said.

Remembering the way this "small" specimen of bear had attacked us after taking two bullets made me hope that I wasn't there when either captain faced a larger one!

"Men, let's get this big boy skinned and get the meat and fur down to the boat. Tonight we dine on white bear!"

CHAPTER NINETEEN

Several days later Clark got his wish. Hunting on shore with Drouillard, they came across a very large white bear and both men opened fire. The bear, estimated at 600 pounds by Captain Lewis, took the first two shots as if he hadn't even been hit and fled, racing out into the river with the hunters in pursuit. The bear's roaring was fearsome to behold, as were the number of bullets Clark and Drouillard and several others in the red pirogue had to fire into him before he finally died. The bear would have stood almost nine feet tall on his hind legs, and the claws on his front paws were over four inches in length!

Up to that point, my only confrontation with those bears had been when I was with Captain Lewis and he shot his first one. I had no desire to come upon one of those monsters on my own. Having seen how fast they could run, I didn't know if I'd be able to reload before the bear could be upon me, should it choose to attack after the first shot.

Other men had said the same thing, while some fools seemed eager to test themselves against the huge bears. I wondered how eager they would be if they found themselves staring at those great teeth heading toward them at a dead run.

Other than the bears, the hunting had become far easier as we moved upriver. The land along both sides of the river was choked with game. Buffalo, deer, elk, antelope, beaver, goose, duck, even mountain lion; a hunter could almost point his rifle in a random direction and pull the trigger, and he would shoot something with which we could fill our stomachs. I know I've spoken a lot about the hunting on this journey, but that was one of my main tasks, and I was focused on it. I was still being utilized as one of the principal hunters, and I ranged far and wide from the boats, mostly out of my own desire to see the land and not through any need to travel far to obtain meat. And in the evenings the captains would drill me for information about the countryside through which I had passed, wanting every detail I could relate to them. I learned quickly to keep my eyes and senses open so I could adequately answer their questions and satisfy their endless curiosity.

During my wanderings I crossed numerous small streams that emptied into the Missouri, and passed many ponds formed by the industrious work of the area's beaver population. There seemed to be just enough vegetation for the animals to build their dams and lodges. And they were everywhere, a trappers dream come true.

The days flowed past as we made our way through this paradise. On some days rain fell, and on others we would be forced to camp early or depart late due to winds so strong the canoes would become swamped. We met up with and killed more of the white bears, and on every occasion we were amazed at the strength and stamina of those giant beasts. On one occasion a massive bear had been shot eight times and still chased Richard Windsor right off a bluff and into the river. Those bears were a wonder to us.

Occasional mishaps occurred, such as canoes catching waves and filling with water or narrow escapes when a bank would cave in just as a canoe or pirogue passed underneath. Injuries and illnesses were few and far between, beyond sore muscles and strains, and the general health and morale of the men remained high. As we moved into the country where the ground was dominated by a low spiny plant Lewis called prickly pear, pulling the boat upstream with the tow cords became a challenge, but one which we endured, as we had no other choice.

In other words, we had reached a point where we were all in prime physical condition and prime mental condition. We were fully dedicated to the task ahead of us, and our goal was the same as the goal of our esteemed captains, to cross the mountains and reach the ocean. None of us could imagine any obstacle that we couldn't overcome.

* * *

A cold wind blew down the river as I stood on the edge of the bluff above the camp, watching the boats resting below. I was taking my turn at guard duty. It was well past the middle part of the night and the camp was as quiet as a camp full of sleeping, snoring men can become. On the far side of the camp, William Bratton was sharing my guard duty, and I knew he would be as awake and alert as I was. We were coming into country known to belong to the Blackfeet Indians, a nation not rumored to be very friendly toward white men. We had passed some Indian camps further down the river that appeared to have been constructed with fortifications, a necessity only if those natives had expected to be attacked and were fully prepared to defend themselves.

The night wasn't quiet, as nights never are quiet on the prairie, but the sounds I could hear were all sounds that I expected to hear. Crickets, wolves, the light splashing of waves against the rocky shore, the droning of wind through the trees. The camp was located on the shore just above the boats, and a fire was kept burning through the night. All was peaceful.

I turned away from the camp and walked north, keeping my eyes moving as I looked out across the dark prairie. The land was difficult to distinguish from the sky, both being as dark as dark can become, it seemed, and I had to depend on my hearing even more than my eyesight to remain alert for danger.

The night was a good time for contemplation. I thought about how far we had come since leaving Wood River, not only in miles but as a team. I thought about the development of the men. George Shannon, who had almost starved the summer before because he was such a lousy hunter, and who had spent the winter perfecting his skills and was now almost as at home behind the rifle as I was. John Collins, who had been in trouble at Wood River even more than me and who had been labeled by Lewis as a blackguard, who now received praise from both captains for his attitude and dependability. Drouillard, our half-breed, now as much a member of the team as any man and much revered for his skills as hunter and interpreter. Half-breeds were viewed with contempt by the white people in the east, but out here he was just George, a superb hunter and man.

Even the Frenchman's squaw, the one they called the Bird Woman, was becoming like a member of the Corps. Her cool-headedness in a crisis was one example of her attributes, such as when the white pirogue had almost overturned and she had single-handedly saved some of our most prized possessions, including the captains journals. Her ability to find and prepare roots and plants that added to our meals in a positive way was another of her attributes.

I smiled to myself in the close darkness. Yep, we were quite a team.

"Hey! In the camp! Fire!" Bratton's voice rang out across the silent prairie, shocking in its suddenness and unexpectedness, and I whirled around, my heart leaping in my chest. Running as fast as I could to the edge of the bluff, I looked down at an amazing scene.

A large leaning tree had ignited, apparently from sparks tossed up from the fire. It blazed in the darkness like an inferno, its roaring and crackling already surprisingly loud. Then I saw something that turned my blood to ice.

Directly under the leaning tree was the captain's tent.

I could see Bratton racing across the camp as men leaped from their blankets, shouting questions and confused commands. I quickly slid down the steep embankment and ran into the camp, grabbing Tom Howard by the arm.

"Buckets!" I shouted. "Get some men and grab buckets!"

Howard nodded and raced off toward the river, yelling for assistance as he ran.

Bratton had reached the captains tent and ran inside, shouting out the warning. Very quickly, the captains and their tent-mates, Drouillard, Charbonneau and the Bird Woman, ran outside, Lewis's dog right at his master's heels. Drouillard and Clark, thinking fast, dragged the tent away from the danger. Just seconds after they had the tent moved, the tree fell with a rending crash, throwing sparks and burning branches in all directions.

It took us a good portion of the night to extinguish the fire, which had spread to several areas around the camp, catching shrubs and grass on fire and threatening to spread even further. Countless buckets of water were handed up from the river and tossed on the flames until the last flickering spark was extinguished.

I stood with Clark later as we examined the place where the tree had fallen. For one of the very first times since I had known him, the captain appeared unsettled.

"We would have died, John," he said. "If that tree would have come down on us, we would all be dead right now."

"Yeah, you're right. But it didn't. Be thankful for that."

He didn't seem to hear, and when I walked away he was still standing there, shaking his head.

In the morning, the captains gathered the men around and publicly praised Bratton for spotting the fire and warning them in time to escape. It was the first time I actually saw William Bratton look embarrassed.

* * *

Unfortunately, that wouldn't be the captain's last close call with danger. Just a couple of weeks after the fire, a large bull buffalo swam across the river late one night, coming ashore directly at the camp. He started up onto the shore, then, apparently startled by the scent of humans or maybe by the glow of our fires, he took off at a run straight through the center of the camp. His massive hooves pounded the ground, coming down just inches from the heads of men still deep in exhausted sleep. The sentry that night, Reubin Field, was unable to fire at the bull for fear of injuring some of the men. Instead, he shouted at the buffalo, and the massive animal veered off, charging back across the camp in the direction he had come. By now the rest of the men were coming awake, leaping up from their blankets and shouting in alarm, and the bull veered again, charging across the camp straight toward the captain's tent.

This time, it was Lewis's dog, newly recovered from a vicious bite he had sustained from an injured beaver, who saved the day. As the buffalo neared the tent, going full speed and apparently planning on running straight through it, the dog charged out, barking and snarling viciously. The bull skidded to a stop and wheeled away from the dog. He ran one final time across the camp, again narrowly avoiding several men, before vanishing into the darkness of the prairie.

Miraculously, nobody was injured, and the only damage was to a gun belonging to Clark's slave, York. Once again, we had been very lucky.

* * *

On June 3rd, we came upon a wide and shallow river intersecting with the Missouri from the north. All along our course we had been passing numerous rivers that fell into the Missouri from both sides, yet this was the first major river we had encountered since the Yellowstone and it posed a problem.

The Indians back at the Mandan villages had spent hours with our captains discussing the route into the Rocky Mountains in minute detail. Whether through drawings on the skin of an elk or by drawings made in the dirt with a stick, using rocks or piles of dirt to indicate mountains, those Mandan's had been very clear on what the Missouri would look like all the way to the Great Falls. And, according to both Lewis and Clark, not one had ever mentioned a major river coming in from the north.

Captain Lewis stood on the shore, hat in his hand, peering first north up the new river, then southwest at what we believed to be the Missouri. He was scratching his head.

"Any thoughts?" Clark asked.

"I have no idea," Lewis replied, confusion in his voice. "Big White never mentioned anything about another river right here."

Clark stared up the north river. "I don't understand," he said. "They had to have known it's here. It's too big of a river to miss."

Lewis stood in silence for a few moments. Then he turned to face us. "All right, men, let's make camp right here, and make it a good one. We're going to be here for a while until we figure this out."

We made camp while the captains talked. After a while they called the sergeants over and included them in the conversation. We could see them walking back and forth, staring at the two rivers, even climbing to the top of a nearby bluff to peer as far as they could along both of the rivers.

"What do you think, John?" Willard asked me.

I finished unloading the last box from the white pirogue and shook my head. "I have no idea, Alex," I said. "It's a mystery."

"Not really," George Gibson said. "Look at the water."

We all looked at the two rivers. "What about it?" Willard asked.

"The water coming down that branch to the north is thick and muddy," Gibson said. "The water coming from the west is clear."

"So?" I said.

"So what has the water been like all the way up from St. Louis?" he asked.

I suddenly realized what he was saying. "Muddy," I said.

"Yes! So the north fork has to be the Missouri."

Willard was shaking his head. "I'm not so sure," he said.

"How can you not be sure?" Gibson said. "The water from the north is muddy. The Missouri is muddy. Mud equals Missouri. Case closed."

"If it were that simple," Willard reasoned, "would Clark and Lewis be standing there scratching their heads?"

Willard had a point but I tended to agree with Gibson.

Later, after the camp was put together and we had several fires blazing, the captains returned from their expeditions. Both looked perplexed. Lewis called everyone together and we stood before him.

"All right, lads, here's the problem. We are two months into our travel season. We still have to cross the Rocky Mountains and travel down the Columbia to the ocean before winter. If we make the wrong choice between these two rivers and it takes us a month or two to learn of our mistake, we're ruined. Now, the Mandan never mentioned another river, so we are in a position where we have to determine for ourselves which route to follow. I have talked over our options with Captain Clark and with your sergeants and the consensus seems to be that the north branch is the Missouri. With a show of hands, how many of you men feel the same?"

Almost every hand went up, except for mine, Willard's, and a couple others.

"That's what I expected to see," Lewis said. "So, here is what we will do. We'll make camp here, get our hunters out tomorrow to bring in some food, and then I will be sending small parties up each branch in an effort to determine which is the Missouri. Somewhere up one of those is the Great Falls. We need to find those falls."

I nodded in approval. Captain Lewis made good sense.

"When those men return this evening, we will hear what they say. If they can not make a determination, Captain Clark and I will set out tomorrow to learn what we can. So let's get some dinner and some sleep," Lewis concluded. "Tomorrow we'll get started."

* * *

"I'm convinced the fork we want is the western, not the northern," Captain Lewis said later that evening. The men he had sent out to scout the two rivers had returned with no conclusive evidence for either branch. We were in a quandary.

Clark took a swallow of his whiskey and nodded slowly. "I tend to agree, don't ask me why."

"What about the muddiness of the water coming from the north branch?" Sergeant Gass asked. "That darn Missouri has been muddy all the way up. Wouldn't the muddy river be the one we want?"

"Here are my thoughts," Lewis said, and we all turned toward him, eager to hear what he had to say. "The north fork, as far as we can tell, meanders out across the plains. The small streams that empty into it come from those plains and carry their dirt into it. The west fork comes more from the direction of the mountains, and seems to be spring water or snow run-off, hence the fact that it's the clearer of the two. The Mandan were quite adamant in their assertion that the headwaters of the Missouri are in the mountains."

"Inconclusive," Clark said. "We don't know that the north fork doesn't turn back toward the mountains. It could still be the one we want."

"I thought you believed the western fork to be the correct one," Lewis said with a smile.

"Just playing the role of devil's advocate, my dear Meriwether. We must look at both sides of the argument, or both forks of the river, as it were."

"You're right," Lewis nodded. "Which is why we will set out in the morning to find out."

Clark nodded in agreement, and the matter was settled.

I sat for a while thinking about both arguments. I was torn. I could understand Lewis's logic, but I also understood what Clark was saying.

Drouillard sat down beside me. "What do you think, John?" he asked.

"I don't know what to think, George," I said.

He nodded, a smug grin on his face. "I understand. But I already know which branch is the right one."

"You do? How?"

"Indian intuition," he said gravely, tapping his forehead solemnly.

"Bullshit."

He laughed, and then nodded toward the captain's fire, where Lewis and Clark were sitting with Charbonneau and Sacagawea. The squaw was nursing her baby boy and humming softly to him, a tune I had heard her hum in the past that seemed to soothe little Jean-Baptiste.

"I asked her."

"Her? Why her?"

George chuckled. "You all forget her story. Why is she along with us, John?"

"So she can help us negotiate with the Shoshone for horses to cross the mountains."

"Exactly true. And how can she help us obtain horses from the Shoshone?"

I saw what he was getting at and it was suddenly obvious. "Because she's Shoshone."

"You're fairly smart for a white man," Drouillard grinned. "She was kidnapped from the Shoshone by the Hidatsa and sold to Charbonneau. This is her country we are going into. If anyone here would know this country, it would be her. So I asked her."

I waited, but he didn't say anything more. "And?"

"And the correct fork is the one to the west," he said smugly. "That's the Missouri."

I thought about what he said. "Have you told Lewis?"

George snorted. "Lewis is a white man from the Virginia aristocracy. The Bird Woman is a squaw. To Lewis, a squaw is barely smarter than that dog of his. He is not going to listen to her."

I admired Captain Lewis, but I knew George was correct.

"So what do we do?" I asked.

"We rest for a while, make some new clothes, make some stronger moccasins to help with those damn prickly pear, and wait for her to be proven correct. What else can we do?"

CHAPTER TWENTY

I spent the majority of that next week hunting, and the bottomlands at the juncture of these two rivers proved to be as thick with game as the rest of the lands along the Missouri. Elk were plentiful, as were buffalo, deer, geese and ducks, and there were a large number of bighorn sheep that lived in the rocky hills to the west. None in our party wanted for food.

Several days after setting out on their reconnaissance missions, the captains returned. Both were more convinced than ever that the western fork was the correct route to follow, but Lewis wanted to be positive before making his final decision. I could tell that the thought of wasting several weeks travel on a wrong decision was weighing heavily on him.

Again, the captains called all the men together. A large fire burned cheerily on the bank of the river as we gathered around to hear his words.

"Men, we face a dilemma. Having traveled near sixty miles up the north fork, I am more than ever convinced that the west fork is the one to take. Captain Clark is leaning toward my way of thinking, but I know that the majority of you believe the north fork to be the true Missouri and the course we need to follow into the mountains. So I want to make a proposal to you. I say we cache the red pirogue and an amount of our gear at this fork to make our travel easier. Then we will commence to travel up the western fork. I will travel ahead with a small group in order to seek the Great Falls and learn for certain that the west fork is the correct route.

"Lads, you've followed Captain Clark and me over two thousand miles up this Missouri River, and you've had faith in us and trusted us every step of the way. May I intrude on that trust once again and ask you to trust us enough to embark up that west fork?"

Captain Lewis's question was met with a resounding cheer from the men, and I could see that he was touched and pleased by the response.

"Then in the morning we will cache the gear and set out to conquer those Rocky Mountains!" he said, and another cheer ripped the night.

Later, as the fiddle squeaked and the men laughed and danced, Drouillard nudged me with an elbow. "What do you think now, John?" he asked.

I had to laugh. "I think if'n we'd just listened to that squaw, we'd be at those Great Falls by now."

"You're gettin' smarter, Colter. Trust us red folk. We know what we're talking about."

* * *

In the morning, a group of us set to work digging a hole to cache the spare gear in, locating it up on a rise far enough from the river so that winter floods wouldn't damage the contents. Other men were engaged in hunting or finishing sewing the last of the clothing and moccasins for the journey ahead, and John Shields was repairing several of our more necessary metal items that we were planning to take with us. Shields had served us well as a blacksmith at Fort Mandan, repairing and making new items for the Mandan people in exchange for the corn they brought us, and he proved himself just as useful now.

The red pirogue was hidden away, secured to some trees, while the other boats were pulled from the water and any needed repairs were made. Captain Lewis chose four men to accompany him ahead of the main party up the western fork, and I admit to being a mite disappointed not to be one of those chosen. Captain Clark would lead the remainder of the crew up the next day. After Lewis's party disappeared up the river, we finished burying the items in the cache, then spent the rest of the afternoon preparing ourselves to depart in the morning.

"Are you well, John?" Clark asked me that evening.

"I'm feeling right as can be, Captain," I said.

"Good. I'm checking with all the men to make sure. You know Charbonneau's wife is ill."

I nodded. She had fallen sick several days earlier, though I had no idea what her illness might be.

"I'm awful worried about her," he said, shaking his head, and then moved on to talk to Hugh Hall.

We set out early the next morning and headed up the west fork. The going was relatively easy and without event. It was a repeat of the routine we were all used to, of rowing and pulling the canoes against the current. We were entering a valley with tall cliffs and mountains on each side, including some cliffs of a white rock that were so straight and true that they almost gave the appearance of being carved. The squaw remained ill and did not appear to be getting better, and we all despaired for her future, and that of her son.

Two days travel followed, slow days fighting against the current, when we were met by Joseph Field coming down the river. Captain Clark immediately called a halt until he could reach us.

"Well?" Clark asked anxiously.

Field grinned widely. "It's the falls, all right. This here's the Missouri!"

A loud cheer went up, a cheer of relief, and then we settled back in to our work. We were very glad to hear that we were going the right way, though there was also a certain level of surprise. We had been so sure that the other branch was the Missouri. I looked at Sacagawea reclining in one of the canoes and thought about what Drouillard might have to say, and I had to grin.

"What about a portage around the falls?" Clark asked. "Is it gonna be a problem?"

"Captain Lewis went up above the falls, and he said there are several falls and it's near twelve miles from the bottom to the top," Field said, and we all looked at each other. A portage of twelve miles with all this gear and boats? It wasn't a pleasant prospect.

Clark didn't think so, either, I could tell. But Captain Clark wasn't the type of man to let his concerns or doubts infect the morale of his men. "Well, boys, you've all been saying how much you want a break from rowing," he called out cheerfully. "Looks like you're going to get your chance."

General laughter sounded among the canoes, accompanied by several groans and catcalls.

We halted later that day at the first of what would prove to be a number of waterfalls, and Clark made camp. We were all completely exhausted from our journey up the Missouri from the forks to this point, and we were glad to stop. The river was far too fast and churning to attempt to row any further anyway. The last miles of our journey had been made pulling the boats through the shallow rapids with tow ropes, and the banks in this area were covered in slippery rocks and prickly pear. Every man had bruises and shallow cuts from falling on the rocks, and our feet were a misery from the combination of sharp stones and prickly pear thorns. Rattlesnakes were everywhere among the jumbled rocks and we had to be always on the alert for their hollow rattle noise. We had had several close calls already and none of us wanted to be the first one to be bitten. It had been a trying several days!

The next morning, we were rejoined by Captain Lewis and the four men he had taken with him, and the captains immediately went into discussion about the best way to portage around the falls. Clark dispatched John Potts and me to explore the south side of the river to deem if a portage was practical on that side and we set out immediately.

The land on the south side of the river was mostly flat plain, though several deep ravines cut across the land, draining water into the Missouri. The muted roar of the falls remained constant to our right as we walked. I could see by John's eyes that he did not relish the idea of moving all of our gear across this land, infested with rocks, ravines and prickly pear, but we also knew the choice wasn't ours. Having come this far and endured so much, there was no way the captains would turn back now, and I don't think the men would allow the idea, either. We were of a single mind by this time, and we had no other thought than to reach the Pacific.

Back in the camp that night, we made our report to the captains.

"The land is mostly flat and level," I said, "but those ravines are going to be a problem. We'll have to swing wide across the plain toward the east to pass by them."

John Potts shook his head. "I don't know how the Mandan's ever imagined a portage of a half-day, like they told you," he said. "That's near to fifteen miles to get above those falls, Captain."

Lewis nodded soberly. "I know, John. All I can surmise is that they travel far lighter than we are and were able to lift their canoes onto their shoulders, walk up, and continue their journey. That obviously won't work for us."

"I have assigned six men the job of cutting down some trees and making wheels to place under the canoes," Clark said briskly, obviously not wanting the dismal report we were making to affect the men, or us. "We'll use them to roll the canoes, filled with our gear, right across that old prairie."

"We're going to cache some more gear right here," Lewis said, "including the white pirogue. When we get above these falls, we'll put together my iron boat and continue to the mountains."

I was curious about Lewis's iron boat. He had mentioned it on other occasions, and it seemed to consist of numerous iron bars that would be fitted together and covered with skins. We had lately been collecting as many elk skins as we could to sew together to make one large skin to go over it. If it worked, that would be a wonder to see.

We would just have to wait and see.

CHAPTER TWENTY-ONE

"Colter, Willard, Shields, McNeal, Joe Field, you're with me!"

Captain Clark gathered us around him early the next morning. The sun was shining down from a clear blue sky, and a cool breeze rustled the leaves in the cottonwoods that lined the banks. Lewis was preparing to set out with another group of men in order to find more trees for the construction of the wheels and wagons we would be using to transport our gear to a point above those massive falls where we could again take to the water.

"We need to scout out the route we are going to take," Clark told us. "I am estimating one week to get all of our gear above those falls. This portage is not going to be easy, lads."

We nodded, especially Joe Field and me, who had both walked that prairie.

Clark led us away from the camp and up a shallow climb to the top of the prairie. To our right we could see the mist that always hung above the falls, and beyond that the snow-covered mountain peaks that we would have to somehow cross to reach the ocean. Captain Lewis had painted a picture in our minds of one single wall of mountains, easily crossed, then an easy drop down the other side to the Pacific. I hoped he was right.

"I can see how the men worry about this portage," Clark said as we reached the high plateau. "They're allowing their worries to obsess them. So I need your help."

We listened expectantly.

"I'm not asking you men to lie in any way. But if you could see fit to leave out some of the worst aspects of this prairie, it may help to bring the other men's thoughts up a ways. This portage is going to be hard, and if we can keep the men's hopes and morale up, it will be far easier on them."

We all nodded in agreement, and for the first time I really understood the strain these two captains worked under. It was an eye-opening realization.

"Thank you, men," Clark said. "Let's get on our way."

As we walked I thought about the responsibility of their positions. Not only did they have to fulfill Jefferson's demands for knowledge, they also had to keep the spirits and health of the crew foremost in their thoughts. They would never be able to express their own fears and doubts because that would transfer to the men, who looked to the captains for inspiration and leadership. If Lewis or Clark started to grumble and complain the way we regularly did, our faith in them could be lost and then the expedition would be ruined. I thought about all that and my esteem for the captains increased a thousandfold.

* * *

Loud crashing suddenly came from behind me, followed by a guttural roar, and I whirled around. Two days had passed since we had scouted out the portage route, and I was at the southern end of a long willow island, dressing out an elk that I had killed. Next to where I stood, to the east, the Missouri raced past to crash over another set of falls just below, while on the west side of the island the water was as calm as a pond.

Captain Clark and several of the other men were at the opposite end of the island, also hunting, and I had heard several shots earlier and knew they had found meat. But now something was racing toward me at a high rate of speed and I hadn't reloaded my rifle after shooting the elk. This could be trouble!

As I whirled around I caught a glimpse of tan fur, then a massive white bear broke into the open, coming straight at me. I had heard one of the Mandan warriors call this bear a "grizzly," apparently due to its fur texture appearing grizzled or choppy, and the name seemed to fit its demeanor as well. The bear caught sight of me, roared loud enough to shake the trees, and charged.

Having no other choice and not pausing to think, I ran for the calm water on the western side of the island, knowing that to jump into the fast-moving portion of the river to the east would send me over the falls and spell my certain death. I could hear the shouted voices of Clark and the other men coming nearer and I could only hope they would reach the bear before the bear reached me.

With another ear-splitting roar, the bear raced after me. I splashed into the river, sending up a spray that glistened in the sunlight, wishing for the ability to walk on water, and the bear followed right behind, gaining ground with every stride. I began swimming as rapidly as I could, but I knew it was futile. I had seen these bears swimming in the lower portions of the Missouri and they were almost as fast in the water as they were on land. He was going to catch me, and then that would be the end of John Colter.

A shot rang out, then another. The bear skidded to a stop at the edge of the water and whirled to face the others, then broke and ran north into the protection of the trees that covered the island. Willard sent one shot after him and we could all hear the bear's crashing progress fade away as he ran.

I came out of the water, feeling as if I had just been granted another life. "Awful good to see you, Captain," I said shakily.

Clark grinned. "Wasn't sure we were going to get here in time, John," he said.

"But you did," I said. "And I'm right grateful." I picked up my gun and reloaded it. Never again would I fail to reload as soon as possible after firing a shot. I had learned my lesson.

Clark stood with his hands on his hips and looked around. "I guess we'll call this 'White Bear Island,'" he said.

Field grinned and nodded. "Great name, Captain. It sounds better than 'Colter's Last Stand Island,'" he joked.

"Or 'Colter Eaten by Bear Island,'" I said.

Clark clapped me on the shoulder. "It does at that, John. And speaking of eaten, let's get this elk of yours back to camp and get something to eat."

* * *

We returned to the lower camp to find that Captain Lewis had everything in order and ready to begin the portage. The white pirogue had been stowed, the unneeded gear had been cached in a hole dug in the ground, and the wheeled contraptions he called wagons had been constructed to aid in the portage. The men who had stayed at the lower camp had been busy hunting and drying meat and had laid in a good supply to keep us going during the portage, as the men would be too busy transporting the gear around the falls to do much hunting.

We began the portage the following day, and it was just as difficult and exhausting as we had expected it to be. The captains had determined that the crews starting out for the upper camp, which had been established on White Bear Island, should leave early in the morning in order to make the camp before nightfall. The high prairie did not have any cover or readily accessible sources of water, and they didn't want the men to have to make camp in that inhospitable plain.

The captain's estimate of a one week portage turned out to be quite optimistic and it ended up taking us a month to transport all of our gear to that point above the falls where we could continue on our journey. Each day, we would take the canoes, loaded with our gear and belongings, three miles up a small stream we named Portage Creek to be loaded onto the wheeled carts. Then the tedious and back-breaking labor would begin.

The gear would be loaded onto Captain Lewis's carts and hauled up onto the high prairie by use of the same tow ropes we had used to haul the keelboat and pirogues up the long Missouri. From the top of the bluff all the vast and open country could be seen and it was a sight to behold, if you weren't pulling hundreds of pounds of gear on imperfect wheels, that is. The high mountains to the west glistened in the sunlight, the buffalo were numerous, and the clouds sailed by on a vast endless sky. It was a beautiful land.

Underfoot, the prickly pear was our greatest enemy, piercing up through moccasins and stinging like all the devil. Along with the pear were the sharp rocks and the fractured, uneven earth, ground up by the hooves of the buffalo that wander these plains by the millions. With the tow ropes over our shoulders we resembled oxen, bent forward under the load and pulling with all our might to move those unwieldy carts across the land. Sweat would pour from us, stinging our eyes and making our grip slip on the ropes, and not one of us escaped the painful indignity of falling on our faces when rocks would unexpectedly slide out from under our feet. Our heated curses filled the quiet air!

On the open plateau, we were fully exposed to the weather as well, be it pounding sunlight baking our backs and heads or drenching rain soaking us to the skin or heavy hail that would sting our exposed skin and force us to take cover beneath the carts. The wind was a constant on that high open land, and when it blew into our faces, forcing us to pull into it and blowing dust and fine sand into our eyes, it made the journey even more difficult.

The axles of the carts were made from the mast of the white pirogue and were not very strong. Likewise, the wheels and frames had been cut from cottonwood trees, the only trees readily available on this windswept and barren land, and were therefore weak and prone to breaking apart. Numerous times we were forced to stop and affect repairs, using up valuable time.

By the time we reached the upper camp with the first loads, all of us were deeply and intensely aware just how difficult this undertaking was going to be. It had taken us all day to bring just a small amount of gear to the camp on White Bear Island, and we still had to return to the lower camp the next day to get another load. The captains were wise in establishing a rotation of work, alternating hunters with the crews assigned to pull the heavy carts across the portage, thereby giving everyone a chance to get away from the hard physical work on a regular basis, but it was still an exhausting time for us. All of us were limping from the soreness in our feet, and when we were pulling the wagons we would invariably drop to the ground in sheer exhaustion when a break was called, sometimes falling into an instant sleep where we fell. I don't think I can recall another time when I was that tired and sore! Rowing up the Missouri was a breeze compared to that portage!

On several days, the wind was at our backs, and we rigged up a sail to help propel the carts across the land. Captain Lewis seemed especially delighted at our ingenuity and applauded us. Both captains continuously expressed their appreciation for the work that we were doing, and I could see that they were very sincere.

* * *

"Big storm coming, men!" I called out.

Everyone looked toward the west, where black heavy clouds were rolling toward us. The wind was quickly picking up, carrying even more dust and sand into our faces, and thunder rumbled in the threatening clouds. The air between the clouds and the ground had seemingly vanished in what looked like a solid wall of rain.

"This is gonna be a whopper!" Pete Weiser yelled out.

He had no sooner spoken than we were hit with hail, unlike any hail I had ever experienced. The hail stones were huge and were driven down toward the earth with a force that was impossible to believe. I saw John Potts crumple to the ground after being hit on the head, and then all the men were scrambling for cover, yelling out in pain and consternation as the unbelievable storm of hail continued to assault us.

Heavy rain started falling along with the hail, rain that seemed to flood down as if released from giant buckets. I fought my way against the rain and frightful hail to where Potts lay and grabbed him under his arms, pulling him to cover beneath one of the carts. He was moaning, barely conscious, and blood ran from a nasty lump on his head.

The storm roared and raged for close to an hour and none of us moved, afraid to leave the scant cover provided by the carts. The hail fell until the ground was white with it, as if it had snowed. By the time the black clouds had finally boiled off toward the east, we were thoroughly cowed. Nature had won that battle.

Leaving the carts and gear where they were, we headed back for the lower camp, or maybe "retreated" is a better way to describe it. Potts was hurt the worst but we were all bruised and bleeding and in need of aid, and with the track turned into a sea of mud, there was no way we were going to move those carts another inch, anyway. Our only option was to get off that plain and get some care for our wounds.

Back in camp, we learned that Captain Clark had had a close call of his own. Exploring a canyon with Charbonneau, Sacagawea and their baby, they had taken shelter under an overhang of rock when the storm hit. A flash flood had raced down through the canyon, and only by climbing desperately up a stone wall were they able to escape with their lives.

That night, we gathered around the fire and shared out extra drams of whiskey and toasted our narrow escapes. I listened to the voices of our little party, many of them raised to an extra-loud level with their relief. I thought about fate, and how many close calls we had had so far on this journey, and I had the distinct feeling we would have more before we were done.

Up above, the clouds had cleared and stars shone down on us. It was a beautiful night.

CHAPTER TWENTY-TWO

After what seemed like a painful eternity, we finished portaging our gear past those amazing waterfalls. It had been a month of endless toil and back-breaking labor and we were all more than ready to get on with our journey. We were fully aware that the month we had lost on the portage could make the difference between returning to Fort Mandan that year or wintering at the ocean and we were almost desperate to be on our way.

"We have to assume our plans at this point will change," Captain Lewis said to us. "We fully expected to be across the mountains and on the Columbia by this time." He looked about as disappointed as I had ever seen him and I felt badly for him. Earlier that week he had been forced to abandon his prized iron boat after repeated attempts to cover it with elk and buffalo skins had met with failure. No matter what we did, the boat leaked and sank, and Lewis was depressed and angry.

Captain Clark and several men had made a canoe camp further along the Missouri from the portage camp and had carved out two more canoes from cottonwood trees to take the place of the iron boat, and now all the gear was loaded. We were ready to depart.

"We have to plan to spend the winter somewhere near the mouth of the Columbia," Lewis went on. "Hopefully a ship will stop to trade with the natives in that area and we can secure passage back to the eastern coast. If we do not see a ship or can not secure passage, we will have to return across the continent in the spring. Unless our circumstances undergo a miraculous change, I don't see that we will have any other option."

We all understood what he was saying. We had discussed the same thing among ourselves and as far as I could tell all of the men were fine with the idea.

It was a cool morning, the sky clear, though it had rained hard all through the previous night. A strong wind was blowing at us from the southwest as we stood on the bank a few miles up the river from our previous camp at the White Bear Island. The eight canoes were riding in the water, and they seemed as eager to get under way as we were.

"So, without waiting any longer, let us be on our way."

We launched the canoes out into the river with a feeling of joy. This was what we had been waiting for, to get back on the river. Despite our dislike of rowing against the Missouri's current, it still beat pulling those darn carts across the prairie like donkeys or oxen! It was the middle of July, the last of our whiskey had been consumed on the fourth in celebration of Independence Day, we were all sore in many places on our bodies, and the most difficult part of the journey lay ahead, but somehow just getting back on the water made our spirits seem higher than ever.

The country we were passing through was far different from the wide lush plains of the lower Missouri. Here the land was rocky and abrupt, covered with scraggly hills and small mountains and nearly devoid of grasses and timber. It was a dry land, almost desert-like in its scarcity of vegetation. Where the river had cut through the hills, it had left behind steep cliffs and jutting rocks that seemed to rise straight up out of the water. It was a beautiful land in a severe way, and I imagined that the winters here would be terrible to behold.

Captain Lewis had been very clear as to the next step in our mission. We needed to locate a band of the Snake Indians and trade for horses to assist in making the short portage across the Rocky Mountains to the headwaters of the Columbia. Lewis seemed to think the portage would take a day or two, but that was what we had been told about the portage around the great falls and the men were beginning to lose faith in the native's ability to calculate time.

Our course through the rocky valleys passed uneventfully.

Charbonneau's woman at one point said she recognized those mountains as the home of her people, which was good to hear, as it meant we might be near the Three Forks and the opportunity to secure horses.

"The Snake's know we're here," Lewis said one day, staring up at the rocky hills as though his gaze could convince the Indians to come out.

"They've undoubtedly heard our hunter's guns and probably think we're Blackfeet coming up to make war on them," Clark surmised. "Don't worry, my friend. We'll find them."

Lewis nodded, though he looked unsure.

* * *

I had never seen so many beaver in one place in my entire life.

We had at last reached the Three Forks, and we were amazed at what we saw. This broad bottomland, ringed by mountains, was a paradise of visual beauty and wildlife, the beaver being the main animal we saw. The opportunities for trapping in this wide valley were breath-taking. A man could get rich in a place like this, I reckoned. I had no way of knowing it on that hot afternoon, but this valley would play a huge role in my future, and in this valley I would have several brushes with death. No, all I knew then was that this was a land of plenty.

The three streams that came together at this place to form the Missouri meandered and split numerous times, forming many small islands and swampy marshes. Cottonwood was the main tree in the valley, though Captain Lewis did point out willow and alder trees as well. We took the fork that led toward the southwest, as this led in the direction we wanted to go, and soon made camp on a flat prairie.

"Unload the canoes and set up a camp," Lewis said. "I plan to stay here for several days."

We were all happy to hear that, as the journey up the Missouri to this point had seemed to become more difficult with each mile. A few days of rest would be very welcome by all of us. The only thing that might have made us happier right then would have been the discovery of a forgotten cask of whiskey in our gear, which, sadly, did not occur.

Captain Clark, who had traveled ahead of the main party in order to seek out the Snake Indians, came into the camp that afternoon, and he looked about as tired and sick as any man I had ever seen. His gait was more of a stumble than a walk, and sweat ran off of him in rivulets. Captain Lewis persuaded him to rest in the shade of a canvas awning near where I was flensing an elk hide.

"No sign of the Snakes," Clark said, his breathing shallow and rapid. He was sipping slowly at a flask of water and mopping the sweat from his face.

Lewis sighed. "I'm beginning to despair, Mr. Clark," he said quietly, his voice almost drowned out by the whisper of the wind and the gurgling of the nearby stream. "I fear our entire enterprise is in danger of failing."

This was the first time I had ever heard either captain make a statement like that and I felt a chill pass through me.

"If we can not find those elusive Snake Indians and get horses before the snows close in those mountain passes, we shall have to go back," Lewis continued. "I shudder at the thought of admitting failure, but I can not send these brave men to a certain death by pushing forward too late in the season."

"We'll find them," Clark said reassuringly.

"I hope you're right," Lewis sighed.

I continued flensing the hide, my thoughts troubled. A little while later I saw George Drouillard coming up along the bank of the river, a deer carcass thrown across his shoulders. He dropped the carcass onto the stony bank and glanced toward the captains. "Captain Clark feeling okay?" he asked.

"He's kind of sickly," I said. "He should be all right soon."

Drouillard nodded and stepped into the shade thrown by the awning. "I have some interesting news," he said.

"Go ahead," Lewis said.

"I was speaking with the Bird Woman just now and she said that this is the exact spot her people had camped when they were attacked and she was taken prisoner."

Clark smiled at Lewis. "See? I knew they came here. We'll find them sooner or later."

"Have you seen fresh signs of the Snakes, George?" Lewis asked.

Drouillard shook his head. "No, sir, but I think they're up in those hills." He gestured toward the west.

"Why do you think that?" Clark asked.

George shrugged. "I don't know, I just feel it."

"Well, I hope you're right," Lewis said, but he seemed to be in a better mood than he had been before George had arrived with his news.

* * *

"So which one is the Missouri?" John Potts asked, looking out across the wide plain. From our vantage point on top of a flat bluff, the courses of all three rivers could be seen, twisting and wandering over the low valley.

"None," I said. We had left camp earlier in the morning to hunt and had so far killed three elk and a deer.

John looked at me from the corner of his eyes. "Well, one of 'em's gotta be the Missouri," he said reasonably. "We did get to this place by following the Missouri, remember?"

"I remember," I said. "But Captain Lewis has said that, as all three are just about equal in size and flow, he can't point out one as being the Missouri. So he and Captain Clark have named the western one the Jefferson, the middle one the Madison, and the eastern one the Gallatin."

"Hmm," Potts said noncommittally, scratching his head and peering down at the rivers.

"You don't like those names?" I asked.

"They're all right," he said. "I suppose."

"And what would you have named them?" I asked.

He grinned widely. "The Potts, the Colter, and the middle one could be the Johns."

I laughed out loud and shook my head.

* * *

By the last day of July we were ready to continue up the Jefferson River and into the mountains. All of us were aware of the advanced season and knew the importance of finding horses, so nobody complained when camp was struck and we set out.

As we worked our way toward the wall of mountains to our west, the sheer number of beaver in the Three Forks area became ever clearer to us. Beaver dams and beaver houses lined every river and stream, and many of the rivers that fell into the Jefferson had been rerouted by those dams, leaving ponds and small lakes behind.

Game became ever scarcer as we left the low valley and moved deeper into the canyons of the mountains. Drouillard and I hunted almost every chance we had, and when Drouillard was taken along with Captain Lewis in search of the Snakes, most of the hunting fell to me. I went out every day, usually joined by any one of a number of the other men, but we often came back empty-handed. We saw signs of elk and deer, and often spotted the fleet-footed mountain goat high up on inaccessible hills above us, but most of the game animals seemed to stay away from the rocky ravines and canyons through which the Jefferson cut its path.

The walls of the canyons were sometimes sheer cliffs of several hundred feet in height, and the sun beating down on the rock faces made the air stifling and hard to breathe. We fought our way against the rushing current, drenched in our own sweat, and our progress was torturously slow. The oars were mostly useless and we spent the majority of our time in the river, physically pulling the canoes upstream with tow ropes. The rocks on the bed of the river were slick and round and we often fell, twisting ankles and knees. Fatigue seemed to set in a little earlier every day, and when we made camp we often fell into a sleep of sheer exhaustion within moments of resting our heads on the ground.

Just when we would begin to despair of ever coming out of those inhospitable canyons, the rock walls would fall back and we would find ourselves in some low wooded valley, and we would again have plenty of deer and elk to eat. For a while we would feast, and feel the strength returning to our battered bodies. Then we would move further along the river and the walls would close in once again and our tribulations would start anew.

We saw signs of Indians along the route, buoying our hopes of meeting with a band of Snakes and trading for some horses. We were somewhat encouraged by Sacagawea's recognition of numerous landmarks along the way, including a large rock formation in the shape of a beaver head near which she claimed her people often made their summer camps. But it wouldn't be until the middle of August that we finally met our first Shoshone.

CHAPTER TWENTY-THREE

I wish beyond all wishes that I could have been in the party with Lewis when he met up with the Indians for the first time. Instead, I had to hear about it second-hand from Drouillard, who was there.

After seeing Indians on several occasions but unable to get close enough to speak with them, Lewis finally came across several native women as they dug for roots in a small clearing. One of the women immediately ran from them, but Lewis was able to greet and communicate with the other two, mostly with the help of George's sign talking. When Lewis gave the women some small trinkets as gifts, they knew his intent wasn't to harm them, which was fortunate for the captain and the men with him! Because right after that about sixty warriors came riding up, apparently alerted by the woman who had escaped, and they were armed and ready for war. The two women showed the warriors the gifts they had received and Lewis and the men were welcomed warmly.

Captain Lewis and the men were led to the Snake's encampment and spent some time with them, smoking a pipe and getting to know one another. Drouillard said the conversation was difficult due to the language barrier, which I can fully believe. But they were able to get the main points across.

"Those Shoshone were none too happy to learn there was a bigger party of white men coming up the mountain," Drouillard told me. "They're a reclusive people, used to hiding in the mountains from their enemies, who always seem to be better armed than they are."

"They don't have rifles?" I asked, surprised. I had assumed that all of the natives had weapons.

"A couple old muskets," Drouillard said dismissively. "Nothing to amount to a damn. They were existing on berries and roots up there, John. Shields and I set out that first day to do some hunting just to get food into them, I felt so badly for them."

Lewis spent a lot of time learning as much as he could about the country between the mountains and the ocean. The Shoshone camp sat on a river that flowed toward the west, but the chief had told him the river was not navigable, which didn't make Lewis very happy.

"The only route seems to be through a pass to the north," Drouillard said, "but from the way it was described it won't be easy."

"Nothing about this mad journey has been easy," I said, and he smiled.

* * *

While Captain Lewis was meeting his first Shoshone, the rest of us were struggling up the ever-shallower river, dragging our heavy canoes for mile after mile. All of us were praying that we would find those Shoshone soon so we could abandon those cursed canoes and travel across land on horseback. The days were hot, and mosquitoes and biting flies made our lives a misery, and there wasn't a man among us who wasn't bruised and bleeding from slipping and falling on the slick rocks.

"Captain Clark, look!" Joseph Field shouted, pointing up the mountain.

We all stopped and looked. Several Indian men had appeared from behind a small ridge of stone and were coming down toward us. As they drew closer I could see that one was Drouillard.

"Well, I'll be!" Clark said. "Looks like Captain Lewis has found us some Shoshone!"

Drouillard came down to where we sat, the Indians trailing behind uncertainly. I had seen deer enter a glade that way, with the expectation of being attacked and ready to spring in any direction to escape. Captain Clark noticed it, also.

"Let's all be nice and calm, lads," he said quietly. "Those are some frightened Indians."

With much cajoling, Drouillard brought the Snakes down to the canoes. With the Indians standing to one side, eyes darting in all directions, Drouillard gave a brief rendition of Lewis's meeting with the Shoshone, including the Indian's timidity and their fear of an ambush. "He said to get down here and get you up there as quick as possible before they all melt into the trees and disappear," George finished.

"Then we shouldn't disappoint him," Clark said. "Listen up, men. I will be going back up with George and these Indians. Charbonneau, I want you and your wife with me. The rest of you, continue bringing the canoes up the river until I can learn what Captain Lewis has in mind to do."

"Getting' out of hauling these damn canoes, eh, Captain Clark?" Hugh Hall joked.

"Captain's prerogative," Clark replied. He grinned at Drouillard. "Lead on."

* * *

Later that afternoon, the captains returned to the river with the full band of Shoshone. By then we had advanced maybe another two miles up a river that was swiftly turning into a mere trickle of water and the labor was incredible.

The Shoshone that the captains brought to us were very friendly, and seemed excited to see us. Sacagawea seemed extra emotional, and we all found out later that the leader of this particular band was actually her brother. The Shoshone had long since imagined her to be dead and her reunion with them was a cause for much celebration.

As we set about unloading the gear, the captains spread an awning for shade and began their council with the Indians. As I worked I listened as best I could, and it seemed to be a very awkward process. The Indians would speak in their language, which Sacagawea would translate into Hidatsa. Charbonneau, who knew Hidatsa, would translate from that language to French. One of our French boatmen, Francois Labiche, would then translate from French to English for the benefit of the Captains. When the captains spoke the whole process had to be completed again in reverse.

I shook my head and continued my work. At that rate, any negotiations would take well into the night.

That evening, Captain Clark came to where we were camped. "The Indians paint a very gloomy picture of the land on the other side of the mountains, namely the scarcity of food and timber for making canoes. They say that the rivers running down to the ocean are filled with tall cascades and narrow canyons. I'm not certain if they are being truthful or just love exaggeration, so I'm setting out in the morning to take a look for myself. Sergeant Gass, Sergeant Pryor, you're going with me, and I want Windsor, Cruzatte, Colter, Collins, Shannon, Reubin Field, Weiser, Hall and Goodrich. I want you to bring your gear, plus axes and whatever tools you might think necessary for the purpose of building canoes. We leave at ten o'clock tomorrow morning. Any questions?"

We grinned at each other, happy to be away from dragging those boats up any more rivers. There were no questions.

Clark nodded. I had the feeling he could sense our pleasure.

* * *

The captains had bargained with the Shoshone for horses, and when we set out the next day it was without the burden of carrying all of our gear. The majority of the Indians accompanied us, leaving Lewis behind with some of the chiefs to continue his negotiations for more horses and possibly a guide to lead us across the mountains to the Columbia.

We crossed over a broken, rocky ridge and descended into a narrow valley. Short stubby trees and thorn bushes covered the rocky hills. The creek we traveled beside was narrow and it crashed and tumbled over boulders and waterfalls. The idea of traveling down this stream was laughable.

"Maybe it gets better further down," Clark said, but his voice told a different story.

Sacagawea said something to Charbonneau, who translated in his very broken English. "She say…hills like this…all way to bottom. No river…for canoe."

Clark nodded but didn't say anything.

We made camp that night near the stream, at a fork where another equally inhospitable stream fell into the one we were following, and woke in the morning to a thick layer of frost. The air was bitingly cold and a stiff breeze came down from the high peaks around us. Goodrich and I were sent out to hunt while the rest of the party gathered their gear to continue down, and we quickly were able to kill two deer, which served as our breakfast.

Our travel that day took us up and down narrow valleys and over rocky hills. Numerous streams cut through the barren landscape, all of them totally impassable with any kind of boat. When we crossed over the tops of the divides, we could see similar hills and cliffs extending in every direction. The captain's assumption that we would only have to cross one ridge and join the Columbia for a fast trip to the ocean appeared to be crumbling.

In our exploration we met and talked with various parties of Shoshone who were making their own ways through the mountains, seeking food. Some ran and hid at the sight of us, but once our Shoshone companions convinced them of our friendliness, they came out of hiding to greet us. All of them were happy to share what food they had with us, despite the fact that they didn't have enough to feed themselves, and that simple sincerity was touching. Back in the east, most folks would let a stranger starve before giving up their own food.

"It's not looking good, lads," Captain Clark said, standing at the edge of one of the tumbling creeks. All around us shattered rocks and cliffs jutted up and knobby trees littered the slopes, none of which could be used to carve out a toy canoe, let alone one large enough to carry the men and gear. Not that the wild rivers in this land would be navigable by canoes, anyway. The captain was correct. It did not look good.

Clark pointed at a small stunted tree that huddled beside the path. "Look at that poor thing," he said, then motioned around us. "They're all like that, only good enough for maybe a one-man canoe. I can build enough small one-man canoes to get us down the rivers except that the rivers are all rocks and cascades."

"Think we'll be crossing the mountains on horses, sir?" Sergeant Gass said.

"If Captain Lewis can secure horses for us." Clark scratched his head, and then turned away from the view below. "I don't see that we're going to have a choice, Sergeant. We sure can't take a canoe down these rivers. Let's head back for the camp."

We turned back. Clark sent me out to do some hunting but the game was as scarce as I'd seen since setting out from Wood River. It was no wonder these poor people were starving. I managed to shoot one deer during the afternoon and that shot was from about as far away as I could possibly be and still make the shot. These people, with their crude weapons, didn't stand a chance. I had no idea how they survived.

* * *

Eventually our party was fully reunited and we started for the Columbia River via horseback. It was the only choice we had, and none of us were real excited by the prospect. We had all stood at the peaks of the hills around the Shoshone camp at one time or another and looked toward the west, seeing range after range of snow-capped mountains vanishing into the distance. The idea of crossing those mountains was intimidating, but there wasn't a man among us who would turn back at this stage.

Captain Lewis had secured enough horses for each man to ride one, and some extras for carrying baggage and possibly for food should we have difficulties procuring meat. And he told us a funny story of how he had, at long last, conquered the mighty Missouri.

"The creek that becomes the Jefferson got narrower as we ascended the mountain," he said, as we sat at the fire in our camp. "Finally we reached the spring that spilled out from under a shelf of rock. So I was able to stand with one foot on either side of the mighty Missouri!"

The Shoshone who had stayed with Captain Lewis in order to help bring our gear across were anxious to be on their way to the hunting grounds down the mountain to the east. This was the time of year when they normally went onto the plains to hunt buffalo for food and skins to get themselves through the winter, and they were delaying their hunt to help us. The captains finally allowed them to go on their way, retaining the services of an older man and his son to act as our guides through the mountains to the land of those the Shoshone called the Nez Perce.

Captain Clark gathered all the men around him the evening prior to our departure. "All right, lads, here's the scenario. We can not descend the rivers to the ocean from here. Our only option is to cross the mountains on horse until we reach the waters of the Columbia on the other side. Winter is coming on at this high altitude, so we don't know the kind of weather that'll be waiting for us out there in those mountains, but we can expect it to be awfully cold. Food might be scarce."

"You trying to frighten us, Captain?" Shannon called out.

Clark grinned. "Not my intention, Mr. Shannon. I just want you all to know what we're facing. Anybody want to turn back?"

We all looked at each other then back at him. "Are you kidding?" Potts said. "I didn't come this far to turn back now."

Nods all around as Captain Clark smiled. "That's what I thought."

"Although I could probably get back to them Mandans by winter," Hugh McNeal said, rubbing his chin thoughtfully. "Had me a nice toasty squaw down there."

"Your squaw's busy toasting someone else right now," Collins said, and we all laughed.

"So we're determined to see this through?" Clark said.

We responded with a cheer that sent several crows flapping away, their indignant caws echoing down at us.

On August 30, we set out.

CHAPTER TWENTY-FOUR

We left the Shoshone camp behind us and took to the trail on a day that was clear but quite cold. A thick coating of frost had covered the ground that morning when we awoke, and our breath misted in the air as soon as it left our mouths. We had dined on a deer killed by Drouillard earlier that morning, and we all felt content and ready to face the challenges ahead, whatever they might be. Of course, we had no way of knowing at the time just how daunting of a challenge we were about to face.

The old Shoshone guide, whom the captains referred to as Toby, was on the lead horse. He had told the captains that there were two potential routes to the ocean, one to the south through desert land with no water and very little game, and another to the north through rough mountains. He gave us an estimate of ten days to reach the junction of a major river via the northern route, and another five days to reach what his people called the "stinking water," otherwise known as the Pacific Ocean. It was another estimate that would turn out to be quite optimistic.

Our journey through those mountains was one that I will never forget. The route we followed took us up and down narrow ravines covered in piles of rocks, through valleys filled with tall timber, and over mountains covered in deep drifts of snow. We passed several bands of Indians in the first days who were headed east to join the Shoshone on their buffalo hunt, but after a while we were the only humans to be found in that wild and desolate land. Narrow streams dropped and splashed down rocky defiles and over shattered stones and fallen logs. Within days of departing from the Shoshone, the game animals had vanished to wherever they go in the winter and the hunters, including me, had to travel farther out every day to find any kind of food to sustain the men.

Occasionally, in the beginning, we would come unexpectedly on a wide clearing where the horses could dine on grass, and then we would be right back into the mountains where every step on the jagged rocks offered the chance of a broken leg. Some of the roads were so bad that horses were crippled. On several occasions horses and riders slipped and rolled down the sides of hills, but miraculously nobody was hurt. In one such incident our last thermometer was broken, and in another we lost Captain Clark's writing desk.

We had one fortunate encounter with a band of what our guide called the Flathead tribe. They were coming up through the mountains to hunt buffalo on the plain, and we were able to trade some of our worn-out horses and some small items for some of their horses that were fresh. Those people were hungry and impoverished, and even their dogs were so starved that they ate several pairs of the men's moccasins.

The captains spoke with them through the several layers of interpreters and gave them the typical speech, though I was a little confused as to why they were bothering. My understanding was that the United States had purchased the territory up to the base of the mountains. These Indians came from the western side of the Rockies, out of Jefferson's jurisdiction. But, hey, I was just a private, so I kept my mouth closed.

The other act the captains performed that amused me was their habit of "making" chiefs. They would pick out men they felt were the leaders of a band and name them chiefs, and give them medals or flags. I often wondered what the other members of the tribe would say if those men were foolish enough to walk back into their main village and proclaim that some passing white men had named them as chiefs, and now the rest of the people had to obey them. And I wasn't the only one to have those thoughts.

"I wonder what President Jefferson would say if I walked up to him and said that some red man out here had named me President," Silas Goodrich said one afternoon. "Think he'd let me run the country?"

Shannon had laughed. "He'd probably slap you behind bars," he said.

"Hopefully these Injuns ain't fool enough to call themselves chiefs to their people," Silas said.

I nodded in agreement.

Food became our greatest concern as we pressed deeper and deeper into the inhospitable mountains. Most deer and elk were too smart to try and travel through this fractured land, and we found them but rarely. Mostly we had to subsist on pheasant and grouse and an occasional beaver, and, of course, the ever-present berries and roots. Early in the journey we ate the last of our greasy pork that we had carried clear across the continent, and there were those among us who would almost rather have gone hungry than try to force down that vile meat. The hunters were given horses so they could hunt further and further from the main party, but the land was so hilly and rough that there were times when the horses were more of a hindrance than a help.

Ironically enough, the tall trees on this side of the pass would have made fantastic canoes, except for the fact that the rivers were still too rocky and rapid to navigate.

Then the heavy snows began and the travel became really interesting. Paths made treacherous by the loose gravel became even more dangerous when covered by ice and snow. Our moccasins would get wet from walking in the snow and then they would freeze, presenting us with the very real danger of frostbite.

Some mornings we would wake up to find our clothing had frozen to the ground in spite of the fires we kept roaring through the night, and every bone and muscle in our bodies would cry out in stiffness and pain. We would move around like frail old men, struggling to force our aching joints to function in the manner they are meant to, and then we would eat a meager breakfast, gather up our horses and gear, and set out again. Our trail might climb to a snowy pass, then drop back down again and we would find ourselves in a valley where the freezing rain would fall all through the day. Or we might follow the course of the river through heavy falls of snow, where all of the world around us would vanish behind a white curtain.

* * *

"There," Drouillard said softly, pointing ahead and to the right.

We had been on this trail through the mountains for six days and George and I had been sent out to hunt. It had been two days since the last time we had eaten fresh meat.

I peered in the direction he was indicating and saw a slight movement, a hint of tan hide. The underbrush here was thick and difficult to see or move through, and the snow was falling heavily. I had no idea what he was pointing at.

"Elk," he whispered.

I nodded, though I wasn't so sure.

Drouillard moved forward several steps then froze. I could see that every ounce of his concentration was on the trees ahead. I hoped he was right about the elk, because those men coming along that rocky trail were desperately in need of fresh meat, but now even the faint hint of tan had vanished.

Barely breathing, I watched George raise his rifle and fire. A loud crashing noise came from ahead, moving off to our left, and George waved me forward. "Got 'im, John. Let's go."

We ran forward into a small clearing in the pine woods. Bright red blood was splashed on the snowy ground, and a trail of blood led off to the left. We followed the trail, down toward the river. I could hear the sound of the river as it fell and splashed over the rocks, and the sound of the injured elk's stumbling passage through the thick brush. Then, without warning, the crashing stopped.

"He's down," Drouillard said.

We found the elk at the edge of the river. The big animal had fallen with his head in the water. I waited while George said his prayer to whichever spirit he prayed to, and then we set to work butchering the elk.

"Pretty lucky he came along," I said. "Our boys are gonna be real happy for this meat."

Drouillard grinned. "That wasn't luck, my friend," he said.

I raised an eyebrow. "Oh, really?"

"Yep. That was the Great Mystery."

"The Great Mystery," I repeated. I had no idea what he was talking about and I wondered if our recent hunger had affected his head.

He nodded as he worked. "Yep. You white folks don't know about the Great Mystery. I'll try to explain. We are in desperate need of this meat, am I correct?"

"Yes."

"So the meat sacrificed itself for us. The Great Mystery knew we needed this elk to cross our path and so he sent it to us. That is how the circle works. And that is why I pray to the Great Mystery after I kill an animal, to thank him for the gift, and I also thank the spirit of the elk for dying for us."

"So let me get this straight," I said. "Your Great Mystery sent this elk so we could kill it and eat it."

"Right."

"Because the Great Mystery knew we were desperate."

"Right."

"So if that's the case, why couldn't the elk kill itself so we wouldn't have to use up a bullet?"

Drouillard shook his head in disgust, though I could see his grin. "I don't know about you, Colter," he said. "You're either smarter than all of us or you were dropped on your head when you were a child."

"Probably the latter," I said, and we laughed. I never thought I'd see the day I'd be sharing a joke with a half-breed, especially one that was half-Shawnee, but these were strange times and my life was following an entirely different path than back when I had been killing Shawnee's for the United States government. Besides, I liked old George. Strange times, indeed.

CHAPTER TWENTY-FIVE

"Looks like we could float down from here, Captain," Sergeant Ordway said.

The river we had been following for over a week had grown wider and deeper as we moved along and was now almost a hundred yards across. The bed of the river was gravel, and when we were forced to ford across it the water was up to the horse's bellies.

Captain Lewis nodded thoughtfully as he looked at the water but he didn't say anything.

We were breaking camp on a cold and rainy morning. Stark mountains reared up on both sides of the river, barren of trees. The only trees in this place were those that hugged the banks of the river, unlike the thick forests we had passed through just the day before.

"What's your thoughts?" Clark asked.

"I see what Sergeant Ordway is saying," Lewis said, "but I think we need to stay with the horses. It's too soon to take to the water."

Clark gazed at the river. "Looks pretty wide and deep to me."

Lewis smiled. "Yes, and what do you normally expect to see in a wide and deep river in these parts?"

Captain Clark thought for a moment, and then nodded. "Salmon," he said.

"Yes. Salmon. The fact that there are no salmon, or any fish, in this river tells me that there are some mighty big falls downstream a ways."

"Smart thinking, Captain Lewis," Clark said. "The horses it is."

As we moved to load our gear onto the horses, I heard Clark say to Lewis, "You can't worry about it. It doesn't matter now, my friend."

"I know. But it still bothers me, William. Four days! Imagine!"

"Yes, but if we had found it, we wouldn't have met those Shoshone and secured our horses. Things work out as they work out, Meri."

"I suppose so."

Nate Pryor walked past me and I nodded toward the captains. "What's that about?"

He glanced toward the captains before answering. "Old Toby told them that this river meets another one just as wide a ways below us, and there is a direct route from that junction to the Missouri that can be walked in four days."

I stared at him in amazement.

"The Hidatsa had told Captain Lewis about it and said it originates near the Gates of the Rockies, but he couldn't locate it on our way through."

That was even more of a shock. We had passed the area called the Gates of the Rockies over two months earlier.

Nate nodded. "Yep, that long ago," he said. "Now you know why Captain Lewis is so mad."

Now I understood, and I understood why Captain Lewis would be upset. Four days from the Missouri to the river we were following, bypassing the Great Falls, the Three Forks, and the mountain crossing. It was like a cruel joke.

* * *

I froze where I was standing and tried my best to appear harmless.

The three Indians rode out into the open and moved slowly toward me, their arrows pointed straight at my chest. Their faces held no expressions and their dark eyes never blinked. One wrong move and I would look like a porcupine.

Earlier, Captain Lewis had sent all of the hunters out in differing directions in order to find food for the party. I had traveled about three miles toward the north without seeing even a sign of deer or elk and I was hoping the other hunters were having better luck than me. I had just decided to turn toward the east and try my luck along the high ridges when these Indians had appeared.

One of the Indians said something in a strange, guttural language and motioned at me. I had no idea what he wanted me to do.

"White man," I said. "Friend."

He shouted at me again and jerked his hand toward the ground. I thought I knew now what he wanted me to do and I didn't hesitate, not with three arrows pointed at me. I slowly lowered my rifle to the ground and stepped away from it.

The Indians seemed to relax a little and they rode to where I stood. The man in the lead dismounted and walked to stand in front of me. For a moment we stood looking at each other, and I could see the same uncertainty in his eyes that I knew he must be seeing in mine. In that instant of mutual understanding, I almost started to laugh. Here we were, two humans standing in a snowy clearing on the western slope of the Rockies, and we couldn't even carry on a simple conversation.

The Indian saw me smiling and he smiled back at me. Now, I'm no sign-talker like Drouillard, but in that moment I felt inspired. Improvising as best I could, I tried to show this Indian that I was traveling through with a large group of white men heading to the west, toward the ocean. I tried to show him that we were friends, not enemies. I have no idea how much of my signing made sense to him, but when I indicated that I wanted to take him down to meet the captains, he seemed to understand and he nodded.

The man I considered to be the leader swung back onto his horse and motioned for me to join him. I picked up my rifle and grasped his arm, and he swung me up behind him. Without any further hesitation, we set out for the river.

Captain Clark was the first to see us and the expression on his face was one of surprise and amazement. As the Indians dismounted, Old Toby was called forward to help interpret.

It took over an hour for the Indians of the two different nations to communicate through signing but eventually we learned that the three men I had encountered were considered by the captains to be of the nation called Flatheads. They were in the mountains pursuing two Snake Indians who had stolen twenty-three horses from them. They had heard the gunshots of our hunters and had been frightened, thinking that the Blackfeet, ancient enemies of theirs, were in the mountains. Captain Lewis and Captain Clark joined the conversation as several of those hunters returned to camp. By some luck had managed to kill four deer, a beaver and some grouse, and a feast was prepared. I thought about what Drouillard had told me concerning what he called the Great Mystery and I reflected how it did seem a little bit much of a coincidence that we would finally find meat at the same time that we were visited by these Indians.

The Flatheads were happy to share the venison with us, and the talks between them and the captains went on into the evening. The captains were able to ascertain from them the location of their village on the plains west of the Rockies, and the Indians told them it would take six days to reach it. As we had already been in the mountains longer than the Shoshone had said we would be, none of us were willing to place a lot of credence in that estimate.

"Two of these Indians are going to continue their pursuit of the Snakes," Captain Clark said later that evening. "The third has agreed to go with us to lead us to his people on the plain."

Shortly after that, the two who were going in pursuit of the horse thieves departed, and the man I had ridden back to camp with stayed with us. He seemed to be a man of much humor, and he conversed at length with Drouillard and Old Toby as we sat around the fire.

In the morning it rained, and we spent a lot of time searching for several of the horses that had wandered away in the night. It was late in the afternoon before we set out, and to my surprise the Flathead man grew disgusted with our seeming disorganization and departed in a bit of a huff, setting out to catch up with his friends. I could see that Captain Clark was disappointed with the loss of what had seemed to be a promising guide. Lewis on the other hand dismissed the man as a "typically lazy savage" and then seemed to push the incident from his mind.

I spoke with Drouillard later and he had a different story. "That Indian sat watching our confusion in rounding up a couple horses and decided that we were destined to die before we got out of the mountains," he said. "He didn't want to die with us."

* * *

After that strange meeting the country became even more rugged and food even more scarce. We climbed high rocky hills and passed through barren country with no water and no game. We often melted snow to cook with and to drink, and near a small creek we killed one of our colts for food after two days of hunt resulted in one scrawny pheasant. The captains named the creek Colt Killed Creek in honor of the colt that died to save us.

* * *

I woke up with a strange feeling that something wasn't right. The world around me was quiet and still, without even the sound of a hunting hawk to break the silence. And I felt heavy, as if a blanket had been thrown across me during the night.

I opened my eyes but could not see a thing. The world in front of my eyes was utterly white. And that was when I figured out what had happened. The snow that had begun falling in earnest the night before must have buried me! For a brief moment panic set in, as I recalled Old Toby saying that the snow in these mountains sometimes drifted twenty feet or more in depth, but when I sat up my head broke through into daylight and I could see again.

The snow was approximately three feet deep and had robbed the landscape of definition, turning it into a strange muted world where every sharp edge had been rounded and softened. Piles of boulders had become singular large mounds, and fallen trees had blended into the ground so as to become practically invisible. More snow was falling, huge flakes that seemed to float down serenely from the sky and which gave the impression to me that they might continue to fall for a long time to come.

Drouillard had gone out to hunt before first light and returned with two deer, so we were fortunate to have some food to warm ourselves with. The horses had found grass beneath the thick pines where the snow hadn't fallen as deeply and they contentedly ate their breakfast while we broke camp. All of us were eager to be out of these mountains and back down into a milder climate, but our Indian guide wouldn't guess how long it would be before that happened.

"I don't think he knows," Lewis said, shaking his head as he stared at Old Toby. "I just hope he's not taking us in circles."

"Well, unless this river runs in circles, we should be okay," Clark replied, nodding toward the swift-flowing stream.

Lewis managed a grin. "You're right. Water does flow downhill, does it not?" He shook his head again. "I just can't stop thinking how we've already been on this trail twice as long as he said we would be and we're still in these damn mountains."

"I think he was referring to Indian time, Captain Lewis," Drouillard ventured.

"What does that mean?" Lewis snapped. He was definitely not in a good mood this morning.

"Indian time," Drouillard said. "Indians travel light and fast. They're not burdened down with all this gear that we carry. Added to that, they usually pass through these mountains in the summer when the weather is less of a factor. A journey through these mountains, in summer weather, would probably take them far less time than it will take us."

What he said made sense, and I could see Lewis mulling it over.

Clark laughed. "Well, Indian time or no Indian time, we're not getting any further by sitting here worrying about it." He raised his voice. "Finish up your breakfast, lads! It's time to get on our way!"

* * *

The traveling that day was not easy. The snow had not only made the track more treacherous but had hidden it completely in places, so that we had to wait while Old Toby and Captain Clark could find it again. The heavy snow sat thick on the branches of the trees, and it would fall off onto us as we passed, almost as if it had planned to do just that! Within a short time after departing the camp we were all soaked and cold.

Sergeant Gass was riding in front of me as we climbed a steep slope to another rocky pass, and I could see him shaking his head as he gazed around at the forbidding terrain.

"Not like home, eh, Sarge?" I said.

He uttered a short laugh. "Terrible country, Mr. Colter. Terrible country."

I grinned, though I didn't completely agree. I found the austerity of these high mountains rather beautiful.

The terrain continued to grow more rugged, and we lost much time traversing narrow switch-back trails, sometimes traveling ten miles in ground distance to advance one mile toward the west. The horses were struggling with their footing, and we had several close calls where a horse would slip completely off the trail and fall down into a ravine. Nobody was hurt in those falls, but each time it happened we all held our breaths, knowing that any of us could be seriously injured or killed in an instant. And a serious injury in these mountains was as good as death.

CHAPTER TWENTY-SIX

Captain Clark summoned me forward, along with Drouillard, Reubin Field, John Shields, John Potts and George Shannon.

"We're going to head for that valley down there," he said, pointing toward the west. In the far distance we could just see a wide, deep plain with high mountains rearing up again on the far side.

"Toby says that plain is where we can pick up the Columbia," Clark continued. "I want to get down there and kill some food to send back to the rest of the party, or we'll be in serious trouble."

I knew what he was referring to and I agreed. All of the men looked gaunt and thin, and many were sick from the meager diet and hard exercise.

"I'm taking you men because you're my best hunters. Now let's get some meat for our friends."

We set out immediately and headed for that wide fertile plain. The going was not easy, and the trail remained as broken and treacherous as ever, but seeing that deep valley and knowing that our journey through those inhospitable mountains might be nearing an end lifted our spirits considerably. The air seemed to grow warmer as we descended the mountain, and I could see signs of game along the edges of the trail, the first I had seen in days, which lifted my spirits even further. Images of venison cooking over an open fire filled my head and I resolutely pushed it away. I needed to keep my mind clear. But, oh, I was so hungry.

Our first luck with hunting, though, was unexpected. We had just descended another of the endless switch-back trails and entered a narrow wooded ravine when we came across a wild horse. Without hesitation, Clark raised his rifle and fired, and the horse dropped.

"Hang 'im up in a tree, boys," he ordered. "Those fellows behind us will have some dinner tonight."

We did as he said, though I felt a little perturbed. I would have liked some dinner myself.

We continued on. The valley widened around us, spreading out into a flat and level plain, which was much relief to the feet of our poor horses. Pine trees were abundant, and long grass filled the open areas. We crossed numerous narrow streams and passed several empty Indian lodges, all of us luxuriating in the mild climate after so many days in the high mountains.

"Keep your eyes opened," Clark said. "If we can find Indians, they might have some food we can send back to the men."

"That would be good," Drouillard said. "I'm sure not seeing any deer."

That surprised me, too. I would have thought that this wide valley would have been filled with deer at this time of year, but all we saw were a few scattered tracks.

"Speaking of Indians, Captain," Shannon said, "look ahead."

Three young Indian boys were standing stock-still beside a broken and stunted pine, staring at us as if we were ghosts. As soon as they saw that we had noticed them, they took to their heels and ran.

"Damn," Clark muttered, jumping off his horse. "They'll have their entire village in an uproar." Handing me his rifle, he lit out after the boys.

The rest of us dismounted also and followed after Clark. Within a few minutes we caught up to him. He had found two of the boys hiding in the tall grass and was squatting down in front of them, holding out his hand. The boys were huddled together, shaking with fear, and I could see in their dark eyes that they fully expected to be killed at this moment. And I can't imagine that we were a vision that inspired hope in them, seven dirty, hairy men appearing out of the mountains like specters!

"Do we look that scary?" Potts asked softly.

"Have you looked at yourself recently?" I said.

He grinned and shook his head. "Nope, and I don't really want to."

"Keep it down," Clark said. He was still holding his hand out to the boys, and I could see that he was offering them several small pieces of colored ribbon. Their curiosity and desire for the ribbon was slowly overcoming their fear. One of them finally extended his hand, slowly and fearfully, and took one of the pieces of ribbon, and his friend, not wanting to be left out, followed suit.

"I think we'll be okay now," Clark said quietly, smiling at the boys.

Drouillard signed something to the boys and they nodded, and then sprinted off toward the north. We remounted our horses and followed after them more slowly. The sun shining down from a flawless blue sky felt wonderful on my face, and even though the temperature was probably near 40 it felt like a warm spring day compared to the mountains we had just come out of.

We were met several minutes later by an older Indian man, who, after signing with Drouillard, motioned for us to follow him to his camp. As we rode, Drouillard told us that the older man was of the nation known as Nez Perce, and that their main chiefs had just left to go to war against some enemies of theirs in the south and would be returning in several weeks. As we rode into the small village, I could see the open fear on many of the faces of the old men, women and children who were there, and I could understand. All of their warriors gone, and now these strange alien men riding into their midst.

The man led us to a large lodge in the center of the village and ushered us inside. As we sat, several women entered and set food in front of us. The women appeared very timid and frightened, and they kept their eyes down, not looking at us.

The food was a trifle meager but seemed like a divine feast to our starved eyes! It consisted of dried buffalo meat, salmon, berries, and a large amount of an onion-shaped root that Drouillard said was called camas. The camas apparently grew abundantly throughout the area and was a staple of these Indian's diet. We fell to eating like starving wolves at a fresh carcass, and I have to admit that I didn't even think about our friends still in the mountains, not at that moment, at least.

Later, as we sat near the fire just outside the village, all of us felt very sick to our stomachs, a penalty for eating like hogs that afternoon.

* * *

In the morning, we still felt awful, but that didn't stop us from eating a breakfast of dried salmon and some more of the camas. The memory of our near-starvation was still fresh, and having food was a blessing we weren't about to pass up.

After we ate, Captain Clark dispatched all of us to hunt, while remaining behind to learn what he could about the rivers leading down to the Columbia, and to allay some of the fears and suspicions of the Indians.

"They're not sure about us yet," he said that morning. "They're afraid of us, and I think if their warriors were here we might be in a lot of trouble."

We spent the morning hunting with no luck. The deer and other game animals seemed to have fled from the valley, or had maybe been hunted out by the Indians living there. When we returned to the camp, Captain Clark told us that there was another chief, called Twisted Hair, at a village near a large river half a day from where we were, and that we would be going to his village to speak with him and learn more about the rivers running to the ocean. Clark dispatched Reubin Field with one of the Indians to find Captain Lewis and the other men and lead them to Twisted Hair's village.

We set out late in the afternoon. The directions given to Captain Clark took us along the banks of a narrow stream, through a wide plain covered in tall grasses and the camas root plants. We rode through the day, and near dusk met with an Indian man, whom Clark hired to lead us to Twisted Hair's village.

* * *

Eventually we were reunited with the rest of our party and we celebrated our conquering of the Rocky Mountains, a task far more difficult than any of us had expected when we set out from the Mandan villages. Whiskey would have made the celebration more joyous, but we had been so long without it that it didn't really matter. All of us were sick to our stomachs from the abrupt change in diet but we laughed and danced well into the night.

* * *

Chief Twisted Hair drew a map on a white elk skin, depicting the course of the river from his village to a large waterfall, at which he said white traders could often be found. The goods they traded made their way up the Columbia and its tributaries to tribes such as Twisted Hair's, goods like the pieces of copper that adorned the chief's buffalo-skin robe.

"Numerous nations live along the courses of the rivers," Drouillard translated, speaking with the chief through signing. "They live mostly on the salmon and meat they trade for with the inland nations, using the goods from the white traders as currency,"

The best news to me, though, was the chief's report that the wide rivers were navigable by canoe clear to the ocean, with only very short portages to contend with. As I reclined by the fire, trying to ignore the pains and rumblings in my stomach, I daydreamed about the unimaginable luxury of floating down a river, with the current bearing us along. No rowing upstream against the water's flow, no horses, no walking on prickly pear or on snow-covered boulders. It sounded almost too good to be true!

In the morning, Captain Lewis, in spite of his internal discomfort, gave his speech about cultivating friendships among all the native nations. He and Clark handed out numerous gifts, and we purchased food and skins for our journey.

The captains planned to set up camp on the banks of the river and build canoes for our journey to the ocean, and Clark set out with the intention of finding good timber.

* * *

"Come on, John," Potts said to me, holding out my rifle. "We're going hunting."

I looked up at him from where I lay near the edge of a narrow stream.

The sun was warm on my face, and small clouds sent shadows dancing across the long grass. My stomach hurt so bad I just wanted to lay there for about a year.

"Come on," Potts said. "We need to find some deer or something. If I have to eat one more damn salmon or camas root, I think I'll lose my mind. Get up, John."

Groaning, I pushed myself to a sitting position. The movement sent waves of nausea through me and I threw up violently. My stomach felt a little better afterward, but I still had no desire to get up.

"Go on ahead," I said. "I'll catch up."

Potts grinned. "Look, John, I feel awful, too. All the men feel awful. That's why we need some venison. Our stomachs can't handle the change in diet, especially after starving through the mountains."

"You've been listening to Lewis too much," I said.

"Actually, it was Captain Clark who told me that," he said. "Now get up or I'll shoot you and we'll have you for dinner."

I struggled to my feet and stood swaying, mentally debating the option of just jumping into the stream and drowning myself. Drowning couldn't have been worse than the stabbing pain in my guts. But I understood what Potts was saying, and I reluctantly reached out for my rifle.

Once we started walking, I felt a little better, though I did have to stop and vomit on two more occasions. But the cool air felt good as we entered the trees, and by the time we returned to the camp that afternoon with three deer, I felt much revived. The venison was a huge hit among the men, and we ate with gusto. I watched the men as they ate, and I could almost see the life flowing back into them, in spite of the cramps still wracking their bellies, and I was glad that Potts had forced me to go hunting with him.

CHAPTER TWENTY-SEVEN

The tall tree fell with a rending crash that I felt through the soles of my feet, and we were finished. This was the last tree we needed to cut down to make canoes. Already, there were three brand new canoes floating at the shore and one more very near completion. We were almost ready to head down to the ocean.

I had just caught up to the main party after being sent back to the mountains to find a lost horse, and to retrieve a canister of shot left behind when we were struggling our way through the snowy passes. It had been an easy trip, not like our first journey through those mountains, and I was a little surprised at how much work had been completed on the canoes in the short time I'd been away. It looked like I wasn't the only man eager to get to the ocean.

Numerous Indian camps surrounded our canoe camp, and as I rode in and dismounted I heard grumblings from some of the men about the Indians. Apparently there had been several instances of items being stolen by the Indians, including a tomahawk that had belonged to Sergeant Floyd, and the men weren't very happy about it.

"Damn savages'll steal anything not nailed down," Collins said, looking toward the nearest Indian camp with disgust plain on his face.

"A lot of them are here for Clark's doctoring," Gass said, and I nodded. Captain Clark had become very popular among the natives in the area after word had spread that he was a medicine man. Shortly after our arrival he had used some of the medicine we had carried along to cure eye problems in several natives, and it hadn't taken long for the word to get around.

I was a little surprised to see Old Toby, the Shoshone guide, sitting to one side of the camp with his son. It looked like he was making arrowheads.

Drouillard saw the direction I was looking and nodded. "Yep, he's still with us."

"Why?"

He shrugged. "The captains haven't paid him yet so he can leave."

"Do we still need him?"

Drouillard shook his head but didn't say anything more.

We cooked up the venison that I had brought with me, then Captain Clark handed me an axe. "How are you at building canoes, John?" he asked with a grin.

"Gotta admit that I'm better at hunting," I said honestly.

"Don't matter. There's hardly any game around here worth mentioning. We're all back on fish and roots." He laughed at the expression on my face and nodded toward the newly-felled tree. "You can start by lopping off some of those smaller branches, and then Sergeant Gass'll tell you what to do next."

* * *

Work on the dugout canoes raced forward. We had switched from trying to hew out the wood with our small, inferior axes and had adopted the Indian manner of burning the interior of the tree and scraping out the burned wood. Our hunters went out every day but the game continued to remain scarce and elusive, and we were forced to revert to our diet of camas and salmon, much to our displeasure. At one point the captains killed a horse to provide us with meat, and on another day we purchased a dog for food. I had been raised with dogs as companions and workmates, and it was hard for me to kill and eat one, and I wasn't the only man to feel that way.

As the final canoe neared completion, we branded our thirty-eight horses and left them in the care of Twisted Hair, who said he would watch over them until we returned. We also cached our saddles and some other gear and supplies in a hole we dug near the canoe camp.

And on October 7th, we set out onto the river.

* * *

Oh, what a glorious sensation it was.

The canoes floated downstream on the current, requiring very little input or exertion from us. The wooded hills and old Indian camps slid by on either side in a lazy fashion. No tow ropes, no poles, just an occasional sweep of an oar or a minor course alteration. The river ran rapid in some places, and in others we encountered rocks which required us to get out and pull the canoes clear, but all in all this was the easiest travel we had had since leaving the camp on Wood River in the spring of 1804!

And for the most part, the rest of our journey down the river passed in much the same manner. We would awaken in our camp, eat what breakfast we could find, then pile into our canoes and set off. Some of the mornings were quite chilly, and on some days we ran down the river in a cold rain. Rocks and rapids were common, but only rarely did we encounter a high falls at which we would have to empty the canoes and portage them around.

We still had our share of minor incidents. Sergeant Gass's canoe hit a rock and split open, and several men who couldn't swim had to be rescued. The articles on board the canoe got wet, causing us to delay for two days while we repaired the canoe and allowed the items to dry.

Old Toby and his son, who had traveled with us from the Shoshone camp, departed while we were repairing the canoe and headed for their home without saying a word or collecting their pay, and I could see that Drouillard was unhappy with the manner in which they had been treated. In fact, that was the only time I saw him in open disagreement with the captains. Clark wanted to send someone after them to give them their pay, but Twisted Hair, who had rejoined us at one of the Indian fish camps, advised against it, saying the other Indians up the river would just take the items away from them. I could see that Clark was a bit taken aback by that, but he succumbed to the knowledge of the native and acquiesced.

Another couple of days travel took us to the juncture of a major river that came in from the south. The land had become steadily more arid as we moved toward the west, and the high hills on either side of the river were mostly devoid of trees other than in the draws and ravines where water flowed. The captains called the south river the Lewis's River, in honor of our Captain Lewis. We made a camp near the mouth of Lewis's River and sent out hunters, but their luck wasn't any better here than it had been further up into Twisted Hair's land.

"What, all the damn deer go over the mountains to hunt buffalo, too?" Shields asked as we tromped fruitlessly through the hills south of Lewis's River.

"Maybe they're all at the ocean waiting to greet us," I suggested.

He snorted. "I'm so damn tired of fish and roots, and I still can't get used to eating dog."

"Better than starving."

"Barely." He stood for a while, staring at the treeless hills, and then turned away. "Let's head back. Maybe we'll cook up that dog of Lewis's for dinner."

When we got back to the camp, the captains were standing waist deep in Lewis's River and staring upstream. Shields and I walked down to the shore.

"Any luck hunting?" Clark asked.

"Not a thing," I said.

"Twisted Hair has been trying to describe the source of this river," Lewis said, holding his hands down so the current ran through his fingers. "From what we can gather, this is the same river that flowed from the Shoshone camp, the one William here tried following up in the mountains. You think that's possible?"

We shrugged. "I guess anything's possible, Captain Lewis," Shields said. "It looks like it comes down from the mountains."

Lewis nodded. "Yes, I think it does." He waded out of the water. "Let's head back to the camp."

* * *

The following morning dawned clear and mild and we set out early. It was a beautiful day to be on the river, and the current was gentle and steady. There were very few rapids on this section of the river and our travel was almost idyllic. Most of us had adjusted to the strange diet we had been forced onto on this side of the mountains and we no longer suffered the excruciating pain we had experienced immediately after encountering the Nez Perce, though we were looking forward to traveling into a country where deer might be plentiful.

Along the banks of the river we saw small villages of Indians, all busily engaged in fishing or checking their weirs for caught salmon. We stopped at several of the fishing camps and purchased fish from them. Those Indians, unlike their counterparts on the Missouri, absolutely would not give anything away, and expected to be paid for every small kindness. Likewise, they would pilfer anything that was not watched at every moment. The captains surmised that they had been influenced by their exposure to British and Spanish traders who reached them from the Pacific, and therefore had learned that everything has a value to white men.

* * *

"I don't feel that we have a choice," Captain Lewis said.

Several of us stood looking at a small wooden house that sat above the river. It had obviously been constructed by an Indian in a place where he could set up weirs in the river.

Clark nodded. "I agree. Tear it down, lads."

Earlier, one of our canoes had gotten sideways in a bad rapid and had overturned, dumping all of its contents into the water. Tools, shot, powder, and other supplies had been lost. What we had been able to recover was laid out on the shore, but we needed firewood to help it dry. In that land of no trees, the only wood for miles was the old cabin.

As we set to the job of tearing it down, Lewis said, "I swore that we would not take anything belonging to a native person without paying for it, but these Indians don't seem too concerned about taking things that belong to us. If this one comes along and complains, we'll just tell him to collect his reimbursement from his thieving friends upriver."

We got the fire blazing and set to drying out our clothing and gear. This journey down the river to the ocean was becoming more difficult than we had all hoped it would be, but it looked like nothing on this journey was going to be easy.

Shortly after that, we reached another junction of two rivers. The river coming down from the north was the widest river we had encountered yet, and where it joined with the river we were on we made camp. Below this point, the combined rivers made a lazy turn toward the west and disappeared between high sloping hills on both sides, rocky hills devoid of timber or any plant other than some scraggly grass and bushes.

A large band of Indians were camped at the point where the rivers joined and they came to our camp, singing and dancing around our fires. They were friendly and open and seemed genuinely happy to greet us. Those Indians told us that the large river coming down from the north was the Columbia, and the river we had been following was called the Snake. I watched as Captain Lewis absorbed that information, and then followed him later as he broke away from the festivities to walk down to the shore. Squatting down, he lowered one hand into the waters of the Columbia and let it rest there, the steady current washing around him.

"Everything okay, Captain?" I asked.

He looked around at me. "Oh, hello, John. Everything is fine. I was just marveling that, after all this time, we have reached the Columbia."

I nodded. "It has been an incredible journey."

"Yes. Yes, it has. And I was just thinking how nice it would have been for Charles Floyd to have seen this."

I wasn't sure what to say to that. I turned to go back to the camp, sensing that the captain wanted to be alone with his thoughts.

"Wait a moment, John," he said. Wiping his hand dry on his shirt, he walked toward me. "Back in Wood River, I strongly suggested to Captain Clark that we not bring you along on this trip."

I nodded, wishing I could read his expression in the dark. "I can understand that, Captain."

"I was wrong. I had judged you based on your actions at the camp, and Captain Clark asked me to give you another chance." He smiled. "I'm glad that I did."

I felt a lump in my throat. "Thank you, Captain Lewis. That means a lot to me."

"Good," he said. He clapped me on the shoulder. "What do you say we head back and get something to eat?"

"That's a very good idea. I hear they're cooking up old Seaman tonight," I added teasingly.

"They better not cook my dog!" Lewis said, laughing.

We walked back to the camp together.

* * *

We spent several days at the juncture of the rivers, meeting with various Indians, purchasing meat and supplies, and repairing our clothes and weapons. The weather was growing colder by the day, and as we were in the middle of October we all knew we needed to get to the ocean as quickly as we could and either find transport back to the United States or build a fort for the winter. Our options were running out, and we all knew we had no hope of getting back to the Mandan villages this year, as had been our original plan. Finally, we floated our canoes out onto the mighty Columbia and continued west.

It took us three weeks to descend the Columbia from the juncture to the ocean, and it was a perilous journey. The Columbia was home to many small islands and numerous rapids, most of which we were able to navigate without having to resort to portaging. Indian villages and fishing camps lined both sides of the river, and on many evenings we had Indians visiting us at our camps. Some brought dried salmon or berries with them as gifts while others attempted to steal small tools or items and had to be chased away. At other fishing camps, the natives would run in terror at the sight of us, as though we were some kind of demons.

On occasion we would send out hunters but for the most part we didn't bother, knowing that game was very scarce. We could understand why the natives of this land were forced to exist on fish and berries, though we ourselves were growing weary of the diet. All of us longed for fresh meat, for deer or elk or antelope, anything to escape from the endless drudgery of fish!

* * *

"What do you think it is?" Clark asked.

We stood on the banks of the river, at the upper end of a long island, looking at the strangest thing I had ever seen. We had spotted it from the center of the river and Captain Lewis had immediately called for us to turn toward shore.

"Must be a burial crypt," Lewis said. He took his hat off and wiped his brow with a sleeve. The day had started cold but was quickly warming.

The odd structure was about ten to twelve feet wide and maybe sixty feet in length, and appeared to be constructed of old canoes and pieces of wood leaning against a center ridge pole. Inside were hundreds of bones, some still wrapped in decaying robes while others were piled in the center. At the eastern end, twenty-one human skulls were arranged in a circle. Fishing nets, wooden bowls, spoons, robes and small trinkets, some made of copper, decorated the entire space, as if left as gifts for the deceased.

"Look here," Lewis said, pointing toward something at the west end. We looked and saw that the object was the skull of a horse. "They must sacrifice the horse belonging to the dead person and place it here," he continued.

I felt a little strange, standing there in a burial place, and I stepped back a couple feet. In my mind, burial crypts were sacred, even if these did hold the bones of savages.

"Fascinating," Captain Clark said.

Lewis was walking around, peering at every thing with his usual interest. As he did, one of his feet bumped against a robe-wrapped shape that was resting on a willow mat. The robe split, spilling out the bones of the body inside, but Lewis didn't even glance down. I felt a chill go up my spine.

Finally, the captains finished their inspection of the crypt and we went back to the canoes. As we shoved off, I took one last look at the strange building. I was happy to be leaving.

CHAPTER TWENTY-EIGHT

We had come down the Columbia quite a long ways, passing from the high barren desert-like country to a lower land of tall pines and rocky cliffs. High waterfalls fell down sheer cliff faces on both sides of the river, and a heavy mist hung continuously over the hills. Rain fell on most days and fog was an ever-present concern, obscuring the view of the river ahead, but on the plus side the hunting drastically improved the closer we moved toward the ocean. On one afternoon George Drouillard and I killed five deer, and the venison was welcomed enthusiastically by the other men.

None of us wanted to think about going back up this river and across the mountains in the spring, so we pushed the thought from our heads. With luck, there would be a trading vessel at the mouth of the Columbia and we could secure passage back to the east coast aboard her.

But none of that mattered on the afternoon of November 7th, when Captain Clark stood up in the prow of his canoe and shouted in glee. As we all looked at him in surprise, he shouted, "Can't you hear it, lads?! It's the ocean!"

We stopped paddling and rested the oars across the canoes. Above the mild splashing of waves against the boats and the cries of gulls, we could hear a steady pounding noise coming from ahead.

"Those are the waves!" Clark said exuberantly. "We've made it!"

Cheers echoed across the water as we celebrated, and I know I wasn't the only one who felt a sense of amazement. We had traveled across the continent, up the Missouri to its source, across the terrible Rocky Mountains and down the western rivers to reach this place. We had done it!

"Praise the Lord," I heard George Shannon whisper.

But, as it turned out, our celebration was a bit premature.

* * *

"Well, lads, seems like we're in a bay," Captain Clark said the following morning, shading his eyes with one hand as he stared out at the gray waves. Gulls hung suspended above the water and the heavy smell of salt filled our noses.

"Sure smells like the ocean," Potts said.

"Oh, the ocean is close," Clark commented. "Maybe only a couple of miles away. What do you say we go and find it?"

That sounded like a fine plan to us and we shoved the canoes out into the choppy water. Spray broke over the gunwales, drenching us, and the waves tossed the canoes to and fro, making them difficult to row. Our stomachs rolled right along with the boats, and several men quickly became sick from the erratic motion. This was not going to be pleasant.

The shores in the bay were steep and rocky, and the cliffs plunged straight down into the water, offering no place to beach the canoes. The swells grew worse the further we proceeded, driving us toward the northeast, and we fought against them with all our might, fully aware of the danger of being smashed against the rocks. Men cursed and sweated, spitting out mouthfuls of salty water as we struggled to keep the canoes from tipping over.

Captain Lewis was searching the shore with his eyes, and he pointed to a tiny cove, almost invisible behind the high waves and flying foam.

"In there, men!" he shouted above the roar of the surf. "Put 'em in right there!"

The beach barely deserved the name. Only a few feet wide, it was a litter of driftwood and shattered rocks, pounded by the waves and soaking wet from the incessant spray. We brought the canoes into the small shelter provided by a jutting ridge of rocks and clambered onto the rough ground, pulling the canoes up behind us.

I took a look around and shook my head. The place in which we found ourselves was not ideal by a long ways. The waves were powerful and high, crashing with incredible force against the rocky land. The cliff behind where we had landed was perpendicular and impossible to climb, not that we would have abandoned our canoes in any case. There was no water other than from the waves, and we had all unwillingly swallowed enough of it to know that it was brackish and undrinkable. But, as they say, beggars can't be choosers, and any land was better than those vicious waves.

We unloaded the canoes, piling our gear up on mounds of driftwood in an attempt to keep it out of the worst of the water. By this time rain had started to fall, adding to our physical misery but allowing us to collect some fresh water to drink. Later in the evening a storm lashed us, driving the waves at us in a furious manner while throwing the heavy driftwood logs about like toys, endangering our canoes and our lives. Only through sheer exertion and will did we manage to keep from losing the canoes completely to the fury of the waves and wind.

"Lovely place you brought us to, Captain Clark," Joseph Field said loudly, his voice barely audible above the roar of the waves. He was soaked to the skin and looked like a drowned rat.

"Glad you like it, Joe," the captain said, grinning.

"I was thinkin' about building me a house here, what with the beautiful view and mild weather and all."

"Plenty of wood to build it with," Clark rejoined. "Make sure you invite me to see it when you're finished!"

* * *

The terrible weather continued through the night and into the next day. Reubin Shields was able to kill a couple of ducks in the morning and we dined on that meager fare, washed down with the rain water we had captured in our cups and bowls during the night. Not much of a breakfast, but it was all we had.

Finally, in the late morning, the storm abated somewhat and the waves lessened in their intensity, allowing us to bail out our swamped canoes and set out, away from that awful stretch of shore upon which we had been so miserable. We didn't get very far, however, before we again encountered massive crashing waves that forced us to seek shelter. Twice more that day we tried to escape from our predicament, only to be defeated by the waves. Finally we made another wet camp against the cliff walls, surrounded by the ever-present driftwood. We were all getting frustrated by our lack of progress, as though nature was determined to make sure we couldn't complete our journey to the ocean. I had never encountered a river mouth as vicious and evil as this one and I was amazed at the sheer brutality of the waves and wind.

Several Indians visited us at our place of misery that evening and sold us dried fish. We were all amazed at their ability to take their small canoes out onto those pounding waves and travel on them with no seeming concern, succeeding where we continued to fail. I wished I could go with them, away from this horrible place of waves and drifting trees and rocks that fell down on us from the cliffs above. I had never witnessed a place so inhospitable.

Another fierce storm pounded us through that night, accompanied by hail and torrential rainfall. The waves were so high and dangerous that we had to move our camp around a point of land and into a small cove, where the beach was barely big enough to hold us. We weighted our canoes with rocks and sank them beneath the water, hoping in this way that they wouldn't be battered to pieces by the waves and driftwood logs.

"Remember what you said about leaving me behind at Wood River?" I said to Captain Lewis that evening, as we huddled miserably behind what little shelter we could find.

He nodded.

"No offense, but I kinda wish you would've," I said.

Lewis grinned.

* * *

I set out the following day in our smallest canoe with Willard and Shannon in an attempt to explore toward the west. Several of the Indians who had visited our campsite had mentioned white people near the ocean, and the captains wanted to learn if there were in fact any white people still there. The waves were just as awful as they had been since we had arrived in that place and we fought for every inch of westward movement, positive we were going to be flipped over and drowned at any moment, or dashed against the rocky cliffs.

We made about three miles before we gave up. The water was just too rough for us to defeat. We were able to find a better place for a camp, on a low stretch of ground fairly well protected from the waves, and we saw two camps of Indians near there. Several of the Indians were out on the water in their canoes, making it all look so easy, and one stopped near us to sell some fish. There were three men and two squaws in the canoe, and their shifty appearance made us suspicious. It wasn't until they had departed from us and set out toward the east that we realized they had stolen my basket and gig right out of our canoe.

I was furious, but there wasn't a lot we could do. The canoe of Indians had already disappeared around a narrow spit of land, and we had no hope of catching them. Shannon suggested we put ashore for the night and make a camp and return to the main party in the morning, and Willard and I reluctantly agreed.

It was a miserable camp, but we were probably more comfortable than the rest of our party. We were able to get away from the breakers and waves and find shelter beneath some pines, and even though our clothing was rotting away to nothing from the dampness we passed a fairly pleasant night.

In the morning, we were held on shore by another of the seemingly endless storms and I decided to set out over land. Heading east on land was sure a lot easier than paddling west, and I was happy to be on my feet and out of that damn canoe. When I finally reached the camp, I was surprised to see the same Indians there who had stolen my gear the day before.

Their eyes grew wide when I appeared, and they headed quickly toward their canoe, but I wasn't about to let them get away. Hoisting my rifle, I waded into the waves and grabbed their bow rope, then leveled my rifle at the closest Indian.

Captain Clark stepped into the water beside me. "I assume you know these people, Mr. Colter," he said.

"Damn right I do," I growled. "Filthy savages stole my gig and basket yesterday when they were selling us fish. And I intend to get it back."

Clark just nodded and looked expectantly at the Indians. After a few moments, one of the squaws reached down into the bottom of the canoe and came up with my gear. I took it from her and threw the rope toward them, and Captain Clark motioned curtly, ordering them away. Sullenly, the Indians grabbed up their oars and paddled out of sight.

"I really hate these thieving savages," Lewis said sourly. "Makes me glad the Louisiana Purchase doesn't extend to this side of the Rockies."

* * *

The entire party stood on a high bluff on a cool afternoon several days later, looking out at the gray and endless waves of the Pacific Ocean. Heavy clouds raced by overhead, and the wind that came off the water blew our hair and beards and ruffled our clothing. The high crying of gulls could be heard above the booming crash of the breakers, and we could see otters and seals splashing in the heavy swells. It was an awesome sight.

"We've done it," Captain Lewis breathed, and I could see an emerging happiness on his face that I hadn't witnessed in a very long time. "We have done as our President has commanded, and crossed the continent by land to the Pacific."

"Let's have a cheer for our captains, lads," Sergeant Gass said, and we all let out a loud whoop, our voices battling against the continuous roar of the surf.

"Thank you, men," Captain Lewis said, and I could tell he was touched by our gesture. "But the cheer should be for you. We wouldn't be here if it weren't for the incredible effort and labor put forth by you men. And I'll stand before the throne of God and state that I am humbled to be associated with men such as yourselves. You are the true heroes here."

We all cheered again, and I could feel a fierce pride swell within me. It wasn't until that moment that I fully realized just what we had accomplished as a team. Living immersed in each day, struggling against fierce rivers or heavy mountain snows, wondering how we were going to make it through to the next day or find our next meal, it was easy to lose sight of the true scope and breadth of our accomplishment. It was only looking backward at it that I truly understood. We had done what all those naysayers in the east had said was impossible. We had done it!

Lewis went on. "At this time, as we realize that our westward journey is complete, we have to consider our next options. I propose we stay near the mouth of the Columbia until one of two events occurs. One, we encounter a ship that is going to the east coast and can provide us passage, or, two, spring arrives and we depart upriver to return to our homes by the land route. I have seen, above this bay, a place where white people have been as recently as this summer, but there are none there now, so we may not see a ship before spring.

"Therefore, I want to ask for a vote. Do we send a party south across the bay to explore that southern shore to determine if making a camp there is feasible, or do we return up the Columbia and make camp further inland? Or, do we stay here on this side of the river? I need your opinions, men."

We all voted, including the squaw Sacagawea and Clark's slave, York. In the end the voting was split between returning upriver, which was my choice, or crossing the Columbia to the southern shore, but all of us agreed that an exploration of the southern shore was in order.

"Thank you, lads," Captain Clark said. "And I agree with your opinions concerning the south shore. If, unlike this side, game is plentiful there, it might be best to remain in close proximity to the ocean, in case a ship would arrive." Drouillard and I had both related our disappointment to the captains at the lack of deer or elk near that northern shore, and I hoped the hunting would be better on the southern side. I was so sick of fish!

CHAPTER TWENTY-NINE

The terrible weather continued to assault us as we attempted to make our way across the mouth of the Columbia to the southern shore. Heavy rain, cold wind, and crashing waves all combined to make our lives extremely miserable. Our clothing, robes and blankets were all but disintegrated from the continuing dampness, and many of us were sick with coughs and chills. We had to get under cover soon.

We followed the northern coastline back toward the east, deeper into the Columbia, and then finally made our way across to the opposite shore, landing near a point of land that Captain Lewis named Point William, after Captain Clark. We made a dismal wet camp near the point and sent hunters out, while the rest of the party went to work mending our damaged canoes and trying, futilely, to dry our bedding and gear.

"We can't depart that horrible place soon enough for me," Drouillard said to me. We were making our way inland, looking for meat. Elk signs were everywhere, but so far we hadn't spotted one, or any deer, either.

"Don't like rain and cold, George?" I grinned.

He shrugged. "Rain and cold I can deal with, but not every day!"

I nodded. I had to agree with that.

* * *

We finally located what we considered to be a prime location for a fort, and the captains put us to work clearing trees and starting the construction. There was a fresh-water stream within a short walking distance that emptied into the Columbia, and the game animals seemed to be most abundant around that stream and further to the south. There were plenty of tall trees that could be felled in order to make the walls of the fort, and the ocean was nearby in case a ship might appear. The land upon which the fort would sit was about thirty to forty feet above the river, so we knew we wouldn't have to worry about a high tide swamping our fort. Captain Clark declared that he wanted the fort completed by Christmas, and since we were all more than eager to be indoors and out of the incessant rain, none of us complained about the hard work. We had just less than a month in which to build the fort if we wanted to make his deadline, and all of us wanted it finished even sooner than that!

Sergeant Gass was again put in charge of the construction and every man pitched in, including the captains. Those of us who were designated as hunters spent a lot of our time in the forests when we weren't helping with construction, and we were happy to discover that the local Indians assertion about game being plentiful in the area was turning out to be true. The men reveled in the elk that we were able to kill, and just about every one of us mentally swore off fish forever after dining on the wonderful elk meat. It was a vow we all knew we would eventually have to break, especially if we had to return up the Columbia in the spring, but for that moment we were all bound together by our hatred of nasty dried fish!

The rain continued almost non-stop throughout the construction of what the captains would later come to call Fort Clatsop, the name coming from that of a local Indian tribe. We worked on that little fort from the first hint of dawn until long after the feeble daylight had ended, felling trees, shaving off bark and branches, notching and laying the logs. We were also kept busy mending and making new clothing and moccasins, and the steady supply of elk and deer skins were very welcome for that purpose.

Captain Clark and several men traveled overland to the ocean and established a camp for the purpose of making salt. Along the way he and the men blazed a trail, which allowed us to travel to the salt camp without worrying about getting lost in the often-foggy woods. Those forests, so thick and dark and lacking landmarks, could get a man turned around quicker than any place I had ever been. Even the vast prairies of the lower Missouri weren't as likely to get a man lost, as there you could see the sun and gain direction from it.

By the middle of December the log walls were up on the fort, and the captains praised us all for our hard work. Sergeant Gass was struggling with the local wood, as it didn't lend itself to being split, so placing roofs over the huts was going to be a problem.

"Damn trees just splinter," he said, shaking his head in disgust. "Ain't never seen anything like it."

By December 24th, we at last had all of the huts roofed and the logs chinked with mud to fill in the gaps, and we moved into our fort. The joy at having a solid roof over our heads was indescribable and we celebrated well into the night. On several days prior to the 24th snow had fallen, and hail, and we could not have completed the construction of the forts at a better time.

"All warm and cozy, lads?" Captain Clark asked, sticking his head in through the door of the hut I was sharing with Potts, Shannon, Weiser, McNeal and Collins. I could see snow glistening in Clark's red hair and more falling behind him. It was the same question he had asked us at the Wood River camp when the first of the huts had been completed there.

"Just like being at home in my daddy's parlor, Captain," Weiser said comfortably from his reclined position on his bunk.

Clark laughed. "Good! Then you get first guard duty!"

We all laughed at the expression on Pete's face.

* * *

Life at the fort settled down into a routine after that. The weather remained lousy, with rain just about every day, and I wondered why anyone would choose to live in such a damp and disagreeable climate. Of course the natives didn't have much of a choice; it was, after all, their ancestral home, but I couldn't imagine white people ever settling there. Members of the local Clatsop tribe visited us on a regular basis, and many of our men took advantage of the local women's loose morals and seeming fascination with white men and the gifts we could give for their favors, and I admit I was one of them. The women weren't as likable or attractive as the fondly-remembered women of the Mandan villages, but they were women. As we entered another year away from our homes, any women suited us just fine.

As a result, of course, venereal diseases ran rampant through the camp, and there were very few of us who escaped having to go Captain Clark for treatment.

The hunting remained easy and fruitful, and we all bolstered our energy through our consumption of elk and deer meat, with the occasional duck or goose thrown in. We also built up our wardrobes of robes and other clothing, and many of us sewed numerous pairs of moccasins, our memories of the dreaded prickly pear being too near to hand. All of us were of the opinion that we would have to return to the United States via land in the spring, though Captain Lewis still held out hope that a trading ship might appear at the mouth of the Columbia.

"Don't you think the winter storms will keep them away?" Captain Clark asked one afternoon. It was December 22nd, we were finishing building the chimney for the fireplace in their cabin, and the captains were helping.

"Maybe," Lewis conceded. He was holding up one end of the heavy wooden mantle over his fireplace while Hugh McNeal and I fitted stones around it. "That Indian chief who was here yesterday said the ships sometimes stop well into the winter."

Clark snorted in derision. "You mean the one who wanted us to trade him a rifle for some berries and a mat?"

"That's the one."

"Let me just say this," Clark said, as Lewis set his end of the mantle down on the completed base. "If any of these Indians hereabouts told me it was raining, I'd throw your dog outside and wait for it to come back in wet before I would believe them."

Lewis laughed. "Well put, Mr. Clark. Well put." He studied the finished fireplace, and then nodded to us. "Fine work, lads. Thank you kindly."

"Grab a couple more of the men and meet me down at the canoes," Clark said to me, throwing his cloak over his shoulders. "I want to head down the stream to those abandoned huts we saw yesterday and collect some boards for our roofs. It's time we get you fellas under cover."

* * *

The rain had decreased but not stopped as we loaded two of the canoes with boards taken from several old Indian huts. The huts sat perched on the edge of the river a mile or so down from the fort and appeared to have been used as fishing huts by the native people of the area. Clark, Gibson and McNeal were in one of the canoes, while Potts and Joseph Field were with me.

"That should be about enough to finish the job," Clark said, wiping muddy hands on an old rag. He surveyed the contents of the two canoes and nodded in satisfaction. "Yep, I say we head back."

We climbed into the canoes and set off for the fort. We could see another dark bank of clouds moving toward us from the west, and John Potts rolled his eyes in mock surprise.

"Oh, my, it might rain," he said. "Won't that be a welcome change?"

Joe Field laughed. "Rain? What's that?"

I just shook my head. I was so sick and tired of rain.

"You know what the biggest problem with this weather is?" Field asked.

"The fact it never stops raining?" Potts said.

"Besides that. We can't preserve any meat."

He was right. With the mild weather, we were always losing meat that rotted away in the warm temperatures. At Fort Mandan we had been able to stockpile meat and keep it frozen, and in that manner the hunters didn't have to spend all their time looking for fresh game. Here, Drouillard and the other hunters had to be out every day, and they had to bring back just the amount of meat that we could consume in a day or so.

"That's a problem," I agreed.

"It is," Joe said. "It means we have to hunt further and further away from the fort. These elk ain't stupid. They know that white men mean danger. And I'm sure they're passing that message along to their elk friends and relatives all through these woods."

It sounded crazy but I knew what he meant. We had to travel miles away from the fort to find elk anymore. They did seem to be avoiding us.

We got the wood up to the fort and set to work turning it from scraps into roofing material. Sergeant Gass was overjoyed to have some flat boards to work with.

"Where did a bunch of savages get flat boards?" he wondered as he directed the placement of the boards over one of the huts.

Captain Clark shrugged. "Who can guess? Maybe from traders, or maybe from a shipwreck. Don't matter, though. Wherever they came from, they're a roof, now."

Joe Field looked at two leftover boards. "And I think those two might make pretty neat writing desks for our esteemed captains," he said.

Clark smiled. "That would be nice."

* * *

On Christmas Day we moved the last of the men into their huts, and oh what a wonderful day that was! Dry and warm on Christmas, and let me tell you there had been a few of us who had started to wonder if we would ever be dry and warm again!

Sergeant Ordway very quietly gathered all of us together at dawn on Christmas morning directly outside the captain's hut, and on a signal from him we split the air by firing off our rifles, and then added three loud cheers. We followed that up with a rousing rendition of "Joy to the World," sung off-key but with exuberance.

The captains came out of their hut grinning widely, and they applauded us when the song finished. I don't know if they were applauding our singing or the fact that we were finished!

"Merry Christmas!" they shouted to us.

"I believe we've all earned a rest on this holy day," Captain Lewis said. "We'll leave you fine men to your own devices on this day." He looked up at the sky, from which rain fell steadily. "Maybe you can fill a cup with this lovely rain and imagine it to be the finest of whiskeys."

Most of us spent the day relaxing in our huts and talking about past Christmases with our families and friends gathered around. The talk left a melancholy feeling in us as we relived those warm and happy memories, but I believe Silas Goodrich summed it up best when he held up a cup filled with rain water and toasted us all.

"On this wet and disagreeable Christmas Day, I salute you, my new family. All over the world, civilized men are spending this day with family and friends, but none of them are spending it with men as fine and noble as you. When I am back in the bosom of my other family, hopefully by next Christmas, I will look back fondly on this day and I will raise a proper toast to you all."

Well said.

* * *

The year of 1805 ended in an unspectacular fashion, with all of us snug in our cabins, when we weren't out hunting or doing chores in the rain. We did our best to dry our belongings but to no avail, because as soon as we had everything dry we would have to go out in the rain and we would get wet all over again.

The rain and storms continued into the new year, and the wind blew our smoke right down our chimneys and into the huts, making life a misery at times. The rain and smoke, combined with the ever-present fleas that infested everything and everyone, made us long for the open sunny plains, and we often reminisced about those days, conveniently forgetting how much we struggled and sweated as we brought the unlamented keelboat up the Missouri. But I guess that's how it goes. On the plains we complained about the heat and mosquitoes, in the mountains we complained about the cold and the snow, and at Fort Clatsop we complained because it wasn't either hot like the plains or snowing like the mountains!

Just before the turning of the year, the salt camp was completed at the coast, and the captains set up a rotating roster to man it. All of us were excited at the prospect of having salt to season the elk meat with, though we were reluctant to leave the comfort of our little fort to live at the ocean when it came our turns to go. I didn't mind it a lot because I loved being near the ocean. There was something so raw about it, something so elemental.

We finished putting up the palisades around the fort, driving the last log in during a torrential downpour. Captain Lewis was happiest about the completion of the gates, which meant that we could put the local Indians outside at night.

"We'll establish some rules," Lewis said. "All natives must leave the fort at sunset, when the gates will be closed for the night, and can not return until sunrise, when we will open them. That will finally help to control their intrusive nature!"

I had my doubts.

CHAPTER THIRTY

Captain Lewis stood before the assembled men on the first day of January and read aloud the new post orders.

"Now that our lovely little fort has been completed, Captain Clark and I believe it is time to establish some post orders that will determine how things will be run. We think it proper to direct that the guard shall, as usual, consist of one sergeant and three privates, and that the same be regularly relieved each morning at sunrise. The posting of the new guard shall take place in the room of the sergeants who are commanding the same. The sentinel shall be posted, both day and night, on the parade ground area in front of the commanding officers quarters, where a shelter has been built. Should the guard at any time think it proper to remove himself to any other part of the fort, in order to better inform himself of the designs or approach of any party of savages, he is not only at liberty to do so, but is hereby required to do so. It shall be the duty of the sentinel also to announce the arrival of all parties of Indians to the Sergeant of the Guard, who shall immediately report the same to the commanding officers.

"Any questions?"

There were none.

"All right, then I shall continue. The commanding officers require and charge all men in the garrison to treat the natives in a friendly manner. This is important, men, so pay attention. You will not be permitted at any time to abuse, assault or strike them, unless the natives strike or attack you first. Nevertheless it is perfectly all right for any individual, in a peaceable manner, to refuse admittance to, or put out of his room, any native who may become troublesome to you. Should the native refuse to go when requested, or attempt to enter your rooms after being forbidden to do so, it shall be the duty of the Sergeant of the Guard to put that native out of the fort and see that he is not again admitted during that day unless special permission is given. The Sergeant of the Guard may for this purpose employ such coercive measures as he shall deem necessary to affect the same, up to but not including the taking of life. In other words, if you have to bodily lift them up and throw them from the fort, do so.

"All clear, men?"

"All clear, Captain," Sergeant Ordway said, and we all nodded.

"Very good. Now, we need to speak about theft. As you all know, the natives of this area have sticky fingers, and things tend to disappear when they are around. Should any native be detected in the act of theft, the Sergeant of the Guard shall immediately inform the commanding officers of the theft. It will then be up to the commanding officer to determine how the thief should be punished.

"At sunset on each day, the sergeant, along with Charbonneau and two members of the guard, will gather and put out of the fort all Indians except any that may be specially permitted to remain by the commanding officers, and those Indians put out shall not be admitted again until the main gate is opened the following morning.

"At sunset, or immediately after the last of the visiting Indians have been dismissed, both gates shall be shut and secured, and the main gate shall be locked and remain locked until sunrise the next morning. The water-gate may be used freely by the garrison at all times, though from sunset until sunrise it will be the duty of the sentinel to open and shut the gate after each person has passed through. It is very important that we never leave that gate opened longer than is absolutely necessary.

"Any questions now?"

"What about the canoes?" Nate Pryor asked.

"That's coming up next, Mr. Pryor, but thank you for asking," Lewis said. He continued, "It shall be the duty of the Sergeant of the Guard to maintain the key of the smoke-house, and to make sure the guard keeps regular fires therein when they are necessary for smoking meat. Also, it is required at least once a night for the guard to visit the canoes and make certain that they are safely secured. Each morning, after he is relieved, the Sergeant of the Guard must make a verbal report to Captain Clark and me relating that all assigned tasks have been completed and to alert us of anything unusual that may have taken place during the shift.

"All right, to other duties, and here is where Captain Clark and I get to enjoy the privilege of rank." Lewis grinned. "The guard who is going off-duty in the morning will, on every morning after being relieved, furnish two loads of wood for the commanding officer's fire."

A chuckle went through the men.

"No man is to be exempt from the duty of hunting and bringing meat from the woods unless approved by myself or Captain Clark. Also, no man except the cooks and interpreters are exempt from standing guard.

"Each mess has been furnished with an ax, and they are directed to maintain that ax in the room belonging to the commanding officers. This also applies to all other public tools of which they are in possession. At no time shall any tool be taken from the officer's quarters without the knowledge and permission of Captain Clark or me, and any individual who does borrow a tool or tools is strictly required to bring them back the moment he has finished with them. At no time will they be permitted to keep them out all night.

"Any individual selling or disposing of any tool or iron or steel instrument, arms, accoutrements or ammunition shall be deemed guilty of a breach of this order and shall be tried and punished accordingly. The only exception to this is for the tools loaned to John Shields for the repair work that he performs."

Captain Lewis looked up from his notebook. "Are there any questions?"

There were no questions.

"I included the portion about the tools for the simple reason that we will most likely be returning to the United States by land. If we do, we will need every tool we currently have. Some men in this command have become used to receiving the favors of the squaws hereabouts, and those squaws want something in return." He looked at us sternly. "The first one of you who tries to pay for a squaw's favors with a tool may have to learn how to live without your man parts."

There was some theatrical groaning and covering of crotches, along with general laughter.

"Then, if there are no further questions, be about your business. And, gentlemen, remember this. By the end of this wonderful new year of 1806, we shall be at home with our families and friends!"

A tremendous cheer went up from the assembled men, and I cheered right along with them. I had no way of knowing then, of course, that I wouldn't see civilization again until 1810.

* * *

Later that day I set out to hunt, and it would prove to be an exercise in futility. I was reminded of what Joe Field had said about the game animals warning their friends and relatives about us, as I spent four days hiking through the rainy forests and only came back with a duck and a goose to show for it. I returned to the fort at the end of the fourth day hungry and tired, and it didn't cheer me much to learn that Drouillard had killed an elk just a mile from the fort.

* * *

The Indian squaw, Sacagawea, stood in front of Captain Clark, hands firmly on her hips and a fiery light in her eyes. I saw for once that our Captain Clark had met his match.

Sacagawea rattled off something in her Shoshone tongue, the words rapid and clipped. From where I was seated in one of the canoes, I could see that Clark was relenting. He looked mighty hen-pecked right about then.

Two of the canoes had been prepared and were ready to set out. Several of the local Indians had told us about a whale that had washed ashore on the coast, and the captains were determined to get over there and bring back some of the meat and blubber for our uses. There were twelve of us waiting in the canoes, and it appeared that Sacagawea was determined to join us.

"She says that she has traveled a long distance with us, and she wants to see the giant fish, and the ocean," Labiche translated. "She says she has earned that right."

Clark pursed his lips and looked at us. "Men, what do you think?"

"There's always room for one more, Captain," Nate said.

"All right, then," Clark said. "You can go."

Head held proudly, Sacagawea stepped into the first canoe.

Captain Clark shook his head in amusement, and then climbed into the same canoe. "Shove off, lads," he said. "Let's go see that whale."

* * *

The coastline was extremely rugged and abrupt, with cliffs that grew straight up out of the crashing breakers leaving no land in between. From the salt camp, we headed north up that rugged coast, often having to climb and descend nearly vertical hills to keep the sea in sight. It was a very difficult journey, with the continuous and ever-present danger of injury. Along the way we came across numerous small dwellings of Indians, and some of them were boiling down whale meat that they had already procured. These Indians along the coast were as stingy as their brethren around the fort and wanted ten times an object's worth in trade, and in almost all cases we walked away without securing the item of which we were interested.

"You'd think these savages hold some kind of rare jewels instead of small bits of dried fish and whale blubber," Clark said in disgust.

It took us two days to travel from the salt camp to what was left of the whale. Our first glimpse of the giant fish stopped us dead in our tracks with awe, even though only bones remained. The natives had picked the carcass clean, but to us it was still an awe-inspiring sight. Sacagawea seemed extra impressed, not only by the fish but by the very immensity of the ocean itself, and I had seen her on several occasions staring out at the rolling waves with something close to disbelief in her eyes. I wondered what she was thinking, this woman who had never seen a body of water larger than the streams and lakes of her homeland. I wondered what I would be thinking if I were in her place.

We stayed that night near the whale's carcass, and Captain Clark worked to purchase some of the meat and blubber from Indians in the area, but to no avail. They all wanted far too much in return. One group did say they would come to the fort and trade for some of the blubber, so Clark still had hopes of securing a share.

"I tell you," Captain Clark said that night as we sat near our fire, "I'm not looking forward to the trip back to the fort with great anticipation."

"You do have to be part mountain goat to survive around these parts," Windsor said.

"It would help," Clark grunted. He was starting to say something more when a shrill scream came from the direction of the small Indian camp, followed by frenzied yells and shouts. Several Indians who were near us ran towards the camp at full speed, their feet kicking up sand as they went.

"What in the tarnation..." Clark said, rising to his feet. We were all on the alert, weapons in hand, staring toward the Indian camp.

More shouts sounded, accompanied by much running around by the Indians.

"Is everyone here?" Clark asked.

We looked at each other, and then I said, "McNeal's absent, Captain."

"Dammit," Clark said. "Sergeant Pryor, take Colter, Frazer, Windsor and Potts and get over there. Find out what's going on."

We set out at a run, heading toward the camp. As we reached a small stream that emptied into the ocean we saw Hugh McNeal running toward us from the opposite direction, eyes wide.

"Hugh, are you all right?" Nate shouted.

"Yes," McNeal said. He sounded shaken.

"What's going on over there?"

Hugh shrugged. "I don't know. They're all upset and yelling about something."

We got Hugh back to the fire and gathered around it, weapons ready for whatever might happen. We had no idea what was taking place in that Indian camp, but we weren't taking any chances.

"What happened, Hugh?" Clark asked tensely.

"One of the squaws that always comes to the fort was over there with a friend, and they invited me to share some of the whale meat. Then the friend wanted me to go to another cabin with him, but the squaw grabbed me like she didn't want me to go. So I pulled away from her and headed out and that was when she screamed and went running out, shouting like a pure crazed fool."

It took us a while to learn what had happened, but it turned out that the friend, a man visiting from another village, had planned to kill McNeal and steal his blanket and other items. The squaw, who had learned of the plan, saved McNeal's life by warning the other Indians through her shouts. The visitor had run away as soon as the alarm was sounded, and I was sure we would not see him again.

We didn't sleep much that night, and I could see the anger in Clark's eyes. In the morning he said, "Let's get back to the fort, boys. If I could make spring get here sooner, I would. I can't get away from these sneaky savages quickly enough."

* * *

We made it back to the fort without incident and life returned to normal. The hunters had been having a hard time procuring meat, and Potts and I set out the next day to hunt. If we stayed in that place much longer, I thought, there wouldn't be any meat at all for miles around. Our hunt was unsuccessful, but by great fortune Drouillard was able to kill seven elk just the next day and once again we had meat. We were also able to make tallow, as we had burned our last candles early in the month. All supplies were low, and we still had a continent to recross.

"I would like to leave here around the first of April," Lewis said one afternoon. I had managed to shoot a deer just a few miles from the fort, and we were all enjoying our first venison in several months.

"I would like to leave here now," Lewis continued, "but to do so would be impractical in the least and highly dangerous as well. The chiefs around here claim that the snow is laying several feet deep on the high plains of the Columbia, and we can only imagine how terrible those mountain passes would be during these winter months."

"So April it will be," Clark said. He cocked his head and listened to the sound of the rain hitting the roof of the fort. "Though I dare say I'll miss this lovely climate."

Lewis snorted laughter and returned to his meal.

* * *

That night, laying on my bunk and listening to the low rumble of thunder, I thought about what I would do when I returned to civilization. I would have money to spend and a grant of land as my reward for my service during the expedition. I could settle down, find a wife, and start a family. But for some reason, when I thought about my future, the image that kept filling my mind was the Three Forks of the Missouri and the great number of beaver that lived there. There was a fortune swimming in those rivers, and the man who could get in there and trap them, then get those skins down to St. Louis, could set himself up like a king.

With that image in mind, I drifted off to sleep.

* * *

The days rolled past in a dreary pattern of rain with occasional snow and even more occasional sunshine. Some of the local natives had told the captains that the summers along the coast were hot and sunny, and weeks would pass without a drop of rain, a circumstance difficult for us to believe.

I spent several weeks at the salt camp on the coast after Gibson and Bratton, who were assigned there, got sick. We made salt by scooping up bucketfuls of sea water and boiling it in our largest kettles that we had carried all the way across the continent. Once the water had boiled off, we were left with salt. It was a tedious process, and even with the kettles boiling twenty-four hours a day we would be rewarded with very little salt in return. I didn't particularly care for my time at the salt camp simply due to the lack of elk in the area of the coast; we were lucky when we could kill a deer for meat, otherwise we had to trade with the stingy Indians for dried meat, fish or roots.

Hunting was a continuous challenge around the area of the fort due to the steep hills, tangled underbrush and fallen trees that filled the forests. We often struggled for hours through the forests to travel a mile or less, and when we would shoot an elk we often faced serious difficulties in getting the meat back to the fort. On several occasions meat was lost to us because we couldn't get to it after we killed it, either due to the terrain or because the weather was so terrible that we couldn't take the canoes along the Netul River or onto Meriwether's Bay to reach it. We also lost elk meat to the natives, who would not hesitate to steal any meat they might find before we could return for it. The elk refused to cooperate by walking into the fort to be shot, so all we could do was deal with the situation as best we could, but it was still frustrating.

However, all the trials and tribulations passed by in the same manner as the calendar days, and we survived them all. In fact, I could not envision a circumstance that we wouldn't have been able to survive. After what we had already been through, I wouldn't think it amiss to say that we all felt a bit invincible.

CHAPTER THIRTY-ONE

Toward the end of February the captains sent Sergeant Ordway and a group of men to the salt camp. It had been decided to dismantle the camp and bring what salt we had made back to the fort, along with all of our equipment. The salt camp was finished.

"How are Gibson and Bratton?" I asked, as we broke down the camp and packed up our gear.

"They're recovering," Ordway said. "They'll be fine."

I was glad to hear that. It had been almost two years since we had lost Charles Floyd, but that memory remained. I didn't want to lose any more of these men who had become my friends.

We stopped at the top of a high hill above the salt camp and looked back. The waves still rolled in and crashed on the shore as they had been doing for countless years. Gulls hung overhead, and pelicans dove into the chilly water as they fished. It was beautiful. It was also the last time I ever saw the Pacific Ocean.

We made the arduous hike back to the fort through heavy rain and strong winds and stashed our gear away. During my absence, Captain Clark had completed his map of the route from Fort Mandan to the coast, and it was fascinating to look at. I could remember so many of the places he had drawn, despite the fact that a lot of the days had blended together in my memory. And having a map would be nice as we attempted to retrace our route back in the spring.

* * *

February rolled by and became March. Several of the men were sick during this time, including Sergeant Ordway, McNeal, Bratton, Willard and Gibson.

"We haven't had this many men sick at the same time since Wood River," Captain Lewis said one evening. As usual, the rain was falling heavily outside, and we were all staying undercover. I was working on another pair of elk-skin moccasins for myself, double-soling them as protection against the inevitable prickly-pear we would face on our return trip.

"What's the cause, you think?" Clark asked. He was seated in front of his map, making small corrections by flickering candlelight.

Lewis shrugged. "Could be any number of things. Influenza. Colds brought about by all the time the men are spending out in the cold and rain. Maybe some illness particular to this part of the continent that we know nothing about. Some of it could be reactions to the different venereal diseases caught from the native women. With the complaints of fever and headaches, I'm leaning toward influenza."

Clark looked at me. "What about you, John? How are you feeling?"

"I'm feeling right as rain, Captain," I said.

He laughed. "Did you have to use a rain analogy, John?"

"Sorry. Rain is kind of on my mind."

"Rain is on all of our minds," Lewis said, looking out through the open door at the muddy parade grounds. "I dream of the day we're away from all this rain."

"And when we're back on the Missouri, straining against sand bars and mosquitoes, with the hot sun cooking our brains, we'll look back fondly on this lovely rain," Captain Clark said. "I for one happen to relish this weather."

Captain Lewis and I looked at each other, and then looked at Clark. "Maybe I need to prepare some medicine for you," Lewis said. "I think you're coming ill yourself!"

* * *

The month of March passed at Fort Clatsop much as the March of the previous year had passed at Fort Mandan, with preparations being made for departure. All of the men had become quite adept at making clothing and moccasins, and I daresay we were better prepared in that manner than we had been for a very long time. Our gear and equipment was taken out and inspected, and any articles which had become damp were placed out to dry. We all worked with the date of April 1 in our minds, for that was the day the captains had chosen as our date of departure from Fort Clatsop.

* * *

"You're about the busiest man in this entire party," I said to George Drouillard one afternoon.

We were about three miles up the Netul River from the fort, dressing out an elk that George had shot. For once we had a clear day, and the sun felt warm against our backs as we worked.

"Busy hands don't have time to get into trouble," he said solemnly, then grinned.

"Then I can't see you ever getting into trouble," Potts commented. "When you're not hunting, the captains have you running to just about every Indian village in these parts, buying canoes, buying fish."

"That's what he says he's doing," I commented slyly.

"What do you mean?" Potts asked.

"I think maybe he's got him a few female friends in those villages."

Drouillard smiled. "Not me, friend. I'll let you have those diseases. I'll be just fine without syphilis or gonorrhea."

"Seriously, George, do you ever get tired of being errand boy for Lewis and Clark?" Whitehouse asked.

He shook his head. "I don't view it as being their errand boy. I'm doing tasks that have to be done, and I'm the one best suited for dealing with the local Indians. As far as hunting goes, you white boys would starve without me around."

I laughed, though Potts and Whitehouse looked a little miffed at his words. And I reflected for a moment on the phenomenon of Drouillard. Back in the east, a half-breed like George would be treated little better than a slave like York, and if that half-breed spoke to white men the way George spoke to us, it wouldn't be unusual to find him hanging from a stout tree branch with a rope around his neck. But out here things were different. George was well-respected and well-liked. He was the best hunter in the bunch, and his ability to communicate with the Indians we had met along the way had saved us much grief. In short, he was one of us.

"I kind of agree with Colter," Whitehouse said, giving me a sideways wink. "After all, them captains have been trying for weeks to buy a canoe from those savages up by the bay, and George here pops in, says howdy, and comes back with a canoe. Maybe the parents of some sweet young squaw are trying to entice you to stay, eh, George?"

George just smiled and shook his head.

"Or maybe they gave him the canoe so he'll go away and leave their daughters alone," I said.

Our laughter echoed across the low valley.

* * *

Sergeant Ordway pulled me aside the next morning, along with Thompson, Collins and Shannon.

"The captains have a special mission for you boys," he said. "We're getting real close to leaving this place, and those savages refuse to sell us another canoe unless we pay a ridiculous price. We need another canoe. So the captains have decided that we have no choice but to steal one."

I was surprised. All along our journey, the captains had sworn that they would not take anything belonging to a native person without either paying for it or accepting it as a gift. I didn't say anything, but I was a little uncomfortable with this decision.

Ordway must have felt the same way. "The way I look at it, those savages have stolen tools and other equipment from us since the day we came onto the Columbia. I'm not a man who likes to steal from anyone, but these people owe us."

"Where should we steal it from?" Shannon asked. He didn't seem too bothered with the mission.

"Head over toward the coast, to that wide prairie we crossed on the way to the salt camp. There's always a village there."

We nodded. I knew where he meant, and so did the other men.

"All right, then. Be careful."

It took us about ten minutes to gather our gear, then we set out. It was raining very lightly, and a thick fog hung above the tree tops. Water dripped from every tree branch, a constant symphony which we were all becoming used to.

We reached a small fishing village near midday and hunkered down in the underbrush to survey the scene. The small group of huts was quiet, with nobody in sight. Near one of the huts, a canoe sat tied to a small fir tree.

"What do you think?" Thompson said.

"Looks pretty quiet," Shannon said. "They must be out on the river."

"Well, let's stroll in there all friendly like and take a look around," Collins said, rising to his feet. "If nobody's home, we'll take that old canoe back to our captains."

So we did what he suggested, strolling into the small village as if we belonged, and it only took us a few minutes to realize that the huts were all deserted. Collins swiftly cut the rope holding the canoe to the tree and Shannon and I lifted it onto our shoulders. Within a minute we had left the huts behind and vanished into the thick trees.

* * *

Captain Lewis was busily hanging a sheet of paper on one wall of his and Captain Clark's cabin when I walked in with the elk skin he had requested.

"Ah, thank you, John. Just toss it over that chair."

I did as he said, then walked to where he stood. "What's that, Captain?"

"This is a note I am leaving for any white man who may find this fort. I have given copies to all the Indian chiefs in the area to pass along to any white person they may meet. It reads, 'The object of this list is that through the medium of some civilized person who may see the same, it may be made known to the informed world that the party consisting of the persons whose names are hereunto annexed, and who were sent out by the government of the United States in May 1804 to explore the interior of the continent of North America, did penetrate the same by way of the Missouri and Columbia Rivers, to the discharge of the latter into the Pacific Ocean, where they arrived on the 14th of November, 1805, and from whence they departed the blank day of March 1806 on their return to the United States by the same route they had come out.' I intend to fill in that blank when we know the exact date we will leave."

"It will also help to inform the world, should we for some reason not make it home, that we did indeed reach the Pacific," Captain Clark said, walking up behind us.

"We'll make it home," Lewis said. He went on, "Below that note, as you can see, I listed all the men's names. 'Captains Meriwether Lewis and William Clark; Sergeants John Ordway, Nathaniel Pryor and Patrick Gass; Privates John Shields, William Bratton, John Colter, Hugh Hall, John Collins, Joseph Field, Reubin Field, Silas Goodrich, Alexander Willard, William Werner, John Potts, Thomas Howard, Peter Weiser, George Gibson, George Shannon, John Thompson, Richard Windsor, Robert Frazier, Hugh McNeal, Peter Cruzatte, Francois Labiche and Joseph Whitehouse; interpreter and hunter George Drouillard; interpreter Toussaint Charbonneau; Shoshone squaw Sacagawea and her baby son.'" Lewis gazed at the list for a moment. "Looks a little incomplete without Sergeant Floyd's name on it."

"Yes, it does," Clark said somberly.

* * *

"Men, we have not lived like kings since arriving in this place, but I have to believe that we have lived far better than we might have expected that we would." Captain Lewis had gathered us outside the main gate of the fort. The flag had been taken down for the final time that morning, and our small fort, our home for all these rainy days, was being handed over to the Clatsops. We were going home.

"We have accomplished every task to which we set ourselves for this place, except for the hope I had of meeting with a trading vessel. I would have liked to have purchased some more supplies for our return trip, but that was apparently not to be. Other than that, I believe our time here has been well spent.

"President Jefferson asked me to gather as much information as I could about the areas we visited and the people who live there. Captain Clark and I have been able to write extensive notes for him about everything from native languages and customs to the incredible variety of plants, birds and animals we have encountered. And I have to extend my heartfelt gratitude to you men for all you have done to help us in that task. Your attention to bringing us any new animal you were fortunate enough to shoot and every new leaf or branch that struck your eye has allowed us to complete a treasure chest of information for Mr. Jefferson, and for all of civilized society.

"Our intrepid salt makers have brought us enough salt to make our homeward journey more pleasurable, just as our fine hunters have provided us with meat that we could dry and skins that we have made into fine clothing and moccasins. Some of you remain ill but I believe that you will feel much better as we return to the lands beyond those mountains where we can once again secure the wonderful meat of the bison and deer.

"I won't stand before you and tell you that our return journey to our homes and families will be one of ease and comfort, but when I reflect on all we have been through to this date I can not foresee any obstacle that we can not overcome. You are some of the finest men currently residing on this continent. Now let's go home!"

It was March 23rd, 1806.

CHAPTER THIRTY-TWO

Oh, the joy that flowed between the men in those canoes! We were going home! Excited banter went back and forth, each man trying to outdo the other with exaggerated tales of home and holiday meals and how the girls in their town were prettier than the girls any place else. If those canoes had been powered by enthusiasm we would have flown over the Rocky Mountains on air!

Not even the cold and rainy weather could dampen our happiness at finally leaving that wet and disagreeable place to return to our homes. It had been three years since I joined the Corps of Discovery, and some of the men had been with the enterprise longer than that, and despite our pleasure at what we had accomplished together, we were all ready to finish this task and continue with our lives.

Our progress up the Columbia was slow; once again we were rowing against the current of a mighty river. Other than the rocky scenery and low-hanging mist, this might have been the Missouri in 1804 all over again! We stopped at numerous places along the way, to take meals with Indians and to hunt. The captains wanted to time our arrival at the Rocky Mountains with the melting of the snow, since none of us wanted to attempt a crossing of those ghastly peaks in winter!

Many of the Indians that we met were coming down the river, and they told us that the food situation farther up the Columbia was dire. Many nations had consumed all of their winter stocks of fish and the new salmon run had yet to begin, and these people were traveling down the

Columbia for the roots and berries they could not find farther up the river. I could tell that this news greatly worried the captains, who were caught between two difficult scenarios. If we stayed down in the lower Columbia region until the salmon run began, the Nez Perce who were guarding our horses might cross over the Rockies for their spring buffalo hunt before we reached them. If we continued up, we faced a grim food situation and could be mighty hungry by the time we secured our horses and could make our way to the Three Forks area. Also, Gibson reminded me, if we waited too long we wouldn't get down the Missouri before it froze over, and we would be forced to winter with the Mandans again.

At camp that evening, Captain Lewis laid out our options and told us what he and Captain Clark proposed to do. "We shall remain here for as long as it takes to obtain a large quantity of dried elk and deer meat," he said, gesturing toward the woods to either side of the river. We were at the juncture of the Columbia and a river he had named the Quicksand River, and the hunting was good. "Once we have determined that we have a sufficient supply of dried meat, we will continue up the Columbia. I would like to purchase canoes from the natives as we move east, and then exchange those canoes for horses with those nations higher up, until we have enough horses for transportation across the mountains, and for food if need be."

There was once a time when I would have balked at the idea of eating horse, but those days were long past, having ended with the starvation we had faced crossing the Rocky Mountains the previous year. The horses and colts we had killed and eaten during those desperate days had saved our lives, and were the only certain source of food we could depend on in those high and wild mountains.

"When we get within five or six days of the Nez Perce nation, I will send five men ahead to gather our horses and have them ready for us, in order that we might make our way across the mountains as early as the snow allows. In the meantime, I will task our hunters with the vitally important job of finding as much elk and deer meat as possible in a short period of time," Lewis continued. "I want all of our hunters out at first light. I am sure you all remember our passage across the Rocky Mountains last year. We do not want to find ourselves in that situation again."

Captain Clark set out around this same time to explore a large river that entered the Columbia from the south, a river apparently called the Multnomah by the natives. This river, he reported upon his return, had been hidden from us by several islands, and we had therefore missed it both on our descent down the Columbia and on our return. If not for several local Indians telling us about it, we might never have learned of its existence. The river, according to Clark, was wide and fairly deep, and appeared to be the main river that drained the land between the low mountains near the coast and the higher inland mountains, and was peopled by numerous small nations of savages.

"A lot of those nations have been decimated by the smallpox," he reported following his return from exploring the river. "We saw several villages that had once been large and densely populated that now only have a couple dozen people, and many of the survivors have the pox scars."

Lewis nodded soberly. "The Clatsops told us the same thing," he said. "The coastal tribes must have come in contact with the disease through trading ships, and it just traveled up the rivers as they traded into the interior."

"And without vaccinations or tolerance against it, they stood no chance," Clark said. He shook his head slowly.

* * *

Several days later we camped near an Indian village we had visited on the way down. Those people were friendly toward us, though they had no food to share. They also told us about the dire food situation higher up the river, and informed us that people were starving and dying up there for lack of food.

As I walked through the village, a man came out of one of their small huts. Catching my eye, he immediately ducked back through the door, in his haste almost tripping over his own feet. Suspicious of him, I hefted my rifle and prepared myself for whatever might come. When nothing happened, I stooped down and peered in through the door of the lodge. I could see the man, huddling in the far corner, and I also saw one of our tomahawks hanging on the wall above his head like a trophy on display.

I remembered back to the previous fall when we stopped at this same village, that a tomahawk had been stolen, and the sight of it so blatantly displayed in this savage's house infuriated me. Striding into the hut, I grabbed the tomahawk off the wall.

Shouting, the man grabbed my wrist, trying to wrest the tomahawk away from me, but I wasn't having it. Thrusting my free arm across his chest, I threw him across the hut, and then leveled my rifle at his head. If he had moved toward me again I would have shot him, that's how angry I was right then, but he saved his own life by remaining where he was.

Back at our camp, I told the captains what had happened, and they turned toward the chiefs who were at their fire. A flow of words raced from their mouths, and even though I couldn't understand a word they were saying I knew denials when I heard them. Lewis kept thrusting the stolen tomahawk in their direction while Drouillard sign-talked with them, and after a while they finally admitted the obvious, that the theft had occurred.

"They tried to claim they had bought it from some other nation down below," Drouillard said, "but when I told them it had been stolen right here, they finally confessed."

"Keep an eye on everything," Lewis said sternly. "They stole from us before, they'll steal from us again." He then ordered the chiefs and their people from our camp, and they reluctantly moved away, eyes downcast in shame.

"Good work, John," Captain Clark said. "I'd reward you with an extra dram of whiskey, but..."

I grinned. "I understand, Captain. You can owe me one back in St. Louis."

"You have a deal," he said.

* * *

We continued along the Columbia, eventually reaching the narrow rapids that we had navigated with such difficulty on the way down. As the walls of the canyon were so narrow at many of these rapids, pulling our canoes up through the tumbling water was difficult at best. It involved tying a stout rope to the bow and struggling along the shore, pulling the heavy boat while slipping and falling on the wet and mossy rocks. Bruises and minor injuries were common and the fatigue was numbing, but we had no other choice.

The natives in the area of the rapids were the most insolent and unfriendly that we had met during our journey, and were also the greatest of thieves. We had to be constantly on our guard against them, and at one point they even stole Captain Lewis's dog. We managed to get the dog back, and all the other items they attempted to steal, and Captain Lewis was so incensed by the episodes that he informed their chief in no uncertain terms that he would kill the next person who stole anything belonging to us. The chief swore that his people were good and that we would have no further problems, but we stayed vigilant just the same.

As we moved up the river we could feel the air turning dry, and rain became less and less of a problem the further east we traveled. The towering pines of the lower Columbia gave way to smaller, more stunted trees, and the landscape became more desert-like. The captains spent a lot of their time attempting to purchase horses from the natives along the way but were mostly unsuccessful, as all the natives wanted far more for their horses than we were willing to pay. It looked like we were going to have to stick to the rivers until we reached the Nez Perce country.

Near the end of April, we stopped at another small fishing village we had visited in the fall. The people there were in a bad state, sitting and staring down the river as if they could will the salmon to come up. Here we had to portage our loads around another dangerous rapid and pull the canoes through with tow ropes, while the captains continued bartering for horses. Once we had the canoes secured above the rapids, we sat down to a dinner of dried elk meat. We were exhausted from pulling the canoes against the racing current.

A happy shout came from the river's edge, and we all looked to see a man running up toward the village, holding a wriggling salmon high above his head. The people in the village spilled from their huts, all laughing and talking excitedly. Drouillard walked over to the villagers and began signing with them, then walked back to where we waited.

"I think we can guess what the excitement's about," Sergeant Gass said.

"Yep, the first salmon of the season."

We looked toward the village, where all the people were gathered around the man who had brought the fish. He was cooking the fish over a fire.

"They estimate the main run should begin in about five days," Drouillard continued.

"Wonderful," Potts said, disgust in his voice. "Fish again."

We all laughed.

"They all gonna try and eat that one fish?" Windsor asked.

"Just watch," Drouillard said.

The villagers stood in a circle as the salmon cooked, and when the man took it off the fire the children of the village were brought forward. Using a sharp knife, the man cut the fish into small pieces, handing one piece to each child. By the time the children had all received a portion, the fish was gone.

"Well, how about that," Shannon said.

"See, we're not all uncivilized savages," Drouillard said.

* * *

We moved on from that place and continued east. Captain Lewis was in an increasingly bad mood and kept mostly to himself. He was angry with the local natives, who had again shown their true natures in their dealings with us and had stolen numerous small articles. Even Captain Lewis's repeated threats to beat or shoot any thief we caught didn't stop them from stealing anything they thought they could get away with, and when he actually did beat one man and threatened to kill them all and burn their village to the ground, they only hung their heads in mock shame. Tomahawks, spoons, knives, robes; they all at one time or another became the victim of some savage's sticky fingers.

"I have never felt this level of contempt for any living creature," Lewis said, staring with hatred toward a nearby cluster of huts. "I can almost wish the salmon would travel up a different river this year and pass by these putrid savages completely. Starvation would suit them right."

We had just finished rounding up the few horses we had been able to purchase, minus one. That horse had been taken from us by an Indian who said he had won the horse in a bet before the previous owner sold it to us. I was with Captain Lewis when he retrieved the items we had traded for the horse, and the original owner didn't seem the least bit repentant at his underhanded ruse.

Eventually we had enough horses that we were able to do away with some of the canoes and travel mostly by land, which raised no objections from us! Captain Lewis managed to sell two of the canoes to the natives, and when he could not sell the third he ordered it destroyed and the wood used for our fire.

"I absolutely refuse to give anything to these people," he said as he watched the canoe burn. "I'd rather destroy everything we have then allow anything to be given to them for free."

* * *

Potts and I were sent ahead the next morning with one of the two remaining small canoes for the purpose of finding fresh meat for the party, while the remainder of the Corps came up along the bank with the horses and gear. We had come about three miles when Potts, who was in the bow, lifted his oar from the water and pointed ahead. "Not a good sign, John," he said.

I looked to where he was pointing. Far ahead to the east, we could just make out the distant mountains we had crossed in the fall, and they were completely covered in snow. Heavy clouds wreathed the highest peaks, and I would have bet all the money I was due to make on that journey that more snow was falling from within those clouds.

"I don't like the looks of that," he said.

"Well, you been saying that you're sick and tired of rain," I reminded him.

He made a face and shook his head. "Not funny, John."

"Let's put ashore and see what there is around here to shoot," I suggested.

"You mean besides one of them thieving Injuns?"

We beached the canoe near some low banks and dragged it ashore, tying it securely to a stout tree. "You wanna stay here to guard the canoe or do you wanna hunt?" I asked him.

"I'll hunt," John said.

"Figured you would," I said. "Get on your way, then." I watched as he set off toward a fairly large wooded valley to the south and took a seat on the ground by the canoe. I hated the fact that I had to waste my time guarding our canoe against theft when I could be out there hunting for food instead.

The day passed slowly and around mid-afternoon Potts returned empty-handed. About that same time the rest of our party came up the shore, Lewis in the lead. His face was dark with anger.

"No luck, Captain," Potts said.

"I'm not surprised," Lewis grunted. "Even the animals want no part of these filthy savages."

I bit the inside of my cheek to keep from laughing.

Lewis looked off toward the snow-covered mountains on the horizon and breathed a deep sigh. "I'm just so weary of it all, John," he said. "I just want to get over those mountains and leave this desolate land behind."

"Before you know it, we'll be racing down the Missouri for home, Captain," I said, trying to cheer him up a little.

He nodded absently. "Yes, I suppose we will." He looked at the men coming up the trail behind him. "Let's make camp right here," he said, "and get a fresh start in the morning. Maybe I'll be in a better mood by then."

CHAPTER THIRTY-THREE

"Now this is more like it," Captain Lewis said two days later.

We had reached the main village of the Walla Walla people and had been met by their principal chief, whose name roughly translated to Yellept. Yellept had met with the captains during our journey down the Columbia and now he greeted us happily on our return. The people remembered us fondly, many having been doctored by Captain Clark, and they made us welcome in their village.

The chief spoke to his people and told them to help us in any way they could, and followed his own example by carrying several arm loads of wood to our camp. They also seemed happy to sell us horses for a far more reasonable price than their brethren below. Yellept told the captains about an Indian road that would take us across land to Clark's River, cutting more than eighty miles off our return trip, and the captains were eager to be on our way.

"You should have seen old Lewis's face when that Yellept fellow said he wouldn't provide canoes to take us across the river unless we agreed to stay for another day." Frazier slapped his knee and laughed out loud. "Thought he was gonna burst!"

We were on the north side of the Columbia, and directly across from our camp to the east we could see the mouth of the Snake River. The Walla Walla's had a Shoshone captive living among them who could speak their language, and who could translate to us through Sacagawea. It had made things a lot easier.

"Then old Yellept brought Captain Clark that big white horse and only took a sword and some powder and lead as payment. Suddenly the captains like Indians again!"

We all laughed. The captains were spending the night in Yellept's village, leaving the rest of us down on the riverbank. Cruzatte had taken out his fiddle and we were dancing and having a fun time. Some of the native men had come down to join us and were dancing right along with our men. It made a pleasant change from the suspicion and hatred shown between the Indians of the lower Columbia and our party since departing Fort Clatsop.

In the morning, we crossed the river and headed east over the grassy prairie land. By this time we had procured twenty-three horses, which carried all of our gear and instruments, and any of the men who might be feeling tired or too sore to walk. Some of the Indians traveled with us, but with these people there wasn't the constant need to guard everything we owned against thievery. In fact, on several occasions Indians found and returned knives lost by men in our party, and Yellept even sent three young men after us to return a trap they found that we had carelessly left behind two days earlier! Even Captain Lewis commented on the integrity and honesty of the Walla Wallas.

We followed a low valley alongside a pleasant stream, though there still seemed to be a surprising shortage of game. We had purchased dogs to eat along the route, and Drouillard managed to kill an otter and a beaver, but we saw no signs of deer or antelope. The natives with us didn't seem concerned, and seemed perfectly happy with their diets of fish and roots, but I wanted some real meat.

Finally, several more miles up the stream, Labiche came trotting out of a small draw to our left with a doe thrown across his shoulders, and a cheer went up from the men. At last, we would have something real and substantial to eat. Lewis stopped the party while Labiche dressed out the deer and then led us onward, and I'm sure I'm not the only one whose mouth was watering at the thought of the fresh venison tied to Labiche's horse.

At camp that night the venison was as delicious as we had anticipated it to be and we ate with gusto. The evening had come down quite cold, with a brisk wind blowing along the river, and the fires warmed our outsides while the deer meat warmed our insides. All of us hoped strongly that our days of fasting were behind us, but every time we caught a glimpse of the distant mountains covered in snow we knew we could go hungry again soon.

We entered a deep valley and followed it down to Lewis's River, an area we all recognized from our journey toward the ocean the previous fall. At Lewis's River we met up with some familiar Indians, including the chief who had traveled with us as far as the falls of the Columbia on our westward journey. Those Indians also seemed happy to see us, and again we feasted and danced well into the night. For the natives the celebration seemed to center around our return, while the members of our party were celebrating the fact that we were heading home.

The Indians belonged to the bands with whom we had left our horses in the fall, and who had promised to take care of them and have them ready for us on our return. From this place we could clearly see the mountains to the east, and, as we had already seen, they were completely covered in a thick blanket of snow. I didn't think we would need those horses right away.

George Gibson was of the same opinion. "Better find ourselves a comfortable place to camp," he said, gazing off toward the mountains with his hands on his hips. He was shaking his head slowly back and forth.

"What do you mean?" Thompson asked.

"You got eyes. Look and see. We won't be crossing those rocks any time soon."

We all looked at the snow-covered mountains. What he said made sense.

"How long, you think?" I asked.

Gibson shrugged. "Drouillard told me that the Indians hereabouts think it'll be well into June before we can make the crossing."

Shannon let out a low whistle. "June? We'll never get down the Missouri before the ice sets in."

"That's what Lewis is saying. He's really itching to get across to the Three Forks area."

Something in Gibson's voice caught my attention. "How badly is he itching, George?"

Gibson shrugged again. "Who can say? Maybe enough to try those mountains with the snow still thick on the ground."

We stood in silence for a while, contemplating what he had said. We remembered our journey westward through those mountains the previous fall, and we knew that the crossing would be a hundred times more dangerous with heavy snow obscuring the path. The horses wouldn't be able to find footing, and we wouldn't be able to see where the path ended and a cliff began. Crossing now would be suicidal.

"Lewis ain't crazy enough to try it, is he?" Shannon asked, not sounding as if he believed his own words.

We all shrugged.

"I did hear one funny story," Joe Field said.

"I like funny stories," I said.

"You all remember old Toby, our guide from last year. You also remember how we kept him along with us long past the time we needed him and he finally got fed up and lit out without getting paid."

"Couldn't blame him," Thompson said.

"Yeah, me neither," Field replied. "Anyway, it seems he got paid after all. On his way back through here, he took two of Lewis's best horses with him."

We all laughed. That was the kind of nerve we all admired.

* * *

"You know where we're at, don't you, John?" Captain Clark asked, smiling widely.

I looked around and spotted the creek that fell into the river. "Yeah, I guess I do."

That evening we made camp near the mouth of the creek the captains had named Colter's Creek back in the fall, and of course my friends had to have some fun at my expense.

"Ghastly," Windsor said, taking a drink from the water of Colter's Creek and grimacing. "Tastes kinda like antelope piss."

"You drink a lot of antelope piss, Pete?" I asked.

"Not if I can help it." He took another drink. "Yep, definitely tastes like piss. All the way across the continent and the only creek that tastes like piss is named after Colter. Coincidence?"

"Maybe that's why all the Injuns around here have that pinched-up expression on their faces," Shannon said.

"You mean because the creek tastes like antelope piss or because it's named after this reprobate?"

"Maybe both," Shannon said. He knelt down and took a sip of water from Colter's Creek and swished it around in his mouth for a moment. "Nope, you're wrong, Pete."

"Wrong?"

"Yeah. Ain't antelope piss. Tastes more like badger to me."

I shook my head. "You're all a bunch of idiots, you know that?"

"Don't mind him, Pete," Shannon said. "He's just mad 'cause his creek tastes like badger piss."

I gave up.

* * *

Several more days travel brought us up to the village of Twisted Hair, the Indian chief who had traveled with us for a while in the fall, and to whom we had given the ultimate care of our horses. His reception of us was cool, to say the least, and he immediately got into a heated argument with the other two Nez Perce chiefs that had come up with us. Cut Nose and Broken Arm were their names, and we all stood to one side watching as the three Indians shouted and gestured at each other. Our interpreter, a young man of the Nez Perce nation, refused to speak a word, telling us that it was not his place to become involved in a dispute between chiefs. I could see Captain Lewis getting madder and madder, his face going red, and I was glad to see Drouillard come back from his morning hunting excursion. Now we might get somewhere.

Utilizing Drouillard's hand-talking skills, Lewis managed to bring the three chiefs together at our camp. Lewis was anxious to learn the state of the horses, as we had been told by several Indians that they were scattered all across the wide plain. We were also concerned about the saddles that had been cached near here. Rumor had come to us that the saddles had been discovered and stolen.

"We need to know where our horses are," Lewis said to Drouillard. "I don't know why these chiefs are angry with each other, but find out if you can."

Drouillard nodded and began signing with the chiefs. After a while he turned to Captain Lewis. "According to Twisted Hair, when these other two came back from their war excursion last fall, they got mad at him for taking command of our horses. I guess they're above him in rank, somehow, and they felt like he was shouldering in on their authority."

"So where are the horses?" Lewis demanded.

"Scattered across this area, according to Twisted Hair, though most are said to be close by," Drouillard replied. He paused. "That other chief, Cut Nose, tells a different tale. He says Twisted Hair has two faces, and he has allowed his young men to ride our horses for hunting and that he has not taken care of them."

Lewis shook his head in exasperation. "Damn politics! And what of our saddles?"

"He has said that they were found during a flood last year and he has moved them to a place of safety. Some may have been lost to the flood but he isn't sure."

"We'll see about that," Lewis said sourly.

"Twisted Hair has said if we travel to his lodge, he will gather the horses that are in his area, and then we can continue up to Broken Arm's lodge while he sends men out to gather all the rest," Drouillard continued.

"Is that your recommendation?" Lewis asked.

Drouillard appeared surprised by the question. "Yes, sir."

"Then that is what we shall do. Tell them, George."

Drouillard passed along the information and the chiefs seemed satisfied with it.

* * *

The following day we went to Twisted Hair's lodge and camped nearby. Alexander Willard went with Twisted Hair to retrieve the saddles and some powder that had been cached in the fall, and they returned to camp late in the evening with only about half of the original number of saddles. One of those missing belonged to Captain Lewis, and we could see his temper starting to rise.

In spite of his words stating that these people were among the finest natives on the continent, I could still see that he held them in low esteem, as he seemed to do with all native people. He was quick to lose his temper with them, and he seemed to believe they should all do his bidding at all times, even though we were not in the land newly purchased and controlled by the United States. Drouillard and I had held long conversations while we were hunting about the native people's viewpoint on our journey and the speeches given by Captain Lewis, and he had made me look at our journey in a different light.

"Think about it, John," he'd said one cool afternoon. "You're living your life as you have for generations, on land your ancestors lived on and are buried under, and then suddenly these crazy white men appear one day and tell you that they own the land now and you have to do what they say. That there's a new Great Father way back east who rules you, now, and you are one of his children and must obey him. What would you think about that?"

"I'd think they were out of their minds."

"That's right. And these Indians think Lewis is out of his mind."

I grinned. "Maybe they're right."

"I'll tell you, John, I've seen the arguments among these people and some of the guarded looks they give us, and I'll bet everything I have that they still aren't sure if they should just kill us and get it over with."

Now, there was a pleasant thought, considering that we were drastically outnumbered. My mind kept returning to that throughout the day, mulling on it.

In the afternoon, several men from Twisted Hair's village brought in a large number of our horses, and it was obvious they had been ridden hard and not cared for all that well. Several had sores on their backs from the rough Indian saddles. Lewis wasn't pleased with their condition but he held his temper.

We stayed several days with those Indians, and Captain Clark spent most of his time doctoring to them. Many of them had sore eyes and other complaints, and Clark did the best he could for them from our limited stock of medical supplies. In many cases, his doctoring brought much-needed food and supplies from the natives, who had no other way to pay him for his services. And these people really needed all the help they could get, not having the benefit of medicines or medical knowledge. I felt sorry for them.

Around the middle of May we moved our camp several miles up the river, to an ancient fort apparently constructed by Indians. It was a circular wall of earth about four feet high and maybe thirty feet in diameter, and it was situated close enough to the river to make it easy to obtain water. A level plain extended away from the fort, with plenty of forage for the horses, and we settled in. From the fort we had a clear view of the mountains to the east, mountains still thickly enveloped in snow, and Lewis said he planned to stay in this location until that snow had melted back enough for us to venture east.

Before it was all said and done, we would be at that fort for an entire month!

CHAPTER THIRTY-FOUR

Our biggest concern while camped at the old Indian fort was food.

Every day, teams of hunters went out in all directions, and on most days they came home empty-handed. Captain Clark had ordered us to only hunt in pairs due to the surprisingly large numbers of the white, or grizzly, bear that lived in that region, but even bear meat was hard to come by. Our principal food source was the camas and other roots that had made us so sick in the past, and horse meat when we could purchase a horse from the natives to kill.

We had hopes that the annual salmon run would eventually reach us, and one of our hunters reported that he had witnessed an eagle plucking a salmon from a stream. Deer tracks were sometimes spotted in the hills above us but only rarely did we have venison. It was a situation we had all lived through before but not one which we enjoyed.

Shannon and I shot a deer and a bear late one afternoon but the coming of night made pursuit impossible, and by the time the sun rose again falling snow had covered the trail, so more meat was lost. That snow was quite worrisome to us, for if it was snowing down where we were, that meant it was most assuredly still snowing in the higher elevations above. The level of the river was rising regularly, however, which Captain Lewis contributed to snow melting in the mountains, and I hoped he was right. We needed to get across those mountains to where there was food!

While we were camped in the old fort, Sacagawea's baby got sick, and the captains doctored it as best they could. That child had journeyed thousands of miles on his mother's back and was a source of wonder and joy for all of us, and we worried about him. Eventually he did recover, but whether from the captains doctoring or his own volition we'll never know.

Near the end of May one of the local chiefs that the captains called Hohâstillpilp told us that the large horse herds that ran free around the camp all belonged to him, and we should feel free to kill any of them that we felt we had to in order to survive. It was a grand gesture that sent Captain Lewis into a state approaching rapture.

"Can you believe that?" he asked, a wide grin filling his face.

"It is pretty astonishing," Captain Clark confirmed.

"Astonishing? That doesn't begin to describe what he has done, William! Think about it! We have been given free rein to kill as many of his horses as we need. Name one person in our civilization who would make an offer like that. There are none! Our own neighbors among the exalted gentry of Virginia would allow us to starve before they would give us a freedom like that!"

"We must use that license sparingly," Clark warned, and Lewis nodded.

"You're right, of course," he said. "We mustn't be greedy, or take advantage of his hospitality. But just think of it, William! It is truly, well, astonishing!"

* * *

More time went by, and the snow continued to cling stubbornly to the high mountains, almost mocking us as we sat and waited for it to melt. The hunting remained sparse, and we all grew used to the constant pang of hunger. On the positive side, we did manage to find and reclaim a stolen tomahawk that had vanished when we were passing through the area in the fall. It was a tomahawk that had belonged to poor Sergeant Floyd, and just seeing it again sent a wave of melancholy through the camp along with joy at having it back.

* * *

"'Bout time our luck started to change," Willard said.

I looked up from dressing the deer I had shot to see Joe Field come into the clearing, another dead doe across his shoulders. That made five deer we could take back to the camp, along with a black bear Willard had shot further down the valley.

"Now, I ain't saying I got anything against horse meat," Willard continued. His hands were red with blood as he butchered his latest deer. "I just prefer venison."

We'd had this conversation before, and we all knew Willard's dislike for eating horses. "There's just something not right about it," he would say, pounding his fist against a leg. "Horse's ain't game animals."

"Better than dog," I said now, as Joe dropped his doe on the ground of the clearing and set to work butchering it.

"Anything's better than eating dog," Joe said. He looked off toward the mountains. "You'll be damn glad to have horse meat once we get in those mountains," he continued, casting a glance toward Willard and grinning.

Willard grimaced but didn't say anything.

We finished dressing the deer and loaded the meat onto the horses we had brought up with us. It would take us about three hours to get down to the camp, and we didn't expect to get there before dark.

"Gonna rain again tonight," Field said, looking up at the overcast sky.

"Better than snow," I ventured.

"Yeah, you're right there."

"Old Lewis wasn't too happy with the news that Indian brought in."

"Can you blame him?" Willard said.

The day before, a young Indian man had met up with some of our hunters and had told them how he had attempted to cross the mountains to the east and had been forced to turn back by the heavy snows and treacherous conditions.

Joe cinched the last strap over his load of venison and nodded down the mountain. "You gents ready to head down?"

I nodded and we set out for the camp.

* * *

On June 10 we left the camp in the old Indian fort and set out for the mountains. Captain Lewis planned to camp near the area where we had met up with the Indians coming out of the mountains in the fall, in order to secure guides and to dry some more venison. After that, it was into the mountains.

Our journey east through the mountains wasn't expected to be as much of a trial as our trip west had been, mainly due to our knowledge of what we were getting into which allowed us to better prepare. We had plenty of horses, and we had labored all through the previous month to dry meat and gather roots and berries. Our biggest concern was forage for the horses, as we would at one point pass over a high ridge with no grass or food for them to eat.

But in spite of our concerns we were all excited to be on our way, and nobody advised caution. A month of sitting on that prairie and staring at the mountains had made us all even more eager to defeat them, and there was nothing that would stop us. So we thought.

Before we had moved very far out of the low foothills, we were encountering snow that still lay in the low and shadowed areas. Some of those patches of snow were from two to three feet deep in places. Captain Lewis also pointed out that the huckleberry, honeysuckle and white maple were just beginning to break forth their blooms, while down in the valley those same plants had bloomed weeks earlier. Captain Lewis voiced his concerns about what that boded for the mountains above but he didn't elect to turn back. None of us wanted to turn back.

A little further into the mountains the snow lay heavier and deeper across the track and we all glanced at each other a trifle uneasily. We were still technically in the foothills, with the mountains looming high above us, and seeing those eight and ten foot deep drifts didn't gladden our hearts any. We reached a small meadow near where we had killed the wild horse in the fall, and though there wasn't a lot of grass showing above the snow for our horses to graze on, we stopped for the night. Grazing possibilities would be fewer and farther between the deeper into the mountains we moved, so we had to take an opportunity when we had it in front of us, meager as it might be. The creek we had previously named Hungry Creek ran past the small meadow, its waters clear and ice cold, and with the ease born of long practice we set up camp.

William Bratton sat by me at our fire that evening.

"You're looking a lot better, Will," I said. He had fallen ill at Fort Clatsop with terrible pains in his back and legs, and had been in an almost crippled state for a long time. Only recently had he been able to walk for any distance.

"I'm feeling a lot better," he said.

"You think it was those sweats that helped you?" Reubin Field asked him. Captain Clark had treated Bratton with long sessions in a sweat lodge during our stay with the Nez Perce, and he was convinced it was the sweats that had helped Bratton regain his faculties.

Bratton shrugged. "I really don't know," he said. "I guess it could have done. Captain Clark sure thinks so."

"I've seen stranger things," Silas Goodrich commented.

"Yeah, every time you look in a mirror," I said.

Silas grinned while the other men around the fire laughed.

"Think we'll make it through them mountains?" Bratton asked.

"I know I'm not staying on this side of 'em," Field commented. "I got me a sweet young lady friend back east waiting for me. I'm going across those mountains if'n I have to tie myself to one of them mountain goats and ride it across."

John Thompson laughed. "Your lady friend is probably married to some other fella," he teased. "Remember, we were supposed to be back in St. Louis over a year ago. They probably think we're all dead by now."

"You think so?" Nate Pryor asked, and it wasn't hard to guess that he was thinking about the young wife he had left behind.

"Maybe. Don't forget, they all told us we would never make it. They're probably all back there congratulating themselves on being right."

"Well, I hope you're wrong about that," I said. Nate was staring into the fire, and I tried to cheer him up. "And if they do think we're all dead, then just imagine how much sweeter the homecoming will be!"

"There is that," Silas said, nodding.

We sat in silence for a while, looking into the crackling flames, and then Reubin spoke again. "I know one thing for dead certain," he said.

"What's that?" I asked.

"The first thing I'm gonna do when I get to St. Louis is find a bottle of whiskey and drink away the memory of Indians, prickly pear, mountains, canoes, dried salmon and you ugly sons-a-bitches!"

"Amen!" Silas said heartily.

* * *

Our determination to get across the mountains was strongly tested the next day, however, when we ran into snow even deeper than before. In some places the trail was invisible under as much as fifteen feet of snow, and for the first time since leaving the Wood River camp in 1804 we admitted defeat and fell back.

"I think to continue on at this stage would be futile and dangerous," Captain Lewis told us, staring ahead at a world of white. The wind was blowing the snow across the trail, and drifts higher than our heads filled the low valleys. "The possibility of losing our way in these mountains is too great, and if we lose our way we will most likely lose our lives. That is the worst scenario. We might also survive but lose our horses to falls or lack of forage, and if we lose our horses we lose all the information and knowledge we have gathered since departing Fort Mandan a year ago."

"What do you suggest, Captain Lewis?" Sergeant Gass asked.

"Much as it pains me, I suggest we fall back to the valley and secure the services of an Indian guide." Lewis spoke plainly, without emotion, but I could see the disappointment in his eyes. "That is the only sure way to get through the mountains with the least danger and risk. If we wait for all this snow to melt and proceed by ourselves, we will not make it home by the time the Missouri freezes, and we will be forced to spend another winter in the Mandan country. And I know none of us want that."

So we turned back and headed down the mountain, and it was the first time on this entire journey that we did turn back! None of us liked it but we also knew the captain was right. The majority of our gear we placed on high scaffolds that we constructed, deciding it was safer to do that than to carry it back down with us, and it's a good thing we did. The traveling down the mountain was treacherous, as I was to learn rather quickly, and rather painfully.

The first indication of trouble came when I felt the horse's legs begin to slide out from under us. The horse let out a snort and then whinnied in fear, and then, in an instant, we were off the trail and tumbling down into a deep ravine. Sky and ground flashed past my vision in a revolving pattern, and I bounced off the hard ground, flew through the air, and then bounced again. Rocks and sticks fell with me, striking me, and at one point I landed on top of the horse before flying off into the air again. Fortunately the horse never landed on me or that might have been the end of old John Colter! When I finally reached the bottom of the ravine, landing with a splash in Hungry Creek, pain was flaring up and down my body and I felt sure I had broken several bones.

Gingerly, I sat up, trying to feel every part of my body at once. Blood trickled down into my right eye from a cut on my forehead, and my jacket and trousers were both torn in several places, but to my astonishment nothing seemed to be broken. I was sore, there's no doubt about that, but I seemed to have escaped serious injury. Next I looked around for my horse, sure he was badly injured or dead, but he was standing about ten feet further along the creek, watching me placidly. He had several cuts on his side but none appeared life-threatening. I was more than surprised.

"You all right down there?" Captain Clark called, his voice echoing in the canyon.

"Yeah, seems so," I yelled back up.

I stood up slowly, still positive I must have some kind of injury, and went to collect my horse. My rifle was still strapped to the horse's side and appeared undamaged, but my blanket was missing. I looked around but didn't see it, and I cursed roundly. I was really going to miss that blanket, I felt sure. Probably five miles down the river by then, and heading for the ocean!

It took me a while to get back up to the trail, and I had to travel about a mile down the center of the river to find a place to do so. When I reached the main party, Captain Clark shook my hand warmly. "Damn glad to see you, Mr. Colter," he said. "Thought we'd lost you there for a minute."

"No such luck," Nate said good-naturedly.

I ignored him. "Thought I was a goner, too, sir," I said.

"You're not hurt?"

"I'm sure I'll have a few bruises but nothing seems to be broken."

"Good! Now let's get down this mountain before anyone else takes a tumble!"

* * *

Drouillard and Shannon were sent ahead of the main party to locate a guide or guides who would lead us across the mountains, and Lewis sent a rifle with them to be given as partial payment for the guides' services.

"Tell them they'll get two more rifles and ten horses once we clear the mountains," Lewis instructed.

"Yes, sir," Shannon replied, and they were off.

The rest of us set up a camp on a level plain, with plenty of grass for the horses, and prepared to wait. Hunters were sent out, and I was one of several men assigned to fish in the nearby stream. We were fully committed to staying in this place until either an Indian guide came up or the snows melted enough for us to continue on by ourselves, but again fortune was against us. The hunting in that location was so poor that within two days we had exhausted our provisions and were packing up camp again and heading down to the low valley floor.

We were barely out of the mountains when we met up with two Indian men. They told us that they had seen Drouillard and Shannon and had been hired on as guides, but for some reason those two had not returned with these Indians. The Indians agreed to guide us across the mountains, and told us they would wait with us for Drouillard and Shannon to return.

Returning to the prairie was a wise choice as far as the hunting was concerned, and within a day we had killed eight deer and three bears. We also learned that the salmon run had reached the rivers in the area and Joseph Whitehouse was sent to the river near Collins Creek to bring back some of those fish. We could now begin to build up our food stores once again for the trip across the mountains.

Drouillard and Shannon returned several days later with three Indians who had been secured to act as our guides. One of those was the brother of Cut Nose, and the other two were well-liked young men who had each presented the captains with a gift of horses while we were at Broken Arm's lodge earlier in the spring. Captain Lewis was especially happy to see those two men, as he liked them very much and considered them to be men of great character and honesty.

Now we could set out once again for home.

* * *

"Now that's a fine sight," Collins said, smiling and nodding his head.

We were all staring in undisguised awe as a tall pine tree burned in front of us, its branches crackling and throwing off a huge amount of sparks. The flames roared up the tree, engulfing it quite rapidly, and the bright sparks swirled out into the darkness.

"Impressive," Shannon said.

"Hey, George, what's with the fireworks?" Hugh McNeal called out.

Drouillard walked to where we stood, his eyes riveted to the sight of the burning pine. "The natives around here have a tradition of burning a tree before they set off across the mountains. They say it will bring good weather."

"And how's that work, exactly?" I asked.

"How the hell would I know?" George grinned. "I'm Shawnee, not Nez Perce."

* * *

The next day we set out once again.

CHAPTER THIRTY-FIVE

Having the Indians to act as guides helped all of us feel a little better about crossing the mountains, and I have to say those Indians knew what they were about. They led us along the same route we had followed earlier in the month, and we were all happy to see that a significant amount of snow had melted in the meantime. We passed the spot where I had taken my tumble, and retrieved our gear from the scaffolds we had built, and later that evening we came to a clearing exactly where the guides had said it would be. New green grass was growing in an area on the south side of a tall hill, providing food for the horses, and the general atmosphere among the men was one of great cheer. Now we finally felt like we were on our way home.

The following day we stopped at a place important to the Indians, where a cone-shaped pile of rocks had been built. A large pole made of pine sat atop the mound, and the Indians gathered around it, smoking a pipe and casting the smoke to the winds. From this place we could see countless miles in all directions and every where we looked we saw nothing except magnificent and daunting snow-covered mountains. The valleys between those mountains appeared as an impenetrable maze, and we all realized how valuable our guides would be to us. I can not imagine that we would have been successful if we had continued without them.

We headed east from the monument, if that was what it was, and down a steep ravine, crossing a fast-moving stream at the bottom. The guides didn't hesitate at any of the branching trails and canyons and we followed where they led. We traveled up rocky hills, down along swollen creeks, across low valleys and trails deep with snow, and that evening camped in a clearing very similar to the one we had stayed in the night before. Here again was grass for the horses to graze on, and we passed a fairly pleasant evening.

"You feeling any better, Captain Clark?" I asked at the fire that night.

He nodded. "My head doesn't hurt nearly as badly as yesterday," he said.

"That's good. You were in quite a lot of pain."

"That I was. I can live a long time without feeling pain like that again and it wouldn't bother me in the least."

"What's the outlook for tomorrow's travel?" Potts asked. He was also getting over an injury, having cut his leg quite badly on the same day I took my tumble down into Hungry Creek.

"The guides tell us we'll be walking on top of snow, mostly."

"I gotta say, I do get a bit nervous walking on top of ten feet of snow," Weiser commented.

Clark nodded in understanding. "I know how you're feeling. But just think about all the rocks and branches and downed trees lying buried under that snow. I daresay our travel is easier going over the snow than having to fight our way through what's under it."

Potts nodded. "That's true."

"We won't get as far tomorrow as we did today," Clark continued. "The guides say we'll reach a fine field of grass about midday and then after that it will be a long ways before we come across any more food for the horses. So we'll camp in that field, let the horses get in some good graze, and then head out early the next morning."

"As long as we're heading home, that's fine with me," Collins said.

"We are heading home," Captain Clark confirmed.

* * *

Two days found us descending a long switch-back trail to a wide and low prairie, which was also the location of some hot springs we had passed in the fall. The last of the snow had been seemingly left behind earlier that morning, and we walked through meadows green with fresh grass and budding trees. We set up a camp near the hot springs, turning the horses loose to enjoy the tall thick grass. As far as the humans were concerned, we took our leisure in the hot springs, lowering our sore and battered bodies into the blissfully hot water. The Indian guides also took advantage of the springs to soak away the memories of the icy journey, though they interspersed their bathing with repeated trips to a nearby stream. There they would dive into the frigid water before returning to the hot springs to soak some more, then repeat the process once again. None of our men attempted to mimic their actions!

On the 30th of June we reached the campsite we called Traveler's Rest and the captains decided to stop there for several days, in order to fully rest the horses and allow us time to hunt and gather meat. All of us were quite relieved to have made it through the mountains a second time, and we spent a lot of energy celebrating and congratulating ourselves on being an exceptional species of men! Not one of us will ever forget the hunger or cold we suffered in those mountains if we live to be a hundred, but we survived.

* * *

"All right, men, here is what will happen next."

We were all gathered around our large fire at Traveler's Rest and Captain Lewis was speaking. The day had started out cool but was warming up nicely, and we were enjoying the brief respite from traveling. Our hunters had killed an amazing twelve fat healthy deer that morning, and we had full stomachs and were thrilled to be back in this land of plenty.

"I plan to travel from this place with a small party and take the most direct route that I can to the great falls of the Missouri. I will take Hugh McNeal, Silas Goodrich and John Thompson with me, and those three men will remain at the falls with the assigned task of preparing wheels and carts to portage the canoes and gear. I will also take several other men to travel with me up the Marias River to explore that country and determine, if we can, whether any extension of it lay above the 50th parallel. Do I have any volunteers to join me?"

Just about every hand went up and he smiled in satisfaction. After a moment of thought, he selected Sergeant Gass, Drouillard, the Field brothers, Werner and Frazier.

"The remainder of you will accompany Captain Clark to the Three Forks to retrieve the gear we cached there in the fall. At that place we will split the party again, and nine men with Sergeant Ordway will descend the Missouri River, gather up the men at the falls, portage around the falls, and rendezvous with me at the mouth of the Marias. The rest of the party, to include York, Charbonneau and Sacagawea, will travel with Captain Clark across land to the Yellowstone River, descend that river, and meet us at the juncture of the Yellowstone and Missouri. Finally, Sergeant Pryor with two men accompanying him will travel by land to the Mandan villages then on to the Assiniboine lands to carry a message to Hugh Heney of the Northwest Company to ask the leaders of the Sioux to meet us at the river. I would like to invite them to send a delegation to travel to Washington to meet Mr. Jefferson.

"I know this is a tall order and that there is a risk in splitting our party, but I want to gather as much information for President Jefferson as I can during this return voyage. I will ask that you all remain as vigilant as you possibly can during the time we're apart, because I do want every one of you to arrive safely in St. Louis.

"Are there any questions?"

There weren't, and we immediately set about preparing to split our parties. Over the course of the next day we divided our powder and lead, made certain our weapons were in good order, and handed out dried meat and roots to all the men to sustain them when hunting was meager. Then, on the morning of July 3rd, we bid our good friends farewell and went off in our opposite directions. We didn't know if we would see each other again, the dangers being what they were on those wild and open plains, but with everything else we had been through we didn't imagine that we could fail.

* * *

For the next five days those of us in Captain Clark's party traveled south and east, crossing numerous streams both small and large as we journeyed. Some of those streams were so rapid and deep that we had to travel up them several miles to find a place to ford, and even then the water would often wash across the horse's backs, wetting our gear. A lot of precious time was spent drying our clothing and tools before starting out again, and the process would often repeat itself at the next river crossing we came to.

The low country was alive with flowers and grasses, and the horses had all they could eat. The sun was warm on our faces and the hunting was good, and nobody went hungry any more. Charbonneau's squaw told Captain Clark that she knew the area through which we traveled from her time living there with her people and she gave a detailed description of the route we needed to follow to reach the place where we had stashed our canoes. The captain wisely accepted her advice and directions and soon we were passing through a gap in the mountains that led us down to a wide and beautiful plain. Snow-capped mountains lined the horizon, just as she had said there would be. She also said that this wide plain was where her Shoshone people often gathered roots to supplement their meager meals.

We crossed that wide valley over the course of the next day and passed over another ridge before dropping down to the headwaters of the Jefferson River. Sacagawea had led us right to where we needed to be, and she basked in Captain Clark's effusive thanks and appreciation. I had watched the Indian woman change during her time with us, becoming more than just a squaw who stayed in the background and did as she was told. On several occasions, as she became used to us, she had voiced strong opinions, and I secretly enjoyed watching her exercise her will.

We followed the Jefferson River up to the place where we had camped the previous September, and where we had sunk our canoes and cached some of our gear and provisions. And one of the provisions we had stashed there was our tobacco! I swear I could almost smell it as we came up that winding creek! We had no sooner set up camp than Clark, with a knowing grin, ordered us to dig up the cache, and we set to the task with gusto. The only way we would have dug that cache up any faster would have been if there was whiskey in it.

"Now I'm beginning to feel like a civilized man again," Potts said, eyes closed as he enjoyed his tobacco.

"You said it," Collins agreed.

I glanced over at the canoes resting on the shore. There was surprisingly little damage to them for having spent several months submerged under streams that had surely frozen over during the intense cold of winter. "I wonder who's heading down the Missouri and who's heading for the Yellowstone."

"I guess we'll find out soon enough," Shields said.

* * *

The next day we traveled down toward the Three Forks, some of us on land and the rest in the canoes. This land was much as I had remembered it, and the beaver and otters filled the streams as thickly as they had in the fall. We traveled past the rock outcropping that the Shoshone called Beaver's Head and eventually arrived at the Three Forks. Camp was established and hunters went out, returning with a feast of deer and beaver.

That night, Captain Clark split up our party once again and assigned the men who would be traveling down the Missouri with the canoes. To my disappointment, which I kept well hidden, I was one of those so chosen. I would have much preferred to travel over to the Yellowstone and see that land instead. In my mind I was already figuring out a way to get back up to this country to trap once this journey was complete, and knowledge of the Yellowstone might have been invaluable to my plans. The choice, however, wasn't mine to make, and so I climbed into the canoe to which I was assigned and we set out.

* * *

With Sergeant Ordway in charge, we slipped into the current of the Missouri River and headed downstream. For the first time in almost a year we were back on that much-hated yet much-loved Missouri, the river that had caused us so much grief the previous year but which had also ingrained itself so strongly into our hearts and souls that it seemed like it would always be a part of us. In later years, after my adventuring days were over, I would build my house close to the Missouri River, seemingly unable to exist very far from its steady flow and current. Hardly a day would go by that I wouldn't walk down to the banks to watch that river pass, knowing full well what that water had seen on its journey down, and I would stare upstream and imagine in my mind this wild and lovely and vibrant country.

Our journey down the Missouri, though not idyllic, was a far cry from the struggle we had endured fighting our way upstream against its current in the fall. The hunting was easy along the banks, and the wind, though fierce at times, stayed mostly at our backs, pushing us along. Our old friend, the mosquito, was waiting for us in the low canyons, but all in all it was a pleasing and relaxing journey.

On the 19th of July we swept around a bend in the river and came down upon White Bear Island, the island that had been our camp at the top of that terrible portage the year before. Sergeant Gass was there, with Frazier, Goodrich, Werner, Thompson and McNeal, and we had a happy and boisterous reunion with them. We were relieved to see them healthy and well, and they said the same about us, telling us of their constant worry that we might be injured or dead. We reassured them that Clark and his party had also been well and fine when we parted, then we settled down around a fire to enjoy a dinner of buffalo and venison.

"Where's Captain Lewis?" Ordway asked.

"He took the Field brothers and Drouillard and headed up the Marias River a few days back," Gass said.

"Left you here to portage, did he?"

Gass laughed. "Yeah, I guess I'm being punished for something. We dug up last year's cache and found it mostly okay. Some things got wet but the wheels we made for the carts are fine."

Ordway grimaced. "You mean we can't just fill these canoes with our gear, cross our fingers, and push them over the falls?"

"It won't be as bad this time. We did some exploring and found a fairly smooth road, plus we have horses now to pull the carts for us."

Ordway didn't seem convinced.

"Hey, McNeal, tell 'em your bear story," Gass called out.

"It's quite a story," McNeal said, shaking his head, "and I wish it woulda happened to someone else! I was on horseback, riding through some willows down near the river, and never even saw the bear until the horse reared back and threw me. I landed right under the bear, and fellas, I was sure I was a goner! That old bear rose up on his back legs and let loose with a roar that shook the trees, and he had his claws out, ready to rip me to shreds. I was too close to him to shoot him, so I did the first thing that came to my mind and hit him across the head as hard as I could with my rifle. The breech broke right off the gun and that old bear just looked at me like he didn't know what had happened. He started pawing at his head where the guard had cut him and I shinnied my ass right up the nearest tree I could find! That damn old bear kept me up there for three hours before he finally got bored and went away."

We all laughed and congratulated him on his near escape, and I'm sure I'm not the only one who remembered other run-ins with those massive grizzly bears. Those animals truly seemed to hate us.

We rested most of the following day, though we did take the time to attach the tongues to the wagons and work out a way to attach the horses to them. The mosquitoes and flies were a horror, far worse than they had been the previous fall, and they just about drove us out of our minds with their stinging and biting, but all in all we were content.

* * *

We completed the portage in far less time than we had on our trip to the west and gathered together below the falls. It had rained almost every day during the portage and the ground was muddy and cold, but we were so happy to be finished with that task that the weather didn't bother us. The white pirogue, which we had stashed below the falls, was in quite good condition, needing only minor repairs, and we had her ready to go very quickly.

We loaded all of our gear and about a hundred pounds of buffalo meat into the white pirogue and the canoes and set off down the river. Our next goal was to rendezvous with Captain Lewis's party at the mouth of the

Marias River and then continue on to the mouth of the Yellowstone. All of us hoped for an easy journey to where we would be reunited with Captain Clark's party. By this time we were certain we could get to St. Louis before winter and we dug our oars into the water with a new conviction.

CHAPTER THIRTY-SIX

We were a ways above the mouth of the Marias when Captain Lewis and the three men with him suddenly arrived, riding down a steep slope next to the river on lathered and panting horses. Their haste was obvious and we immediately knew that something had happened.

"Met up with some of the Blackfeet," Lewis said as we hastily loaded the boats. "They tried to steal our guns and horses, and we killed one of them. I might have killed a second one, or he might just be injured. Either way, I expect that a war party is on the way to avenge their loss."

Those words encouraged us to work even more quickly and we had Lewis's gear stowed away in record time. The horses were turned loose on the river's bank and the saddles thrown into the water, and then we shoved off from shore to head down to the mouth of the Marias to meet Gass and Willard. By some strange twist of perfect timing, we met with the men, who had ridden down from the falls with the two horses and had just arrived. Quickly apprising them of our situation, we loaded their gear on board the white pirogue.

The red pirogue, which had been left at the mouth of the Marias, was in very bad shape and we decided not to attempt to repair her, especially if a war party of Blackfeet might be descending on us! One cache in that area had also caved in, destroying several items including two large bear skins belonging to Captain Lewis and some other furs and baggage.

"No time to worry about it now, lads," Lewis said. "Let us be gone from this place."

We pressed on, not wanting to waste any time. We passed through the area of high white cliffs that we had marveled at on the way up, and raced on. Thunderstorms and hail assaulted us at several locations, making us miserable in our damp clothes, but there wasn't anything we could do about it so we ignored it as best we could. We were keeping a sharp eye on the banks beside and behind us, but so far we didn't see any sign of pursuit.

"We may have gotten clean away," Captain Lewis said several days later. The river behind us was devoid of life, a welcome sight indeed. In later years the Blackfeet Indians would cause me much grief and trouble, but this time we had escaped from them without injury.

* * *

We hurried down the Missouri for several days after that, and they were wet and miserable days. Rain fell constantly, soaking everything. Just below the mouth of the Musselshell River, we came upon an old Indian camp at which several lodges were still standing and Captain Lewis called a halt, wanting to dry some of our baggage. He had several skins of the Bighorn Sheep that were beginning to rot in the wet weather, and as it is impossible to find those animals in the area we would be passing through, he was determined not to allow them to be ruined.

"I think those Blackfeet are far enough behind us now," he said. "Stopping for a day or so will not hurt us."

While several of the men built small fires in the huts in order to dry the goods, I went hunting, and if I had needed any reminder that we were back in the land of plenty, that hunt told the tale. Within a short walk from the camp I had killed three deer and a beaver, and Sergeant Gass came in with another deer. We also shot and killed a bear that had come right up to the camp as if to investigate what type of strange creatures we might be.

We passed the rest of the afternoon repacking our now-dried goods and loading the boats. Captain Lewis wanted to get an early start the next morning as we were now slightly behind schedule for our rendezvous with Captain Clark at the mouth of the Yellowstone.

"He'll wait for us," Captain Lewis said. "If he doesn't see a note from me, he'll know we haven't passed by yet."

"I'm hoping they're all doing well," Sergeant Ordway said. "That's a mighty big country out there."

Lewis nodded confidently. "I am sure they are fine. There is no better man alive than Mr. Clark. He'll lead them all down safe."

And the funny thing is we all felt the same way.

* * *

"This looks like a good place," Collins said.

Captain Lewis had sent John and me out to hunt that morning and we had paddled down the Missouri to this low land of willows and cottonwoods. If there weren't deer in those trees I would have been amazingly surprised.

Pulling the canoe up on to the bank, we checked our rifles and headed into the woods. The morning air was cool and, for the moment, clear. Dark clouds were on the horizon, and we could hear faint thunder in the distance, but where we were the sun was shining.

"Keep an eye out for them damn white bears," Collins said as we walked.

"You don't like those bears, John?" I asked.

He laughed shortly. "I still can't believe how an animal that big can hide so quiet in the woods and then run as fast as they do. It's a wonder to me."

"Drouillard says they're spirit animals." I'm not sure why I said that, it just popped into my mind.

"That crazy half-breed might be right," he said, his eyes constantly moving as we passed into a small clearing. Deer signs were everywhere, along with elk and buffalo. An eagle floated by above our heads, too high to shoot at, and I wondered what he could see from up there. Hunting would be a hell of a lot easier if I could fly!

"Something has to explain their power," Collins continued. "Those bears just aren't like other mortal animals."

I smiled. "They definitely hate us." I was thinking about one bear in particular, my old friend from White Bear Island.

"Can you blame 'em? All we done since we got up in this country is kill 'em."

I looked at him for a moment, not sure he wasn't having me on. "Now you're sounding like old Drouillard. Them bears don't know from Adam what we do. We been killing deer and elk since we got up here, and I have yet to see one go out of its way to attack us like those bears do."

"Don't get all in a lather, John," Collins said. "All I'm saying is there's gotta be a reason those bears hate us."

"Probably your stench gets 'em all worked up," I grunted, wanting to change the subject. "They're just dumb animals, John. They don't reason things out like you and me. They hate us because they hate all humans, no other reason. So drop the superstitious foolishness."

We continued hunting, and by late morning we had killed and dressed out four deer. We got the meat back to the canoe and loaded it, and then Collins looked up the river. "You think Lewis and the fellas have gone by yet?"

"They should have done," I said.

"Well, let's catch 'em."

We climbed into the canoe and headed downstream. The wind had picked up a little, creating small waves on the river's surface, and the mosquitoes had woken up from whatever passes for sleep for those little bloodsuckers. They were all around us, a continuous nuisance but one we could do nothing about, so we paddled on.

We stopped and made camp that night near a small stream that fell into the Missouri from the north, and there we stayed for two more days, positive the main party was behind us and coming down. On the morning of the third day we decided we had been wrong and launched ourselves back into the river once more.

For two days we rowed down the river and never caught up with Lewis's party. We had eaten all our meat and stopped to hunt more, and came to a decision to wait for a day to see if they might catch up to us. "They have to be above us," Collins said. "Ain't no way they can be this far ahead."

"I don't know. Captain Lewis wanted to push pretty hard to meet up with Clark at the Yellowstone."

"Yeah, but we been rowing our tails off. We shoulda caught them by now."

So we made a camp near the river and settled in again to wait. We had killed a fat doe just that morning on the bank of the river and the smell of cooking meat floated above the camp as we watched for our friends to come into view. I wasn't sure what to think at that point. A part of me felt sure that Lewis was below us, probably waiting for us to catch up to them, but I had to agree with Collins. We had been rowing pretty hard, only stopping to camp in the evening, and we should have caught them by now.

"You don't think those Blackfeet caught up to them, do you?" Collins asked.

"Naw," I said. "We woulda found their bodies, or the canoes, or something. Besides, don't think like that. You wanna bring trouble down on us?"

"Now who's being superstitious?" he grinned.

That night we were assailed by a strong thunderstorm, with hail and lightning, and we huddled beneath our buffalo robes, trying to stay dry. We watched the river, illuminated frequently by the brilliant lightning, but no boats passed in the night. Now I was really starting to worry.

* * *

The next morning we took to the water again, more convinced than ever that our friends were farther down the Missouri. This time we swore we wouldn't stop other than to hunt and catch a couple hours of sleep until we caught up with them. We paddled as hard as we could during the day, almost flying down that wide Missouri River, and still we couldn't seem to catch them. We were becoming extremely concerned, more so with each passing mile.

Finally, after almost eight days from the time we separated, we came around a bend in the river and there sat the white pirogue and the canoes, pulled up on a bank. The relief we felt at that moment could not be expressed in mere words! To see our friends again after all this time of not knowing if they were alive and well, and I have to say they seemed just as happy to see us! Among much back-slapping and anxious queries I spotted Captain Lewis, stretched out on his side on the bank. His face was pinched and white, and a thick bandage was wrapped around his upper leg.

"What happened to the captain?" I asked.

Sergeant Gass appeared to be holding back a grin. "Cruzatte shot him."

"Huh?" I was sure I couldn't have heard him correctly.

"Apparently thought he was an elk."

Pierre Cruzatte had terrible vision as well as being half-deaf, and most of us would decline to go on a hunt with him. "Lewis took him hunting?" I asked.

"Couple days back. They were in some dense woods and apparently Cruzatte only saw the brown of the captain's buckskins moving behind some shrubs. Shot him through the leg. Lewis thought Indians were attacking and had us all up in arms, ready to fight a war."

I walked to where Lewis was laying and squatted down beside him. "You doing okay, sir?"

"Well, I have been better," he said, trying to smile. "I was getting worried about you boys."

"Sorry about that, captain. We couldn't decide if you were behind us or ahead of us."

"You're here. That's all that matters."

"Looks like you were the one we needed to be concerned about."

He smiled again. "I learned a lesson, John."

"What's that, Captain Lewis?"

"Never hunt with a blind Frenchman."

I laughed. "Those are true words of wisdom." I looked around the boisterous camp. "I don't see Captain Clark's party."

"Haven't caught up to 'em yet. But if you'll help me into that boat, I'm more than ready to track them down."

We mobilized the entire camp and were soon back on the river. And .

within another couple of hours we spotted a large camp ahead of us on the bank. It was Captain Clark.

For the second time that day we shared a joyous reunion, tempered only by the injury to Captain Lewis. All of our mutual concerns for the safety of our separated parties could now be put behind, and we laughed and talked late into the evening, overjoyed to find that everyone was healthy and well. I was a bit surprised to see Nate Pryor there, thinking he would be on his way to carry Lewis's letter to Mr. Heney with the Northwest Company, but he quickly filled me in.

"We didn't get two days separated from Captain Clark when some damn Injuns stole all our horses. We tried to track 'em down but they had too much of a lead on us. Messed us up pretty bad."

"How'd you catch up to Clark?"

"We built bull boats."

I gaped at him. "Like the ones the Mandans had?"

"Yep, just like them. We built them and rowed down the Yellowstone until we caught up to Clark." He shook his head sadly. "I'm pretty mad about it all, John, I gotta tell you."

"Wasn't your fault, Nate."

"I know, but I'm still mad. Captain Lewis was depending on me, John. That letter was important."

I clapped his shoulder. "Nothing you can do now, my friend. Don't let it eat at you."

CHAPTER THIRTY-SEVEN

Two days later we arrived at the Mandan villages. Spotting some of the Indians on a bluff above the river we fired our swivel gun in salute, and when we came in view of their upper town we could see many of them on the shore, waving happily.

We stopped at their villages so the captains could get themselves up to date on events, and the news was not good. The Mandans had been attacked by the Sioux, and war had also broken out with the Arikaras. The peace that Lewis and Clark had tried so hard to achieve apparently hadn't lasted much longer than it took for us to row out of sight up the river a year earlier!

The captains sent Charbonneau and Drouillard to the lower villages to invite those chiefs up for a parley, and when they arrived, Lewis tried to convince them to travel with us to the east, to meet our President. None of the chiefs seemed inclined to do so, stating their fear of the Sioux who guarded the river down below. Lewis wasn't interested in hearing their arguments and reassured them that no nation would dare to harm any Indian traveling under the protection of the United States of America. I thought it was a pretty strong claim to make, especially in light of our troubles with the Sioux on the way up. If those Sioux wanted to stop us from passing, they could, with their hundreds of fierce warriors against our few soldiers.

I could see that the Mandans weren't buying Lewis's words, either. In the months since we had wintered near them and had assured them that we had arranged peace in the area, the Sioux had killed a number of their warriors and stole many horses. Our promises of protection didn't hold much water with the chiefs.

* * *

"Can I bother you gentlemen for a moment?" I asked.

Captain Clark looked up from his journal and motioned me into his tent. Captain Lewis was reclining on some furs and skins to one side, favoring his injured leg, though I knew he was feeling better.

"What can we do for you, John?"

"Well, I've been talking to those trappers we met back up the river, and they've invited me to go to the Yellowstone country with them," I said. Several days earlier, right around the same time that our parties were coming back together, we had met two trappers up from the Illinois country, named Joseph Dickson and Forrest Hancock. They were interested in going up to the Yellowstone and Upper Missouri country to trap, and Captain Lewis had shared his knowledge and information with them. They had followed us down to the Mandan villages in the hopes of recruiting another man to go up with them. Hopefully, that man would be me. "They said they'll make me a partner in their business and we'd all share the success together."

Clark nodded slowly. "You've been dreaming about that land up there, haven't you, John?"

"Been dreaming of the fortune to be made," I said, smiling.

"There is a fortune's worth of beaver and otter up there," he said, "but it's more than that, isn't it?"

"I'm not sure what you mean," I said, but inside I thought maybe I did. There was something about that country up there beyond the opportunity to make a lot of money trapping it. There was something about the clear crisp air, the endless vistas, the water as pure and clean as anything on this earth. There was a force in the very silence of the land, the amazing wildlife that filled every glade and hollow. It was a land that crept into a man's soul and took root there, drawing him back, making him never want to leave.

Clark was watching me, smiling slightly, as if he could read my thoughts. And I realized that he was most likely feeling the same way I was, but as an officer and leader of the expedition he couldn't give in to those feelings.

"I have no problem with mustering you out right here and letting you chase your fortune, John," Clark said. "What about you, Meri?"

Captain Lewis shook his head. "I only see one problem."

"What's that?" Clark asked.

"We're still a good thirty days out from St. Louis. If our men start wanting to go their own ways now, we'll never make it back down the river."

I understood what he was saying, and I could sense my golden opportunity slipping away. Then Captain Clark spoke again and my hopes started to rise once more.

"Oh, I don't think that will be a problem," he said. "If I can guarantee that no others in our party do the same thing, do you have any objection to letting John here go and get rich?"

Captain Lewis shook his head again. "None at all."

* * *

Captain Clark called all of the men together an hour later.

"Gentlemen, Mr. Colter here has been given an opportunity to travel back up the river with our new friends, Mr. Dickson and Mr. Hancock. Now, I've told John that I won't stand in his way, and that I can muster him out right here and let him go. But that will only happen if the rest of you agree not to ask for the same thing, and promise to remain with us until we reach St. Louis." He grinned around at them. "Old John's future is in your hands, lads."

"I think we oughta tie him up and throw him in the pirogue," Nate Pryor said, grinning. "Make him go back to civilization with us."

"Yeah, all that walking on prickly pear has given him delusions," Goodrich said.

"Naw, what he wants to do is cross over them mountains and prove that his darn Colter's Creek doesn't taste like antelope piss," Windsor called out.

"Hell, the beaver'll smell his old stinky ass coming from ten miles off and head as far from him as they can." That comment came from Potts. "He'll be broke in two weeks and he'll be begging us to take him back."

I just shook my head, feeling a wash of emotion run through me at my friend's teasing. I really would miss every one of them.

"Let 'im go, Captain Clark," Ordway said jovially. "Hell, I've been trying to get rid of him since Wood River!"

"Yeah, let him go!" McNeal shouted, and the rest of the crew chimed in, all of them giving their affirmation.

"All right, gentlemen," Clark said, raising his hands to silence them. Then he turned to face me. "You're sure you want to turn your back on the pleasures and comforts of civilization?"

"Yes, Captain Clark."

"Then, Mr. Colter, you may consider yourself formally discharged from the United States Army. You may now consider yourself a private citizen of the United States of America, free to wander where you please. I pray you will make your fortune up here and return to us a rich man at some point in the future."

The men all cheered and I swallowed a large and unexpected lump in my throat.

* * *

A beautiful sunrise painted the sky with shades of pink and red as I stood high on a bluff, watching the Corps of Discovery head down the mighty Missouri. Over the three years that had elapsed since joining up with that mad crew in October of 1803, I had come to know and love every one of them. I had worked and lived so closely with them that I could recognize each man from a cough or a laugh. I could recognize the sound of each man's footsteps. They were all like brothers to me, and as I watched them disappear I knew that I might never see any of them again.

Down below the Mandan villages, Dickson and Hancock were loading the last of our gear into the canoes we would be taking with us. Many of the men in the Corps had donated small goods and supplies to us, and Captain Clark had given me twenty of the Army-property beaver traps that I had used on our journey. Soon I would be embarking with my two new partners, virtual strangers to me now, and my new life would begin.

I looked toward the town and could see our old interpreter, Charbonneau, walking with his wife and baby. Sacagawea was carrying little Jean-Baptiste on her back, and when she caught my eye she gave me a little smile and a wave. I waved back to her. Charbonneau had elected to stay in the Mandan villages rather than go down to St. Louis with the captains, and the little family had shared their own farewells with the men with whom they had been through so much.

The pirogue and canoes had disappeared around a bend in the Missouri now and I bid them a last and silent goodbye. For a moment I stayed there on that bluff, thinking about all that had happened in the last three years. I remembered the mud and cold of the Wood River camp and the argument that had almost barred me from the Corps. I remembered the long hot days, struggling against the current of the Missouri River, rowing and poling that damn old keelboat until I thought every muscle in my body would simply fall out. I remembered the skirmish with the Sioux, the cold nights spent in the warm arms of several Arikara maidens, the unparalleled beauty of the wide prairies and mountains of the west. I remembered the terrible crossing of the Rockies, the trip down the Columbia, the wet and nasty winter at our little Fort Clatsop. But mostly I remembered the closeness and camaraderie of the Corps of Discovery, those brave and wonderful men who had become my very best friends.

Turning my back on the view to the south, I walked down to join my new partners.

CHAPTER THIRTY-EIGHT

We set out that same afternoon, heading upriver.

Joe Dickson and Forrest Hancock were two men who were alike in many ways yet who had separate and very distinct personalities. Both men were exactly the same height, just a little shorter than me, and had the same medium builds. Both men had dark hair and thick beards. It was in their personalities that they vastly differed from each other. Where Joe was quiet and almost taciturn, Forrest was outgoing and friendly, prone to quick laughter and always ready with a joke. Joe seemed to be the unofficial leader of the two, at least Forrest deferred to him on most decisions, but Joe also asked for our opinions before decisions were made, and in that way he reminded me a little of Meriwether Lewis.

Traveling upriver in the two small canoes brought back memories of my journey in the previous spring, and so many places along the riverbanks reminded me of events with the Corps. I told my new partners about some of them as we passed those places and they took in every word, obviously fascinated to learn of events surrounding the Corps of Discovery. I learned that we had been big news back in the east after setting out from Wood River, and after Corporal Warfington returned with the keelboat and the first of the captain's letters and discoveries. Joe had heard from other explorers and trappers in recent months that the general consensus had become grimmer, and many believed us to be dead or prisoners of the Spanish.

"There's gonna be a hell of a party when your friends get to St. Louis," he said. "Half that town's been staring up the river for two years, waiting for you boys to get home."

Forrest told me stories of close calls and adventures he and Joe had had since leaving the Illinois country in 1804, including a run-in with my old friends, the Teton Sioux.

"Damn savages robbed us," he said, spitting into the river in disgust. "We musta had a couple hundred beaver pelts and otter pelts and were heading down to St. Louis with 'em, and about a hundred of them Sioux came out of nowhere, lining both sides of the river. We didn't even have a chance to run or hide. They motioned for us to stop and we did, or sure they would have shot us full of arrows."

"One of 'em did shoot me," Joe said bitterly, showing me a black and yellow bruise on his leg. "Lucky for me the savage didn't know how to use his rifle and he shot me with the wad instead of a bullet or I might not be here now."

"They stole all our pelts and I guess we're lucky they left us our canoes and rifles," Forrest related. He laughed. "I guess we're lucky they left us our lives!"

They had heard of our encounter with the Sioux, which had been published after the keelboat reached St. Louis, so they had been wary.

"Not that it did us any good," Forrest said.

We rowed upstream all that evening and camped on the riverbank. The mosquitoes found us as soon as we got our fire started, and even sitting in the smoke from the fire did little to deter the blood-thirsty demons. We dined on an elk that I had shot a few miles below the camp and talked about our plans for trapping on the Yellowstone.

"I would love to reach the Three Forks this season," I said, after regaling them with tales of the hundreds of beaver that lived in that low and bounteous country. "But I'm afraid, with the portage around the falls, that we'd never get there before winter sets in." For a moment I thought about what a winter in the open would be like and a shiver went through me. If nothing else, we were going to be cold!

Joe studied the numbers Captain Lewis had given him, of the miles between the Mandan villages and the forks, and he nodded. "Even if we can cut that portage down to a few days, we'd still be in the mountain canyons when the snow started. I'm thinkin' we'd be better going up the Yellowstone and seeing what our chances are like up thataway. What do you gents think?"

Forrest and I both thought it was a fine idea. I had not traveled the Yellowstone with Captain Clark on our return so I couldn't provide information about the beaver populations, but it was hard to imagine it would be much different from the Missouri or the Three Forks area. Clark had mentioned that beaver were numerous up the tributaries of the Yellowstone and I was willing to accept his word on it.

* * *

The morning dawned clear and cold and we set out very early. We wanted to get as far up the Yellowstone as we could and set up a good camp before the snow set in. Winter was the perfect time to trap beaver, and all three of us planned to trap all we could until spring, then head down to St. Louis and cash in the pelts. At that time I would also collect the pay owed to me by the United States for my service with the Corps of Discovery and start my new life with a nice chunk of money.

Our travels up the Missouri and then up the Yellowstone were fairly uneventful, and nothing exciting happened worth talking about. We all took turns hunting on the shore while the other two rowed up in the canoes, and we made our camps at night in places where we could see a long distance in any direction. We were all aware of the fact that we were three white men in Indian territory, and an advance warning of Indian's approaching might spell the difference between escaping and being killed.

"You been up here, Colter," Joe said. That's one thing that bothered me about him; he never called me John. It was always Colter. "What's the Indians up here like?"

"Depends on their mood, really," I said. Forrest had killed two fat does earlier and we were cooking them as we spoke. "And it depends on which tribe you're talking about. The Shoshone up in the mountains were good to us, but there were a lot of us and we had better weapons than they did.

The Blackfeet will kill us rather than look at us, and they're probably still a bit miffed over Captain Lewis's little skirmish with them up the Marias."

"That was a lot of foolishness," Joe said. He had heard the story of Captain Lewis's run-in with the Blackfeet shortly after meeting up with the Corps above the Mandan villages.

I bristled a little at his tone. "I wasn't there, but I'm sure Captain Lewis handled the situation in the best way possible."

Joe looked dubious.

Forrest threw another log onto the fire. "What were they like, those captains?" he asked. "Lewis seemed kind of short with us, even though he did give us good information and some nice gifts."

"The man just got shot in the ass," I said. "You'd be a little curt, too."

Forrest laughed. "Yeah, guess I would be."

"They were quite different from each other," I went on, "but they both had strong qualities that far outshone any shortcomings they may have had. I'll admit I cottoned to Captain Clark sooner than I did to Lewis, but in the end I recognized that each of them were great men in their own ways. I'm honored to have served with them."

"Did you ever meet up with the Crow?" Joe asked next.

I shook my head. "No, but Captain Clark might have. Their territory is down below the Three Forks, I believe."

"Are they hostile?"

"I can't answer that, Joe. It depends on how we approach them. Most Indians are willing to accept white men if they come to trade. If they come to make war or steal, then the Indians'll kill 'em if they can."

"That's what I've heard. Well, I daresay we'll find out in due time, won't we?"

I didn't respond. I could tell I was going to have a hard time adjusting to Joe Dickson.

* * *

We reached the mouth of the Yellowstone and set up a camp. Joe wanted to stop there for several days to hunt, knowing from his previous travels earlier in the year that the hunting was very good in this low and fertile place.

I worked hard during those early days to get to know Joe a little better and establish some sort of rapport with him but the going was tough. He didn't talk a lot and would often respond to questions or comments with noncommittal grunts. The hunting was as good as we expected it to be, but even over a sumptuous meal of elk and beaver Joe would brood silently. He was a very good hunter and I've only seen a few men who worked as hard as he did, but I just couldn't like him.

"How long you been working with Joe?" I asked Forrest one afternoon. We had been camped at the mouth of the Yellowstone for three days and Forrest and I were hunting on the high ridges north of the juncture.

"Oh, about two years or so," he said. He was looking down across a low valley, where hundreds of bison could be seen grazing on the long grass. They were at least three miles away from us, surrounded by a watchful ring of wolves. "I've known him for about five years, but we only started working together when we left Illinois to head up this way."

"Has he always been like that?" I asked.

Forrest laughed. "Yeah, pretty much. He used to talk more, but since we started having our bad luck he's gotten a bit quieter."

"Kinda makes it tough to get to know him."

"Joe's a good guy," Forrest said. "Sometimes I worry about him, especially when he gets in one of his moods, but I know him well enough to know when to stay away and when to try and bring him out of it."

I thought of Captain Lewis's habits of descending into dark moods now and then and how Captain Clark in some instances could bring him out of them with a word or a joke. At other times there was nothing anyone could do and we would just stay out of his way. It looked like I would have to do the same with Joe Dickson.

* * *

We stayed at the mouth of the Yellowstone for five days. On the morning of the sixth day, we broke camp and set out onto the

Yellowstone, leaving the Missouri behind us. The mosquitoes were like a fog over the water but we were so used to them that we barely took notice. Small clouds drifted above us and the sun cast long shadows as we paddled up the center of the wide river. I was pretty excited, feeling like, after all my travels, I was finally setting out on the journey that would lead to my fortune. All during the lengthy excursion with the Corps I had longingly dreamt of the potential of these rivers, and now I planned to make them my own.

That year autumn lingered around for a long time, not that we were complaining. Yes, it is far easier to track and trap beaver in the winter, when the snow is heavy and thick, but from a comfort standpoint I prefer fifty degrees to ten, or lower. My memories of the winter at Fort Mandan were too recent for me to be all that excited about spending a winter outside of shelter. The valley of the Yellowstone was like an artist's painting that autumn, with trees covered in yellow, red and orange leaves and the snow glistening on the distant mountains. The mornings were crisp and cold, hinting of winter to come, and our first task upon reaching the level plateau where we planned to winter was to find a place to erect a shelter.

"Fellas, what about this?" Joe called out.

Forrest and I walked to where he was standing, near the base of a high cliff. The cliff was of a tan colored rock, fairly soft, and dozens of small caves had been hollowed out near its base by years of erosion. In some places the cliff wall was blackened by ancient fires, showing that other people had sought shelter there in the past.

"We could erect a shelter against this wall," Joe said, tapping one hand against the rock. "We'd have a good view of the valley and be out of the worst of the wind."

I turned and looked across the valley. The base of the cliff sat at the top of a gentle rise that began at the river's edge. A smaller stream fell into the Yellowstone about a hundred yards upstream, and we could see for several miles up and down the river.

"I'd say it's a perfect place," Forrest said, also studying the wide valley. "John?"

"I agree," I said.

So camp was established and we set to work.

CHAPTER THIRTY-NINE

Let me give you a small lesson in the logistics of catching beaver.
Setting beaver traps is an art.

You can't just slap beaver traps willy-nilly along a river and hope some
dumb beaver will wander into one. You have to know something about
beaver and know how to think like a beaver. If you can't, you might as well
float on down the Missouri to St. Louis and take up farming.

Everyone knows that beaver build dams, and most people know that
they build dams to provide themselves with a place to hide from their
enemies. Most people also know that beavers will dig canals from their
chosen pond to sources of wood. It is those canals that I seek when
trapping. The beaver needs constant supplies of fresh wood to make
repairs to its dam and lodge. Therefore, it will make use of those canals
more than any other path of travel.

I also look for beaver dams and lodges that are in a state of good repair.
That tells me that the lodge is active. Ain't no sense setting traps in a
stream the beaver have abandoned!

The beaver is not a stupid animal. It will not walk up to you and allow
you to kill it. You have to work, and work hard, if you plan on making your
fortune in the trapping of beaver. Beavers live in remote and secluded
areas, forced by their very nature to seek the solitude of small streams far
from human habitation. You have to go to the beaver, for it's a sure thing
that the beaver ain't gonna go to you!

We built a stout shelter against the base of that cliff above the

Yellowstone and then went our separate ways for a while. Three men going in three directions will scout out prime beaver country faster than three men walking together. Joe headed upstream with the intention of angling off to the southeast, while Forrest was heading toward the southwest. I was cutting cross-country toward the west. I had a pretty good general picture in my head of the country between the Yellowstone and the Missouri even though I had never set foot there, and I felt sure there would be dozens of good beaver streams draining into those two large rivers.

The three of us worked hard all that autumn and into the winter, and the trapping was as good as I had hoped it would be. The pelts stacked up in the back of our shelter and we could almost taste the riches that would be ours when we finally got those pelts down to St. Louis in the spring. My dream was coming true.

Winter closed in on us in mid-November but that didn't stop us from trapping and collecting pelts. The standard procedure for trapping beaver during non-winter months was to find the spot where the beaver returns to the water following its foraging trips onto land. We called those places "slides," and they were easily identifiable. Once located, the trap would be placed at the bottom of the slide, right where the beaver would re-enter the water. The trick was to convince the beaver to step onto the spring with its hind legs.

Almost every trapper who knew his trade would carry a small bottle containing the essence of castor, a scent guaranteed to attract a beaver from practically miles away. My favorite trick was to push a stout stick into the creek bed next to the trap and smear some of the foul-smelling essence on the top. A beaver returning to what it considered to be "his" river would catch the fragrance of the strange beaver and would have to investigate. The beaver would rise up on its powerful hind legs to reach the scent, and in so doing would step on the pan, releasing the trap.

A beaver's front legs are fairly weak, and a beaver caught in a trap by its front legs will not hesitate to gnaw that leg off to escape. A beaver that lands in the trap with its rear leg is a goner. It'll drag that trap into the deepest part of the river in an attempt to escape and will drown. Then it's just a case of following the drag chain until you find the dead beaver.

Joe, Forrest and I trapped all that fall and into the first part of the winter. We amassed a very nice collection of pelts, as I said earlier, and were settled in for a long winter of trapping.

Then disaster struck.

"Ain't that a right purty sight," Forrest said, smiling and shaking his head as he studied the growing stack of pelts. Along with beaver we were starting to grow an impressive collection of otter, mink and ermine skins as well. Oh, I could just about feel the money I would collect when we reached St. Louis.

From a corner of the shelter Joe grunted.

Forrest glanced at me and shook his head. Joe had become more and more withdrawn as time passed, until now it was just about impossible to get a civil word out of him.

"I found a new stream dropping down into the Yellowstone 'bout ten miles south," I said. "It looks pretty promising."

"South's my area," Joe spat. "Hell you doing down there?"

"I had to circle to the south to avoid that camp of Crow," I explained patiently. I had already told them about the camp, one that concerned me. Those Crow were awful close.

"Damn thief, what you are," he mumbled.

I could feel my anger rising. I had had just about all I could stand of Joe Dickson. Our agreement from the beginning was that we would split our profits into three equal parts, regardless of who brought in the most pelts. If anyone should be grumbling, it should be Forrest or me. Of the three of us, Joe was the least productive.

"I'm getting a little tired of your insinuations, Joe," I said quietly, struggling to hold in my temper.

His head came up and he glared at me. "Are you really?"

"Yes, I am. All three of us are working hard, and we'll share equally in the rewards when spring comes. Accusing each other of theft or other crimes is not necessary." There, spoken plainly and diplomatically.

Joe laughed shortly.

Forrest spoke. "John's right, Joe. We have to live together in this small shelter all winter. We need to get along."

Joe leaped to his feet. "Siding with him, are you?" he shouted. "Shoulda expected it! Both of you, out to steal my damn share!"

"Now, Joe..."

"Joe, my ass!" Dickson was in a rage. "Ever since we set up here, you both been conspiring against me! Well, I damn well intend to put a stop to it right now!" Joe grabbed his rifle then froze into immobility as I pressed the barrel of my own rifle against his chest.

"Bad idea, Joe," I said softly. I was furious. "I think it's time to..."

"Shh!" Forrest hissed, motioning to us desperately. "Listen!"

We all stood as still as stone and listened intently. For a long while there was no sound except for the hiss of wind-blown snow against the wall of our shelter and the low sound of the river. Then I heard what Forrest had heard, the low whicker of a horse.

"Crow!" Joe whispered.

Part of my mind wanted to deny it, but inside I knew he was right. It had to be Crow. Nobody else would be about on horses in this area at this time of year.

Moving to the front of our shelter I peeked outside. My heart fell when I saw what was out there. Lowering my rifle to the floor, I started toward the door.

"What the hell are you doing?" Forrest demanded, grabbing my sleeve.

"Look out there, Forrest," I said.

He stared at me for a moment, and then glanced outside. I could tell by the sudden droop in his shoulders that he had come to the same conclusion that I had.

Pulling back the makeshift door of our small shelter, I stepped outside, keeping my hands in plain sight. Forrest and Joe followed.

Facing us, seated atop their horses in a semicircle, were about fifty Crow warriors. They sat in silence, watching us as we walked out from the shelter, and I tried to read their faces for some hint as to our fates. Their stony visages gave away nothing.

The man directly in front of us motioned to one side and we stepped that way. There was nothing else we could do. He said something and several of his warriors dismounted, hurrying into the shelter. Their voices called out and more of their friends joined them.

I could hear Joe muttering angrily as the warriors appeared, laden down with the pelts we had worked so hard to obtain, and I was pretty upset myself. Months of back-breaking work was being carried to the Indians horses, but I was helpless to do anything to put a stop to it. I don't consider myself a coward by any means, but even the bravest man isn't going to attack a group of fifty-plus heavily-armed warriors!

It took the Crow warriors less than ten minutes to empty us out of the pelts we'd worked months to gather. They showed no sign of anger or any other emotion as they worked, just men doing a job. I still had no idea if they were going to kill us when they were finished, and being without a weapon of any kind meant my fate was out of my hands. All I could do was wait.

Once all the pelts had been loaded onto the Indian horses, the leader motioned toward the west. Immediately, the majority of his warriors tugged their horses around and set out. Five remained behind to watch us, arrows nocked and aimed at our chests, as the main Crow party easily forded the shallow Yellowstone and vanished into the woods on the other bank. If it was going to happen, it would happen now.

The leader stared at us and pointed downstream, toward the Missouri. He gestured that way several times, saying something none of us could understand, but I didn't need words to know what he wanted of us. He wanted us to leave, get out of his country, and not come back.

As I look back on that moment in time, a part of me knows I should have listened. I should have packed up my few belongings, carried my long rifle, powder horn and blanket and headed for civilization. I would have been spared a lot of misery if I had done so.

The Crow made the "go home" gesture a few more times, then he and the remaining warriors turned and rode away, following their now-vanished friends across the Yellowstone. They never glanced back.

After they had disappeared, Joe threw his hat down onto the ground. "Damn it!" he cursed loudly. "Damn it, damn it. damn it!"

Forrest nodded silently, eyes staring in the direction of the departed Crow.

"I have half a mind to get my rifle and go after them damn thieving Injuns!" Joe ranted, and I had had all I could take.

I whirled toward him. "Half a mind is all you've ever had!" I shouted, having to force down the desire to pummel him with my fists. All of the frustrations of the autumn, his attitude and insults, and the theft of our pelts were bubbling inside me, and I would have loved to release those frustrations by beating Joe Dickson into the ground. Instead, I marched into the shelter, gathered up what belonged to me, and walked away.

"Where you going, John?" Forrest called out.

"Away from him," I replied, not slowing my stride.

Behind me, I could hear voices raised in angered shouts but I paid no attention. I strode down the eastern bank of the Yellowstone, heading toward the juncture of the Missouri, and I didn't look back. I had no firm destination in mind, just a vague thought that I might turn west on the Missouri and maybe see what the trapping was like up that way.

"Hold on a second, John," I heard Forrest's voice call out from behind me.

I stopped and turned around. Forrest was hurrying toward me, and to my surprise he had all of his gear with him, rifle in hand, traps slung over his shoulder. Far behind him, Joe stood in front of the small shelter, watching us.

"What do you want?" I said.

"Why, I want to go with you."

"What about your partner?"

Forrest glanced back toward where Joe stood. "Well, I'm a mite tired of Joe," he said simply.

I nodded and we turned our backs on Joe Dickson and walked away.

CHAPTER FORTY

Forrest and I tried our hand at trapping along the Missouri and its tributaries all that long and harsh winter, but we weren't very successful. The beaver all seemed to have gone into hiding, and even the tried-and-true method of tapping on the thick river ice with a stick in search of their burrows failed us. We had enough to eat, as the deer and elk were plentiful in the sheltered river bottoms, and we had built a sturdy shelter near the mouth of the Marias River, but by the time the snows began to melt and the first buds appeared on the trees, I was finished.

"I wish you'd stay for another season," Forrest said, watching as I carved out a small dugout canoe from a cottonwood tree for my return trip down the Missouri.

"No, thanks," I said, easing a kink in my back and wiping sweat from my forehead. "I think I'll just head down, collect my pay from the army for my time with Lewis and Clark, and head back to the Ohio."

"I think you're making a big mistake, John," he said. "You know yourself the riches in this land. All we gotta do is catch a good break and we can be wealthy."

"Yeah, and have the Injuns steal it all again? No, thank you."

Forrest didn't say anything more about staying as I completed the canoe, and he helped me load my gear on board.

I shook his hand warmly. "It has been a pleasure to know you," I told him. "I wish you all the luck and good fortune."

"Take care of yourself, John," he said.

I pushed the dugout away from the shore and climbed aboard. My final glimpse of Forrest Hancock was of him waving as I floated down around a bend. I was sure I would never see him again.

I was wrong.

* * *

The trip down the Missouri was a leisurely one. I took my time, not being in a rush. I had plenty of ammunition and the hunting was easy. Maneuvering the small dugout around the Missouri's obstacles was a dream compared to the pirogues we had rode in during my time with the Corps, and let's not even mention the monstrous keelboat! Not that there were very many obstacles to contend with; the Missouri was running high and fast with the spring melts, and most sandbars and sawyers were deep beneath the rushing waters.

The weather warmed as I floated downstream. I stopped for a while at the Mandan villages, hoping to see Charbonneau and the Bird Woman, but neither was there.

More weeks of slow travel brought me to the high bluff where we had buried Sergeant Floyd. I put ashore there and walked up to the gravesite, wondering if the Corps had done the same on their return to St. Louis in the previous fall. For a long time I sat in front of the weathered wooden cross, not talking, just thinking about all I had done and seen since that day when Floyd had died. I tried to imagine him during the confrontation with the Sioux, or at Fort Clatsop in that cold rainy winter of 1805-06. I tried to imagine what he would have thought standing on the rocky shore, looking out at the pounding waves of the Pacific Ocean. He had missed so much.

I camped that night on the high bluff and set out at sunrise the next morning. I had gone just a few miles down the Missouri when I spotted several large keelboats tied to the shore. Dipping my oar into the river, I propelled myself toward the boats, anxious to see who they were and where they were going.

A voice shouted out from the lead boat and I laughed as I recognized John Potts. He was waving toward me and laughing himself.

"Colter, you old bastard!" he called out. "Get over here!"

I grounded my canoe and was greeted by Potts, who wrapped me in an enthusiastic bear hug. "Never thought I'd see you again!" he said. "George, Pete, get over here and see what the river washed up!"

I laughed again as we were joined by Pete Weiser and George Drouillard, who also greeted me with hugs and hard back-slaps.

"What are you doing here?" I asked.

"We're heading up there," Potts said, pointing toward the west. "Gonna do some trapping and get rich!"

I was about to tell them about my own dismal adventures when we were joined by the leader of their expedition. Manuel Lisa had visited the camp at Wood River way back in 1803-04, and he didn't look any different now than he had then. A small man in stature, he had a strong, almost arrogant, way of carrying himself that made him seem larger than he was. He also had a self-important attitude, though his greeting of me was effusive and warm.

"John Colter!" he said, wringing my hand. "It's a pleasure to see you. Come on, join us for breakfast!"

Lisa led me to the cook fires and introduced me to the other men. I was surprised to learn that this expedition, to establish a trade network among the Indian nations upriver, was funded by William Clark.

"You remember Lewis always talking about creating a trading system with the Injuns," Potts said. "Well, we're doing it."

"Our plan is to travel up the Yellowstone and establish a trading post," Lisa elaborated. "Then, not only can we trap beaver ourselves, we can trade with the Indians for pelts they collect for us."

I thought for a moment about the band of Crows disappearing into the forests with the pelts Dickson, Hancock and I had gathered, and I wondered if they would end up buying my pelts. That would have been too ironic.

"How about joining up with us, John?" Potts said next.

"I don't know," I said slowly, my mind racing. "I was kinda planning on heading down, collecting the pay the army owes me, and going back to the Ohio."

"And do what?" Potts asked. "Be a farmer?"

He had a point.

Lisa smiled. "Your army pay will be waiting for you next season," he said. "Come with us. We could sure use your knowledge of the area up there."

I told them then about the theft of the pelts, and finished with, "The natives up that way don't seem too interested in having white trappers in their land."

"That's because they're not getting anything out of the deal," Lisa said. "Those Indians up that way are like Indians anywhere. They don't like to give away anything for free. If we can show them that they are receiving valuable goods for the pelts we take, then I believe they'll be a lot more amenable to us being there."

I hoped he was right.

"What do you say, John?" Pete said.

"Sure, why not. I'll join you."

* * *

So once again I was heading up the Missouri River, away from civilization. I still held on to my dream of striking it rich, but with a venture like Lisa's the riches would be spread around, with most of the gains going to Lisa and his partners. But I was okay with that. My job on this trip would be to scout out an area for Lisa's trading post, then seek out the local Indian's winter camps and let them know that a new post was open, with excellent trade goods available. For that I would get paid a monthly salary, and I'd have the opportunity to see some new lands for my own trapping endeavors.

St. Louis behind, I headed back into the wilds.

The journey was not without its drama. The keelboat was damaged during an encounter with a floating tree and had to be repaired, then one of the men, a blowhard named Bouche, decided to take an unauthorized hunting trip, delaying us by another week. I couldn't help but compare these men with the men from the Corps, and I found these trappers lacking in the comparison. They had no concept of working as a team, and it wasn't long before I was regretting my decision to join up with them. But I had signed a contract with Manuel Lisa and I was bound to stand by it.

The biggest danger we faced, however, was from the Arikara. That friendly nation, who had greeted Lewis and Clark so cordially and who had sent one of their lead men to visit with President Jefferson, had undergone a drastic reversal of their feelings toward white men. Their man, Big White, hadn't been returned to them, and they were convinced the white men had taken him away and killed him. For that reason, they had turned warlike and greeted us with anger and hostility.

Eventually, through strong negotiations and our own show of force, we passed the Arikara villages and continued up the Missouri. I should have been wiser. I should have known the troubles with the Arikara were a sign, telling me to turn around and go home. But I didn't know any better, so I continued up the wide river with Manuel Lisa.

And I would live to regret that decision.

CHAPTER FORTY-ONE

Manuel Lisa established his trading post at the forks of the Yellowstone River and a smaller river the natives called the Bighorn. He declared that the post would be named Fort Raymond, in honor of one of his sons. We spent the latter part of the summer building the post, constructing sturdy palisade walls in case we needed to defend ourselves. The post was not far from where the Crow had stolen our pelts the previous fall, and we had passed the crude shelter on the way up. It still stood, huddled against the base of the cliff, but there was no sign of Dickson.

Hancock, however, was another story.

Forrest had been at the juncture of the Yellowstone and the Missouri when we came up, and had been convinced by Manuel Lisa to join us. Forrest had obtained a few dozen pelts after I had parted company with him, but nothing like the riches either of us had once hoped to obtain, and he was thankful for the steady employment.

Work raced forward on the post as the air turned colder. I was able to give directions to some of the best beaver streams, and hunting areas, and the meat was plentiful. We were also bringing in a large number of beaver pelts. With winter coming on, the beaver were growing in their thick protective coats, much coveted in the east.

The post was completed just as the first of the autumn rains began to fall, and by the time the snow began to fall from leaden skies, Lisa was ready to open for business. He called together the four men he had chosen to spread word of his post, including Drouillard, Pete Weiser, a man named Edward Rose, and myself, and gave us our instructions.

"Find as many winter camps as you can," he said. "Mainly I'm thinking about the Crow, though I wouldn't mind getting in good with the Blackfeet and Shoshone. Take some trade goods with you to give as gifts, and then send them down here to trade." He rubbed his hands together happily. "Just think about it. If we can set up regular trade with the natives up here, we'll all be rich! Being the first men up here will give us a huge advantage over our competition!"

I prepared my gear that night, intending to be on my way at first light. I checked my long rifle to make sure it was in perfect working condition, knowing my life could well depend on it. I had a full horn of powder, plenty of lead pellets, my trusty flint and steel, and my blanket. I also carried numerous small items I could offer to the Indians as gifts; tobacco, mirrors, awls, needles, beads, small knives and colored dyes among them.

I also prepared myself in other ways, including enjoying my last taste of whiskey, and sitting down with Drouillard so he could teach me some simple sign language for when I met up with the Indians. I had learned a little from watching him during our travels with Lewis and Clark, but those were simple greetings and peace signs. Telling the Indians about a new trading post and giving directions through sign language would be a lot more complicated.

"Make sure you give me the right signals," I said to him. "I don't want to stand in front of some big chief and sign that I want to fornicate with his daughter when I think I'm signing that I come in peace!"

Drouillard grinned. "Guess you won't know until you try it out the first time," he said.

Wise-ass Indian!

The sun was just climbing above the mountains to the east when I set out. Several inches of fresh snow had fallen during the night, and the tracks of deer and other animals stood out against the crisp white background. I was wearing a pair of snowshoes I had constructed during the previous week, utilizing a design I had seen the Mandans use during our winter at their village. I made them by stitching heavy sinew between curved wooden staves, and I was able to travel easily across the top of the snow.

I set out toward the southwest, following the Bighorn River toward the high mountains on the horizon. I knew the Crow lived in that area, and would be wintering in the low valleys where rivers and streams cut through the rock and where there would be shelter from the elements. The mountains to the west were stark and forbidding, covered already in thick snow. It would be a challenging winter!

As I hiked through the snowy woods, I reflected briefly on where I might have been if I hadn't met up with William Clark back in Maysville in '03. I had to grin at the thought. In spite of all the hardships we had endured, I wouldn't have traded what happened after that first meeting for anything.

At night, I sought shelter either against the base of some rocky cliff or beneath a large tree. My thick blanket would provide a degree of warmth, and I didn't hesitate to build large fires for heat and to cook whatever meat I had shot during the day. I wasn't hiding from Indians on this journey.

I left the Bighorn a week later and struck out due west. I could see what looked like a possible pass through the mountains, but I could also see smoke, a dark low smudge against the white background of the mountains. Smoke in the winter meant a village. A village out here meant Indians.

I headed toward that smoke, already thinking about the signs Drouillard had taught me, but also keeping all of my senses alert to my surroundings. Just because it was winter didn't mean all the Indians would be hunkered down in smoky camps. Food still had to be gathered, and hunting parties would be scouring those woods for deer and elk. A lone white man walking through their territory might give some young warrior an opportunity for glory, and I wanted to be ready in case that happened.

More snow fell as I made my way west. I calculated that the camp was three or four days away from the Bighorn, and from the amount of smoke I was seeing against the mountains it was a big one. That was perfect. The more Indians I could send to Lisa's post, the better.

I reached the large Indian camp on the afternoon of the fourth day, and it was as big of a camp as I had suspected it might be. Tipis were scattered over a wide area of a low valley thick with cottonwoods, and I could see dozens of horses tethered in amongst the trees. Voices rang out as I appeared out of the woods, though I had the feeling they were expecting me. I couldn't imagine a camp this size not having sentries out in the woods watching for any enemy that might approach.

My suspicions were confirmed when a dozen warriors rode toward me on horseback, weapons ready. They had obviously known I was coming. I could feel my heart pounding in my chest as they neared, the expressions on their faces fierce and threatening. Keeping my rifle pointed toward the ground, and trying to appear as non-threatening as possible, I gave them the hand signs Drouillard had taught me and held my breath.

The warriors reined to a stop in front of where I stood. A dozen sharp arrows were pointed at my chest, and I knew I might be just seconds away from resembling a porcupine. A dead porcupine! Then one of the warriors stepped his horse forward and signed what I knew was a question about my intentions.

Sweating but keeping my face neutral, I ran through the signs taught me by George, praying I got them right. The Indians stared at me without expression as I did so, their stony faces revealing nothing.

I was just about to run through my presentation again when the lead Indian grunted something unintelligible to me. His hand sign, however, was unmistakable. As the other warriors took up position around me, I swore silently and tried to prepare myself for death.

Just then, another voice shouted from the area of the camp, and the warriors backed off a step or so. Another man was riding out toward where we stood, his painted warhorse floundering through the deep snow. As he neared us, I could see that he was a much older man than the young warriors around me, with dozens of feathers adorning his hair and robe.

The older Indian drew rein in front of me and said something. Not knowing what else to do, I went through my hand-signing once again. The older man watched me in silence, then spoke to the warriors. To my infinite relief, the warriors turned their horses toward the village.

Motioning for me to follow, the man who had saved my life spurred his horse toward the tipis. I followed along, relief at my deliverance uppermost in my mind. I could tell from the ornamentation that these were Crow, and I thought I recognized one or two of the warriors as members of the party that had stolen our pelts a year ago. Not that I was going to make any accusations. I'm not crazy.

In the camp, I followed the older warrior to a large dwelling near the center of the village. It appeared to be a communal meeting hall in the manner of many of the plains tribes, and I didn't hesitate to follow the Indian into the gloomy interior. Several other older men sat around a small fire, and they looked at me with undisguised curiosity as I entered. The man who had led me in motioned me to sit.

Food was brought as the Indian men talked in low voices. The squaw who handed me the stone bowl of stew was very pretty, with large brown eyes, and I smiled at her. The stew was hot and delicious, and I ate every last bite before handing the bowl back to the woman with a nod of thanks.

The man who had saved my life turned toward me. "Bear Walks Alone," he said, holding his hand to his chest.

"John Colter," I said, mimicking his action.

"Col-ter," he said, nodding and smiling. He said something to the other men and a low chuckle spread around the room. Then Bear Walks Alone faced me again. His hands moved slowly in sign language and I struggled to follow his meaning. It was a laborious process, with many frustrating stops and starts on both parts, but finally I was able to discern that he would visit Lisa's trading post. He also told me that I would be allowed to spread the word of the new trading post to other Crow winter camps, and I watched intently as he drew a crude map in the dirt of where some of those camps might be located.

I gave Bear Walks Alone some of the tobacco and a new steel knife as thanks for the information, and also passed tobacco out to the other men in the lodge. The atmosphere in the lodge had turned friendly with the handing out of gifts, and I allowed myself to relax. It appeared I wasn't going to be killed. Yet.

* * *

That night, the young squaw who had brought me the food earlier made another appearance, ducking in through the opening of the small lodge I had been given for the night. She said something I couldn't understand, then quickly shed her clothing and stood naked before me.

Sometimes words are completely unnecessary. I was out of my own clothing in record time and as I lowered her to the soft blanket I silently blessed the hospitality of Indians.

CHAPTER FORTY-TWO

For the rest of that long and cold winter, I tramped through those mountains in search of Crow camps. Bear Walks Alone had given me a small totem, a stick adorned with hawk feathers that were arranged in such a way as to show that I traveled with his blessings. That totem would save my life on several occasions when I could wave it at Crow warriors who were racing at me from out of the trees, arrows nocked and ready to shoot into my body!

I traveled west out of Bear Walks Alone's camp and into some of the wildest and strangest land I had ever encountered. I passed through an area where the very earth spit out great clouds of noxious steam, where water would suddenly gush from cracks in the earth and spew into a sky dense with steam and fog. The river in that area smelled so strongly of sulfur it was difficult to breathe, and strange black rocks that were hot to the touch seemed to force themselves right out of the ground. I had never seen anything like it in all my travels and adventures, and I'm sure I got a glimpse of what Hell must look like!

I climbed a low pass out of that strange land and dropped down into a spectacular wide valley. The snow there was deep and the winds down from the surrounding mountains was bitingly cold. I had ingrained Bear Walks Alone's map into my memory, and in this valley I turned north. High mountains were on all sides of me, and I climbed steep slopes and crossed more snow-filled passes as I moved. From the tops of those mountains I could see far in every direction, picking out individual peaks

I could use as landmarks later. I also spied several deep valleys, valleys Bear Walks Alone had told me might be the location of winter camps.

My snowshoes kept me moving swiftly on top of snow that could have been anywhere from a few feet to dozens of feet deep. I crossed wide clearings that almost certainly held frozen lakes beneath the snow, and I passed like a silent spirit through vast forests where massive trees soared hundreds of feet into the sky. Towering waterfalls fell from breath-taking heights, and roaring rivers, moving too rapidly to freeze, crashed down into stunning valleys. Other rivers, frozen solid, made roads I could follow with little difficulty, and I made good time. It was a wondrous land.

One late afternoon, I stood high on a peak, watching a large pack of wolves trail a herd of elk across a valley floor below. The wolves harassed the elk relentlessly, forcing the great beasts to continuously move, tiring them out. Eventually, a grizzled old bull collapsed from the endless pursuit and the wolves set to their feast with a vengeance as the rest of the herd lumbered out of sight into the woods. Survival of the fittest was the rule.

The winter passed slowly as I traveled from Crow camp to Crow camp, spreading the message about Lisa's trading post while memorizing as much as I could about the land I passed through. I was treated well by the Crow that I visited with, especially after showing the totem given to me by Bear Walks Alone. In one camp near the northern shore of the large lake that filled the bottom of the valley I recognized several of the warriors who had robbed me of my pelts on the Yellowstone and I'm sure they recognized me, but nothing was made of it by either myself or them. The past was in the past.

As the winter began to mellow and the temperatures started to rise, I made my way back to Lisa's trading post. I had completed the task set before me, had visited over a dozen large winter camps and countless small hunting camps, and I looked forward to sleeping under a roof once again.

* * *

In the spring, Manuel Lisa pulled me aside and asked me to head out again, this time to the Three Forks area. The trees were bursting with their new leaves, the snow was almost all melted, and the traveling would be far easier than my trek during the winter, but I was hesitant. I knew how fortunate I had been to meet up with Bear Walks Alone and to receive his blessing to visit the Crow camps, but the Three Forks area held both Shoshone and Blackfeet. They might not be so kind.

"Some of the Crow are coming in now," Lisa said to me. "They tell me that many more are following later in the spring. This is the perfect opportunity to get word of this post out to other nations." He was grinning and practically rubbing his hands together in anticipation. "If you can convince other nations to come here and trade, John, we'll all be rich!"

Well, that was why I had come up to this land, after all, wasn't it? To get rich. I agreed to go.

Two weeks later I set out on the Yellowstone. I was using my memory of the trail Clark had used in '06 on his travels from the Three Forks to the Yellowstone, and I cursed again the fact that I had been sent down the Missouri that year instead of being allowed to travel with Clark. It would have made my current task a lot easier, I can say that!

I eventually found a pass that resembled the one described to me by Clark, the pass pointed out to him by our squaw, the Bird Woman. Crossing the pass, I descended into the Three Forks area.

For a month I traipsed back and forth across that wide valley, making forays into the surrounding mountains, but, like had happened when I was with the two captains several years earlier, there was no sign of Shoshone or Blackfeet. There were many signs that Indians had been in the area, like old cook-fires and faded tracks, but those signs weren't recent.

I was sitting on the bank of the river Lewis had named the Gallatin, considering my options. The sun was shining down from a sky devoid of clouds, and I was glad for that. It had rained for the previous week, soaking me and all of my gear to the point where I thought I might never dry out! But now the sun was out, and my gear was spread on the rocky bank to dry.

I was cooking a deer I had shot earlier that morning when I heard the unmistakable sound of horses approaching from the west. The gurgling and splashing of the river, combined with the crackling flames of my fire and the sizzle of cooking meat, had muffled the sound until it was too late for me to even think about hiding. By the time I grabbed up my rifle and rose to my feet, the Indians were upon me.

But I was lucky. They were mostly Crow, along with some Shoshone. As they circled around me, arrows pointed at my chest, I waved the totem given to me in the fall by Bear Walks Alone, and the arrows were lowered. I could breathe again.

I was surprised to see a band of Crow as large as this one in the Three Forks area. I estimated that there were seven to eight hundred warriors in this band. Through signing, though, I was able to determine that they had been raiding Blackfeet camps in the mountains for horses and they were now planning to head for Lisa's trading post.

I agreed to travel with them. They reported seeing recent signs of Blackfeet in the valley, a large band, and I could tell the Crow and Shoshone were nervous about meeting up with them. We broke camp the next morning and set out.

For three days our travel was uneventful. We moved east, toward the pass that would lead us over to the Yellowstone, and the days were warm and sunny, as if Providence was smiling down on us. The fourth day also dawned clear and sunny, but Providence was no longer on our side.

Voices rang out in warning as hundreds of Blackfeet raced out of the trees. Gunfire blazed and arrows filled the air, along with the thunder of hundreds of horses and the screams of dying men. I dove for the sparse cover of a clump of thorn bushes as soon as the hordes of Blackfeet came into view, but I was unlucky, the victim of either bad luck or an Indian with fantastic aim.

Do you have any idea how much it hurts to get shot in the leg? I'm here to tell you, it hurts like the dickens! And the worst part was getting shot during a battle I had no desire to be a part of! The last thing I wanted was to be the only white man in a war between Crow and Blackfeet, but that option was no longer mine. I was in the middle, I had been shot, and if I didn't defend myself I would die.

Crawling into the small amount of cover provided by the bushes, I quickly ripped some material from my cloak and wrapped it around my leg. Later, I might have time to inspect the severity of the wound, if I lived long enough, but for now I needed to concentrate on survival! The leg burned, but I could move it, and there didn't seem to be all that much blood soaking through my pants.

The battle raged most of that morning, and sometimes I was in the thick of the fighting while other times I was on the fringe. All around me men were dying, and bullets and arrows filled the air. Blood soaked the ground, and it was hard to tell friend from enemy in that madness of killing and death.

Eventually, though, the Blackfeet withdrew, gathering up as many of their dead and wounded as they could before disappearing as swiftly as they had appeared. Finally, I was able to crawl out from the shelter of the thorn bushes and examine my wound. The bullet had creased a path along the back of my thigh, a shallow but bloody trench that burned like fire but wasn't serious. I did a better job of wrapping it, and then limped down toward the river to determine the final result of the raid.

The Crow and Shoshone had lost several dozen men, and they were already busy gathering their dead and tending to their wounded. The Blackfeet dead were left where they lay, and already crows and ravens were circling, eager to feast on the still-warm flesh. Several wounded Blackfeet had been found and they had been immediately dispatched, something that went against my white upbringing, though I knew better than to try and intervene. I had the feeling it wouldn't be appreciated if I tried to force my views on these Indians.

Late in the afternoon we traveled about three miles and set up camp on a small hill. From the hill we could see several miles in all directions, and would have advance warning if the Blackfeet tried to attack us again. I didn't think they would, as they had suffered more casualties than us, if the number of bodies I saw littering the ground was any indication. No, I had the feeling those Blackfeet were heading for home as fast as their horses would carry them.

The night passed quietly, broken only by the moans of the injured men, and even those were subdued in the Indian manner. My leg was aching, a dull ache that bothered me like a mosquito in my ear but which wouldn't slow me down. When the sun arose, we set out once again for Fort Raymond.

CHAPTER FORTY-THREE

At Fort Raymond, tensions were running high. A long-simmering hatred between Manuel Lisa and Edward Rose was now boiling right out in the open, waiting for just the right spark to explode. I have no idea when or why the animosity between Rose and Lisa was so powerful; John Potts had told me that the two just seemed to hate each other from day one.

The Crow and Shoshone that I had brought in spent about a week at Fort Raymond, trading dozens of beaver and otter pelts for mirrors, beads, blankets, but mostly powder and lead. They proved to be humorous and lively men, dancing around their fires late into the night, and when one of our men who played a mean fiddle joined them, the yells and whoops echoed along the river. Some men, like Potts, avoided the Indian camp, their dislike of Indians too strong to overcome. Others, myself included, enjoyed the rough camaraderie of these wild men. As time passed I had learned more and more of their language and was able to communicate with them, and we shared many stories. I was sad to see them pack up and leave, their trading done, but they invited me to visit them in their villages any time.

Two days after the Crow and Shoshone departed, the feud between Manuel Lisa and Edward Rose reached its climax. I wasn't in the room when it all started, so I don't know what was said between the men. Rose had just returned from a trapping expedition, and had apparently told Lisa that all his pelts had been stolen. Lisa, who had just finished preparing his keelboat to depart to St. Louis with a heavy load of pelts, intending to return with more trade goods, was reportedly incensed. I don't know. All I know was there was suddenly a great uproar, with men yelling and cursing, and by the time I ran into the room, Rose had Lisa down on the floor and was choking the life out of him.

Edward Rose was a huge bear of a man, far larger than the short Lisa, and struggle as he might Lisa had no chance of loosening Rose's iron grip from his throat. Several of us rushed forward to help, and we managed to wrestle Edward off the smaller man. Lisa scrambled for the door.

With a roar, Rose leapt to his feet, fully intending to chase down and kill Manuel Lisa. As he made for the door, John Potts stepped in front of him.

"Calm down, Edward…" he said, and then dropped to the floor as Edward punched him square in the face.

Before any of us could move, Rose was on top of Potts, pummeling him with both fists. Blood flew from John's nose and mouth, and I know Rose would have killed him if five of us hadn't jumped on him, bearing him to the floor and allowing John to crawl away.

"Damn it, Rose, calm down!" Pete Weiser shouted.

Rose climbed to his feet, his face bright red with rage. Brow drawn, he glared at us, and then ran from the building.

I helped John to his feet. "You all right?" I asked.

John angrily wiped blood from his face with a sleeve. "Yeah, I'll be fine. Let me get my gun, though, and I'll blast that son-of-a-bitch!"

"Hey!" a voice yelled from outside, followed by the deep roar of the swivel gun. The large gun had been taken from the keelboat and mounted onto the front porch of Fort Raymond, both as a showpiece for the Indians who visited and as a defensive weapon. Voices yelled in anger and John and I raced outside.

On the river, the keelboat was on the move, pulling away from shore and heading downriver. Manuel Lisa could be seen on the stern, poling like mad, and the men with him were rowing as if their lives depended on it. Edward Rose had commandeered the swivel gun and was firing at the departing keelboat, his murderous intent still fully intact. Once again several of us tackled him, sending him sprawling into the mud at the foot of the steps, and I watched as the keelboat vanished around a bend in the river.

Rose scrambled to his feet, mud caked all over his clothing and in his hair. Huge fists balled, he whirled to face us, and found himself staring at three rifles. The anger drained from him like water from a bucket and, saying nothing, he stalked away.

Three days later Edward Rose left Fort Raymond in the dark of the night.

* * *

By autumn, most of the local Indians had visited Fort Raymond and traded with us, and the storeroom in back was filling again with pelts and skins. Manuel Lisa wasn't expected back from St. Louis until the following spring, and I wanted to get some trapping of my own in before winter sealed us into the fort.

"What do you say, John? Wanna get out of here?"

Potts leaned back on his bunk and looked up at me. "What you got in mind?"

"I was thinking about heading over to the Three Forks and doing some trapping," I said. "Beaver are thick as skeeters over there."

"Didn't you almost die over there in the spring?"

"Don't be such an old woman," I teased him. "Those Blackfeet are long gone. Come on, John, let's go get us some beaver."

The following morning we rented two horses from some of the men who were planning on spending the winter in the fort. We loaded them with all the gear we thought we might need and headed up the Yellowstone. Following the same trails I had used in the spring, John and I made our way to the Three Forks and set up a camp. I showed John the location of the battle, the flattened field still littered with the bones of the dead Indians, and he shuddered. "You sure them damn Blackfeet are gone?"

I waved around us with an outstretched arm. "You see any?"

"That ain't funny, John," he said, peering in all directions. "Them sneaking savages could be anywhere, and we won't know it until they shoot us full of arrows."

I shook my head in amusement. "They're gone, John. It's fall. It's the time when they move their villages to winter camps. They're not gonna be hanging around the Three Forks."

He looked dubious. "I hope you're right," he said.

* * *

I was positive the Blackfeet had returned to their homes for the winter, but, as John said, it never hurts to be wary. We scouted the rivers for slides and dams with the utmost care and set our traps at night, collecting our catches in the early morning before retreating into our well-hidden camp to hide during the day. Several weeks passed without incident, as the air turned cooler and the leaves fell from the trees, then, on a chilly and frosty morning, our luck ran out.

We were working our way along the Jefferson River in a dugout canoe we had built on our arrival, checking our traps. Several dead beaver already rested in the bottom of the canoe, to be skinned after we returned to camp, and John was just pulling another trap up from the river bottom when I heard a sound.

"Psst, John," I whispered.

He looked at me and made to speak. I motioned him to be silent and jerked a thumb toward the shore. "Listen," I hissed.

We sat for several minutes, listening intently, and then the sound came again. It was unmistakable, the thud of hooves on hard ground.

"Buffalo," Potts said dismissively.

I shook my head. "I ain't so sure. I think we should seek some cover."

Potts snorted laughter. "It's buffalo, John. Quit being an old woman. Now help me pull this trap..."

The low heavy thuds came again, closer. John ignored them and continued pulling the heavy trap into the canoe, making enough noise to be heard at old Fort Clatsop! I was about to shush him again when the Blackfeet appeared on the bank.

"Damn," Potts said slowly. He let the trap drop back into the water.

"See?" I said, making sure my hands were in plain view. "Maybe you'll listen to me someday?"

One of the Indians rode forward and motioned us to come to shore. "Maybe they only want to rob us," I said hopefully.

The Indian motioned to us again, and reinforced his gesture by pointing his rifle in our direction.

"We can't go to shore," Potts hissed. "They'll kill us for sure."

"They'll kill us if we don't," I said. Taking up the oar, I rowed the canoe to shore. As I started signing our peaceful intentions to the Indian in front of me, another Blackfoot stepped into the river and yanked John's rifle out of his hands.

Moving quickly, I grabbed the rifle from the Indian and handed it back to John. As I started signing with the Blackfeet again, Potts suddenly shoved the canoe away from shore and into the middle of the river.

"Don't do that, John," I said. "Get back over here."

"Uh-uh," he said. "They gonna kill us, John. I ain't gonna die without a fight."

The Indian who seemed to be the leader motioned angrily, pointing at Potts then at the bank.

"I'm trying," I mumbled. I motioned to Potts again. "They'll kill us sure if you don't get over here," I said. "You gonna try to fight all of them?" From what I could see, there were close to five hundred Blackfeet gathered on the shore. Fighting them would be ludicrous.

Potts started to speak when one of the warriors, apparently tired of waiting, shot an arrow that slammed into John's hip. "I'm shot!" he yelled out, dropping to the floor of the canoe. Scrambling to his knees and raising his rifle, he fired one time, blasting a warrior out of his saddle. Within seconds, dozens of arrows were fired at John Potts and he fell again, dead, his body riddled with arrows.

"Damn," I muttered, feeling anguish race through me at the death of my friend. At that moment, I was sure I was about to die.

Enraged at the death of their warrior, several of the young Indian men jumped into the river and pulled the canoe to shore. They hauled John's lifeless bloody body onto the bank and set about mutilating him, chopping off his arms and legs and hacking into his body. His head was removed and thrown up onto the shore, where warriors on horseback trampled it until it was no longer recognizable as a human head. Other warriors kept their arrows pointed at me, pinning me frozen to the spot. I was absolutely certain I would be the next to die, tortured in obscene and imaginative ways, and I silently vowed to die with as much dignity as I could.

After the Indians had had their sport with John's body, I was pulled up onto the prairie and stripped naked. They took all my clothes, including my boots, and I held my breath, wondering what part of me they would cut off first.

Then, one old Indian grabbed my arm and led me several feet away. Through hand signing, he inquired if I was a fast runner.

Not sure where the question was leading, I shook my head.

The old Indian laughed and said something to the warriors. Then he pointed across the flat land in the direction of the Madison River and motioned me to walk away.

I was sure it was a trick. I stood still.

Shaking his head, the old man motioned again, instructing me to go. I had no idea what to do. I was going to die no matter what I did, of that I was sure, and so I figured I would play along. Turning my back on the Indians, I started walking away.

The ground was rough and rocky and covered with prickly pear. Within several yards my feet were cut and bleeding, prickly pear thorns sticking out from them, but I continued walking. I fully expected to feel arrows piercing my body at any second and I walked with shoulders hunched, every muscle tense. When I had gone a hundred yards or so without being shot, however, I glanced back.

About fifty warriors had dismounted and were shrugging out of their cloaks and blankets. Several were limbering up their muscles, stretching their arms and legs, and it suddenly dawned on me what was about to happen. This was a race, and those warriors would be their fleetest of foot. They were going to chase me, like hounds after a rabbit, and the reward at the end of the race would be my scalp.

Drawing a deep breath, I ran.

CHAPTER FORTY-FOUR

Looking back at that day, I feel pretty safe in saying I ran faster and harder than I had ever run in my life. I ran with a swiftness that surprised even me, though I suppose it shouldn't have. I was, after all, running for my very life.

I ran as the blood pounded in my veins and my lungs gasped for air. Rocks and prickly pear cut and stabbed my feet, and I knew I was leaving a trail of blood behind me. I could hear the whooping and trilling of the Indians and I knew the chase was under way. Now was the time when I would have to draw on all of my strength and reserves if I wanted to survive. And as I ran I swore to myself that if I got out of this I would leave the west and return to St. Louis once and for all!

I shot a quick glance back over my shoulder and saw the Indians coming, spread out in a line behind me and yelling for all they were worth. Yeah, they were having a grand old time, chasing my white naked hide across that torturous ground! I struggled for more speed, though I was running as fast as I could. I just knew I was going to die.

Head pounding, blood now starting to run from my nose from the power of my exertions, I ran and ran and ran. More swift glances behind showed one young warrior pulling ahead of the rest, quickly gaining on me. His face was wrapped in a joyous grin and he waved his spear as he ran, already envisioning, I'm sure, the sight of that spear impaled in my body. I didn't intend to let that happen.

I could hear his footsteps gaining on me and I slowed. My last glance back had showed me he had pulled out a hundred yard lead over the next closest Blackfoot, and I knew I could never outrun this man. I would have to trick him. Stopping suddenly, I whirled around to face him.

Startled by my action, the Indian stumbled just as he cast his spear toward me. The spear clattered to the ground at my feet as he fell, and, swift as a snake, I grabbed the spear and drove it through his body, pinning him to the ground. Then I grabbed his blanket and took to my heels once again.

I was approaching the Madison River by this time, and I was also approaching the very limits of my endurance. Every breath was an agony, every step a torture. My feet and legs were burning like fire, and I was soaked with my own blood that poured from my nose and mouth. From the angry yells I could hear behind me, the Blackfeet had found their dead warrior, and I knew they would chase me with a renewed ferocity. I only had one chance.

Reaching the Madison, I ran straight off the bank and into the icy water. I could see a huge pile of driftwood jammed up against a small island downstream from where I was and I floated down that way. I knew I didn't have much time; the Indians weren't that far behind me. Drawing in a deep, ragged breath, I dove under the driftwood. If the wood was solid above me, I would drown under here, but I was out of options. All I could do was hope and pray.

Within moments, I had found a small pocket of air beneath the heavy logs and I pressed my face up into it. I could hear the shouts of the Indians and I knew they had arrived on the river bank. I had no more strength for running; if they found my hiding place they would kill me, and there was nothing I could do about it.

For close to three hours the Blackfeet searched up and down the river banks, yelling to each other, and I could detect the anger and frustration in their voices. Several walked back and forth across the driftwood under which I was hiding, and I was afraid they might set it on fire in an effort to find out if I was underneath it. But eventually they went away.

Tired, sick, exhausted, I stayed beneath that pile of driftwood for several more hours, until I felt confident that the Indians had in fact gone away. Then I slowly swam out from beneath the driftwood and surfaced, listening with every ounce of my strength. Silence save for the rippling of the river and the call of birds. Keeping my head moving as I attempted to look in all directions at the same time, I made my way to the bank and crawled up to the top. I peeked over the top, prepared to make a headlong retreat to the safety of the driftwood if I saw as much as one Indian. But the prairie was deserted in all directions.

Breathing a silent sigh of relief, I slumped down on the rocky bank. Yes, it was definitely time to go home.

* * *

It took me almost two weeks to get back to Fort Raymond. I knew I couldn't cross the pass to the Yellowstone, because if the Blackfeet were still hunting me they would have warriors guarding that pass for sure. Instead, traveling by night I crossed the mountains south of the pass, over rocks covered in several feet of snow. I didn't have my rifle to shoot game, and I wouldn't have risked the noise if I had, so I ate roots, mostly, and tree bark. By the time I stumbled into Fort Raymond, I was a skinny, gaunt caricature of myself, unrecognizable to the other men.

A week after that, I headed for St. Louis.

EPILOGUE

Well, as you may have guessed, that wasn't the end of my adventuring in the lands of the Yellowstone and Three Forks. No, like a fool I went right back there again, guiding a group from the Missouri Fur Company, right back to the Three Forks. Pierre Menard was leading that group, with me as the guide, and we had such upright, good men as Thomas James and James Cheek with us. And, like before, we were attacked by the Blackfeet and I barely escaped with my life. The Blackfeet were on a rampage against all white people by that time and had even killed my old friend George Drouillard near Fort Raymond. It took me several more close escapes to finally get it through my thick skull that I didn't belong in their land.

So now here I am, older and wiser. And now you've heard my story. It's about time for me to get back home; Sally and little Hiram'll be wondering what's become of me! But one last thing before I go.

In my long and adventurous life, I was fortunate enough to meet many fine people, and see places few have ever seen. Legends have been told about me, and my role has been expanded far out of proportion to truth, but it's those other men who deserve the credit for all we did, men like Lewis and Clark, Potts, Shannon, the Fields brothers, Drouillard, Hancock, Ordway and Gass, Charles Floyd. They were the heroes. Old Captain Clark is still hanging on down there in St. Louis, but most of those other great men are gone now, and I probably will be too before long.

Longevity doesn't seem to be a gift shared by the men of the Corps of Discovery.

Yep, my time feels like it might be close. And when I do go I hope they bury me where I can look out over this beautiful Missouri River. It holds my soul.

AFTERWORD

John Colter was a real person.

He lived, breathed, walked this earth, and died. Those are indisputable facts. What are also indisputable facts are that he met up with Meriwether Lewis and William Clark in Kentucky in 1803, joined the Corps of Discovery, was almost dismissed from the Corps following a dispute with Sergeant John Ordway, and went up the Missouri with the Corps in 1804. It is a fact that he distinguished himself as a valuable member of the team, and that he did not return to St. Louis in 1806 with the rest of the Corps, instead joining two trappers to return to the Missouri country to make his fortune. It is a fact that he spent the next several years trapping along the Yellowstone and Missouri Rivers and in the area of the Three Forks, and that he had several famous run-ins with the Blackfeet Indians, including one that resulted in the death of his fellow Corps friend, John Potts. It is a fact that he explored the area that is now Yellowstone National Park, possibly the first white man to do so. It is a fact that he died in May of 1813 from an unknown ailment. Those are all facts.

What makes this book a work of "historical fiction" is all of those things that happened in between the known facts, all of those small details that can only be imagined. We don't know the conversations he had with people like Lewis and Clark, or Sergeant Floyd, or John Potts. We don't know for certain what caused the fight with Ordway, or what he had to say in his defense that allowed him to stay with the Corps and even be assigned to Ordway's "mess," or squad. All we can do is surmise, based on the journals of the Corps of Discovery and the verbal legends passed down from generation to generation from the people who were there.

The characters in this book, with the exception of the Crow chief Bear Walks Alone, were all real people, and their interactions with Colter have not been altered other than using my own imagination to embellish those contacts. I have not added new characters from the pure fabric of imagination, again with the aforementioned exception, or placed characters in roles they did not possess in real life. I felt the addition of Bear Walks Alone was necessary, since Colter did meet with the Crow and his first meeting with the Crow would have had to have involved an exchange of names. Any other alterations from what was actually said or done are unavoidable, since those people who were there are no longer around to question! But I have done everything I could to make this book true to reality while moving it beyond the realm of boring facts into something exciting and fun.

Writing in the first person did create some disadvantages, foremost among them the inability to describe important scenes that took place when John Colter was not present. I have had to import those scenes into the story through conversations Colter had with people who were there, or through other means. In this manner, some of the historic detail has been lost in the translation. Two large examples of this are Lewis's encounter with the Blackfeet on the Marias River, and Clark's exploration of the Yellowstone River. Colter was elsewhere during these times, and his knowledge of what took place could only have come through conversations with those who were there.

* * *

Like most of you, my first exposure to history was through school textbooks, and their dry, boring focus on two factors; what happened and the date it happened. I sat in classrooms memorizing dates and events that meant nothing to me, and they only stayed in my head long enough to pass the next quiz, then I discarded them. History was dusty to me, existing only as a simple recitation of what happened on what day. The living, breathing people whose actions created that history had no dimension. Later in my life I was exposed to history again, but this time it was through works that took those boring dates and facts and transformed them into stories that were exciting and interesting to read. Those authors accomplished that feat by looking at a small journal entry, for example, and maybe in that entry it said that it was a cold day, some snow, the river was running fast, and the hunters came back with two deer. They then created an entire scene that brought that short journal entry to life, as it might have happened. And that is how I set out to write this book. I wanted to make the story of John Colter into a fun, readable adventure as opposed to a book filled with dull facts. I have made every effort to remain as true to history as I can, while adding enough detail to keep the story flowing and to bring his history to life. Some historians may frown at this approach. I can't help that. The reader will have to make up their own mind.

* * *

John's time with the Corps of Discovery is fairly well documented in the journals kept during the years 1803 to 1806 by such people as Meriwether Lewis, William Clark, John Ordway, Patrick Gass, Charles Floyd and Joseph Whitehouse. When John split with the Corps in 1806 and went back up the Missouri with Dickson and Hancock, the facts are harder to locate. The letters and journal entries concerning John's activities were few and far between, and for this period, from 1806 to 1808, I have had to depend on interpretations done by historians and which are themselves filled with conjecture and supposition.

All the details of John's time with the Corps of Discovery have been interpreted by me utilizing Gary E. Moulton's truly amazing "Journals of the Lewis and Clark Expedition." A special thank you to the University of Nebraska for their exceptional website that allowed me to follow the journals in the easiest, most complete way imaginable. While sparse on details at times, it was those original journals written during the expedition that have kept people like John Colter alive in the minds of Americans. I also owe a debt of gratitude to several excellent authors: Stephen E. Ambrose (Undaunted Courage), James Alexander Thom

(Sign-Talker and From Sea to Shining Sea), George Laycock (The Mountain Men), Larry E. Morris (The Fate of the Corps—What Became of the Lewis and Clark Explorers After the Expedition), and Burton Harris (John Colter—His Years in the Rockies.) Those books helped to bring John Colter and the western part of the continent during the years 1803 to 1808 to life in my head. Those excellent books are a must-read for anyone interested in learning more about John Colter and the Lewis and Clark Expedition. Jim Wark and Joseph A. Mussulman's "Lewis and Clark from the Air" is another excellent resource to aid in seeing and understanding some of the physical obstacles those men in the Corps had to overcome on their journey. I would also recommend Alvin Josephy's "Lewis and Clark Through Indian Eyes," James Ronda's "Lewis and Clark Among the Indians," and anything by the excellent author Joseph Marshall III, to gain a better understanding of the impact of the expedition and white encroachment on the native peoples of this continent.

Since I do not have the financial means at hand to quit my day job and explore the areas John Colter explored, I have to depend on other sources to give me a feel for the country he passed through, whether with the Corps or on his own. Ken Burns' fantastic PBS film, "Lewis and Clark— The Journey of the Corps of Discovery," is a wonderful resource for those of us who have never journeyed on the Missouri, as, again, is Jim Wark and Joseph A. Mussulman's "Lewis and Clark from the Air." And I want to offer a special thank you to all the staff and volunteers at the Fort Clatsop National Memorial, which fortunately for me was just a couple hours from my home in Oregon during the writing of this book. Their assistance and information has been invaluable.

By writing this book in the first-person form, as though seen through the eyes of John Colter, I have attempted to utilize wording and descriptions as they might have been used in the early 1800's. Thus, such derogatory terms as "Injun," "savage" and "squaw" have been used during re-created conversations, mainly because that is how white people spoke back then. Those terms are not intended to be taken as insults against any person or race of people. Another problem is that there is knowledge available today that the men in that time did not have access to. One example of this is the use of the phrase "Teton Sioux" when describing the Lakota nation. In the early 1800's, Teton Sioux was the title given by white people for the Lakota, and that is why it was used in this book. Remember, this book was written as if John Colter were sitting at a campfire back in 1810-1811 with friends and talking about his adventures. Also, if I include terminology or phrases that have evolved since the early 1800's, again that is entirely my mistake and is not intended. I'm old, but I'm not old enough to have been around in 1803! Likewise, any mistakes made in describing people or places are entirely the fault of the author.

I need to thank the following people: Thomas Pieper, my high school history teacher, for sparking my interest in the history of the American West; Ken and Allie Alumbaugh, Rick and Kathi Miller, Krissi Hesse, Robert Pagano and Maria Duer for being such great friends over the years; and everyone at Salem Friends of Felines in Salem, Oregon, and Best Friends Animal Society in Kanab, Utah, for taking such great care of the animals!

Finally, I have to give my ultimate thanks to my wife, Deborah Lynn Amiet, for putting up with all those long hours when I would be holed up in my little office, working on this project instead of spending time with her! She has shown me complete faith, support and love, and I could never hope to repay her. I love you.

This book is dedicated to the memory of Dr. Murray Bett.

www.donamiet.com
www.bestfriends.org
www.sfof.org

9 781607 490715